CHERYL BIGGS

HEARTS DECEIVED

ZEBRA BOOKS
KENSINGTON PUBLISHING CORP.

ZEBRA BOOKS are published by

Kensington Publishing Corp.
475 Park Avenue South
New York, NY 10016

Zebra and the Z logo Reg. U.S. Pat. & TM Off. Heartfire
Romance and the Heartfire Romance logo are trademarks of
Kensington Publishing Corp.

First Printing: May, 1994

Printed in the United States of America

PLAYING WITH FIRE . . . AND DESIRE

"Damn you, Belle St. Croix," he said again, his voice ragged with emotion. "Damn you."

Startled, his words seemed to snap Belle from the mists of desire that still enveloped her mind. "I don't—"

"What's your game, Belle?" He dropped her hands as if their touch suddenly repulsed him and fixed her with a riveting stare. "What the hell is it you want, lady?"

Instantly sobered by his harsh words, Belle bristled in indignation and hurt. "Game? What in blazes do you mean, game?"

Traxton scoffed. "Exactly what I said, Belle. Game. I don't know what you're up to, or after, but whatever it is, it isn't going to work."

"I haven't the faintest idea what you're talking about."

"I don't know if my brother is in love with you yet," Traxton said, overriding her spurt of indignation, "but he's damned well on his way, and you know it. Yet you're not satisfied with that, are you?"

Belle felt her temper begin to flare out of control. "I don't care what you know, Traxton Braggette, or what you think you kn—"

"It isn't going to work, lady," Traxton ground out. "I don't know what your game is, but I'm not playing. And," his eyes became shuttered and cold, "I would suggest you stop playing, too, before someone gets hurt."

* * *

"This exciting tale has a mixture of mystery, conspiracy, humor, and sizzling sensuality that will curl your toes and zap your mind into overdrive. [Ms. Biggs] whets your appetite . . . and leaves you in suspenseful anticipation for the next book. Wow! what a story!"
—*Rendezvous*

This book is dedicated to my family, each of whom has contributed in their own unique way to both my career and to this series:

Mom, your continual support and encouragement are always deeply appreciated, as is the legacy you handed me of loving a good book . . . and for always being willing to trot off with me somewhere to do research. Oh, and if I never said it before, thanks for letting me watch Hopalong Cassidy instead of practicing the piano.

Dad, you've always been there for me whenever I've needed anything; you raised me on cowboys and history; and never told me I couldn't do something I really wanted to do. Thank you, from the bottom of my heart.

Chantel, thanks for all your help, the crazy costumed autographings, the loan of the jacket, the free publicity and recommendations, the munchkins, but most of all, for being my daughter and giving me the fuel to bring Belle into her own.

Ken, my handsome, though quiet, son. You're darkly handsome, swagger sexily, and you're mysteriously quiet, yet that devilish gleam is never truly gone from your eyes for long. Thank you for lending me part of your personality and looks so that Traxton could actually "live," and for always being a wonderful son.

Stacy, my other handsome, though not so quiet, son. Someday some woman will become a very lucky bride, but until then you're still my "baby," albeit a tall, dark, and handsome one. Thanks for lending me part of your personality for Travis; he is all the better for being you.

Rhonda, thanks for just being you, and my stepdaughter, and especially for all your enthusiasm and support of my books. I wish you lived closer.

John and Sara, good luck in your own romance, and thanks in advance for giving Jack what he wants, more grandchildren.

And Jack, my own special hero, my best friend, my husband. Thank you for your faith, support, and encouragement, but most of all, your love. I couldn't do it without you.

Prologue

The fireplace poker swung through the air. Its slender gold rod momentarily caught the ray of sunlight that streamed through the transom window over the entry door and reflected it in a brilliant spark. Thomas Braggette looked up just as the black hooked end neared, but it was too late. It smashed against his skull, parting the thick mat of his white hair, slashing through his flesh, and shattering the fragile curve of his skull.

At the impact a low grunt escaped Thomas's lips. Pain, hot and searing, filled his head as blood gushed onto the shoulder of his frock coat. A kaleidoscope of radiant, near-blinding colors assaulted his eyes as they rolled upward. His knees buckled, his heart stopped, and he pitched forward.

A hand, still shaking with rage, dropped the blood-stained poker to the floor and stepped away from Thomas Braggette's body. "You should never have betrayed us," trembling lips whispered. "Never."

One

"Belle, are you sure about this plan of yours?" Lin asked. She twisted the green satin cord of her beaded reticule. "I mean, really sure?"

"Yes." Belle picked up her portmanteau and began to walk toward a packet that sat docked at the end of the wharf. The blue silk folds of her skirt rustled softly with each step. Instinctively she knew Lin wasn't following. Dropping her heavy satchel, Belle whirled around, white-gloved hands on hips, and sent her twin sister a piercing stare. "Melinda Sorbonte, for heaven's sake. Are you coming, or do I have to do this by myself?"

Lin hesitated for a few seconds longer, then shook her head and bent to pick up her own satchels. "Why am I doing this?" she murmured softly, then uttered a silent prayer, which she always did whenever she allowed herself to become involved in one of Belle's schemes . . . which was all too often. But this one was the most daring yet. "Yes, I'm coming, *Belinda Sorbonte*," she said, mocking her sister's use of her full name. "Don't I always?"

Belle picked up her satchel again. "Yes, but you always have to worry both of us to death first."

A young steward, his curly brown hair sticking out wildly from beneath a white cap, waited at the end of the gangplank to assist passengers board. His gaze hopped from Belle to Lin and back again as he obviously tried to decide if he really saw two identical women approaching. It was a usual occurrence when the two sisters went anywhere together where they weren't known. Belle recognized the look and ignored it. After all, her gown was blue and Lin's was green, so they weren't really identical today, not like when they truly wanted to be and wore matching outfits. She handed the boy her satchel and stepped onto the riverboat.

"Well, someone has to worry a little, since you certainly don't," Lin said quietly. She placed her hand in the steward's offered one and allowed him to assist her onto the deck. A gracious smile of gratitude curved her lips as he handed Lin back her valise. She hurried after Belle, who had already started down the aisle leading toward the cabin doors. "I only meant that, well, maybe we should hire someone to do this. After all, we're not really—"

"Papa needs *our* help," Belle snapped. "Anyway, how would anyone else get access to the Braggette plantation without having to confess who they were and why they were there?" She shook her head. A rich wave of silver-gold hair spread across her shoulders like a platinum-silk shawl. "No, my plan is the only way. And we will succeed, Lin, you'll see."

Lin sighed. "I hope you're right."

"Oh, you worry too much." Belle chuckled lightly and continued her way down the deck in search of their cabin. "Don't my plans always work?"

Lin's brows rose. Her aquamarine gaze met Belle's as her headstrong sister glanced back over her shoulder at Lin's silence.

"Oh, all right," Belle said. "So there was that time I talked you into taking Papa's prize stallions out for a ride and we got caught." She laughed again. "But we wouldn't have if we'd gotten an earlier start, which we didn't because you couldn't make up your mind if you were going or not."

"And the time we went swimming at Calzeau's pond with no clothes on?" Lin urged.

"Well, we wouldn't have had such an audience if you hadn't blabbed to Eddie Pellichout that we were going." A devilish smile curved her lips. "I think almost every boy in Natchez County was at the pond that day."

"And Papa, too," Lin reminded her.

Belle ignored her sister's admonishing tone. The attention from the crowd of adoring boys had been fun, but the tongue-lashing afterwards from her father had not. She stopped in front of one of the cabin doors that faced the outer deck. "5B. That's ours." She slipped the key the ticket agent had given her into the lock but found the door hadn't been secured. She pushed it open.

A tall, gangly man who was dressed only in his underwear, which was faded, red, and threadbare, jumped off of the room's bunk and stared at them.

Lin felt her cheeks turn pink. She gasped in embarrassment and hurriedly averted her gaze. "Oh, my goodness," she murmured.

Belle stared defiantly at the man. "What are you doing in our room?"

"Ain't in your room, lady. This here's my cabin." He reached out a gnarled hand to swipe a key off the top of the dresser beside him and stepped forward to dangle it in front of Belle's nose. "See? 5B." He jabbed a finger at the small plaque on the door. "5B."

"I don't care what your key says, you're still in the wrong—" Belle looked at the key in her hand and instantly realized her mistake. "Oh, I'm sorry. The ticket agent said 5B, but gave me a key to 5D." She picked up her valise and turned from the door, then paused and looked back at the man, smiling sweetly. "But a gentleman would have locked his door."

"And a lady woulda been more careful whose room she was prancin' into," the man shot back. He slammed the door, nearly catching the corded blue hem of her gown.

"Hmph! It's obvious he's no gentleman." With a toss of her head and her nose held high in the air, Belle retraced her steps along the deck toward the stairs. A small sign stated that the D cabins were on the next level of the packet.

Lin hurried after her. "Belle, are you sure we should be going to New Or—"

"What would you rather have happen, Lin?" Belle said over her shoulder as she climbed the steps of the widely fanning staircase toward the second deck. "Have Papa rot in that jail? Or be hanged for a murder he didn't commit?"

Under any other circumstances, the ride downriver on the *Cotton Queen* would have been enjoyable and the prospects of visiting New Orleans exciting. Instead, shopping and socializing were the furthest things from both Belle and Lin's minds. Lin was fraught with worry over what they were about to attempt, and Belle was consumed with rage at what had been done to their father. While Lin paced the cabin floor, Belle walked the deck, releasing her anger on anyone and everyone who dared to approach her, including the packet's captain.

It took only ten hours for the *Cotton Queen* to travel from the Natchez docks, where the Sorbonte twins had boarded, to the wharves of New Orleans, but to Belle it seemed like forever.

Lin stood quietly on the second deck, her satchels at her feet, and watched the boat move slowly toward shore. The huge red paddlewheel at the bow of the *Queen* churned steadily through the water and filled the quiet morning air with a steady *whoosh-whoosh* sound. Belle moved to stand beside Lin and dropped her own satchels on the deck with a thud. "Damn, I never realized what a long and boring trip this was."

"Cursing doesn't become you, Belle," Lin said quietly.

"I doubt hunting down a killer becomes me either," Belle snipped, "but that's what we have to do." She looked quickly at Lin. "Isn't it?"

"Yes," Lin answered.

The word had been spoken so softly that Belle wasn't sure she'd actually heard it, but she decided not to comment on Lin's obvious lack of enthusiasm for her plan. Her sister was cooperating, and that was the main thing. Belle turned her attention to the city coming into view. New Orleans hugged the river that was such an important part of its life, and then sprawled outward. There were at least a hundred other packets docked around its seemingly endless wharves, which ran the length of the entire city, and more than a dozen schooners anchored offshore. Belle waved a hand in front of her face and screwed up her nose. "Phew, I can smell those horrid street canals already," she said, referring to the open trenches that lined the streets of the city and carried everything from wash water to human waste toward the river.

Lin smiled. "Oh, you cannot!"

Belle laughed. "No, but we will soon enough. Thank heaven it's not summer yet, or we would be getting the odor full strength right now."

Lin looked pensive. "I hope there isn't an outbreak of yellow jack while we're here."

"I think it's too early in the year for the fever," Belle said. "Not hot enough yet."

The boat bumped against the wharf, and Lin grasped the railing to steady herself.

"Well, we're here," Belle said needlessly, "so let's go." She bent down to retrieve her satchel, but a masculine hand had already wrapped itself around the handle. Another was reaching for Lin's bag. The man's fingers brushed Lin's, and she jerked away instantly.

"Allow me, ladies."

Belle looked up into the face of the same man who had been seated at their dinner table the previous night. It was obvious from his attire—black frock coat and trousers, silver-threaded vest, white silk shirt, and black string tie at his neck—that he was a gambler. The black Stetson he wore even had a diamond stickpin in its silk band. Standard riverboat gambler attire. She'd seen plenty of professional gamblers whenever she and Lin had traveled with their father on business. At any other time Belle would have smiled flirtatiously and taken advantage of the man's offer to carry her bags, though she knew Lin would harangue her forever about her lack of propriety. This time, however, due to their mission, Belle wasn't in the mood to flirt. She took the valise from him.

"Thank you, sir, but I believe we can manage on our own."

They hurried down the stairs and toward the gangplank.

"He knows there are two of us," Lin whispered.

Belle waited to answer until they had debarked and begun to make their way across the wharf. "It doesn't matter. Most likely he'll be taking another packet upriver to fleece some poor sucker at the gaming table."

"But what if he doesn't? What if he stays in New Orleans? He could ruin our plan," Lin insisted.

Belle sighed. "Will you stop worrying? And pull that veil down over your face."

Lin reached up and pulled down the green tulle net attached to her bonnet. It didn't really hide her features, merely obscured them.

"Good." Belle paused. "There's some carriages for hire over there." She pointed toward one end of the wharf.

A half-dozen buggies of various size, adornment, and condition were parked to one side of the wharf's ticket booth. Several drivers stood talking next to one carriage while others remained in their vehicles, dozing while they waited for a fare.

"Take a carriage to the St. Louis Hotel," Belle said, "like we planned. I'll go out to Shadows Noir and get settled there."

Lin's brows pulled together as she frowned. "Belle, are you sure we should do—"

Belle waved a dismissing hand at Lin. "Remember, you're not Melinda Sorbonte now. Check into the St. Louis as Lin Bonnvivier, and I'll introduce myself to the Braggettes as Belle St. Croix. Then when I come to the hotel, I'll be Lin and you'll be—"

Lin sighed. "Belle, I swear, this is too confusing. Why don't we—"

"No," Belle snapped. "It is not confusing, not if you pay attention to what you're doing. Don't you want to help Papa?"

"Well, of course I do. It's just. . . . Oh piddle." Lin whirled around and walked toward one of the carriages.

"I don't know why I bother to argue with her," she mumbled.

Belle waited until Lin boarded and the driver had wheeled the carriage away from the banquette and onto the street before she approached one of the other drivers.

"I want to go to Shadows Noir," she said. "The Braggette plantation."

The man jumped down and tossed her satchels under his seat, then helped her board.

"Is it far?" Belle asked.

"Few miles outta town," he said, past the cigar that hung from one corner of his mouth. "Mebbe an hour's ride."

Belle settled back against the well-worn seat and tried to relax, but the effort was in vain. Neither she nor Lin were actresses, yet what they were about to do would take the skills of a professional performer. A small sigh escaped Belle's lips. She closed her eyes and ordered her nerves to quiet. They couldn't afford to fail. This plan *had* to work. It must, because if it didn't, if either she or Lin were caught, their father could die.

Two

"Did you see the way old Mrs. Gadreaux looked down her nose at me after the funeral service?" Eugenia Braggette let the lace panel fall back into place at the window, then reached to tuck a wayward lock of silver-streaked black hair into the chignon at her nape. She moved to a rosewood-trimmed ladies' chair and sat down. The chair's green silk cushion was instantly hidden by the voluminous folds of her gown's skirt, a flattering gray barege trimmed with black velvet cord, the dark colors broken only by the gown's snowy white lace cuffs and wide collar.

Her daughter, Teresa, handed Eugenia a cup of tea and opened her mouth to respond but was forestalled by her brother's reply.

"People are bound to talk, Mama, since you and Teresa refuse to postpone the wedding." His deep chuckle was silenced as he lifted a crystal tumbler to his lips and took a slow swallow of bourbon, then held the glass cupped in his hand and studied the liquor that had settled back into its deep bottom. Sunlight streamed through the tall windows that lined one wall of the room and turned the rich amber bourbon to molten gold. The morning light also settled on the broad expanse of Trace's shoulders to give the whiteness of his shirt an almost blinding brilliance. It touched the strands of his neatly cut hair and transformed them to soft waves of depthless ebony, and momentarily lent his aristocratic features a patrician hawkishness.

Eugenia's brows rose defiantly. "Your father's death is no reason to postpone Teresa's wedding, Trace Braggette, and you know it. The man didn't give a picayune about his family, and you're well-aware of that, too. Why should we put up a pretentious front of mourning him when his passing was more a relief than anything else?"

"He didn't even plan to be here to present me to Jay," Teresa said, the words a blend of anger and hurt. Gray-blue eyes only slightly lighter than her brother's blazed with defiance, and long black sausage curls bounced off of her shoulders as she tossed her head. "Not that I wanted him to."

"I consider that my privilege, Tess," Trace said. He smiled and lifted his glass toward her. "And I'm looking forward to it. I just hope that fiancé of yours appreciates what he's getting. After all, there are any number of young men in the parish who would feel honored to be marrying you."

His words brought a smile to Teresa's face, as he'd planned, and light laughter to her lips. But all too quickly the smile was replaced with a frown, which was more the usual for her these past few days. "Do you think the others will come, Trace? I mean, really?"

He shrugged. "They wrote that they would."

"They'll come," Eugenia said. "Nothing in the world could keep your brothers from coming to your wedding, honey. Nothing."

"They might not have come if Father was still . . ." Trace hesitated, then continued, "But we don't have to worry about that now, do we?" He smiled widely. "I agree with Mama, Tess, they'll come."

"Oh, I'm so looking forward to seeing them again," Teresa said, and clapped her hands. "It's been so long since they were here."

"Yes, it has," Trace said.

Eugenia looked up sharply, having caught the underlying thread of annoyance that laced her eldest son's tone.

"Your brothers did what they felt they had to do," she said quietly. "The same as you did, Trace."

"Not quite the same, Mama," he answered. Lifting the tumbler to his lips, Trace downed the last of the bourbon, set the glass on a nearby table, and rose to his feet. "Well, if you'll excuse me, ladies, I'd best get back to the books. Tomorrow I have to go into town."

"More questions?" Eugenia asked.

"The sheriff wants to look over father's office, though I don't know why. He searched it once and found nothing that would tell him why Sorbonte murdered father. I don't know what he thinks he's going to find by looking around it again."

"What are you going to do about the office, Trace? Rent it out?"

"Eventually, but right now I don't have time to go in there and clean out all of his papers."

Eugenia nodded and Teresa remained silent. It wasn't a task either of them wished to volunteer to do.

Trace turned to leave the room but paused as a knock sounded on the main door and echoed through the wide foyer. He looked back at his mother and sister. "Are either of you expecting anyone?"

They both shook their heads.

"It might be another condolence caller," Eugenia offered.

Trace groaned in disgust. "They didn't really like him when he was alive, though that's no surprise, so why do they feel bound to flock around and profess hollow words of sympathy now that he's dead?"

"Because they're being proper," Teresa said, "which I agree is silly. The man's dead and buried. I'd rather just forget he was ever here, let alone that he was my father.".

Trace turned toward the door and disappeared into the foyer. A pretty sentiment toward one's own father, he thought wryly. But then, if truth be told, wasn't that how they all felt? Thomas Braggette had been a cold, hard man. More so to his family than to anyone else. In spite of his father's numerous enemies, there had been times Trace had thought no one could hate Thomas Braggette as much as his own kin did.

A knock sounded again. Trace moved toward it and was instantly cut off by Zanenne, the housekeeper. "Never you mind," she said, and scurried past him.

Since he truly didn't want to receive another condolence caller, Trace happily relinquished the task of answering the door. He stepped out of view of whoever was on the front gallery and waited as Zanenne proceeded to the door. She'd been the housekeeper at Shadows Noir since long before any of the Braggette siblings had been born. Though she was sixty-one and as thin as the trunk of a young birch tree, Zanenne moved with more speed and agility than most people half her age. She shoved a waxing rag into the pocket of the muslin apron that was tied around her waist and lifted a hand to her head, as if to reassure herself that the red turban covering her hair was still in place.

Trace stood near the wide staircase that gracefully curved its way from the front portion of the foyer up to the second floor of the house. He leaned a shoulder against one ornately carved balustrade and watched Zanenne pull the door open. If the caller was someone he didn't care to see, all he had to do was take a step back and he'd be completely out of sight.

"Yes, ma'am?" the housekeeper said.

"Hello, I'm Belle St. Croix." Belle handed the housekeeper her invitation to the wedding and guest accommodations at Shadows Noir. Well, actually it wasn't *her* invitation. It belonged to a distant cousin of the widow Braggette who was a fairly good friend of Belle's. The woman couldn't attend the wedding, and Belle had managed to talk her into giving her the invitation, claiming she was going to New Orleans anyway and had actually met the bridegroom several times. She assured the woman she would write the Braggettes and explain. And of course she had, though using a false last name. Belle smiled at the housekeeper. "I believe I'm expected."

Zanenne took the invitation and looked down at it. Her dark face screwed into an expression of concentration as her brown eyes scanned the linen card. She recognized the word *Braggette* printed at the bottom, but that was all. The rest of the fancy writing with its exaggerated spirals and loops meant nothing to her, although she also recognized the invitation as being one of one hundred and fifty Eugenia had sent out for Teresa's wedding.

Upon hearing a young woman's voice, Trace immediately pushed himself away from the staircase and straightened. As far as he knew, none of the guests were due to arrive for several more days. Obviously his mother had neglected to correct him on that issue. He took a step to the side so that he could peer around the housekeeper.

The afternoon was bright, but the wide overhang of the second-story gallery shaded their guest from the brilliant light and left her in near silhouette to his view. Sunlight at her back created a golden halo that surrounded her and turned the waves of her hair into strands of flaxen silk.

Shimmering but weaker light from the fanlight window of the rear entry door at the opposite end of the foyer revealed to Trace only that her gown was blue and her figure subtly curvaceous. Her face remained within the shadows created by the wide-brimmed bonnet she wore.

Zanenne nodded and moved aside, then motioned for Belle to enter. "Welcome to Shadows Noir, Miss St. Croix," she said. "If you'll wait here, I'll tell Mrs. Braggette that you've arrived."

Belle left her satchels on the gallery where the carriage driver had placed them and stepped into the foyer, thankful to be out of the sun. It might only be nearing mid-April, but the air was already sultry and overly warm. She stood quietly and let her gaze move over the foyer while the housekeeper went to alert her hostess that they had a guest. The entry hall was very similar to the one in the Sorbonte plantation in Natchez. It ran the entire length of the house with identical entries at both ends, was extremely wide, high-ceilinged, and richly furnished. A huge grandfather clock of a dark, reddish wood she didn't recognize stood against one wall, its gold weights and massive pendulum gleaming. A petticoat table was set against the other wall, its mirrored bottom reflecting the opposite side of the room.

Thomas Braggette had obviously been a man of means. But that information brought her no insight into the reason for his death or who had killed him. Belle continued her assessment of the foyer.

A chandelier of polished brass hung from the ceiling. Each crystal sconce, of which there were at least forty or fifty, held three candles, and another row of identical sconces lined the sill of the fanlight window over the door. The one thing that made the foyer different from most was the floor: rather than hardwood it was made up of large black-and-white marble tiles.

At her entry into the foyer, Trace had stepped quickly behind the door to his study, then stood at such an angle that, although he was out of sight, he could still see their newly arrived guest. He felt the breath in his throat catch as Belle moved from the shadows into the light. He had seen many beautiful women in his time, courted a few, and even been betrothed to marry one, but this woman was more than beautiful. She was breathtaking. Her hair was the palest blond he had ever seen, long and flowing free down her back, silver strands touched with highlights of gold. His gaze moved to her eyes and again he found decision on a distinct color impossible. They were at once the color of a clear summer's sky and a freshly unfurled lilac leaf. He was instantly reminded of the aquamarine ocean waters he had once seen surrounding a Caribbean island. He had never encountered eyes quite that color before, and they intrigued him. Etiquette dictated that he step into view and introduce himself as well as welcome her, but he remained still and silent. The recent conversation with his mother, not to mention the events that had surrounded the Braggette family of late had left his disposition sour at best, and though he could appreciate the woman's beauty, he was in no mood to play the chivalrous gallant for her and while away the afternoon with inane small talk.

Trace quietly closed the door to his study and settled down behind the sprawling cherrywood desk his father had imported from France years ago. He opened the ledger that held the accounts of the plantation and stared, unseeing, down at the numbers. A few minutes later he slammed the ledger shut and gazed across the room at the book-lined walls and black-faced marble fireplace. His mind was not on facts and figures, not on the business of the plantation. He stood and walked to the window. They were coming back. Damn it all to hell. They were all finally coming back, and he wasn't sure how he felt about it. He knew he should be elated. He hadn't seen his brothers in many years, and as children they'd always been close. Especially he and Traxton.

But then they'd had to be close. It had been a form of self-protection. Them against their father. They'd lied, fought, protected, and soothed each other, but as they'd grown older, they'd found that no matter what they did, they couldn't win, not against Thomas Braggette. The others had left Shadows Noir and never returned, but Trace had stayed. His hand clenched into a fist at his side. He'd stayed, but it hadn't been because he'd wanted to.

He pulled a cheroot from the crystal holder that sat on a small étagère next to the window and slid the thin cigar back and forth under his nose, breathing deeply of its brandy-soaked fragrance. Utilizing the silver clippers that always lay next to the jar, he snipped off one end of the cheroot and slipped the other between his lips. "They're coming back," he said softly to himself, holding the cheroot still with his teeth. His fingers dipped into a small box of lucifers that sat near the cigars, retrieved one, and scraped its sulfur head against the heel of his boot. The lucifer burst instantly into flame, and he held it to the snipped end of the cheroot and inhaled deeply.

He hadn't seen Traxton for almost eight years. Travis had left the plantation a little over six years ago, and Traynor had been gone four years. Twenty seemed to have been the magic number for Thomas Braggette. Trace sniffed in disdain as he remembered his father and imagined what must have been in the man's subconscious: *if you haven't destroyed your children by the time they turn twenty, devastate them instead.* And Thomas Braggette had come close to doing just that with each one of them. Thank God he wouldn't be around in three years when Teresa turned twenty.

Trace threw the cheroot to the brick gallery just beyond the wooden doorsill, then walked over to it and ground out the burning tobacco with his heel. He couldn't blame his brothers for leaving, though Lord knows he'd wanted to. They had left, but he'd remained at Shadows Noir. After everything his father had done to him, and to Myra, he'd stayed. His fist slammed against the doorjamb . . . he'd stayed because someone had to. And he was the eldest. It had been his responsibility. He would have given anything to have been able to leave like the others, to have escaped, but he'd known he couldn't. He didn't like to think about what might have happened to his mother or sister if he hadn't been there, if they had been forced to live with Thomas Braggette alone.

"And now they're coming back," he said again, so softly that anyone standing only a few paces away wouldn't have heard even the whisper of his voice.

Lin looked up at the sprawling building as the carriage drew to the curb before its wide, canopied entry. An elegant black sign with gold lettering over the door proclaimed the structure the St. Louis Hotel. It was four stories in height, taller than most of the buildings in her hometown of Natchez, took up the entire width of the block, and was constructed entirely of brick. A gallery made of wrought iron and fashioned in an intricate pattern of cornstalks and flowers adorned the second floor, and a large dome capped the roof.

A tall, dark man dressed in bright red, white, and gold

livery stepped from the shadows of the canopy and offered his hand to Lin as the carriage stopped.

"Welcome to the St. Louis," he drawled as she accepted his hand and descended. He turned away. "Markus, take the lady's satchels inside."

"Thank you," Lin said. She walked into the hotel behind the steward. She had only brought two satchels, but the boy was so small, maybe eleven or twelve at most and built like a swamp reed, that he was barely able to carry them. A fleeting sense of guilt assailed her as she watched him struggle. Next time she'd pack less. Markus ignored the crowd of people milling about the lobby and proceeded directly toward a huge ornate counter that lined one far wall of the room. Lin, however, after taking only a few steps into the cavernous chamber, stopped abruptly. Her mouth opened in awe as she looked around, instantly mesmerized by the sight.

The lobby of the French Quarter's famous hotel was the largest she had ever seen, and the most luxurious. The building was four stories in height, and the center of the lobby was actually a massive rotunda, open to the ceiling and crowned by a dome of stained glass arranged in an intricate design. A huge chandelier of five tiers and immense width hung from the center of the dome and reflected a myriad of brilliant colors as sunlight filtered through the colored glass above and touched each crystal prism. The upper floors of the hotel opened onto the lobby, their galleries edged with elaborately designed iron railings and balustrades beyond which could be seen the windows of the shops that crowded the veranda's length. Elegantly gowned men and women strolled casually along the wide galleries, talking, laughing, and peering over the balustrade to gaze at the auctions on the main floor. White Doric pilasters graced the walls of the first story, rising at least twenty feet and stopping just beneath the slightly overhanging second-story gallery, as if to support it. Between each pilaster the walls were paneled in dark oak, upon which were hung large oil paintings of the city's past heroes and prominent citizens.

The steward noticed Lin pause and did likewise, but after a few seconds of standing still, his arms laden with her heavy satchels, he grew impatient. "Ma'am?" Markus said, knowing full well he should have remained silent.

Lin looked at the boy and smiled, forgetting that the veil over her face obscured her features. Unable to appease her curiosity, she didn't move to follow him but rather turned her attention to the bustle of activity that was taking place in the center of the vast lobby. A large group of men were gathered in front of a raised dais above which stood an auctioneer on an even higher dais. A young black woman stood alone on the lower platform, her arms wrapped tightly about her waist, head held high while her eyes remained fixed on some sight in the distance that only she could see. One man, well-dressed and obviously quite wealthy, walked up to the dais and lifted the woman's skirt. He ran a hand over her legs, as if examining her for injuries or weaknesses, much as Lin had seen her father do to horses when considering a purchase. Another in the audience loudly asked the auctioneer if the woman had ever been bred.

Lin's gaze moved to the next group of people and the next auctioneer. His merchandise was furniture. A group on the other side of him was bidding on paintings brought from France, and still another on household goods.

"Ma'am?" the steward said again. One of Lin's satchels began to slip from his grasp and Markus grappled to resecure his hold on it. "The desk?" he said hopefully. "It's this way." He turned and began to make his way across the lobby again, but glanced over his shoulder with every other step to assure himself she was following.

Lin made her way through the crowd, though she would have preferred to stand rooted to the spot and watch the proceedings around her. While they had been growing up, Henri Sorbonte and his wife had taken their daughters to Boston and New York on several occasions, but in neither of those cities had Lin seen anything as grand or as fascinating as the St. Louis Hotel. It wasn't just its elegance or that everything in the hotel glimmered with wealth and grandeur. It was more a uniqueness of style, an aura of old-world French class and New Orleans Creole flamboyance.

"Sold for twelve hundred dollars." The auctioneer's gavel crashed against the top of his desk and sent a jarring echo throughout the lobby.

Lin, startled at the sound, whirled around. She watched a short, stockily built man make his way through the crowd that stood before the auctioneer's block. He handed the auctioneer a fistful of greenbacks then reached up and wrapped a gnarled, stubby-fingered hand around the young black girl's wrist. Lin turned back to the desk clerk, who was still smiling and waiting for her reply to his inquiry of her name.

"Lin," she said finally. "Lin Bonnvivier of Vicksburg, Mississippi." She suddenly bit her lip and frowned. She shouldn't have said Mississippi. Or even Vicksburg. Especially Vicksburg. It was too close to Natchez. She should have said Baton Rouge or St. Louis or even Memphis.

"Beautiful name," the desk clerk said, and smiled.

Lin felt a wave of relief. She had fully expected him to start regaling her with tales of Thomas Braggette's murder and how the killer was from Mississippi, and did she know him because he came from Natchez which wasn't that far from Vicksburg, and didn't everyone from those small towns know everyone else?

"And you are alone, mademoiselle?"

Lin felt a definite sense of uneasiness mix with more than a touch of embarrassment at his question. He was a tall, rather wiry sort, his dark hair slicked back from an angular face. A thin mustache framed his upper lip and accentuated his already too-long beak of a nose and jagged cheekbones. She squared her shoulders. It was improper for a lady to travel alone, she knew, but there was no help for it. At least not this time. Lin smiled and stared past the thick glass of his spectacles to the brown eyes below his raised eyebrows. "Yes, monsieur. Unfortunately my father was taken ill and I was forced to make this trip alone," she said sweetly. "To do business on his behalf. Is my being unescorted a problem for the hotel?"

The eyebrows lowered back into place and he smiled, both his tone and attitude warming immediately. "Oh, no, Mademoiselle Bonnvivier, I was merely inquiring so that the hotel might provide you with the most convenient of accommodations." He looked around quickly, then in a lowered voice said, "And perhaps so that I might extend an invitation to dine with me."

Shocked at his boldness, Lin was momentarily taken back. "I . . ." Her mind raced for a response and finally remembered one she'd heard Belle use countless times when trying to rid herself of an undesired suitor. "I'm sorry, monsieur, but I believe my fiancé would find it quite unacceptable should I consent to dine with you."

The clerk bristled and tugged at the lapels of his frock coat. "Oh, certainly, Mademoiselle Bonnvivier, I didn't mean . . ." He turned toward a collection of highly polished, mahogany slots that covered the wall behind him and drew a key from one. "Room 210," he said stiffly, and handed the key to Markus. The boy groaned as he took the key and eyed her satchels again, which he had just set down. It was obvious he didn't relish carrying them up the stairs.

The desk clerk shot him a reprimanding glare and smiled coolly at Lin. "Markus will see you to your room."

"Thank you." Lin turned, more than ready to get away from the lecherous desk clerk, but as she waited for the steward to pick up her satchels, her wandering gaze caught and settled on a man just exiting the hotel bar. It wasn't so much the fact that he was handsome that held her attention, for she had met many handsome men. She studied him, a tiny frown pulling at her brow, and then realized why he intrigued her. He looked out of place in the elegant hotel.

He was taller than many of the other men in the lobby, and though there was an air of aristocracy in the way he carried himself and in the clean, sharp lines of his features, there was also a savageness about him that sent a shiver snaking up Lin's back. She had no doubt he was a man to whom most would give a wide berth. This impression was intensified by the holster that rode low on one hip, a revolver settled into its sheath and tied to his thigh. Leather chaps hugged his long, lean legs from waist to ankle, the outer seams adorned with silver conchos that caught the light and sparkled brilliantly. Silver spurs attached to his boots jingled with each step he took, and a black Stetson rode low on his forehead, almost but not quite leaving his face in shadow.

Blue-gray eyes, hard and assessing moved over the occupants of the room as he continued to walk toward the door. As if sensing danger, or merely feeling the need to be prepared in case it arose, he settled one hand atop the mahogany handle of his gun.

Lin continued to watch as he passed a woman entering the lobby. His free hand rose to touch the brim of his hat, and he nodded an acknowledgement. The woman smiled, said something to him, and continued toward the crowd of auctioneers.

Most likely one of the city's lawmen, Lin decided, and shuddered. Handsome as he was, she'd hate to be on his bad side. She turned back to follow the steward.

Three

"Miss St. Croix, it is so nice to meet you," Eugenia said. "My daughter and I were just enjoying a cup of tea. Would you care to join us before being shown to your room?"

"That would be wonderful, Mrs. Braggette, thank you," Belle answered. She glanced one last time around the foyer, having had the impression earlier she was being watched, then turned to follow her hostess into the parlor.

Eugenia paused in the doorway. "Please, call me Eugenia, dear. And may I call you Belle?"

Belle nodded. "Of course." It would simplify matters immensely not to have to be constantly alert for someone calling her "Miss St. Croix." She pulled off her kid gloves and shoved them into the figured blue reticule that hung from her wrist.

"Belle, this is my daughter Teresa." Eugenia beamed proudly. "The bride." She turned to her daughter. "Teresa, this is our guest, Belle St. Croix."

Teresa stood and smiled.

"Hello, Teresa," Belle said, "it's so nice to meet you. I wish you the best, and I want to thank both of you for your hospitality."

"It's nothing, really," Eugenia said. "You're a friend of cousin Helene's."

"Yes, and Helene sends her regrets for not being able to come, of course." Belle sat on the settee Eugenia motioned her toward. "Is your fiancé here, Teresa?"

"No, he had business in town today, but he may join us for supper. I understand you know him?"

Belle laughed, hoping she didn't sound nervous. This was her first test. "Actually, I met your fiancé some years ago and I doubt if he would even remember me." Helene had told her as much about Jay Proschaud as she knew, which wasn't that much. Hopefully Belle's little white lie would hold up, otherwise their plan could fail even before it got started.

"It doesn't matter really. We always love to have guests, and I'm sure my brothers won't mind at all." Teresa smiled slyly and handed Belle a cup of tea.

"Your brothers?" Belle echoed, emphasizing the plural. She knew Thomas Braggette had four sons, but Helene had said three of them hadn't been home in years and most likely wouldn't come to the wedding. Belle had counted on only Trace Braggette being there. She tried to smile. Fat lot Helene knew. Now it appeared she had even more people to fool.

"My sons left home quite a few years ago to make their own way in the world," Eugenia offered, "but they wouldn't miss Teresa's wedding. They should be arriving anytime now."

"How nice." Belle felt her smile threaten to turn into a grimace at just the thought of facing *all* of Teresa's brothers. The wedding, however, was not the topic of conversation in which she wanted to engage the Braggettes. "Oh, I'm sorry," Belle said, as if suddenly remembering. "I should have offered them earlier, but please accept my condolences on Mr. Braggette's death." She watched both women for a reaction. "I heard about it just before I left home. Terrible thing, just terrible. Have they caught the man who did it yet?"

Eugenia and Teresa exchanged what Belle considered a very knowing glance before either answered.

"They have made an arrest," Eugenia said.

"Oh, how wonderful." She leaned forward conspiratorally. "Then you know why Mr. Braggette was killed?"

"He most likely swind—"

"No, we don't," Eugenia said, cutting Teresa short, "and I'd rather not talk about it." She smiled. "I'm sure you understand, dear. My husband was a senator and a very powerful man. He made a lot of enemies in his time, but I don't like to dwell on that. Teresa's wedding is a much more pleasant subject, don't you agree?"

"Yes, it is," Belle said, realizing that neither Eugenia Braggette nor her daughter seemed too upset about Thomas Braggette's murder. In fact, she'd swear Teresa had been about to say something derogatory about her father when Eugenia had cut her off. Belle sipped her tea. Could it be that they truly didn't care why he had been murdered? A darker thought entered Belle's mind: or did they know a lot more about his demise than anyone suspected? She tucked the suspicions away to dwell on later. "Well, if there is anything I can do to help you with the wedding preparations, please let me know." Belle smiled widely. "I just love weddings."

"That would be wonderful, dear," Eugenia said. "I'm sure we could use your help, but now we'd best let you retire to your room. I'm certain you'd like to rest awhile before freshening up for supper."

"Yes, thank you," Belle said. She stood. "Will it just be the three of us, then, for supper?" She glanced back at Teresa as Eugenia escorted her to the door. "Or four, if Teresa's fiancé joins us?"

"My eldest son, Trace, will be dining with us," Eugenia offered. "I apologize that he's not here now to greet you, but he's been rather busy since his father's death, taking care of things."

"I understand," Belle said. "My mother passed on a few years ago."

"I'm sorry, dear," Eugenia said. She touched a hand to Belle's arm. "Do you still have your father?"

Belle smiled. "Yes, but he's often away." Especially now that he's in jail, she thought bitterly.

Zanenne, as if answering a silent summons, entered the foyer from another doorway.

"Oh, Zanenne, good," Eugenia said. "Please show Miss St. Croix to her room and see that she has whatever she needs to be comfortable."

"Yes, missus," Zanenne said.

Belle followed the housekeeper up the staircase and then down a long, elegantly appointed hallway, the upper portion of its walls covered with French silk paper, the bottom paneled in highly polished cherrywood. They passed two sets of doors, and Belle was shown into the third room on the right. It was decorated in varying hues of ivory and accented with complimentary tones of blue.

Zanenne crossed the room and drew back the heavy blue damask drapes that covered the room's two windows. She secured the draperies and the lace panels beneath them over gold hooks attached to the wainscoting, then opened the windows up into the wall above. "Let in some air," she said, and shoved open the jib doors that, when closed, made up the wall below the windows. "Bujo be bringing up your satchels."

Even before the words left her lips, a man appeared at the door to the bedchamber, one muscular arm wrapped around two of her satchels, while the third dangled from his other hand. Belle's first impression of him was *square.* His neck and shoulders were massive—his head was more a large cube than an oval—his features were wide and coarse, and his skin was blacker than a moonless night. The gray coat and trousers he wore, to say nothing of the white shirt, seemed strained as they hugged his muscular form. He smiled as his gaze met Belle's, and a slash of white broke the darkness of his face.

"Bujo, I presume," she said, and laughed lightly.

The man nodded, his eyes gleaming with amusement. "Yes, missy. Bujo, that's me."

"Put them bags on the bed and be done with it," Zanenne said curtly.

"Yes, Gramma," Bujo said, still smiling. He crossed the room and set the satchels down as instructed.

"Now be gone with you," Zanenne said, "and next time remember, I ain't your gramma when we're at the big house."

"Yes, Gramma." He smiled again. "I mean, yes, ma'am."

"Humph!"

Zanenne promptly set about removing Belle's clothes from the valises and placing them in the huge armoire that stood against one wall.

Belle pulled a fan from her reticule and walked to one of the open windows. Gathering the folds of her gown so as to ease the wide hoop through the passageway, she stepped out onto the gallery. The landscape of Shadows Noir was similar to that of her own family's plantation, and yet at the same time it was much different. Large oak trees dotted the terrain, their gnarled limbs draped with flowing curtains of Spanish moss. A formal garden of roses and other flowers was set to one side of the house, and fields of cotton could be seen spreading endlessly toward the horizon. Everything she could view from her own window at home, and yet here the moss was thicker and more abundant, the oaks seemed more massive and gnarled, the fields more sprawling. In Natchez the terrain was rolling; here it was mainly flat.

Suddenly her attention was drawn to a figure moving along a path beside the formal garden. Unconsciously Belle stepped into the shadow of a white pillar and peered around it. The man was approaching the house, coming, it appeared, from a stable on the other side of the garden. His strides were long, and he carried himself with an air of authority and confidence. His black wavy hair glistened beneath the late afternoon sun, his coiffure neat and precise, as was the gray frock coat that was tailored to accentuate the broadness of his shoulders and narrowness of waist. Her gaze continued to move downward. His legs were long and encased within striped gray trousers held taut by *sous pieds* laced beneath the arch of each black boot. She looked up at his face again as he drew nearer. She had to admit it was one of the most handsome that she had ever seen. The features were patrician, yet strong, his cheekbones high and well-curved, and black brows, like outstretched raven wings, arched over each eye. Even at this distance she could discern that his square jaw was clenched tight and a frown dug into his forehead.

"And just who are you, O unhappy one?" Belle mused softly to herself.

"That's Michie Trace," Zanenne said from directly behind her.

Belle whirled around, unaware that she'd spoken aloud. "Zanenne, I didn't know you were there." She forced a light laugh from her lips and smiled. "He seems to be angry. I hope nothing is wrong."

"Michie Trace got a lot on his mind," Zanenne said

evasively. She clasped her hands in front of her. "I've put all your clothes away, Miz St. Croix, so I'll be taking my leave now. Is there anything else you want? Some coffee or tea, perhaps? Lemonade?"

Belle followed the woman back into the bedchamber. "No, I'm fine, thank you, Zanenne. I think I'll just lie down and rest for awhile."

"Supper's at seven," Zanenne said, "but Mrs. Braggette likes to have sherry in the parlor before supper."

Belle nodded.

"Would you like me to help you out of your gown?"

"Oh, no, that's not necessary. I can manage, thank you." What she really wanted was to figure out a way to search the other rooms on this floor, but knew she'd better not try it yet. Not without first finding out exactly who was in the house and which rooms they occupied. So far she knew there was Mrs. Braggette, her daughter Teresa, and her son Trace. But were there others?

Zanenne opened the door to the hallway. "I'll send Clarissa up to help you dress for supper when it's time, if you like."

Belle nodded and began to release the buttons that held the bodice of her gown secure. She looked toward the open window and the gallery beyond. Perhaps she could stroll along it casually and by passing the windows of the other bedrooms discern if they were occupied. Fumbling to rebutton her bodice, Belle stepped past the curtains, onto the wide gallery, and collided with what felt like a wall of steel.

Trace grabbed Belle's shoulders to keep her from losing her balance as she stumbled backward and the huge hoop cage beneath her gown swayed wildly. "I'm sorry." His deep voice was a drawl of warm honey: smooth, flowing, and rich.

Belle looked up at him. His manners and dress were impeccable, but there was no warmth or welcome in the cool gray-blue eyes that stared down at her, nor in his stiffly held sinewy body.

The moment she had regained her balance, Trace removed his hands and stepped back. "You must be our newly arrived guest. Miss St. Croix, I believe?"

She smiled and proffered her hand. "Yes, Belle St. Croix. And you must be Trace Braggette."

His fingers closed around hers, and he brought her hand to his lips, brushing them across the backs of her fingers lightly, but her smile was not returned.

Belle watched him with intense interest. His nearness confirmed her earlier impression: he was most likely one of the most handsome men she had ever seen, and one of the coldest. Or was it perhaps merely arrogance that lent him an aura of chilled indifference? "You have a beautiful plantation, Mr. Braggette," she said in an effort to stimulate conversation and perhaps find out something about him. "Your mother told me that you've been in charge of it for quite awhile, since your father preferred politics, and I must compliment you. It is one of the most beautiful I've ever seen. Do you have your own mill here?"

"Yes." Trace bowed. "Now, if you will excuse me, Miss St. Croix, I have business to attend to."

"Oh." Her brows soared in surprise. Belle was not accustomed to men rushing away from her company, and she found it unsettling. Regardless of the fact that she suspected Trace of having something to do with his own father's murder and her father being falsely accused.

She watched him walk down the gallery and disappear through an open jib door window. It seemed a safe bet that Trace Braggette was not going to be an easy man to know.

* * *

Trace stalked into his bedchamber and went directly to his dressing table. He reached for his billfold, shoved it into the inside breast pocket of his coat, and turned back to the open window, then stopped. No, not that way. She might still be out there, and he had no desire to run into her again. He thoroughly disliked women who flirted and cooed small talk in an effort to keep a man's attention. Trace turned toward the door that led to the hallway. He'd take the main staircase. His thoughts went back to Belle St. Croix. Imagine, a woman questioning him about a mill! Ridiculous.

He made it to the Callahan place in less than an hour and, with a little bargaining, purchased the old man's prize stallion. The sun was just beginning to sink below the horizon when he rode into the Braggette stable and yelled for one of the grooms to help him with the horses. He handed the animals over to Bujo, who appeared almost before he'd finished calling for someone, and walked up to the house.

The tantalizing smell of Zanenne's gumbo wafted from the cookery, a small brick cottage located behind the main house, and blended with the sweet fragrance of the jasmine blooms that were just opening to the oncoming night and the roses which were pulling in their petals. The enticing odor teased Trace's senses, reminding him that he hadn't eaten anything since breakfast. He glanced at the setting sun again. If he hurried, he'd have just enough time to get upstairs, wash, and change his clothes before his mother expected him in the parlor for their before-dinner sherry.

He gave himself a quick once-over. Yes, he definitely needed to clean up. His shirt was smudged, and he smelled of tobacco, leather, and horseflesh. He began to unbutton the collar of his shirt, then stopped. They had a guest. He hurriedly rebuttoned the collar and retied the gray cravat that had hung loose around his neck since leaving the Callahans. Trace sighed deeply and wiped a bead of perspiration from his forehead. Whoever had set down the dictates of proper dress must have been sadistic, especially if he did it while living in Louisiana anytime other than during the dead of winter. He heard women's voices coming from the parlor as he entered the foyer, but ignored them and made directly for the staircase.

Trace opened the door to his room at the same moment he noticed their guest, Belle St. Croix, step over the threshold of hers.

She turned toward the staircase, unaware of Trace's presence as he watched her disappear down the hallway. She might be a little too outspoken and aggressive for his taste, but she was definitely one of the most beautiful women he'd ever seen.

"Trace, we were just about to give up on you," Eugenia Braggette said. Her words were scolding, but her smile made a mockery of the reprimand.

"Sorry, Mama." He kissed her cheek. "I rode over to Callahan's place to buy Demon back and had to make the trip twice."

"Father had no right selling your hor—"

"I got him back," Trace said curtly, effectively cutting his sister off.

"Nevertheless—" she began again, but abruptly stopped when she saw the glare her brother fixed on her.

"Trace," Eugenia said, "this is our guest, Miss Belle St. Croix."

He turned to Belle, who sat on the settee opposite Mrs. Braggette. "Miss St. Croix and I met earlier, Mama." Trace bowed slightly and smiled. "Good evening, Miss St. Croix."

"Good evening, Mr. Braggette," Belle said. She had taken great pains, with Trace in mind, in her toiletries and dress. Her gown was of ivory silk, its sleeves and hip flounces adorned with yards of Valenciennes lace, the plunging neckline accentuated by a sprinkling of seed pearls and embroidered emerald vines.

Trace smiled, but as before, Belle saw no warmth in the otherwise friendly gesture. "Welcome to Shadows Noir."

She dipped her head in acknowledgment. "Your mother was just telling me that Shadows Noir is over five thousand acres and planted mostly in cotton and tobacco," Belle said.

Trace poured himself a glass of sherry and moved to stand before the cold fireplace. "Yes, that's true." He propped a foot on the brass fender that fronted the grate and laid an arm on the mantel as his eyes studied her.

"And that in addition to being in charge of the plantation, you were once involved with politics like your father."

"Yes, but I found I did not inherit my father's, ah, shall we say, natural ability to succeed in politics." His cool gray eyes bore into hers. The runnings of a plantation, and the machinations of politics were unusual subjects for a woman, especially for such a beautiful woman, and the reason she chose them pricked Trace's curiosity.

"Oh?" Belle threw a quick glance at her hostess, but Eugenia seemed not to notice the underlying tone of sarcasm in her son's words. "I thought it merely took honesty and dedication to be a politician."

"I'm afraid it takes much more than that, Miss St.

Croix," Trace said. "Cunning, callousness, and a need for power above all else." His features hardened as he remembered the way his father had ruined his political career. It was Thomas Braggette who had taken a bribe and arranged for a murderer to escape punishment. And it had been Myra Devereaux, Trace's fiancée, who that same escaped murderer had killed when, on his flight from town, he'd encountered her on the road and robbed her of her horse, her money, and her life. But it had been Trace who'd been accused of taking a bribe and arranging the man's escape, and it had been Trace who people blamed for Myra's death, even though on the day she died, he had died, too, at least inside.

Belle saw the change that came over him and wondered what had brought it about. "I guess I've never thought of it quite that way before."

"Most people don't."

Belle decided that perhaps a slight detour in the conversation was needed. "Mr. Braggette, please forgive me for not offering you my condolences sooner. I offered them to your mother and sister earlier. I'm sorry about your father. His death must have been quite upsetting."

A smile that was actually a half grimace curved his lips. "Thank you, Miss St. Croix. Your sentiments are appreciated, but totally unnecessary."

The words hung like chilled clouds in the air, and for the first time in her life, Belle was at a loss as to what to say.

Zanenne appeared at the door. "Dinner's ready, missus."

Eugenia stood, looking rather relieved at the interruption, and took Trace's offered arm.

"Ladies," he said, motioning for Belle and Teresa to precede them.

A knock sounded on the main entry door as the small

procession was halfway across the foyer. They all paused and turned to look at the door.

Teresa moved to answer it, peeking out of one of the narrow windows that flanked the massive door. "It's Jay," she announced and swung the door wide.

A tall, thin man stepped into the foyer. His dark-brown hair, not quite wavy yet not quite straight, glistened beneath the glow of candles from the chandelier. His brown eyes, with their amber flecks, moved quickly over those standing in the foyer and paused a bit longer on Belle than the others.

She felt an instant dislike for Teresa's fiancé, though for the life of her she didn't know why, since in truth she'd never met him before. Jay Proschaud was not devastatingly handsome like Trace Braggette. In fact, he was not good-looking at all. His body could only be described as lanky, and his features were prominent but smooth. His cheekbones were high, his nose long, his lips thin though distinct, and his skin the swarthy bronze of a Creole.

Belle's gaze darted to Teresa. The girl was very pretty and would someday most likely be quite beautiful. She could certainly have done better than Jay Proschaud, at least if one were to consider his looks. But then Belle knew all too well that looks meant nothing when one was in love. Memories of John filled her mind, and though they still left a shadow of sorrow around her heart, they no longer brought instant tears to her eyes. It had been two years since the man with whom she had believed she would spend the rest of her life had been killed, but now whenever she thought of him, which admittedly wasn't as often as it used to be, she sometimes found herself hard-put to bring the image of his face into her mind.

Jay kissed Teresa's cheek. "Sorry I'm late. I guess you thought I wasn't coming, right?"

Teresa smiled up at him, her eyes shining with love. "I had just about given up and decided your nose was still buried in business. But I'm thrilled it's not. Come on, we were just going in to dinner."

"Good, I'm starved."

"Oh, Jay, I almost forgot. We have a guest," Teresa said. They paused before Belle. "Miss Belle St. Croix, may I present my fiancé, Jay Proschaud." Teresa stood next to Jay who towered over her five foot two form by at least eight or nine inches. "Jay, this is Belle St. Croix."

Belle smiled. This little test had come sooner than she'd hoped. "Good evening, Mr. Proschaud. We've met, but it was quite a while ago, very briefly, and I'm sure you don't remember."

Jay smiled, but the look on his face left no doubt he could not place her. "I'm sorry, Miss St. Croix, but you're right. I don't remember. Please, forgive me, but lately I have thoughts only for Tess. So much so that my brain seems unable to recollect a memory of any other woman, past or present." He leaned down and kissed Teresa's cheek again, and she giggled softly.

Belle's gaze moved from Jay to Teresa. "I think that's very admirable, Mr. Proschaud," she said, despite the fact that her stomach was nearly revolting in response to his syrupy words. "Teresa is a very lucky woman." Belle smiled and prayed that the gesture looked sincere since she had the sinking feeling that her words hadn't sounded so. She had never taken such an instant and thorough dislike to anyone in her entire life.

"Shall we go in to the table?" Eugenia said.

Dinner proved a trying experience. Jay Proschaud fawned over Tess all evening, to the point that he began to remind Belle of a sly child begging for attention while all the time he was plotting how to get into the cookie jar.

Eugenia, through small talk, kept bringing up the subject of the expected arrival of her other sons, which obviously made Trace's already cool mood even cooler. When Belle tried to talk to Trace directly, he responded to her questions with either curt answers or bracing arrogance.

But Belle couldn't give up. She had to know more about him, about all of them. "I would love to take a ride around the plantation tomorrow," Belle ventured, looking directly at Trace, "if that would be possible?" The only way she was going to find out anything about this man was to get him to talk to her, which so far had proven unsuccessful. Perhaps if she could get him alone. She stared at him and waited for a response.

"Of course," Trace said. "Bujo will saddle you a horse. Just go down to the stables. He's usually always somewhere close by."

"Would you mind if I rode with you on your morning rounds?" She tried to smile innocently and felt like a failure. It had been a long time since Belle had been able to look innocent of anything. "I'm an early riser." She caught the smile that tugged at Teresa's lips and the interested stare of Trace's mother as they all waited for his answer.

"I'm sorry, Miss St. Croix, but I'm not going on morning rounds tomorrow," Trace said finally, staring directly into her eyes. "I have to go into town."

Belle nearly choked on the shrimp she had just spooned into her mouth. He was going into town. She swallowed hard. What if Lin didn't stay in the hotel like she was supposed to? What if Trace saw her? How would either of them explain that? She knew the answer to her own question even before her mind asked it: they wouldn't be able to. There would be no explanation but the truth, and then all would be lost. She tried the sweet, innocent smile again. "Would you mind if I accompanied you, Mr. Braggette? I haven't been to New Orleans since I was a child, and I'd love to do some shopping in town. I've been told the Vieux Carré has some of the most fabulous shops in the world."

"I really doubt it's a good idea to accompany me, Miss St. Croix, at least this time. I'll be leaving quite early and be tied up with business matters most of the day. I really don't know what time I'll make it back to Shadows Noir, if I make it at all. My meetings could run late, then I would have to stay over in town."

"Oh." Belle's stomach threatened to flip-flop. She'd just have to pray Lin didn't suddenly get an urge to venture out. Then she remembered who she was thinking about. Lin wouldn't go out of the hotel alone. Traveling about town unescorted was improper, and Lin would never do anything improper, not even if her life depended on it.

The worried little frown on Belle's brow disappeared. She decided to forget about being innocent, curving her lips into her most flirtatious smile and flashing it at Trace. "Well, perhaps we can take a ride together when you return?"

He tipped his head slightly in acknowledgement of her remark, but made no comment. Belle felt her frustration mounting. What did it take to get this man to talk? To smile? To act human, for heaven's sake?

"Good. I'd love to see all of Shadows Noir. It seems such a beautiful place from what I've viewed so far. And since you're the one responsible for making it what it is, Trace," Belle batted her eyelashes in what she hoped was a seductive ploy, "I'd much prefer to wait until you have the time to escort me about so that I can see it with you."

"It would be my pleasure. I'll do my best to be available to you upon my return," Trace said courteously, though Belle had the distinct impression his words were lacking in sincerity.

"When do you think your brothers will be arriving?"

The smile he'd kept on his face, though somewhat stiff, instantly disappeared, and the silver gray of his eyes darkened. "I don't know." The words snapped so sharply they caused Belle to nearly jump from her chair.

She stared at him appraisingly. Trace Braggette was a man full of anger—it was evident in his words, his tone, and in the cold gray and fiery blue of his eyes. Belle felt a shudder trip up her spine. And angry men were usually dangerous men, the kind that could kill . . . even their own fathers.

Four

By the time Belle returned to her room that evening to retire, she was convinced that Trace Braggette had something to do with his father's murder, if he hadn't been the one to actually do it. The man was a gentleman on the surface, but underneath his cool insouciance and impeccable social manners, he was filled with rage. She sensed some of it was directed at his brothers, but not all. It was obvious there had been no love lost between father and son. At least between father and eldest son. She'd have to reserve her opinion of the others until she met them. Belle shuddered. Which would be all too soon. So far everything had gone as planned, except for Trace's trip into town, but there was nothing she could do about that other than pray Lin didn't suddenly feel the urge to flout propriety.

And then there was the little problem of her own outspokenness. She'd never been very good at holding her tongue, and there had been several times that evening she'd nearly bit it off in an effort to stop a sentence that might have given everything away—like who she really was.

Shrugging out of her gown and releasing the waist hook on her crinolines and hoop-cage, Belle let the garments fall to the floor. She stepped from the mound of material, threw her camisole and pantalettes over the settee, and slipped into a batiste nightgown. She was exhausted. The trip, the situation, and the arguing with Lin had all taken their toll, yet tired as she was, her mind wouldn't shut off. She kept replaying pieces of conversation she'd had with the Braggettes, envisioning her father sitting in a cell, and worrying that Trace Braggette would somehow run into Lin when he was in town tomorrow and their entire plan would go up in smoke.

She began to pace. Fifteen steps took her from one side of the room to the other. Trace Braggette seemed the most logical suspect for the murder of his father. There were rumors that Thomas Braggette had destroyed his eldest son's political standing. But was that enough reason to murder one's own father? Or were there other reasons? She had to find out. Trace was still angry with his father, even after the man was dead. Belle had felt his fury. Heard it in his tone, in his words. Another fifteen steps brought her back to where she had begun. And what would his brothers be like? Were they all duplicates of Trace? Did they harbor the same anger? Her head began to throb. She wished she could just march into Trace Braggette's room and accuse him of the murder, force him to confess, and then march him down to the jail so that her father would be released. That was unrealistic, though, as she had only her own suspicions and no actual evidence. She would have laughed aloud at her own thoughts except that it wasn't really funny.

Belle reached to the crown of her head and pulled out the pin that held a good portion of her hair. As she shook her head, the long platinum strands cascaded down her back and over her shoulders, picking up the light from the crystal oil lamp on the night table and glistening like silver.

Belle walked to the window. The jib door had been

secured but the window was still up. She released the latch that held the half door secure and pushed it open, then walked out onto the night-shrouded gallery. The sound of several cicadas filled the night air, interrupted occasionally by the lonely, soulful hoot of an owl. Belle breathed in deeply of the sultry air, letting the intoxicatingly sweet fragrance of the night-blooming jasmine, its vines twined around several of the mansion's large pillars, invade her senses. She looked up at the dark sky, a never-ending expanse of blackness that was sprinkled with a thousand sparkling stars and cradled a sliver of golden moon.

Her appreciative gaze moved to the grounds of Shadows Noir. Belle was well-accustomed to beauty and luxury, the Sorbonte plantation in Natchez being one of the area's most splendid. Even so, the majesty of Shadows Noir left her near breathless. A winding drive led from the main road to the entrance of the house and was covered with crushed white oyster shells. Beneath the night's natural light the shells were transformed into a trail of pale whiteness that snaked its way through a sprawling expanse of grass. The forest green leaves of the giant live oaks that dotted the landscape seemed almost ebony beneath the twilight glow, while the large waxy leaves of the magnolias had been transformed to shimmering planes of silver and the trees' white blossoms, closed against the night, had become balls of soft ivory.

Belle placed her hands on the railing and let herself enjoy the scene. Reaching up and over her head, Belle extended her arms to their full length, dropped her head back so that she was looking up at the gallery's overhang, and arched her spine in an effort to stretch her stiff muscles. A sigh of satisfaction slipped from her lips.

In the darkness of the gardens, hidden by the inky

shadows created by the gnarled, sprawling limbs of a giant live oak and the curtains of moss that hung from them, Trace lazed insolently against the tree's trunk. He inhaled deeply of a thin cheroot cradled between the fingers of one hand. Even though his body was tired, sleep was the farthest thing from his mind.

He held the cheroot up and studied the burning tip of rolled tobacco as he exhaled slowly, letting the white smoke drift from his lips onto the night air where it instantly dissipated.

They were finally free. Their father couldn't hurt them anymore, couldn't destroy everything they tried to do with their lives like he'd done so easily, so callously, while he'd been alive. Trace felt the anger that had been his constant companion for as long as he could remember sweep over him anew at the mere thought of his father and what he'd done to each of them. Now that Thomas Braggette was dead, Trace felt no regret, no sorrow, no remorse. Nothing a son was supposed to feel at the loss of his father. He lifted his hand, intent on returning the cheroot to his lips, when a movement on the second-floor gallery of the house caught his attention.

Instantly alert, Trace pushed himself away from the tree and strained to see through the veils of moss and the black night. Everyone had retired hours ago. The servants had left the house and gone to their own cabins. So who was on the gallery? His hand moved to cover the small pocket of his vest. The derringer was there, as always, nestled safely within the sheath of fabric, waiting to ward off danger. He dropped the cheroot to the ground, stepped on the burning tip, and ground it into the dirt. His fingers closed around the handle of the gun, and he pulled it from his pocket. Every muscle in his body was taut with tension, every nerve cell energized and alert for danger. His index finger curled around the trigger. Trace took a step forward, but remained beneath the protective boughs of the huge tree, obscured by its shadow.

He reached up and touched a curtain of moss with the back of his hand, then pushed it slightly aside to allow himself a better view of the area before stepping into the open.

At that same moment a wisp of cloud that had obstructed the moon drifted onward. A stream of golden light pierced the darkness and fell onto the second-story gallery.

Trace froze in place and felt the breath catch in his throat. He knew he should look away, should turn and leave, but he couldn't. He remained rooted to the spot, his gaze riveted to the woman who stood basking in the moon's soft glow. Its rays penetrated the sheer dressing gown she wore, while at the same time, from the room behind her, the light of an oil lamp shone through the open window and left her figure in silhouette against the diaphanous folds of material. The golden beams of both moonlight and lamplight seemed to dance within the waves of her long silver-gold hair and turn her flesh to the soft ivory of a magnolia blossom.

An uncomfortable tightening of the inseam of his trousers jerked Trace from the mesmerizing stupor and back to reality. His hand dropped away from the prickly Spanish moss, letting it fall back into place, and he whirled around. "Damn it all to hell, what's the matter with me? I don't even like the woman." A string of silent curses, all directed at himself, followed. He damned himself for his lack of decorum, for an obvious failure of self-control, and for the desire that simmered within his body. But he couldn't deny it had happened.

It had been more years than he cared to remember

since the mere sight of a beautiful woman had inspired that kind of hungry passion in him. He had loved Myra with all of his heart. When she'd died, his dreams had died. He'd known with a certainty that was unshakable that he would never love another woman, and he hadn't, but he had also thought he would never be able to be with another woman either. But about that he had been wrong. In his heart and mind those feelings were dead, but his body needed the satisfying physical release only a woman's touch could give him. He had thought of taking a *placeé* and quickly discarded the idea. The mere thought of choosing a woman from the quadroon balls to be his mistress, of setting her up in one of the cottages on the Ramparts and paying court to her, all rang of too much permanence and only reminded him of what he had lost when Myra had been killed.

Another curse and a long sigh escaped his lips. Obviously he had let too much time elapse since his last visit to one of the brothels tucked away in the Vieux Carré. But that could be easily and immediately rectified.

Belle saw the movement in the garden. Her arms flew down and crossed her breasts in an effort to cover them, and she jumped away from the railing. Someone was down there. Someone had been watching her. She felt a shiver of fear. But who? And why?

She moved to stand behind a pillar and peered around it to where she thought she'd seen someone standing. There was no one there. At least no one that she could see. Her gaze quickly scanned the area, trying to pierce each shadow. Could it have been merely her imagination?

The sound of a horse's hooves on the crushed gravel drive suddenly broke the silence.

Belle inched farther back into the shadows of the pillar and waited to see who was approaching the house. She realized almost immediately that the sound had not come from the entry drive as she'd at first thought, but from the side of the house. She whirled around just in time to see Trace ride past. The darkness of his coat and that of the horse he rode merged with the night to make him nearly invisible. Only the whiteness of his shirt and his bronzed flesh in the moon's glow distinguished him from the blackness that enveloped the earth.

She stared after him as he disappeared around a curve of the entry. He had been the one watching her, she felt certain of it, but where was he going now? Why was he leaving the plantation when it was nearly midnight?

Belle stepped back into her room. Well, she didn't know where he was going, but at least she knew he was gone from the house. Everyone else had retired to their rooms hours ago. She smiled and slipped on a wrapper that matched the gown she wore. It was a perfect time to search Trace's bedchamber.

She moved on tiptoe to the door, opened it quietly, and stepped into the hall. The cavernous passageway was illuminated only by a lone candle set within a glass lamp on a wall table. She stared at the closed doors of the other bedchambers, trying to remember which one she had seen Trace enter earlier that day.

Finally deciding on the next-to-last door on the opposite side of the hall, she moved quickly toward it, but before proceeding, she pressed an ear to its oak panel. No sound came from within the room. Her fingers curled around the silver doorknob. Turning it slowly, Belle pushed open the door and slipped into the dark room. For several very long, terror-filled seconds, she stood with her back flattened against the wall and hardly dared to breathe. What if she had been wrong? her mind practically screamed. What if this wasn't Trace's room? What if someone else was in here?

She strained to hear the faintest of sounds and heard nothing, not even the soft rush of someone's breath. Her eyes slowly became accustomed to the darkness, and shapes began to take form and become recognizable: an armoire, a dressing table, a shaving stand, a writing desk, and a bed. Belle took a step into the room, leaned forward slightly, and stared at the surface of the bed. No, there was no one in it. She sighed and felt weak in the knees with relief.

"This is no time to start acting like some silly, ninny," she whispered harshly to herself. She reached toward a lamp on the dressing table and stopped. What was she doing? She couldn't light its wick. What if someone outside saw the light in the window? What if Trace looked back? No, it was too risky, and she couldn't search his room in the dark.

Belle felt suddenly like crying and stiffened against the urge. It wouldn't accomplish anything except to make her feel worse. She'd just have to find an opportunity to search Trace's room in the daytime, when she could see what she was doing.

Moving stealthily, she opened the door and slipped back into the hall. The door's latch made a soft click at her back as she pulled it closed, and Belle nearly jumped out of her skin. Though it was the softest of sounds, to her ears it was like a clap of thunder. She held her breath and waited for one of the other doors to open and an accusing face to glare out at her. When nothing happened, she exhaled silently and made her way quickly back to her room. Sleep did not come easily that night.

Five

Trace looked up from the mass of ledger papers scattered on the desk and fixed his gaze on the man who sat across from him. Sunlight shining through the window behind the attorney, reflected off of his bald pate and turned his large ears bright pink.

Ben Carlisle had been talking for a good five minutes straight, and Trace suddenly realized he didn't have the faintest idea what the man had said. In fact, during the several hours they had been together, they'd actually accomplished very little, and Trace would readily admit it was his fault, not Ben's. His mind was elsewhere, and trying to conduct business while he mused upon his brothers' imminent return and their family situation was fruitless. He raised a hand and the attorney instantly stopped talking.

"What's the matter, Trace?" Ben asked. Perplexed blue eyes squinted through a pair of gold-rimmed spectacles perched on the end of his bulbous nose, and fleshy cheeks puffed even bigger as he pursed his lips and waited for an answer.

"Ben, I'm sorry, but my mind is just not on all of this today." He made a sweeping motion toward the papers that covered the desk, most of which were tally sheets and receipts for cotton and tobacco shipped from the Braggette plantations, as well as for several other family investments and holdings.

"But, Trace, we can't just let things sit idle: you'll lose money. You have to decide on your crop purchases for next season, and determine whether or not you have enough workers and warehouse space. And we have contracts to negotiate."

Trace sighed. "Then you take care of it, Ben." He rose. "Do what you have to do. I'll check in with you next week." He walked toward the door.

"Have they arrived yet?"

Trace paused, looked back, and shook his head. "No, but they'll be here any day now."

"Are they going to stay?"

He pulled the door open. "I don't know."

"And if they do? What about the plantations? Not just Shadows Noir, but the others you own. You're the one who's been running them, holding things together. What happens if they want to stay?"

"There's enough for all of us," Trace said, and closed the door behind him.

Once out on the banquette, he turned toward the river and began to walk. He wasn't quite ready to return home and face his brothers, if they were there. Coming around a corner of the Presbytere, the city's government building, Jackson Square came into view. Beyond it the wharves teemed with activity. The Square was one of Trace's favorite places in the Quarter, a tract of garden set within the midst of the city like an island of serenity. Its paths meandered and curved through tall live oaks, flowering magnolias, dogwoods, chestnuts, and pine, while roses, azaleas, and bougainvillea blooms added their rainbow of colors to the small green vista. It was late enough in the afternoon so that the now well-shadowed Square was filled with people: mothers with their babies, young lovers meeting before the sun sank from the sky and the girls' chaperons whisked them home, and others merely out to enjoy the end of the day.

Trace walked slowly, aimlessly, about the park. Several men were gathered in one corner, arguing loudly over the latest happenings in Washington. Lincoln seemed more adamant than ever that the South bow to the North's demands and free the slaves. Trace shook his head. Did the man realize how many people would lose everything if they were forced to do that immediately, as he was demanding?

He passed a small bench set beneath the overhanging limb of a giant oak, paused, and then settled onto the seat. What if his brothers wanted to stay on at Shadows Noir? It was a question that had been haunting him for days. Could he give up the complete control he had worked so hard to obtain?

He leaned against the bench and let his gaze wander again. It settled on the two-story brick structure that sat to the east side of the Square. Its second-story was adorned with a black wrought iron balcony and was made up of apartments, while its street level was comprised of shops. As Trace stood, deciding not to prolong the inevitable but to go home to see if his brothers had arrived, he caught sight of Belle St. Croix stepping from the door of one of the shops.

Lin exited the candy shop and looked quickly around. The feeling that she was being watched came over her. She reached up and pulled her pale yellow veil down, but the feeling persisted. Clutching her reticule, Lin turned in the direction of the hotel. She shouldn't have left it, shouldn't even have ventured out of her room.

Belle had warned her. Their plan could be ruined if anyone found out there were two of them, and Belle, at the Braggette plantation, could be in placed in danger. Lin felt a wave of disgust with herself. Oh, how could she have been so foolish? She had wanted to see their father, to make sure he was all right and let him know they were trying to help him, and she hadn't even accomplished that.

She began to hurry down the banquette, holding the ruffled skirt of her yellow-and-white striped percale gown up from the ground. She swerved around a woman pushing a baby carriage and a group of young men engaged in heated discussion.

Her fingers tightened their grip on the small package of chocolates she'd purchased for her father at the confectioner's shop. The jailor had refused her entrance, stating that only relatives were permitted to see the prisoners, and she certainly couldn't admit to being a relative. Remembering the musty smell of the jail and its dank atmosphere, Lin felt tears well up in her eyes at the thought of her father being forced to endure such conditions. At least she could send him his favorite treat.

"Excuse me," Trace said, stepping up beside Lin.

Startled from her thoughts, Lin's heart lurched. She glanced up at him briefly but didn't slacken her pace. "Yes, certainly," she said.

"Miss St. Croix, please wait." He touched a hand to her elbow. "I've been wanting to apologize for my behavior yesterday."

Lin kept walking. "I'm sorry, sir, you must be mis—"

"Miss St. Croix . . ."

The name suddenly registered in Lin's mind. *St. Croix.* Good Heavens, wasn't that the name Belle was using? Lin felt a swell of panic in her breast. Oh, Lord. The man thought she was Belle. She stopped short and turned to stare up at him. Then another realization struck her like a blast of lightning between the eyes. He looked very similar to the man she had seen in the hotel lobby upon her arrival, the cowboy with the gun. The panic began to grow. Her gaze raked over him. Was this the same man? He didn't look the same. His clothes were different, refined, gentleman's clothes. Her eyes swept upward and met his. But he'd called her Belle. The panic threatened to overwhelm her.

"I wasn't exactly in good form yesterday when you arrived at the plantation," Trace said, not noticing that Lin's eyes had the look of someone staring down the barrel of a shotgun. "And since you're in town now, no thanks to me, I'd like to make up for my behavior by taking you to dinner."

"Dinner?" Lin echoed. He wanted to take her to dinner. No, her mind corrected instantly, he wanted to take Belle to dinner. What was she going to do? Her mind zipped about in search of an answer. She couldn't go as he'd realize immediately once they started to really converse, that she wasn't Belle. But how could she get out of it?

Trace smiled, and Lin nearly melted, her panic momentarily forgotten. It was the most beautiful smile she had ever seen, and as she gazed into his eyes, she had the distinct feeling that she was drowning in a sea of gray-blue mist.

"Yes, we could dine at the hotel, if that's all right with you," he replied.

"The hotel?" Reality slapped her across the face. *The hotel.* People knew her there as Lin Bonnvivier. The hotel clerk, the young man who had brought a breakfast tray to her room that morning—what if one of them saw her and greeted her by name? What could she say? She began to shake her head in refusal. "No, really, that's not necessary," she said. "I'm sure you have things to do, and I—"

The smile that had been on Trace's face turned to a frown of disappointment. "You're angry."

"No, truly," Lin hurried to correct, uncertain if she were repairing a situation for Belle or aggravating it, "I just meant that I'm sure you're busy and taking me to dinner is really not necessary."

"I agree," Trace said, and took her hand, "it's not necessary, but I would be most honored if you'd consent to join me and most disappointed if you refuse."

At the touch of his fingers on hers, Lin felt a flash of warmth sweep up her arm. She pulled her hand from his and turned to continue on her way. "Thank you, sir," she suddenly realized she wasn't certain who he was, "but I have a few more things to do and. . . ."

For some reason even he was unable to comprehend, Trace was reluctant to allow her to refuse him. His invitation to dine had started out as merely a gesture of courtesy, an act to appease his conscience for being so rude the night before. He looked down into her blue-green eyes and suddenly wanted nothing more than for her to accept his invitation. Trace reached out and grasped her arm, strong fingers wrapping around tender flesh, his hold on her gentle, yet firm. "Please, Belle, dine with me," he said. "I was in a surly mood yesterday when you arrived and I've apologized but . . ." He shook his head as if he was at a loss for further words, but before she could protest again, he continued. "You've traveled a goodly distance to attend my sister's wedding and . . ."

This was Trace Braggette. Lin felt a shudder of nervousness rattle her body. Good Lord, this was the man Belle was convinced had murdered Thomas Braggette and framed their father!

"You are our guest, Miss St. Croix, and my welcome last night was less than gracious. Indulge me," he smiled again, and Lin thought she caught a tiny hint of wicked mischief in the curve of his lips, "and allow me to buy you dinner."

"Really, it's not necessary." If Belle found out about this she'd be so furious, she'd . . . Lin didn't want to think about what Belle would do. She smiled sweetly. "I assure you, I'm not angry and—"

"Good, then since I've just decided I won't take no for an answer and you're not angry with me, we should have a very pleasant supper."

Before she could even think of protesting, Trace cupped a hand beneath Lin's elbow and began to steer her down the street in the direction of the hotel.

He hadn't the faintest idea why he was doing what he was doing. It had been longer than he cared to remember since he'd dined out with a woman other than Teresa or his mother, and why he was so anxious to do it now he didn't know. An apology would have sufficed in regards to his treatment of her the previous night, but for some reason, as he'd looked deep into her eyes, he hadn't wanted to let it go at that.

Lin tried to hide behind the folds of her hat's thin tulle veil as they walked through the lobby of the hotel. Her eyes darted about and her hands trembled. Someone was going to approach her, was going to greet her as Miss Bonnvivier, she just knew it. Then what would she do?

Trace guided her toward the wide, sweeping staircase that led to the second floor.

Lin's heart nearly stopped. The steward, Markus, was on his way down, obviously having just delivered bags to a room. He'd say hello to her. Trace Braggette would discover that she wasn't Belle. Their plan would be ruined and their father would be hanged. Her pulse began to race and a sharp throbbing erupted within her temples. She was going to faint. The reticule she held clasped in her fingers, as well as the small package of chocolates, slipped from her grasp and fell to the floor.

"Are you all right?" Trace asked.

"Oh, yes, quite." She lifted a hand to her forehead and turned to look over her shoulder and back at the lobby.

Markus approached from the opposite direction. "Is anything wrong, monsieur?" he asked.

"No, the lady just dropped her reticule." He scooped the bag of chocolates and the reticule from the floor. "Thanks."

Lin kept her face averted and prayed Markus wouldn't address her so that she'd be forced to turn around.

Trace rose and handed Lin the reticule and package.

"Good evening, monsieur, mademoiselle," Markus said, and continued on his way across the lobby.

Lin felt such a wave of relief her knees nearly buckled. She slipped her arm around Trace's offered one, thankful for the steadying support it gave her.

"Have you ever taken a meal at the St. Louis before, Miss St. Croix?" Trace asked as they ascended the staircase.

Lin's mind raced. How was she supposed to answer that? What had Belle told him? They hadn't been to New Orleans since they'd been children—very young children. Had she admitted that? Or had she fibbed and claimed a close acquaintance with his home city? Oh, how had she gotten into this fix? But that question was easier answered than his. She glanced at him and found him watching her, obviously waiting for her to respond to his inquiry.

"The hotel really is beautiful," she said, hedging, "and has just about everything a person could want, don't you think?"

"You've browsed its shops, then?"

At last a question she could answer without trying to be evasive. "Oh, yes, and I'm afraid I bought more than I'd intended."

"Oh? Where are your purchases?"

Panic instantly returned. Her purchases. Where were her purchases? "Uh, oh, uh . . . they're . . . they're . . ." her mind cast about frantically in search of an answer, "they're being delivered," she finally said.

He nodded and stepped aside to offer her entry into the dining room.

"Good evening, Monsieur Braggette," the maître d' said as they entered. "Your usual table?"

"Yes, Andre, please," Trace answered.

His usual table? Lin felt the trembling in her hands increase. What did that mean, his usual table? Was he staying at the hotel? But why would he stay at the hotel? The Braggettes had a plantation in New Orleans. Her head jerked around and she stared up at the man beside her. Maybe she'd misunderstood him earlier and this wasn't Trace Braggette. He was a Braggette, obviously, the maître d' had called him by that name, but maybe he wasn't *Trace* Braggette. Her heart nearly fluttered out of control. But if he wasn't Trace Braggette, then who was he?

Trace motioned for her to precede him into the dining room and follow the maître d'. Lin lifted the front of her skirt and weaved her way through the maze of linen-covered tables.

The dining room was immense, larger than any ballroom she'd ever seen, and much more elegant. Four crystal chandeliers hung from the ceiling, at least two hundred lit tapers on each one. The flickering flames danced on the tiny wicks and reflected a hundred times within the crystal prisms that hung from each tier like frozen teardrops. Rich, cherrywood paneling covered the walls from floor to waist height, and silk wallpaper depicting a hunting scene rose from there to the ceiling. The floor was gleaming hardwood, the dual fireplaces at opposite ends of the room were faced with white Carrara marble, and damask draperies of emerald green adorned with gold torsade fringe framed each tall window.

A candle within a glass chimney flickered merrily in the center of the table they were shown to, and a small vase of assorted flowers sat beside it.

Trace helped Lin into her chair and then settled into his own. He conversed in French with a waiter, and within minutes food began to arrive at their table. Lin watched Trace from beneath half-lowered silver-gold lashes. She'd had dozens of beaux, but none had been as handsome as Trace Braggette. Then she reminded herself that while he might be the most handsome man she'd ever seen, he might also be a killer and the man responsible for her father being in jail.

The waiter brought the first course to the table. Lin pierced a small chunk of shrimp with her fork but continued to watch Trace.

"So, Miss St. Croix, tell me," Trace said, "how do you know my mother's cousin, Helene?"

The sip of wine Lin had just taken went down the wrong passage. She patted the linen napkin to her lips and swallowed hard. "Please, call me Belle," she said finally, her voice a bit weak.

"All right, but only if you call me Trace."

She nodded. He was Trace Braggette. Lin suddenly didn't know whether that made her feel better or worse, but at least now she knew who he was.

"As I was saying, how do you know Helene?"

"Helene?"

"Yes, my cousin. Teresa mentioned that you knew Helene. Evidently her invitation to the wedding has been extended to you since she couldn't attend and you were traveling here anyway. And I think she mentioned that you'd previously met Jay."

"Oh, well, yes, of course," Lin mumbled. "Umm, actually Helene was good friends with my mother before her passing," Lin said.

Trace nodded. "I'm sorry about your mother. Has it been long?"

She looked at him with suspicion. Was he trying to trick her? Did he suspect Belle of something? Or was his offering of condolence merely that? She smiled. "It's been quite a few years, thank you. But Helene has remained a dear friend of the family."

Lin turned her attention to the meal.

"I've always wanted to visit Vicksburg," Trace said, breaking the silence that had fallen between them. "I have a good friend that lives there, Caylen Wheatley. Do you happen to know him?"

Lin's head jerked up. Caylen Wheatley. Caylen Wheatley. She'd never heard of the man. Should she admit that? What if he was a very prominent person in Vicksburg?

"His main plantation is in Baton Rouge," Trace continued, "so Caylen divides his time between the two cities." He took a long swallow of wine. "In fact, last I heard, he was spending more time in Baton Rouge than in Vicksburg."

"Baton Rouge is very lovely," Lin said evasively. "Does your family own plantations out of the New Orleans area?"

Trace shook his head. "No, all of our properties are here." He put down his fork and smiled at her. "And what about your home, what is it like?"

He was asking too many questions she didn't know how to answer, thanks to Belle. Lin glanced toward the window. The sun was just disappearing beyond the horizon, leaving the city swathed in a pinkish-gray glow. Dusk. That meant nightfall, and a reason to excuse herself, though under any other circumstances she wouldn't want to. She looked back at Trace. "I must thank you for a very lovely dinner, Mr. Bragg—Trace," she quickly amended at a mockingly hurt look from him, "but it is getting late and I'd really better be going."

"Going?" Trace got to his feet as Lin stood. "You're returning to Shadows Noir tonight?"

Lin merely looked at him. Her mind exploded in denial of what she'd just done. "Well, yes, but—"

"Good. I was planning on staying over, but it's not really necessary. I'll escort you."

"Oh, no!" she blurted out.

Trace frowned.

"I mean, no, thank you, but I don't want to interrupt your plans. You were going to stay over. Please don't change your arrangements for me. I can see myself back to the plantation, really."

"It's not a problem."

"No, I insist. I drove in myself; I can certainly get back by myself."

"You came in during daylight, Belle." Trace looked pointedly at the window. "It's evening now, and a lonely dark road is no place for a lady to be unescorted." He took her arm and guided her back through the sea of tables toward the entry door. "Where did you stable the buggy?"

Six

"Oh, uh, the buggy." Lin smiled weakly. It was impossible to get out of this one.

"You didn't ride in on horseback?" He looked askance at her.

"Well, no I . . ." Markus suddenly appeared from the entry to the hotel bar and began to walk across the lobby. Lin snatched at her veil and jerked it down over her face.

Trace noticed, thought it a bit odd, but said nothing.

"I, uh, well, the truth is one of your servants was coming into town and I, uh, I rode in with her. I'm afraid I wasn't thinking of how to get back. I suppose I would have hired a buggy."

"Then by all means, allow me to escort you home," Trace said, and bowed as they stepped past the hotel's entry doors and onto the banquette. Cool night air enveloped them instantly.

Lin stood silently next to Trace as he conversed with the doorman, who in turn conversed with a young assistant. The boy, dressed in the identical red wool and gold cord as the doorman, sprinted down the street toward the hotel's private stable and disappeared into the darkness. Minutes later he returned leading Trace's horse and tied him to the rear of a carriage the doorman had summoned for them. Lin fidgeted with her reticule. She couldn't accompany Trace to Shadows Noir. She couldn't. Belle was there. They would be exposed, and Belle would kill her.

Trace turned to help Lin into the buggy. She hesitated and stared at his outstretched hand. What was she going to do? Reluctantly Lin placed her hand in his. Maybe they'd get waylaid by outlaws on the way to his plantation and one of them would snatch her up and carry her away. Then everything would be all right. She stepped up into the carriage and took her seat. Well, things wouldn't really be all right if she were abducted by outlaws, but at the moment it seemed preferable to facing Belle.

Trace climbed in and sat beside her. "Shadows Noir plantation," he said to the driver; and the carriage rolled forward.

Lin felt her heart sink to the bottom of her stomach. This was it, this was the end, and it was all her fault. They'd get to the plantation, Trace would escort her into the house, and they'd come face to face with Belle. Lin felt every nerve in her body threaten to explode.

Trace relaxed against the back of the seat. Lin sat ramrod straight and tried desperately to think of a way out of the dilemma her impulsive little excursion from the hotel had caused. Why had she gone out? Why, why, *why?* It had been a silly thing to do, and she'd known better. Maybe if she closed her eyes, she would reopen them and discover this was all a dream. Lin counted to ten and opened her eyes. She was still in the carriage, and Trace was still sitting beside her. It wasn't a dream, but it *was* a nightmare. She sighed and wondered if a prayer would do any good.

"Is something wrong, Belle?" Trace asked softly.

Lin started as his voice, a deep velvet caress, slid along her skin and left a delicious trail of gooseflesh behind.

"Wrong? Oh, no, I was just enjoying the scenery." She turned her gaze to the side of the road in an effort to put a little truth into her words. Nothing was going right. She'd just met a man who she couldn't deny she was attracted to, and her sister suspected him of being a murderer. She was on her way to his home, where her sister was masquerading as a wedding guest, and the moment the two of them were seen together, everything was going to be ruined. Tears stung the back of her eyes and she blinked them away.

Half an hour later the carriage passed between two tall brick pillars. Intricately woven black wrought-iron curved from the top of one pillar to the other, the words *Shadows Noir* fashioned from the swirling iron at its crest. The winding drive was a lattice of shadows and filtered moonlight beneath an arched canopy of live oaks, and the surrounding landscape was a shimmering panorama that seemed to go on for as far as the eye could see.

Lin wanted to pray, but she couldn't think of an appropriate prayer. Please God, she finally said silently, please get me out of this. Please. Papa needs our help, and if we get caught now. . . . The tears returned, filling her eyes this time. She blinked rapidly in an effort to stem their tide and failed. One escaped the corner of her eye, and she brushed a finger over her cheek to rid it of the telltale moisture.

The drive curved slightly and the house came into view. Lin stared, instantly mesmerized. It was magnificent, one of the most massive and elegant plantation homes she had ever seen, and a rival to any of the numerous mansions in Natchez.

It was two stories in height, with dormer windows in

its slanted slate roof attesting to yet another floor. The entire house was painted white and was set on a slight knoll which was covered in rich, thick grass, much like a precious pearl set upon a blanket of green velvet. White Corinthian pillars surrounded the entire structure, eight to each side, and edged a wide brick gallery on the first floor. Another gallery graced the second story, and a wrought-iron railing, also painted white, laced its way between each fluted pillar. The entry door was solitary, but extremely wide, and flanked by narrow windows. A fanlight window crowned both the door and windows, its intricately designed and beveled panes reflecting the torch that burned at the end of the walkway leading to the drive. Eight ceiling-high windows adorned the first floor, four on each side of the door. Lin looked at the second floor and realized that it was identical to the first. Cypress shutters, painted emerald green, framed all the windows. Brick steps in the shape of an open fan led from the walkway to the first-floor gallery.

Thick hedges of azaleas lined the front of the house, and even though most of their blooms were closed for the night, it was clearly discernible that when opened to the day they would radiate a profusion of brilliant color.

The carriage drew nearer the house, and Lin felt her heartbeat accelerate to a maddening pace. Her fingers clutched at the beaded reticule in her lap, and she unconsciously began to knead it.

The driver pulled back on the reins, yelled something to the horse, and the carriage stopped before the walkway that led to the entry door.

Lin's gaze darted from Trace to the door and back to Trace. What was she going to do now? her mind screamed.

"Wait here," Trace said to the driver. He climbed from

the carriage, walked around to Lin's side, and reached up to assist her down.

She stood and placed her hand in his. Once again, as had happened earlier, she felt a hot, tingling sensation travel up her arm at his touch. Her gaze leapt to encounter his, blue eyes holding gray, each mirroring the same thoughts, emotions, and confusion. It's nothing, she told herself, and stepped to the ground. Nothing. Just nerves.

Without warning, Trace's head dipped, and he brushed his lips lightly over hers.

Startled, Lin pulled back quickly.

"I'd say I'm sorry," Trace said softly, "but I'm not." He smiled. "You go on in, Belle. I need to pay the driver and take my horse down to the stable."

His kiss had sent her senses reeling, but not so much that she wasn't aware of the predicament she was still in, and Lin felt a rush of relief at being handed the opportunity to escape. She tipped her head in acknowledgement of his words, afraid she'd say something she'd be sorry for if she opened her mouth to speak. A sense of disappointment swept over her as she watched Trace retrieve the reins of his mount and lead the animal toward the stables. She liked him and was having trouble believing that he could have murdered someone. Especially his own father. She glanced over her shoulder at the house and prayed that no one had seen their arrival.

No movement appeared at the windows, and the entry door remained closed.

"Thank heavens," Lin murmured, fighting to get her nerves under control. She stepped into the shadows of a live oak and out of the light cast by the torch. She should warn Belle, but how? Lin looked around quickly, reassuring herself no one else was about. She hadn't any idea what bedchamber Belle was in, so she couldn't throw anything at the windows in the hope of getting her attention. "Oh, Belle," she grumbled, "why do I always listen to you and get myself into these predicaments?" She stared up at the house and tried to decide what to do. Tears filled her eyes again. Lord, she wasn't good at this kind of thing. What was she supposed to do? What would Belle want her to do?

Just then the sound of a door being shut broke the night's silence. Lin whirled around and stared at the entry door, but there was no one there. Movement at the side of the house drew her gaze, and she saw an old black woman appear from beyond some shrubs.

"Daisy?" the woman called in a high-pitched voice. "Daisy, you out there, dog?"

Silence was the woman's only answer.

Lin hastened farther back into the tree's shadow.

"Dang blasted dumb dog," Zanenne grumbled. "Always underfoot when she ain't supposed to be, and never around when she's called."

Suddenly Lin felt something nuzzle the hem of her gown. "Oh, no!" The words slipped from her lips before she had a chance to stop them. She slapped a hand over her mouth and looked down. A small black-and-white dog crouched before her, its nose buried in the ruffled hem of her skirt. The animal's rear end protruded into the air while its long-haired tail wagged rapidly back and forth. Lin looked at the servant who was still waiting for the animal to appear, and then back at the dog. Fear gripped her heart. She took a step back. "Scoot," she whispered, and waved her hands at the animal. "Scoot, doggy. Please, go away."

Daisy whined happily and scrambled around the edge of Lin's skirt.

"No, no, go away." She waved her hands at the dog

again. "Go on . . ." What had the woman called the dog? Daisy? "Go away, Daisy," Lin urged, starting to feel desperate.

"Daisy," Zanenne called again. "I ain't gonna stand here with your dinner all night. Dumb dog. Now where is you?"

Lin stamped her foot. "Go, Daisy, go."

Daisy's tail wagged faster and she playfully pounced at Lin's skirt.

"Daisy!" Zanenne's voice had turned angry.

Lin made to wave her hand at the dog again and suddenly realized she was still holding the package of chocolates. Fumbling frantically, she opened the package and held a chocolate out to Daisy.

The dog sniffed the candy, barked, and opened her mouth to retrieve it.

"Go get it," Lin whispered, and threw the candy toward the house.

Daisy bounded off after the tossed treat and Lin hurried stealthily down the drive, moving alongside of it but keeping well within the shadows created by the big trees.

The heels of her shoes kept sinking into the soft ground, and twice before reaching the main road she nearly lost her balance and toppled backward. It didn't help matters when, having walked only a mile, she began to imagine lurking forms behind each tree and menacing shapes beside each shrub. Her shoulders shook with fear, her teeth chattered from both hysteria and coldness, but she trudged on, knowing it was her only choice.

Halfway back to town Lin was certain she'd never make it the remainder of the way. Her shoes were already ruined, the hem of her gown was covered with dirt, and she'd snagged her skirt more than once on bushes. And she was exhausted. It hadn't seemed that far when they'd ridden out in the hired carriage. But then she hadn't been paying that much attention to the distance as she had been worrying about encountering Belle. Tears filled her eyes again, and she hurriedly wiped them away. For all she knew she could even be lost. What if this wasn't the right road? What if she'd accidentally veered off of the right road and was on her way to God knew where?

She rounded a curve, screamed, and scrambled back several steps.

Twenty feet ahead, illuminated by a stream of moonlight that fell directly onto his ridged back, an alligator, whose length Lin realized was more than twice her own height of five foot two and a half inches, moved slowly across the road. At her scream the reptile stopped.

Lin froze, motionless except for the shivers of fear that coursed through her.

The alligator's head swiveled back and forth slowly, then evidently sensing he was in no danger, he continued on across the road and disappeared into the tall wild grass that bordered it and led into a murky river of bayou water.

Lin shuddered and stared at the spot where the reptile had disappeared from view. Did she dare walk past? Would the thing jump out and try to grab her with its monstrous jaws? She looked behind her, to each side, and then forward again. What choice did she have? Behind her was Shadows Noir. She couldn't go back there. To each side was either bayou or plantation land, the landscape unknown. She began to inch her way forward, then stopped and stared at the spot from which the alligator had emerged. Could there be another one in there? Maybe its mate? Lin could feel her fear turning to terror. She swallowed hard and looked in the direction she'd come. No, she couldn't go back.

Struggling to keep herself from falling into a trembling

faint, Lin moved cautiously forward, summoning all of her courage to move one foot in front of the other. Her eyes darted from one side to the other continually. Ten minutes later, and well past the site of the reptile's crossing, Lin breathed a sigh of relief and began to hurry her pace when another sound brought her up cold in her tracks: the clatter of carriage wheels on the road ahead. Looking around wildly, Lin realized her only choices were to remain on the road and be discovered or run over, or jump into the wild grasses and thick growth of trees and shrubs that edged each side.

A mental image of the alligator appeared. Lin glanced down the moonlit road. The carriage was drawing nearer. She looked at the side of the road, squinting into its shadowed foliage. There really was no choice.

Trace bounded up the entry steps. He hadn't been so attracted to a woman in a long time. After what had happened to Myra, he'd purposely given a wide berth to respectable women, but now his father was dead, and there was no longer a reason to fear what he would do to anyone Trace loved. He strode across the gallery. When Belle had arrived the day before, he'd thought her strikingly beautiful, but definitely not the type of woman that attracted him. She had seemed too outspoken, opinionated, and independent. And definitely too flirtatious. Trace smiled to himself and reached for the doorknob. Yet the past few hours he had spent with her in town had proven him wrong. She had been none of those things. Just the opposite. He'd found her gentle, sensitive, quiet, and almost shy.

He pushed the door open and stepped into the foyer, closing the door quietly behind him. Hopefully she hadn't already retired. He wanted to say good night. Trace turned toward the parlor just as Belle exited it. He stopped and stared at her pale mint day gown. "You've changed," he said, surprised.

Belle paused and looked at him in confusion. "Changed?"

"Your gown," Trace said. "You changed your gown."

She frowned and looked down at the green gown with its white yoke of embroidered orange flowers and green veins. She shook her head and laughed flirtatiously. "No, I haven't changed. It's the same gown I've had on all afternoon."

"It looks different." He stared at the embroided bodice, puzzled, then shrugged. "I hope you've forgiven me now for the way I acted upon your arrival."

"But of course," Belle said.

"I wasn't exactly the most congenial of hosts, but," he smiled warmly, "I hope your impression of me has changed now."

Belle returned his smile.

Trace lifted the tips of her fingers and, bowing his head, pressed his lips to them. "Would you still care to ride the grounds with me?" he asked. "Perhaps tomorrow morning?"

"Yes, I would like that very much." A faint frown of confusion tugged at her brow. She did want to spend time with him, to gather information, but—her suspicions raised—what had changed his attitude so drastically?

"Good." He walked her to the bottom of the staircase. "Thank you for a lovely evening, Belle, and again, I apologize for yesterday."

"Evening?" she echoed. What was he talking about? He hadn't been here since early that morning.

"It really was a pleasant surprise to see you in town this afternoon, especially since I so rudely refused to allow you to accompany me. Thank you for forgiving me and, of course, for dining with me."

Belle's knees felt suddenly as if they were about to collapse beneath her weight and her heart began to pound rapidly.

"Your company made an otherwise dull meal an enjoyable two hours." He smiled widely, and warmth she had not before seen from him twinkled from his gray-blue eyes.

"Two hours," Belle murmured. She felt a tremor of nervous fear race through her body. He saw Lin, her mind screamed. He saw Lin, and he dined with her . . . for two hours!

"Well, the carriage ride home was a long one and I'm sure you're tired. I'll say good night now and see you in the morning."

Ride home? Her mind snagged on the words and refused to relinquish them. Ride home? Lin had come to Shadows Noir with him? She felt an urge to wring her sister's neck. Instead, she forced a smile to her face. "I think I'll just get a book from the library," she said. "Thank you for such a pleasant evening, Trace."

He released her hand, but rather than move away he leaned forward and kissed her lightly. "Good night, Belle," he said huskily.

"Good night," Belle answered absently, though it wasn't the kiss that held her in a state of stupor, but the fact that he had escorted Lin to Shadows Noir.

The moment Trace reached the top of the stairs and turned down the hallway, Belle's gaze darted around the foyer, searching the shadows, looking for some indication that Lin was present. "Lin?" she whispered.

There was no answer.

"Lin?" She hurried back into the parlor and looked

around, then ran into the study, the library, and finally the warming kitchen. There was no sign of her sister. "Damn it, Lin, where are you?" Belle asked, anger lacing each word. She rushed back to the entry door, opened it, and stepped out onto the gallery. The peaceful sounds and inky shadows of night greeted her. She squinted into the darkness. "Lin?" she called in a whisper. "Lin, damn it, are you out there?"

Silence hung heavy on the cool night air.

"Lin? Answer me so that I can kill you," Belle said.

Her eye caught a movement to her left, just beside one of the huge live oaks.

"Lin? Is that you?"

A dog bounded from the shadows, raced past Belle and disappeared into the house.

"Belle?"

She froze, then turned slowly.

Trace leaned casually against the doorjamb, his tall frame silhouetted against the pale yellow light emanating from the foyer at his back. "I came down for some water and heard you whispering out here. Is everything all right?"

Now he probably thought she was crazy, Belle thought. Out of the corner of her eye, she saw a peacock emerge from behind a shrub and strut toward the house.

"Oh, yes," Belle said, "I, uh, I was just mumbling to that peacock." She laughed lightly and threw Trace a flirtatious look. "He seemed rather lonely."

Trace stepped out onto the gallery and moved to stand beside her. "What about you, Belle," he said, a note of seriousness in his deep voice, "are you lonely?"

Belle unconsciously took a step back. "Me?" She laughed again, though this time the nervousness she felt was evident even to her own ears. This was the man she suspected of being a murderer, a man who had cold-bloodedly killed his own father and left hers to rot in prison or hang. She had to be careful. "Lonely? Me?" She took another step back and felt the fluted wood of a pillar at her back. "No, I've never really been—"

Trace closed the distance between them and pulled her into his arms, crushing her breasts against his chest, his hands pressed warmly to her back. "You're a beautiful woman, Belle, a very beautiful woman, and I haven't been seriously attracted to a woman in a long time."

Stay calm, Belle told herself. Stay calm and play the game. Flirt, but keep him at a distance, lest everything be lost. She turned and twisted herself out of his arms, though she smiled playfully and tapped his forearm with her hand. "And you, my handsome friend, shouldn't have been spying on a lady and her beau." She looked at the peacock, who stood several yards away and was now watching her and Trace. "Don't you agree, Harry?"

The bird suddenly let out a wild, ear-piercing shriek.

Trace bowed his head and, with a quick glance out of the corner of his eye, turned back toward the door. "Good night, Belle."

"Good night, Trace," she said softly, feeling relief.

Trace walked across the foyer and approached the stairs, but at the newel post he paused and looked back through the open door. She was still standing in view, but her back was to him. A deep frown creased his brow. He had never met anyone whose personality could change so drastically. How could a woman seem so sweet, so demure and gentle, and only minutes later turn into a flirtatious, saucy vixen? The frown deepened, leaving his eyes in shadow. It was as if Belle St. Croix was two entirely different people, and though he had been near mesmerized by her earlier that evening, he didn't much care for the Belle she had become since they'd returned to the plantation.

Seven

Traxton Braggette pulled his horse up at the entry gates to Shadows Noir. The animal stood patiently for several seconds and then lowered his head and began to graze on a small clump of grass that grew at the base of one of the brick pillars. Traxton leaned forward slightly and rested a forearm on the horn of his saddle, letting the thin leather reins dangle loosely between his gloved fingers. His gaze moved over landscape which his eyes hadn't seen for almost eight years, but which his mind remembered vividly. Memories began to assail him. The good memories were what had enabled him to find the courage to return, but the bad ones, the ones involving his father, which had haunted him since the day he'd left, kept the hate alive and simmering deep within him.

The sun had just begun to inch its way over the horizon, its bright rays bathing the landscape in a haze of shimmering golden light, lending it the feel of paradise. Traxton nearly snorted. Paradise. He shook his head. His memories of life at Shadows Noir were closer to what he imagined it would be like in hell. But now the cause of all of those bad memories, his father, was finally dead. For the first time in a long time hope sparked in Traxton's dark eyes. Perhaps now the facade of paradise could turn to a reality.

He shifted position on his saddle. The horse raised his head expectantly. "Easy, Rogue," Traxton said, "we're not going anywhere just yet."

As if he understood, the huge black-and-white stallion lowered his head again and went back to determinedly munching on the clump of grass at the base of the brick pillar.

Traxton let his gaze roam again in search of the old oak tree he and his brothers had often used as a hiding place from their father when Thomas Braggette had been in one of his moods. Traxton finally spotted it, and a smile came to his face. Sixth oak from the entry, seventh from the house. One side of the massive tree had split while growing, resulting in a natural cavity in the trunk that had provided the perfect hiding place for four little boys and, later, one little girl. He wondered if Teresa had continued to use it. She had been only nine when he'd left.

Traxton reached up and removed a dust-covered Stetson from his head, swept a hand over the thick mass of black hair that the hat had covered, and then set the hat back in place, pulling it low onto his forehead to shade his eyes from the morning light.

He nudged a heel to Rogue's barrel. The horse instantly came to attention and moved forward in a slow but steady walk. The thin layer of crushed oyster shells that covered the drive crunched softly beneath Rogue's hooves, the sound reminding Traxton of how very different Shadows Noir was from the home he had made for himself in Texas. An image of the Rocking T drifted into his mind. The house he'd built at one end of the six-thousand-acre spread was a rambling, two-story clapboard. It was surrounded by craggy ground dotted with cactus and sagebrush, which in spots gave way to lush meadows of tall grass bordering sparkling creeks shaded by willow trees and prairie flowers. It was a harsh land, though like the verdant fields and wandering bayous of Louisiana, beautiful in its own unique way. Mountainous plateaus and endless prairies lent the Texas horizon an infinite, almost end-of-the-world quality, while its sheer cliffs and hidden caves could prove deadly, especially when used by warring Comanches.

Traxton reined up in front of the house and, holding the saddle horn with one hand, swung his right leg over the cantle and stepped to the ground.

At that same moment the door swung open. Zanenne hurried across the gallery and down the steps, her face alight with joy. "Traxton Braggette, you no-good piece of mutton," she grumbled loudly, "I knew you'd come."

Traxton stepped around Rogue, who had already busied himself munching on the lush grass that bordered the walkway to the house. "I'll be damned. Zanenne." He chuckled and grasped her by her upper arms, giving her a quick once-over. "You look good, Zani, but I figured you'd be pushing up daisies by now, what without me here to take your orneriness out on."

"I been saving it all up just for you," she snapped back.

"Good, then come on and give me some," Traxton said, and pulled her into an embrace.

Zanenne slapped his arm and squirmed away from him. "Oh, go on with you now," she said tartly, though the twinkle in her dark eyes belied the caustic words and hard tone. "Your sister's been so worried you wasn't going to co—"

"Traxton!" Teresa appeared in the doorway and called back over her shoulder, "Mama, Traxton's here."

"Uh-oh," Trax said beneath his breath, "speak of the devil."

Zanenne crossed her arms beneath her breasts and gave

him a hard look. "You be nice to her now, Traxton. She's all grown up and getting herself married. Ain't no child to be teasing with no more."

Teresa ran across the gallery, flew down the steps, and threw herself straight into his open arms, wrapping hers tightly around his neck. Laughing happily, Traxton crushed her within the circle of his arms, drew her to his chest, and swung her around.

"Oh, Traxton," Teresa said, "I'm so happy you're home. Trace wasn't sure you'd come, but I knew you would."

He set her back on the ground and, still holding her to him, looked down and with a straight face said, "I don't know who you are, miss, but I'm always happy to hug a beautiful woman."

Teresa giggled. "You ninny," she said, and rose on tiptoe to kiss his cheek.

Traxton laughed. "Tess, you really are beautiful." He slipped his fingers within the long dark curls that cascaded down her back. "Last time I saw you, your hair was in pigtails and you were just a gawky little thing, and now look at you." He stepped back and raked her length with his eyes. "If I weren't your brother, I think I'd ask for your hand myself."

Teresa threw her arms around his shoulders again and hugged him to her. "Oh, Trax, I've missed you so much."

A movement at the door caught Traxton's attention. Removing Teresa's arms from around his neck, he stepped away from her. "Hello, Mama," he said softly.

Eugenia Braggette stood on the edge of the gallery, her silver-streaked black hair swept back in a neat chignon, her gray eyes blurred with tears as a smile quivered on her lips. "Traxton," she said, the lone word choked with more joy than she'd experienced in a long time. She started down the steps, her arms open to him.

Traxton hurried toward his mother and pulled her gently to him. "I'm sorry, Mama."

She held him to her, reveling in having her second son back home once again. "You did what you had to do, Trax," she said softly. "I knew that. It was the only way you could have survived, and God knows, I wanted you to survive."

He held her away from him. "Are you all right, Mama? I mean, *really* all right?"

Eugenia smiled and slipped an arm around his and guided him toward the house. "Now that my sons are coming home, my daughter is getting married, and your father is . . ." she hesitated, ". . . gone, everything will be fine."

Teresa grabbed hold of his other arm. "Travis and Traynor haven't arrived yet, but they should be here any day now. Oh, and wait until you meet Jay," Teresa said. "You'll love him; he's so nice. And smart, too."

"I knew Jay, Tess," Trax said, "a long time ago."

"Oh, then you probably know that his father lost most of their money," a shadow passed over her blue eyes, "no thanks to our father," she added sullenly. "But they've gotten a lot of it back, and Jay's working hard to make more. He will, too, everyone says so. But it doesn't matter. We love each other and that's all that counts."

"Zanenne," Eugenia said, "set another place at the table, will you?" She turned to Traxton. "You haven't had breakfast yet, have you, Trax?"

"No, Mama, and I'm starving."

"Good." They entered the house. "Oh, and, Teresa, go on up and make sure our guest knows breakfast will be served shortly."

"Guest?" Traxton echoed.

"She came down from Vicksburg for the wedding," Eugenia said, "and arrived a couple of days early."

"She?" Traxton's brows rose and his eyes twinkled with deviltry.

Eugenia smiled. "You haven't changed a bit, have you?"

He squeezed her hand and looked around the wide foyer. "And you haven't changed a thing in here," he said. "It looks exactly like it did the last time I saw it."

"Almost eight years ago," Eugenia said.

Traxton felt a flash of guilt. "I always meant to come back and visit, Mama, it's just . . ." he shrugged.

"He would have made you sorry," she said. "I missed you terribly, but it was better that you stayed away. At least that way he couldn't hurt you as much."

Traxton nodded. "At least you're free of him now."

"Yes, we're all free of him now."

Belle slipped a pale blue percale gown over her head and let the voluminous folds of its skirt settle down over the huge hoop and lace petticoats she had fastened at her waist. It would have been easier to dress with the help of a maid, and she was used to having one, but she'd just have to make do without any help for now. Eugenia had offered her the services of one of the Braggette servants, but Belle had declined. At home she was used to babbling away to Clarey, her maid, about everything and anything, and she was afraid that out of habit she'd do that here. That could prove dangerous. She couldn't let anyone, not even a maid, get close enough to discover her true identity or her real reason for being at Shadows Noir. The gown's flounced and heavily ruffled skirt dropped easily over the hoop. Belle straightened the small puffed sleeves at her shoulders and secured the two rows of pearl buttons in the center of the snugly fitting bodice. A torsade of dark blue velvet trimmed the low-scooped bodice as well as the sleeves and lacy hip flounces.

Belle brushed her long hair vigorously, then tied it back with a white silk ribbon, allowing the wavy strands to flow freely down her back. She looked in the mirror, scrutinizing her appearance, and, deciding she could use just a bit of color, retrieved a rose petal from a small crystal dish on the dressing table and pressed it to her lips.

A sharp knock sounded on her door.

"Come in," Belle called out. Giving herself one last assessing glance, she turned from the tall cheval mirror that stood in one corner of her room.

The door opened and Teresa darted in. "Mama wanted me to let you know breakfast is about to be served, Belle," Teresa said.

"Thank you, I'll be right down."

Teresa smiled widely. "My brother just arrived."

Belle stared at the girl and felt a shock of alarm. "Your brother." She caught herself and returned Teresa's smile. "Oh, well, that's wonderful. Which one?"

"Traxton. He's second to the oldest." A spurt of giggles caused Teresa to seem much younger than her seventeen years. "And he looks just like one of those men out of the penny books about cowboys. He even wears a gun, but then I guess he has to, living in Texas and all."

"Yes, I suppose so," Belle said.

"Well, I'll see you downstairs, Belle."

Belle smiled weakly. "Thank you, Teresa, I'll be right down." She looked back at her image in the mirror. Her face seemed paler, and she was suddenly no longer hungry. Her appetite had disappeared the moment Teresa had informed her that another of the Braggette brothers was in residency at the plantation. "Won't show up for the wedding, huh? Well, Helene, obviously you don't know your cousin's family as well as you thought," Belle mumbled. She began to pace the room like a caged tigress. Calm and focused, she told herself. That was the main thing. She had to remain calm and focused. Calm and focused. There was no hope of discovering the truth if she let herself get upset and inadvertently gave away her true reason for being at Shadows Noir. Calm and focused. She told her hands to stop trembling, took a deep breath, and stepped out into the hallway. By the time she reached the staircase landing, she felt better, but just as she was about to descend, voices drifted up to her from near the entry door and she paused.

"At least you're free of him now."

"Yes, we're all free of him now."

Belle felt a shiver run up her spine at the words and stared down at the two figures standing in the center of the foyer. The man towering over Eugenia Braggette looked very much like Trace, yet somehow Belle knew it wasn't Trace. He had removed his hat and held it in one hand by the brim. Belle noticed that his hair, its ragged ends curling over the collar of his shirt and a few wayward locks falling forward onto his forehead, was so dark that the thick waves shone blue-black beneath the bright sunlight streaming in through the fanlight window above the door. Unlike Trace, this man, who she assumed was Traxton Braggette, looked out of place in the elegant surroundings. Yet as her eyes remained on him, she realized that in spite of his appearance, he wasn't out of place at all but was as comfortable with the elegant furnishings of Shadows Noir and its luxury as anyone could be.

Belle reached for the railing, wrapped her fingers

around the polished wood, and was about to take a step forward when Traxton, as if he'd sensed her eyes on him, turned and caught her gaze.

His face, like his older brother's, held an aristocratic handsomeness—yet upon further inspection, Belle saw that Traxton's was just a touch leaner, harder, the sharp curves and deep hollows hinting at an untamed savagery that was lacking in the features of the more genteel Trace. His black brows were thick and arched over a pair of deep-set gray-blue eyes; his nose was straight, near aquiline, though slightly flared at the nostrils, giving him that same air of arrogance that surrounded Trace. His lips were full above a jaw that reminded Belle of a sharp square of impenetrable granite, and his skin was dark, a burnished bronze that was a combination of the Creole blood he had inherited from his mother and long days of riding under the sun.

The collar of a pale gray cambric shirt was unbuttoned at his muscular throat; a vest of black leather stretched taut across his back and broad shoulders; and matching chaps covered his trousers, the snug fit hugging the contours of long, lean, but well-honed limbs. A tooled holster rode low over his right hip, a walnut-handled revolver settled comfortably in its sheath, which was in turn tied securely to his thigh with a thin strip of leather. Silver spurs attached to the back of his boots, and they, as well as the silver conchos that adorned the outer seams of his chaps, caught the light from the window in a brilliant reflection.

Belle felt the breath catch in her throat as his eyes held her prisoner, silently refusing to loosen the invisible reins by which he had captured her gaze. One corner of his lips quirked upward into an odd little smile as the dark eyes finally released their mesmerizing grip on her and slid downward in a bold and impudent assessment that sent a shiver up Belle's spine. Never in all her life had a man done so blatant and thorough a job of undressing her with his eyes. Her cheeks burned with a blush while her mind seethed in fury. She forced a smile to her lips, refusing to allow him to unnerve her further or to see the embarrassment his appraisal had aroused within her. There wasn't a man in Natchez County, or anywhere else for that matter, who had ever gotten the better of Belinda Sorbonte, and she certainly wasn't about to let this . . . this insolent, gauche, unshaven . . . her gaze came to rest on the gun at his hip . . . *cowboy* . . . get to her. Even if he was devastatingly handsome in a rather rugged and barbaric way, and a member of one of the best families in New Orleans.

That last thought brought her up short. One of the best families in New Orleans, yes, but also a family who was most likely harboring a murderer within its midst. Belle pulled her gaze from his, lifted her chin, and proceeded down the stairs. Of course, *he* couldn't be suspected of killing his father since he'd just arrived in town. No, her suspicions would have to remain on Trace, regardless of the fact that the elder Braggette looked and acted like a well-bred gentleman while Traxton looked the epitome of an outlaw, and just the type to kill a man—even his own father.

At the bottom of the steps, she had no choice but to turn toward her hostess. Belle smiled, though as she approached Eugenia and the man she assumed to be Traxton Braggette, her insides began to quiver unaccountably.

"Belle, I'm glad you've decided to join us for breakfast," Eugenia said. "Dear, this is my son Traxton." Eugenia smiled up at him. "Traxton, this is our guest, Miss Belle St. Croix. Belle came down from Vicksburg to attend your sister's wedding. She's an acquaintance of Jay's and an old friend of Cousin Helene."

Belle turned her gaze back to Traxton and wished instantly she hadn't. His eyes were gray, like his mother and brothers, yet the blue that edged his iris was much darker than the others', like that of a midnight sky surrounding a mystical fog. Suddenly, with such intensity it caused her to shiver, Belle became aware of an incredibly fierce aura of sexuality emanating from Traxton Braggette. So tangible was it that Belle, surprised and caught momentarily off guard, felt it wrap around her like two hot hands.

As if fully aware his scrutiny had made her uncomfortable, Traxton's eyes sparkled with haughty amusement. He took Belle's hand in his, bowed his head in what was a gallant yet somehow mocking gesture, and pressed his lips to the back of her fingers. "I cannot tell you what a pleasure it is to meet you, Miss St. Croix," Traxton said, his deep, honey-dark voice an unusual blend of Louisiana smoothness and Texas drawl. "And an honor to have you at Shadows Noir."

"Thank you," Belle said, her tone edged with false sweetness. She pulled her hand from his. "But as I mentioned to your brother, Trace, the honor is all mine."

The reference to Trace as the master of Shadows Noir was not lost on Traxton, but since he had no desire to usurp his brother's position, or even share in it, he decided to ignore the subtly derisive comment. He could not resist, however, offering one of his own. "And have you traveled to New Orleans alone, Miss St. Croix?"

"Traxton, please," Eugenia interrupted, the warning clear in the two curtly spoken words.

Belle's brows rose slightly as her eyes widened in surprise at the taunting question. She smiled at Eugenia. "It's all right, Eugenia." She turned back to Traxton. "Yes, Mr.

Braggette, I am here alone. My father is quite ill and unable to travel at present."

"I'm sorry."

She ignored his apology, which she suspected was insincere anyway, and continued, "We had business in New Orleans that couldn't wait, and therefore I came to see to it myself." Her sweet, almost deriding smile returned, and she looked up at him coyly, though what she would have preferred to do, at the moment at least, was smash him over the head with the vase that sat on a nearby table. Perhaps then he wouldn't be so arrogant and cocksure. She controlled her urges, though with considerable self-restraint, and said, "I do hope that doesn't offend your sensibilities, Mr. Braggette."

"Don't worry, my sensibilities are not easily offended, Miss St. Croix," Traxton answered. Brazen interest glinted from his steely eyes as once again they raked over her. It wasn't often he encountered a woman who was beautiful *and* had fire in her veins, and one look at Belle St. Croix, in spite of the ice blond hair and Carribean blue eyes, had told him that her veins were definitely rivers of conflagration. Now if only she would allow him access to her bed without wanting to lasso him into marriage. He decided the prospect of having her naked body pressed to his was just too tempting not to take the risk. Anyway he had no intention of marrying anyone, now or ever, so there really was very little risk. The worst that could happen was that she'd say no to his desire to share her bed. He smiled. "And to prove my sensibilities are as stalwart as anyones, I would like to invite you to take a ride with me after breakfast around the plantation."

Belle knew immediately, if not by the suggestive tone of his voice, then definitely from the assessing look in his eyes, that he had a lot more than a ride on his mind. She bristled. Well, he could daydream all he wanted, but that's as far as he was going to get with her. Belle opened her mouth to respond, her blue-green eyes flashing with indignation and more than a hint of temper, but was cut off before uttering a word.

"Trax," Teresa said, her lips dropping into a pout, "you can't go running off already, you just got here." She moved up beside him and slipped an arm around his.

"Tessie, I'll—"

"Well, I'll be damned, you did come."

All eyes turned toward the top of the staircase again.

Trace Braggette took the stairs in a steady, but deliberate descent, his handsome face an emotionless mask, only the pale gray eyes showing any hint of feeling.

Belle shuddered, startled at the cool disdain she saw reflected in Trace's features.

"There was any doubt I'd come for Tessie's wedding?" Traxton said. Laughing deeply and ignoring his older brother's obvious aloofness, he grabbed Trace in a bear hug.

"No one calls me Tessie anymore," Teresa interjected, but both brothers ignored her protest.

"Traxton," Trace said, one dark brow cocking haughtily as only a hint of a smile curved his lips, "with you there is always doubt."

"Still mad at me for leaving, huh?" Traxton coaxed.

"I was never mad at—"

"Yes, you were," Traxton said, smiling wickedly. "But you were right. I shouldn't have left you to do it all, and I'm sorry."

"Breakfast is ready, missus," Zanenne said from the door to the dining room.

Much like a predatory animal staking claim to its prey, Traxton instantly moved away from Trace and offered an arm to Belle. "If you don't mind a little trail dust," Traxton said, brushing off the sleeve of his shirt, "I'd be honored if you would allow me to escort you into breakfast, Miss St. Croix?"

Belle looked up at Traxton. This was not what she wanted. *He* wasn't her suspect. She glanced helplessly at Trace only to find that he had turned toward his sister and was offering to escort her to the table.

Cursing silently, Belle placed her hand lightly on Traxton's offered arm, only to have him cover it with his free hand. She felt a surge of heat flash through her entire body. Startled, Belle made to pull her hand away, but Traxton's hold on her remained secure. Her gaze shot to his face. What was happening? Her pulses began to race. Lord, why didn't they open a few windows in this place, she thought, admonishing herself for not bringing a fan downstairs. She glanced down at her hand and saw that it had disappeared beneath his larger, muscular one.

"You appear suddenly flushed," Traxton said softly, leaning his head toward her so that only she could hear the deeply spoken words. "I'm flattered." A mischievous smile curved his lips.

"Don't be," Belle snapped, further angered by the deriding curve of his lips. "I merely find it a bit warm in here." The man was an absolute rake with no more manners than a cottonmouth.

But he certainly is handsome, a little voice at the back of her mind suddenly declared.

Humph! Perhaps in a loutish, rather uncouth way, Belle answered silently. And he certainly is no true gentleman.

"You prefer genteel young men in silk and breeches simpering at your every whim and bowing gallantly?" Traxton said, as if able to read her thoughts.

Startled, Belle's head jerked around. "I prefer men with

manners," she said, and tossed her head in disdain, causing the waves she had allowed to remain loose to sweep across her shoulders like a veil of platinum silk. Though her voice dripped icicles, her insides were quivering and her heart was on a mad dash to outbeat itself, to say nothing of the fiery heat that seemed to have engulfed her entire being.

Traxton laughed out loud, the sound a deep roll of thunder that sent shivers through her body and aggravated her even further.

Eugenia watched her sons, one walking with their guest, the other escorting his sister, and recognized the spark of interest that glistened within the eyes of both men whenever they looked at Belle St. Croix. She'd waited for years to see that look return to their eyes, and now that it had, she was distraught. Belle was only one woman, which meant, at best, one of her sons would be hurt . . . again.

Beneath the thick ruche of partially lowered silver-gold lashes, Belle tried to watch Trace Braggette from her seat at the table without being obvious. Unfortunately her gaze kept wandering toward Traxton, who was very aware of her problem. She felt a shiver of uneasiness course over her every time his eyes met hers. Why did he have such an unnerving effect on her? It wasn't as though she was charmed by him. Anyway, she was here to prove that Trace Braggette had killed his father, not to become infatuated with his brother. Belle forced a smile to her lips.

"Would you be able to ride with me this morning, Trace?" she asked sweetly. "I'd love to see more of Shadows Noir."

"I thought you were going to allow me the privilege of

showing you around," Traxton broke in before Trace could respond, his eyes twinkling with what could only be described as a challenge. Belle felt her temper begin to rise. The man was . . . infuriating. Lifting her chin, she looked down her nose at him, but couldn't help the saucy curve of her lips as she answered flippantly, "Oh, did you?"

His eyes dropped to her cleavage, just visible above the neckline of her gown. "Yes," he said smoothly, "I did."

Belle had a strong urge to flip her fork in his direction and send poached egg, hollandaise sauce, and bacon flying into his face. The way he looked at her . . . at her body, was scandalous. A string of pithy oaths tripped through her head that, had he realized she even knew them, would have turned her father's hair solid gray.

"Well, you thought wrong," she said snippily. Turning to Trace, her tone instantly changing to one of syrupy sweetness. "Now, about that ride, Trace? Could we go? I so want to see the rest of the plantation." Her heart pounded furiously within her breast, but whether in reaction to her encounter with Traxton or the fact that she was trying to entice the man she suspected of murder into taking her out alone, she wasn't sure.

Trace stared at her for a long second before answering, his eyes shadowed and thoughtful. Ever since last night he had wanted to be alone with her again. So why now, when that was exactly what she obviously wanted, too, did he feel uncomfortable? He shrugged the feeling away. Belle was the first woman who had stirred more than lust within him for a long time, and he liked the feeling. Further, he wanted to feel more of it, and he wanted to feel it with her.

He turned to his brother. "Sorry, Trax," Trace said, "but

I asked Belle last night to ride rounds with me this morning and—"

Traxton held up his hand. "No problem." He pushed his chair back, balancing it on its two rear legs, wrapped an arm around Teresa's shoulders, and turned toward her, effectively dismissing Belle and Trace. "So, Tessie, when am I going to get to talk to this man who thinks he's good enough to marry my little sister?"

Belle felt a surge of indignation. The nerve of the man! Dismissing her like . . . like . . . like an old shoe. Not that she wanted anything to do with him anyway, but only moments ago he had been all but drooling down her bodice. She glared at him. A gentleman wouldn't have acted so . . . so. . . . Vexation blurred her thoughts. She took a deep breath and ordered herself to calm down.

She pushed away from the table and rose. At her action Trace also rose. Traxton, not even turning his head, remained seated and talking to Teresa.

"I'll just get into my riding habit, Trace, and meet you in the foyer in fifteen minutes, if that is all right?" Belle said.

He nodded.

At the door leading to the foyer, Belle paused and looked back. They were all engaged in conversation, none looking in her direction. Her gaze came to rest on Traxton. Before she left Shadows Noir, Belle vowed, she'd make Traxton Braggette sorry he'd acted so arrogantly. She'd make him want nothing more than the pleasure of her company—a little smile curved her lips—and then she wouldn't give it to him.

"You've been around here for the past month and you didn't let us know?" Teresa suddenly burst out loudly.

Belle, who had just returned to the foyer, paused and stepped to the wall so as to remain out of sight.

"Well, hell, Tessie, I had some business to do, and I didn't want to see the old man. I would have come eventually, though, when he was in town."

"But a whole month, Traxton," Teresa repeated. "And we've missed you so."

He leaned over and kissed her forehead. "Tess, I was coming for your wedding, and I decided to combine the trip with business. I've been needing some fresh horseflesh on my ranch, so I went over to MacDougal's in Barataria, and up to Conner's in Baton Rouge. Anyway, I'm here now, so quit your fretting."

Belle stood with her back pressed to the wall in the foyer, her mind whirling with the newfound information. A sudden and unexplainable heaviness settled over her heart. Traxton had been in Louisiana during the time of his father's murder. He could have done it just as easily as Trace.

Eight

Lin took a deep breath and yanked the veil of her bonnet down over her face, not that it would do any real good. She approached the hotel's main entry and tried to ignore the doorman's startled gape as he held the door open for her. "Morning, Miss Bonnvivier," he said, tipping his gold-braid-trimmed hat.

Lin smiled weakly. After having been half-scared to death by an alligator, forced to hide in a ditch at the side of the road so as not to be discovered by whoever had been in a passing carriage, and then having had to walk Lord knew how many miles back to town in the dark, alone, and on slippers with one broken heel, she had barely enough energy left to get her up the stairs to her room. The trek to town from Shadows Noir had taken her all night. Her dress was filthy and mud-streaked, as well as torn in several places, and her hair was a disheveled mess of tangles cascading about her shoulders.

She stepped into the lobby. Early as it was, the auctions in the huge rotunda had already begun and a crowd had gathered round. Several more people lounged on settees set strategically throughout the room, and a group of older men were huddled together on one of the galleries overhead, arguing loudly.

"Maybe no one will notice me," Lin murmured hopefully to herself, and hurried toward the stairs.

"Miss Bonnvivier, are you all right?"

Her eyes jerked upward to find Markus, the young steward, approaching.

"Have you had an accident?" he asked.

Lin looked around and felt as if every eye in the room was suddenly focused on her. Her cheeks burned with embarrassment.

"Yes, I had a little accident, Markus, but I'm fine." She turned toward the stairs, paused, and looked back at him. "Could you have a bath sent up to me?"

The boy smiled widely. "Right away, Miss Bonnvivier." He hurried toward the pantry.

Lin turned back toward the stairs, holding tightly to the rail.

"Miss Bonnvivier!"

Lin nearly groaned as the desk clerk called to her. A rippling of dislike tripped up her spine, but she forced a smile to her lips and looked over her shoulder at him. "Yes, Mr. Loushei?"

"Oh, Miss Bonnvivier, whatever has happened to you?" He rushed to her side, and his eyes darted over her. "Oh, my." He shook his head. "Oh, my. Whatever can we do? Did someone attack you?" He began to turn away. "I'll call for the authorities immediately."

"No," Lin said.

He looked back at her, obviously surprised.

"I'm fine, Mr. Loushei, really. I just had a little accident. I'm going up to my room now, and I've requested Markus to arrange for a bath to be brought up." She tried to smile. "Then I'm going to sleep."

He didn't look convinced. "You're sure we shouldn't call the authorities? I mean, if anyone—"

She felt exasperated, yet knew he was merely trying to help. "I'm fine, Mr. Loushei. No one did anything to me. Now," she began to mount the stairs, "if you'll excuse me, I'm very tired and believe I'd best get upstairs and to my room before I collapse."

His hands began to flutter. "Oh, of course, Miss Bonnvivier, of course. I'll just hurry Markus along for you. Can I send up anything else?"

Lin shook her head without looking back. "No, thank you, Mr. Loushei. I just want to rest."

"Coffee would be good," the clerk mumbled to himself, ignoring Lin's refusal of his offer. "And biscuits. Fresh biscuits with jam. Yes, she should eat something." His eyes suddenly shone. "No, beignets. She should have beignets. They'll make her feel better." He looked at one of the stewards. "You, there, run down to the DuMonde and get me some fresh beignets. Hurry. And make sure they're covered with plenty of powered sugar."

The desk clerk rubbed his long, bony hands together and smiled. Perhaps there was a chance for him with Miss Bonnvivier after all.

Within minutes, and with Markus supervising, several maids had carried a slipper tub into Lin's room, filled it with hot water, and poured in a generous amount of scented lilac powders that turned the water's surface into a mountain of foamy white bubbles.

Securing her door, Lin stripped her body of the dirty rags that only hours before had been respectable clothes. All that was salvagable were the hoop, which was soiled but not damaged, and her camisole. Her stockings, as well as her shoes, were ruined, the ruffled hem of her pantalettes and petticoat were ripped and mud-soiled, and the once-pretty yellow dress was beyond description. She tossed everything on the floor in a corner. What had to be cleaned she would give to one of the hotel maids later, the rest could be burned.

Lin lifted one foot over the tub's edge, sighing contentedly as first warm, sweetly scented bubbles and then hot, soothing water engulfed the sore limb. "Oh, now this is heaven," she said, and sighed again. She lowered herself into the tub and felt her muscles immediately begin to relax as she lay her head on the edge of the tub's raised back. Lin closed her eyes and let the water work its miracles on her sore and fatigued body.

Minutes later she was abruptly awakened by a rap of knuckles on her door.

"Mademoiselle Bonnvivier," Pierre Loushei called, "I've brought you some coffee and fresh beignets."

Lin nearly groaned aloud and sank lower into the tub. She always tried to be nice to people, she really did. No matter what, she always tried to find something to like about each person she met, but this man was making it difficult. In fact, every time she was forced to come into contact with him, she nearly shivered in disgust.

"Mademoiselle Bonnvivier?" Loushei called again. "Are you all right?"

Lin forced a sweetness to her voice she did not feel at the moment. "Yes, Mr. Loushei, I am perfectly all right. Please just leave the tray by the door."

"Are you sure?" he called out again, a disappointed whine in his voice now.

Lin felt a shiver of cold revulsion course over her flesh in spite of being engulfed within hot water. "Yes, Mr. Loushei, I'm sure. Thank you."

A rattle of dishes being set down brought a sigh of relief to her lips. She lay her head back on the edge of the tub again and closed her eyes. An image of Trace Braggette immediately filled her mind's eye and a sense of warmth, which had nothing to do with the hot water, invaded her body and filled it with a delicious, teasing tingle. After their father's arrest Lin had listened to Belle's rantings of why she believed Trace was actually the killer and had framed their father. Some of her theories had made sense, some had not, but Lin always went along with Belle, no matter what, and this time had proven no exception. But now, after spending time with Trace, even though it was only a few hours, after looking into his eyes and feeling the touch of his hand on hers, she was finding it extremely difficult to maintain the belief that Trace could murder anyone.

The events of the previous night, before her long trek back to town, unfolded in her mind. Once she'd managed to control her hysteria at finding herself in his company, she'd begun to enjoy herself. Trace Braggette had been the epitome of a gentleman and so handsome that Lin had found herself, at times, staring at him in wonder. She touched her lips with the tips of her fingers and remembered the soft, featherlight kiss he had given her as they'd stood before Shadows Noir.

"And Belle is convinced he's a murderer," Lin muttered. She didn't get angry often, but she was feeling her temper rise. Whether her ire was directed at Belle for believing Trace a murderer, or at herself for letting herself be discovered by him, and then becoming attracted to him, she didn't know.

"Oh, piddle," Lin spat, and then giggled. She never cursed. Ever. Belle would have been shocked. Of course, Belle would be more than shocked if she found out Lin had not only encountered Trace Braggette, but dined with him, and then ridden to Shadows Noir in his carriage. Oh, she hoped she hadn't ruined everything!

* * *

Belle stood on the front gallery of Shadows Noir. "Blazes and tarnation," she cursed beneath her breath. "What's keeping the man?" Trace had gone down to the stables to retrieve their horses and gallantly told her to wait on the gallery, which had been about the last thing she'd wanted to do, what with Traxton lounging in a parlor chair on the opposite side of the window directly behind her. But arguing with Trace had merely brought a frown to his forehead and a shadow over his eyes, so she'd desisted. Belle chanced a quick glance over her shoulder and nearly sighed with relief to see Traxton still seated in the chair and busily talking with his mother and sister.

She turned back and made to look toward the stables when her eye caught a movement on the drive. Raising a hand to her forehead to shade her eyes from the sun, Belle squinted into the distance. "Oh, no." The fingers of her other hand tightened around her riding crop as she began to make out the features of the approaching rider. Waves of black hair were evident beneath the brim of a Stetson the same silver-gray color as the trousers that hugged his long legs. A dark blue cutaway coat accentuated both his broad shoulders and narrow waist, and was complemented by a blue-and-silver brocade vest. Even from this distance Belle recognized the distinct similarities between the tall rider and the Braggette brothers, Trace and Traxton.

"This is not going to be a good day," Belle mumbled to herself. "I can tell already." She knew, without a doubt, that this had to be another Braggette brother and that once Trace returned to the gallery and discovered the new arrival, their morning ride together would be postponed, if not put off altogether. She watched the rider come closer, and as her temper rose, she snapped the riding crop against her skirt in frustration. "Damn, damn, damn, damn, damn!" she swore softly.

"Tsk-tsk, does your father know you have that curse down to such perfection, Miss St. Croix?"

Belle started and whirled around.

Traxton lounged in the doorway, one shoulder leaning against the doorjamb, thumbs hooked into the low-slung gun holster. He stood with one foot crossed over the other.

Belle's heart nearly stopped beating and lodged in her throat. She stared at Traxton as her heart finally slipped back into place and began a thrashing thud against her breast. He had mentioned her father. Did that mean he knew who her father was? Or had it been merely an innocent statement? She took a deep breath and fought for composure as she heard the sound of horse hooves drawing nearer on the drive behind her.

Traxton chuckled. "Don't worry, my sensibilities aren't offended easily, remember?"

Belle's fluster began to turn to temper. "I thought I was . . ."

"Alone?"

"Yes."

"Sorry." He smiled, an imperious curve of his lips that instantly made a lie out of the flippant apology. "I came out to have a cheroot."

For the first time, Belle noticed the long thin cigar dangling from between two of his fingers and the wispy trail of white smoke swirling up from its burning tip.

"My mother doesn't like us to smoke in the house."

Belle lifted her nose into the air and turned back toward the drive. Where in blazes was Trace?

"Did my brother stand you up?"

Her temper flared as he'd known it would. "No, he did not stand me up. He went to the stable to get the horses."

"Uh-huh." He glanced toward the stables. "Always the gentleman, that's Trace."

"I suppose you would have made me saddle my own horse."

He chuckled again. Damn, but he liked her fire. "Most likely."

"Hey, Trax, is that you?"

Traxton pushed away from the doorjamb and ambled across the gallery to stand beside Belle. "Travis, what in the hell took you so long? I've been here for hours."

Travis Braggette swung a long leg over his horse's neck and slid to the ground. "Well, I did have a mite farther to come than you did, big brother." He laughed and walked up the path toward the house.

The two men shook hands and Traxton pulled Travis into a bear hug. "Damn, it's been one hell of a long time, Trav."

"Yeah, too long," Travis said.

"So, how's my brother the saloon keeper?"

"I prefer to think of myself as a casino proprietor," Travis shot back, laughing.

"Guess they're a mite fancier about titles out there in Nevada Territory than we are in Texas, huh?"

Belle moved away from them. Well, at least she didn't have to consider Travis Braggette a suspect, too. Though where Nevada Territory was, she hadn't the faintest idea. What's more, she didn't care. Travis hadn't been here when Thomas Braggette had been murdered; therefore he wasn't a suspect. That's all she cared about for the time being.

Another thought brought her up short; at least she assumed he hadn't been here. She nearly groaned aloud.

Oh, Lord, please, please, don't let him have been in Louisiana when his father was killed, she prayed. She didn't need any more suspects.

Traxton stepped back and gave his younger brother a quick once-over. "What's it been since you passed through Texas, Trav? Three years?"

"Try almost six," Travis returned.

"Six years." Traxton shook his head. "Like I said, it's been one hell of a long time."

"I would have come back sooner to visit but . . ."

Traxton nodded. "Yeah, me, too." He wrapped a brotherly arm around Travis's shoulders and steered him toward the open doorway. "Come on, Trav, Mama and Tess are in the parlor."

The two men started toward the door when Traxton, seeing Belle out of the corner of his eye, stopped. "Oh, sorry," he muttered. "Trav, this is our guest, Miss Belle St. Croix. Belle, my younger brother Travis."

"It's a pleasure to meet you, I'm sure," Belle said, and smiled. Travis Braggette looked very much like Trace and Traxton, having the same dark coloring, gray-blue eyes, and aristocratic features, but his attire was distinctly different from that of his brothers. It was not the attire of the sedate gentleman farmer or the rugged cowboy, nor even the conventional black broadcloth most riverboat gamblers favored. His choice of fashion was more a unique blend of the three styles. The chain of a gold watch hung looped across his chest, accentuating the richness of a silver-threaded dark-blue brocade vest. A string tie of blue silk, the same deep color as his suit, encircled his neck and contrasted starkly with the brilliant white of his shirt. Nestled, but definitely not hidden, beneath the right side of his jacket, a Navy Colt lay sheathed in a holster, secured to his thigh by a leather thong.

"On the contrary," Travis said, "the pleasure is all mine." Bowing slightly, Travis lifted Belle's hand to his lips, and then straightened. "I hope during your visit with us, Miss St. Croix, that we will have an opportunity to become friends."

Traxton laughed. "Doesn't take you long, does it, little brother?"

Belle threw Traxton a cold glance, then gave Travis a flirtatious smile. "I think I would like that very much, Mr. Braggette," she said, her voice oozing charm.

"Call me Travis, please."

"Only if you'll call me Belle."

"Come on, Trav, Mama and Teresa are waiting, and *Belle,*" Traxton said pointedly as he threw her a parting glance, "is going riding with Trace."

Belle lifted her nose into the air again and turned a cold shoulder to Traxton, but as they walked away she couldn't help but overhear their conversation.

"Boy, she sure doesn't care much for you, does she?" Travis said, chuckling softly.

Traxton slapped Travis on the back as they entered the foyer. "I like 'em with some fire and spit, Trav," he lowered his voice, "but this one's got enough fire in her to burn up the whole damn countryside."

"Too hot for you?"

"Well, I'm not partial to getting burned, little brother. On the other hand, I haven't met a woman yet who's too hot for me to handle."

Belle bristled as their laugher drifted out to her.

"Well, Mr. Traxton Braggette," she grumbled, "you've just met one!"

"Belle, are you ready?"

She looked up, abashed at being caught eavesdropping and talking to herself. Damn, these Braggette men had the uncanniest ability to sneak up on her. "Oh, yes, Trace, of course," Belle gushed, and hurried across the gallery.

Trace looked at the horse who stood grazing to one side of the walkway. "Whose horse?"

Belle saw their morning ride and her chance to question Trace privately about to fly out the window. Disappointment filled her. "Your brother Travis arrived a few minutes ago." She tried to smile. "Do you want to postpone our ride?"

Trace looked at her for a long minute, felt a surge of pleasure at the look of disappointment he saw in her eyes and shook his head. "No. I promised you a ride, and I keep my promises. There will be plenty of time to visit with Travis later."

"Trace!"

Belle nearly groaned. Not another one.

She and Trace both turned toward the drive from where the sound of the voice had come. The moment Belle saw him she knew the approaching rider had to be the youngest Braggette brother, Traynor.

Trace stood stiffly and watched his youngest brother's approach. Only when Traynor reined up before him did Trace speak. "Traynor, it's good to see you."

Traynor swung off his horse and jumped to the ground. "Damn, I didn't think I'd ever say this," Traynor said, "but it's good to be back. Not that it can compare with being on the *Sea Witch*." He laughed. "But it's good." He grabbed Trace's offered hand in both of his and held on to it. "I missed you, big brother."

The faintest of smiles curved Trace's lips. "We missed you, too, Traynor." He glanced at Belle. "Please, let me introduce our guest. Belle, this is my youngest brother, Traynor Braggette. Traynor, our guest, Miss Belle St. Croix."

Traynor removed a black slouch hat from his head and swept it in a wide arc before him as he bent in an exaggerated bow. "Mademoiselle, it is truly an honor to meet you. My ship is at your disposal should you ever need her."

Belle couldn't help it, she laughed. "Your ship?"

Traynor straightened. "The *Sea Witch*. We run goods between England and the States."

"You're a sea captain?" Belle asked, intrigued.

"And sometimes a pirate from what I hear," Trace interjected.

Traynor's brows rose in mock innocence as he slapped one hand, its skin as golden as the sun, over his heart. "Me? A pirate?" He laughed soundly. "Tell me, brother, who is spreading such dastardly tales about me? Tell me, and I'll shanghai the scoundrel and make him walk the plank."

Belle saw a spark of amusement glitter within Trace's eyes, but his face remained stolid. He looked at Belle. "I'm sorry, Belle, but I'm afraid we'd best postpone our ride, perhaps until this afternoon."

She nodded and forced herself to smile. How in blazes was she supposed to get into Trace's confidence or search his room with the house filled to overflowing with his brothers? Not to mention his mother and sister, and an entire staff of loyal servants. Belle felt like moaning in despair. Obviously it was going to take longer than she'd thought, which meant her father was going to remain in jail longer.

Trace looped the horses' reins around a hitching rack. "Come on, Traynor. Mama and Teresa are in the parlor with Traxton and Travis."

"I'm last?"

Trace laughed then. "Yes, little brother, as always, you got here last."

"Damn, I guess nothing's changed," Traynor said.

"A few things have changed."

Traynor's smile suddenly disappeared and a frown drew his thick black brows together. "Yeah, I guess you're right. And we've got a few fences to mend, don't we?" Without waiting for an answer, Traynor started for the door.

"Belle?" Trace said. "Will you join us?"

Traynor paused and looked back at her and silently offered his arm.

Belle stifled a sigh. "Of course," she said sweetly. She slipped a hand around first Trace's offered arm, and then Traynor's. "How could little ol' me turn down *two* such handsome gentlemen?"

Traynor beamed, but Belle didn't miss Trace's frown. What was the matter with him now? She glanced at him again out of the corner of her eye as they mounted the steps to the gallery. He couldn't be jealous of his brother, could he? After all, it wasn't as if he'd been trying to sweep her off of her feet since she'd arrived at the plantation. She'd been the one doing all the sweeping, though he had changed a bit since yesterday . . .

Yesterday . . . when he'd met Lin. The thought struck her like a runaway train. Trace was attracted to Lin. Belle smiled to herself. Good. Maybe that would make things a little easier.

"Traynor!" Teresa squealed, running across the room and throwing her arms around her brother.

Letting go of Belle's arm, he hugged her tightly and then set her away from him. "Hey, Tessie, you're all grown up."

A playful pout creased her face. "No one calls me Tessie anymore."

Traynor laughed and chucked a finger under her chin. "Well, I do, Tessie, so get used to it. At least while I'm here."

Belle slipped past Traxton, who was lounging on a tufted wing chair of forest green velvet, and made sure to keep her eyes averted as she pulled the skirt of her blue moiré riding habit aside to keep it from brushing against his outstretched legs, which he didn't bother to move. She settled onto a chair set before the fireplace, which was identical to the one Traxton occupied.

After greeting his mother and other brothers, Traynor remained standing, with Teresa's arm looped securely around his, while Travis sat next to Eugenia on a settee across from Traxton and Belle, and Trace took up a position at the fireplace, resting one arm on the white, intricately carved mantel.

"I must say, Mama," Traynor drawled, "your taste in guests is improving." He winked at Belle who laughed and fluttered her eyelashes coquettishly.

The smile that had been on Trace's face disappeared, but the grin on Traxton's face, which was hidden by the quick sweep of a finger across his upper lip, merely widened.

The woman was as brazen as they come, and though he wasn't sure he really liked it, Traxton couldn't deny that from the moment he'd set eyes on her, Belle St. Croix had stirred a passion within him that was more searing than any he'd felt in a long, long time.

Nine

Lin turned from the window at the sound of a knock on her door. She stared at it without moving, hoping against hope that it wasn't the overfriendly desk clerk again.

"Lin," Belle whispered, and knocked again, "open this blasted door."

Relief swept over Lin. She hurried toward the door, turned the lock, and swung the door open. "Have you found out anything?"

Belle rushed into the room in a flurry, ripped off her kid gloves, and threw them and her reticule onto the bed. She whirled on Lin. "Have you lost your mind?"

Lin's heart plummeted. "You mean last night?"

"Of course I mean last night, you twit. How could you leave the hotel like that after we agreed you were to stay put and out of sight? You could have ruined everything."

Lin wrung her hands together and settled into a yellow brocade chair that sat to one side of the fireplace. "I know but, well, I just wanted to—"

"To what, see the sights? Get us caught?" Belle paced the room, blond sausage curls bouncing with each step. "What were you thinking?"

"I wanted to see Papa and make sure he was all right."

"Oh, wonderful." Belle threw up her hands, stalked to the other side of the room, spun, and started back toward

Lin. "You wanted to see Papa. Now the guard knows we're here."

"No, I didn't use my real name, and anyway, they wouldn't let me see him."

Belle paused, surprised. "Why?"

"They said he couldn't have any visitors but his attorney and his family. I didn't want to tell him who I was."

Belle began to pace again, her temper not at all assuaged. "And of course then you ran into Trace Braggette and you just had to dine with him, didn't you?"

"He thought I was you."

"Well, of course he thought you were me, I'm the one he'd already met. But did he believe you? Are you sure he doesn't suspect?"

"I don't think he's the murderer, Belle," Lin said, ignoring her sister's questions.

Belle stopped her pacing again, propped clenched fists on her hips, and glared down at Lin. "Did he suspect you were me?" she demanded.

"No."

"Okay." She began to pace again. "Why don't you think he's the murderer? Did he say something to you?"

"No, but, well, I just don't feel he's the type to murder someone."

Belle stopped again and stared down at her sister. They had come to New Orleans suspecting that Trace had committed the murder. Now Belle knew it was also possible for the killer to be Traxton. But for some reason she was hard-put to explain, she didn't want to consider that option, though she knew they had to. She purposely softened her tone. "Lin, you like Trace Braggette, don't you?"

Lin looked at Belle cautiously. "Yes, I do."

"Good." Belle smiled as an idea began to take form in her head.

Lin stood quickly. A frown pulled at her brow and her eyes narrowed. "I don't like it when you get that look in your eyes, Belle. What are you planning now?"

"I want you to return to Shadows Noir in my place."

"Me?" Lin's look turned to one of shock. "But they'll know I'm not you."

"Trace didn't."

"But . . ." Lin felt a clot of fear lodge in her throat. "But that was only for a few hours."

"You can do it, Lin. We look just alike. You know when we wear the same outfit no one, sometimes not even Papa, can tell us apart." Belle began to shrug out of her riding jacket. "Now, come on, change clothes with me."

"Oh, Belle, I don't know . . ." But even as she protested, Lin had begun to remove the day gown of pale green muslin she'd donned only hours before. The prospect of seeing Trace Braggette again, even under such nerve-wracking conditions, was just too tempting to resist. "Do you really think it will work?"

"Would I send you out there if I didn't?"

"Yes," Lin said, meeting Belle's mischievous smile.

"Oh, pish." Belle threw the skirt of her riding habit at Lin. "The other three brothers have arrived, so you have to be—"

"Other three brothers?" Lin froze and stared at Belle in disbelief, then began to shake her head. "No, I can't do this. No. Not if there are others out there."

Belle flopped down on the settee. "Fine, we'll just let Papa hang then. Is that what you want?"

"Oh, of course not." Lin stepped from her hoop and reached for the skirt Belle had already discarded.

"Good." Belle smiled and rose. "Then let's get

started." She handed Lin her blouse. "Traxton came in yesterday."

Lin looked at her questioningly. "How will I know which one is Traxton?"

"He's a cowboy."

"A cowboy? A *real* cowboy? Like the ones in those penny books you buy?"

"Yes. He evidently owns a ranch in Texas, of all places." Belle wrinkled her nose.

"Where the Indians live?"

"So I understand." Belle hooked Lin's hoopcage around her waist. "Why anyone would want to live around those savages is a puzzle to me."

"Maybe they're not really savages," Lin offered.

"Right. And they don't kill soldiers and settlers and take their scalps either."

"Oh, Belle, that's so awful," Lin said, tears filling her eyes at the mere thought of some poor soul getting the top of his head cut off.

"Lin," Belle scolded, recognizing the onslaught of an emotional outbreak from her more sensitive sister.

Lin waved her hand at Belle and blinked rapidly. "I know, I know, I'm being too sensitive again." She sniffed, took a deep breath, and slipped into the blouse Belle handed her. "Okay, I'm all right now."

"Good, because we have another suspect."

Surprised, Lin paused. "Who?"

"Traxton. It seems that since he was coming to Louisiana for his sister's wedding, he decided to come early with the idea of buying some horses from some people he knows in Barataria and Baton Rouge."

"So how does that make him a suspect?"

"Don't you see, Lin," Belle said, "he was in Louisiana when his father was murdered, not Texas."

"Oh." Lin brightened. "Then that means Trace might not have done it."

"Might is the right word. You have to be careful, Lin. Remember, someone murdered Thomas Braggette, and if they know who we are and that we're trying to find the killers to prove Papa innocent, they could be dangerous."

Lin fought down the fear that filled her breast. "Okay, how will I tell these brothers apart?"

"It's not that hard, really. Traxton, as I said, is a cowboy. He'll be obvious the minute you see him." A tiny smile tugged at the corner of Belle's lips.

Lin saw the look in her sister's eyes. "You like him, don't you?" she asked.

Belle sobered instantly and frowned. "No. He's crass."

Lin giggled. "You like him."

"I do not!"

Lin held up a hand. "Okay, okay. What about the others?"

"Travis just arrived this morning from Virginia City, out in Nevada Territory, which I understand is near California. He owns a casino there."

"The Braggettes have a gambler in the family?" Lin said, looking aghast at the idea.

"A very handsome gambler," Belle corrected. "Look for elegance and pomp, that's Travis. Brocade vest and jewelry. Oh, and quite obviously a ladies' man."

Linn nodded.

"Traynor arrived this morning, too. He evidently owns and operates a couple of schooners that run between the States and England transporting goods. Trace made some reference to him also being a pirate."

Lin's eyes widened in shock and she clutched at her breast. "A pirate? Oh, good lord."

Belle chuckled. "He's not dangerous, Lin."

"Are you sure?"

"Yes. In fact, he's quite dashing."

Lin eyed her sister warily. "What kind of family is this, Belle? A cowboy, a gambler, and a pirate?"

"And quite possibly a murderer."

A dark shadow came over Lin's eyes. "Yes," she echoed, "quite possibly a murderer."

Belle forced her tone back to one of cheeriness. "As I was saying, I only saw Traynor for a little while, but he had on knee-high boots and a black slouch hat, if that's any help."

Lin buttoned the jacket of Belle's riding habit and looked at her, obviously puzzled.

Belle laughed. "That's the best I can do, Lin. Believe me, they all look alike, yet you can tell them apart."

Lin sighed. "I knew this plan of yours was going to get me into trouble. Anyone else?"

"Teresa, their little sister, the one getting married, remember?"

Lin nodded.

"She's young, about seventeen, I think, and very friendly. And she adores her brothers."

Lin nodded again and positioned Belle's hat on her head.

"Mrs. Braggette, her first name is Eugenia, is a dream. Very gracious. Oh, and the housekeeper's name is Zanenne. Skinny, old, and," Belle laughed, "rather grumpy."

"Okay, I'm ready. Is that all of them?"

"No, there's also Bujo."

Lin groaned. "I'm never going to remember all these names."

"He's Zanenne's grandson."

"Please tell me that's it?"

Belle smiled. "Well, that's all that I've met so far. Don't worry." She patted Lin's shoulder. "You'll do fine. We've traded places lots of times, and no one's ever found us out yet."

"We've never been searching for a murderer before. Or tried to fool so many people at the same time."

Belle's smile faded. She took Lin's hands in hers. "You're right, Lin, so be careful." The sly smile returned. "And stay away from Traxton Braggette. He's a scoundrel."

"Uh-huh."

"I mean it, Lin. Stay away from Traxton. He's trouble."

Lin smiled teasingly. "I have never yet flirted with a man you liked, Belle, and I'm not going to start now."

"Lin . . ."

"Okay, truce." She held up a hand. "You don't like him. He's just a crass scoundrel I should stay away from."

"Exactly." Belle hurriedly told Lin everything that had happened at Shadows Noir since her arrival, including her planned morning ride with Trace that had been postponed. "So get him to take you on that ride, Lin. He'll be expecting you to ask."

She nodded. "What are you going to be doing?"

"I'm going to try and get into Thomas Braggette's office."

"His office?" Lin squealed. "Where he was murdered?"

"Yes."

"What for?"

"For clues, you ninny, what do you think?" Belle snipped, falling back on her sharp tongue to hide her own fear. She didn't relish going to the scene of a murder, and she certainly didn't relish breaking into the place, which she had no idea if she could actually do. But most of all, she wasn't looking forward to going there at night, but it seemed the most logical time. There was too much risk if she tried to do it during daylight.

"Don't snap at me, Belle, I'm doing what you want me to do."

Belle felt instantly contrite, as she always did whenever she took her foul emotions out on Lin. "I'm sorry, I'm just worried about Papa, that's all." She forced a smile to her face and urged Lin toward the door. "Now, you'd best be getting back to the plantation. They were all still visiting when I sort of snuck out, and—"

Lin stopped dead in her tracks. "Snuck out? You didn't tell me that. Why'd you have to sneak out?"

"Because I didn't want one of them to offer to escort me to town, that's why."

"Oh."

"Now, as I was saying, you'd best get out there. Don't admit you went to town. Just say you went riding down the road for some air. And remember, you're me now, so your name is Belle St. Croix."

Lin sighed. "Lord, this is confusing. I was just starting to get used to being called Mademoiselle Bonnvivier."

"You'll do fine."

At the door, Lin hesitated again. "How will I get in touch with you?"

"You won't. Just keep your eyes open. If I need to contact you, I'll find a way. If you get in trouble out there, just leave and come back here. Understand?"

Lin nodded.

"Okay. Get close to Trace. Make him trust you, talk to you. We need to know everything we can about him, especially if the rumors we heard about how his father purposely destroyed his career are true."

Belle watched Lin walk down the hallway and disappear around the corner to the staircase. She sighed in relief, then hurriedly shut the door to the hotel room. Making her way to the chair near the fireplace, she then collapsed into it.

She lay her head against the chair's back and closed her eyes. An image of Traxton Braggette, his eyes sparkling with mischief, arrogance radiating from him, took shape in her mind. The man was an infuriating rake, a scoundrel of the most dastardly sort, an obvious Lothario . . . and she couldn't seem to stop thinking about him. She bounded out of the chair and walked across the room to stand before the dressing table with its tall center mirror.

But Traxton Braggette was not the reason she had been unwilling to return to Shadows Noir.

Are you sure?

"Yes, I'm sure," she snapped, in answer to the little voice that always seemed to pop up and question her motives just when she didn't want to think about them. "There are things to do here in town, and I certainly can't expect Lin to do them." She could just envision Lin swooning into a dead faint if she'd asked her to break into Thomas Braggette's office.

Belle grabbed the reticule that lay on a small table near the settee, made sure Lin had put the key to the hotel room in it, and proceeded to the staircase. At the landing she paused and pulled down the veil of the little green straw hat that sat jauntily on her crown and matched her gown.

Belle proceeded down the stairs. She knew she shouldn't be going out in broad daylight, but there was no help for it. If she were going to break into Thomas Braggette's office that night, she would have to locate the building now in order to be able to find her way back there once it became dark. After all, she didn't want to be out on the streets of the Vieux Carré at night any longer than necessary.

Pierre Loushei, having just delivered a message to one of the auctioneers in the center of the lobby's rotunda, paused as he saw Belle descending the stairs. "Why, Mademoiselle Bonnvivier, good day, but," he laughed nervously, "I could have sworn I just saw you leave."

Belle, her attention on the bustle of numerous auctions which were being conducted simultaneously, didn't hear or see the smiling desk clerk.

"Mademoiselle Bonnvivier?" Pierre reached out and touched Belle's arm.

She started and jumped back. "Wh-what?"

"Excuse me, mademoiselle, I was just saying I thought I'd seen you leave only a few moments ago in your riding habit. I certainly hope nothing is wrong?"

"Wrong?" Belle shook her head. Blast. She didn't know who he was, but he'd obviously noticed Lin leaving the hotel. "Uh, no, I just changed my mind, that's all. About riding, I mean."

Pierre smiled. "Yes, it is a bit warm for riding. You are going shopping, perhaps?"

"Perhaps," she said. Who in blazes was this man anyway?

A sly gleam came to his eyes. "I usually take lunch at a little café down by the Square, the Tranche de Vie. Perhaps you would join me? I'm sure your fiancé wouldn't mind if we just lunched together."

Join him? Fiancé? Belle nearly groaned. Obviously Lin had turned this man down before, but knowing Lin, she'd made it sound as if she regretted having to say no. Much to Belle's frustration, Lin had a habit of feeling sorry for people and always looking for their good side. Unfortunately she also refused to believe Belle, who constantly tried to tell her that some people didn't have a good side. Belle forced a smile to her lips and feigned Lin's sweet, ladylike tone. "I'm sorry, sir, but I have several errands to do today. I couldn't possibly commit to another engagement, but thank you just the same." She started to brush past him.

Disappointed, but not discouraged, Pierre held out his hand, palm up. "Well, I'll just take your key now and save you a trip to the desk. You can pick it up when you return."

The desk clerk. He was the desk clerk. She retrieved the key from her reticule and dropped it into his extended hand. "Thank you, sir."

"Oh, my pleasure, mademoiselle. Would you like me to have a bath sent up when you return?"

"A bath?" Belle's face screwed into a frown of puzzlement. Why would he ask her that?

"Yes, I can have it sent up the moment you return."

"Uh, no, that won't be necessary." Belle began to move away from him. "Thank you anyway." She felt a shiver of revulsion. Why did Lin always have to be nice to *everybody?*

"Oh, it won't be any trouble, mademoiselle. My pleasure, really," Pierre called after her. "Really."

Belle stepped out into the sunshine. The sky was a crystalline blue without a cloud in sight. On the building directly across the street, a flowerbox adorning a downstairs window and filled to overflowing with ferns and blossoming flowers was a rainbow of color. Belle took a deep breath and nearly gagged at the stench that met her nostrils. "Good Lord," she exclaimed loudly through several choking coughs.

The doorman turned toward her. "That's the canals,

ma'am," he said, as if he was used to explaining the city's sewage system to visitors.

"Canals," Belle echoed. She glanced down at the open trench that ran between the banquette edging the hotel and the cobbled street. Human waste and garbage floated in a stagnant river of water that had turned nearly black. "I don't remember them smelling this bad."

"Gonna be a warm day, ma'am. They always gets worse on a warm day."

Belle nodded. Wonderful. She might choke to death on the stench before she even made it to Braggette's office. "Could you please direct me to Rue de la Dumaine?" She knew Braggette's office was on Dumaine, she just didn't know where the street was.

"Certainly, ma'am," the doorman said. "You just go on down to the corner there," he pointed toward the Quarter's main north-south thoroughfare, Rue de la Royal, "turn right, and walk about four or five blocks and you'll come right to it."

Belle smiled, though another breath left her feeling as if she was being suffocated. "Thank you, sir," she said weakly. Snapping open a lace parasol that matched the green gown and settling its thin lemonwood stem upon her shoulder, Belle started down the banquette in the direction he'd indicated. With any luck at all, she'd discern the location of Braggette's office and be back in the hotel without any more unexpected confrontations.

Ten

Lin took a deep breath and ran a slightly trembling hand over the skirt of Belle's riding habit. No one had appeared as she'd ridden up to the front of the house, and obviously no one heard her enter the hall. Belle had said when she'd snuck out that the Braggettes had been visiting in the parlor. Lin stood with her back to the wall, a few feet away from a large, open doorway. Voices filtered out to her. Obviously they were still visiting.

Tears stung the back of her eyes as fear nearly robbed her of breath. Her hands clenched into fists. Get ahold of yourself, Lin, she ordered silently. You've traded places with Belle before, and no one's been the wiser. There's no reason to be afraid now.

A male voice Lin didn't recognize floated from the parlor and startled her from her musings.

"Well, I hope the whole damned mess dies down quickly so we can forget about it, and him, and get on with things."

"Yes, like my wedding."

"You sure are in one hell of a hurry to marry this guy, Tessie."

"I love Jay, Traxton, and I don't see why what happened to Papa should postpone anything."

"Me neither. I was just saying you seem like you're in a real hurry, that's all."

"It will be good to have a soiree here again."

Lin recognized Trace's voice as the one who'd spoken last and, in spite of her fear, felt her heart skip a beat. She didn't really know him and realized Belle was right to caution her against him, but in those few hours she'd spent in his company, she hadn't seen a killer. It was possible she was wrong, she knew, but she hoped, prayed, she wasn't.

"Well, it's now or never," Lin murmured to herself. Straightening her shoulders and smiling widely, she pushed away from the wall, turned, and walked through the doorway into the parlor.

Silence suddenly hung over everyone as they turned to look at Lin.

"Belle," Teresa said, rising from a chair and moving toward her, "where have you been?"

"Oh, I just went for a ride," Lin said. At least she had no problem identifying Teresa Braggette.

"I hope you don't feel neglected, dear," Eugenia offered, "but it's been so long since we were all together."

"Oh, no, I'm fine, really, Mrs. Braggette." Lin chanced a quick glance at each brother.

One of Eugenia's eyebrows rose slightly. "You promised to call me Eugenia, remember?"

Lin felt herself begin to fluster and fought for composure. Had Belle told her to call Mrs. Braggette Eugenia? She couldn't remember. She smiled. "'I'm sorry, Eugenia. I forgot."

Eugenia didn't miss the fact that Belle's gaze remained on Trace just a tiny bit longer than it did on any of her other sons, including Traxton.

"Well, we were just about to have café au lait, dear. Will you join us?"

"Oh, I . . ." Lin's eyes darted from one brother to the other. Could she do it? Trace stood by the fireplace. And she had picked out Traxton easily. He was lounging on a settee, dressed exactly as Belle had described: leather leggings, vest, and boots. His hat was on a nearby table, settled on top of the coiled leather belt of his holster. She looked at the remaining two brothers. She couldn't remember what Belle had said. Panic began to fill her breast. Was Travis the gambler? Or was Traynor the gambler? Or was Traynor the pirate?

Traxton, with a fluidity of grace in contrast to his rugged appearance, rose lazily from the settee. "Your seat, ma'am," he said, with a flourish of his arm and a light chuckle.

"Traxton, behave yourself," Eugenia scolded.

Lin brushed past him and assumed the seat, though she kept her gaze from meeting his. Belle had been right, Traxton Braggette was a scoundrel. But a handsome one.

Traxton's brows rose at his mother's reprimand. "But I am, Mama. I was merely offering the lady a seat."

Eugenia tried but failed to keep a smile from tugging at the corners of her mouth. "Just behave," she said curtly.

"Yes, ma'am," Traxton answered, and chuckled again. He settled back down on the settee next to Lin and turned his attention to her. "Not too tuckered out to take a ride with me in awhile, I hope?"

"Oh, I . . ." Lin looked at him, feeling suddenly very helpless and unsure of herself. "I, uh, that wouldn't really be very proper, Mr. Braggette."

Surprised at the somewhat prudish response, Traxton merely stared at her. *Proper* wasn't exactly the word he had expected to come out of Belle St. Croix's mouth.

Lin smiled shyly up at Trace, then turned her attention to his mother. "You have a very beautiful home, Mrs.—I mean, Eugenia, and if I haven't done it already," and knowing Belle, she hadn't, "I just want to thank you for inviting me to stay here and to attend your daughter's wedding."

"Oh, my dear, we are pleased to have you," Eugenia said.

"Can never have too many pretty girls around," Travis said, and winked at Lin.

She felt a blush heat her cheeks and quickly looked away. Travis. Belle had said Travis was the gambler and a ladies' man.

"And you can help me with wedding preparations," Teresa said. "I have so much to do."

"I'd like that, Teresa." Lin looked about at the brothers again. Each was dark-haired, tall, well-built and swarthy of skin. Their features were so similar that upon first glance they all looked cut from the same mold . . . until one looked closer. Then the differences, other than their apparel, became obvious. Each face had its own look, its own cut and character. Of course, if all were attired identically, Lin wasn't at all sure she'd still be able to tell them apart, except that Traynor definitely looked the youngest. She nearly giggled, remembering how, when she and Belle had been younger, they'd purposely dressed alike to fool their friends.

"Trace is presenting me at the wedding."

Lin frowned. "Presenting you?"

"To Jay, my fiancé," Teresa said. "Usually the bride's father does it, but . . ."

"Oh, yes, I understand. Your father was killed just a few weeks ago."

The room grew deathly quiet. Lin looked quickly at

Trace, wanting suddenly for him to reassure her, to say something that would both clear him of suspicion and prove her father innocent. Instead, his gaze, suddenly cold and hard, fastened on something behind her.

She felt Traxton stiffen, then lean forward, prop his arms on his knees, and stare at the floor. Lin turned to look in the direction of Trace's stare. An oil portrait she hadn't noticed when she'd entered the room hung on the wall behind her, framed by two tall windows. Lin knew intuitively that it was a portrait of Thomas Braggette, though his children looked almost nothing at all like him. Braggette had been a man of immense brawn, his body seemingly more fitted to the work of a roustabout than that of a senator. His hair was white, and his blue eyes held little warmth.

She glanced back at Trace and felt a wave of despair at the animosity she sensed emanating from him as he stared up at the portrait of his late father.

"Yes," Eugenia finally answered, "it is true. But we have decided to put that time behind us now." She smiled at each of her children, though their dour expressions failed to brighten. "I saw no need to postpone Teresa's wedding, nor the visit of my sons."

"Perhaps Miss St. Croix doesn't approve of our lack of propriety," Traxton said, his voice deep and gruff. He settled back into his seat as he spoke and turned a hard gaze on Lin.

"Oh, I didn't mean . . ." Lin rose. "I'm sorry, Eugenia, I didn't intend to bring up unwelcome memories. If you'll excuse me now, I think I'll go up to my room and change."

"You needn't hurry off, dear," Eugenia said.

"No, really, I think I'd like to lie down for awhile." Lin smiled. "I think I rode a little longer than I'm used to."

Trace straightened, Travis and Traynor rose from their

seats, but Traxton stayed seated. All remained silent as they watched Lin leave the room.

"Well, boys," Eugenia said, moments later, "I suppose it's time each of you also changed. I'm sure you all have enough trail dust on you to grow a garden in." She rose, laughing softly. "So scoot. Your rooms are just as you left them. I've changed nothing."

Travis and Traynor rose, kissed their mother's cheek, and walked from the room. Teresa hurried to tell Zanenne to prepare their baths.

Eugenia looked at Trace, who remained standing in front of the fireplace. His eyes attested to the fact that his thoughts were a million miles away. She turned her gaze to Traxton, who still lounged on the settee. "Don't Texas men take baths?" she teased.

A slow smile spread across his lips. "Yeah, Ma, Texas men take baths every once in awhile." A soft chuckle rolled from his lips and he rose slowly to his feet. "That your way of telling me I'm dirty, or just trying to get rid of me?"

"Both," Eugenia said honestly.

He nodded and walked from the room.

"I never thought I'd see that look in your eyes again, Trace," she said softly, once sure she and her eldest son were alone in the room.

Trace looked at his mother. "What look?"

She smiled. "The look that says a woman has caught your interest, that's what look."

He shook his head. "Always trying to play matchmaker, aren't you, Mama?"

She moved forward and touched his arm. "It's all right, Trace; he's gone now. Your father can't ruin it for you this time."

* * *

Traxton paused before the door to their guest's room. A frown pulled his dark brows together. This morning she had impressed him as one fiery little spitfire, a handful of trouble if he'd ever seen one. And definitely a minx he'd like to bed as long as she didn't have her lasso whipping in the wind.

He made to take a step away from the door and paused again as he heard her begin to sing. Not a lively tune as his impression of her that morning would have him expect, but a soft, lilting lullaby, beautiful, yet sad. He always went by first impressions, but it was becoming obvious that his first impression of Belle St. Croix had been wrong.

"Fire in her veins," he said softly, scoffing. "More like lukewarm milk."

At the door to his old room, he paused again, assailed by memories of another Traxton Braggette, a little boy who had constantly tried to stand up to his brooding bully of a father, a teenager who had rebelled at his father's harsh dictates and always suffered for his bravery. At twenty Traxton had become engaged. He'd planned to marry and move as far from Shadows Noir as he could. Less than a year later his father had nearly ruined him. He'd left home then, and hadn't been back since. But now Thomas Braggette was dead, and there was nothing more he could do to hurt his son.

He walked into the room, looked about, and felt himself instantly begin to relax. It was just as his mother had said, exactly the way he'd left it. His room. Traxton walked to the open window, unlatched the jib door, and ambled out onto the gallery. A jasmine vine was curled around the pillar opposite his window. He leaned over the railing. The plant had completely taken over the trellis he and Trace had used as little boys to sneak out, after their mother had put them to bed. They had never dared to use the outside stairs, fearing their father might be waiting for them at the bottom. For some reason they'd never thought he'd be waiting at the bottom of the trellis, and he never had been.

Pulling a cheroot from the pocket of his vest, Traxton bit off one end and spit it over the railing. He settled the cheroot between his lips and dug a finger into the pocket of his trousers in search of the small box of lucifers he always kept there. Retrieving one, he returned the box to his pocket, settled a hip against the gallery's railing, and struck the sulfured head of the lucifer against the rough surface of the pillar. The tiny match burst into flame and, cupping his free hand around it, Traxton lifted it to the end of the cheroot and inhaled quickly several times, drawing the flame to the tobacco.

He had ridden long and hard the night before. He could have taken a packet down from Baton Rouge, but had decided against it. Boats were a fine way to travel for other people, but Traxton didn't like them and didn't take them if there was any other way. He'd had a near miss once when, traveling up the Mississippi, the packet he'd been on had nearly ripped in half when one of its boilers had exploded. He'd been one of the lucky ones who had survived, but he wasn't too eager to risk his life again. At least, not on a packet.

"Beyond the dawn, the Lorelei sings, the Lorelei sings to me . . ."

Traxton's attention was pulled toward the open jib window halfway down the gallery. . . . Belle's window.

Walking slowly, unconscious of his intent, Traxton approached the window. It was open, but the heavy damask draperies had been drawn shut. Suddenly one of them was jerked back, and Traxton found himself staring down at Belle St. Croix, whose outstretched arm had frozen in place at sight of him, her fingers literally clutched around the damask fabric.

"Oh, Mr. Braggette," Lin said, near breathless with shock. She took a step back from him. "You startled me."

Traxton smiled, convinced she had known he was there. "Really?"

Suddenly aware she had nothing on but her camisole and pantalettes, Lin grabbed the drapery she had just pulled back, and yanked it in front of her, clutching it to her breast. "Mr. Braggette, please," she said, her cheeks flaming crimson. "I didn't realize anyone was about." Lin tried desperately to wrap the drapery around her body.

Moments before, while remembering his first encounter with Belle St. Croix, Traxton had felt desire begin to heat his blood as it had then, but he sure didn't feel it now. Not with Miss Prim and Proper hiding behind the curtain. He stared down at Lin. What the hell had happened? Where was the fiery vixen who'd nearly snapped his head off that morning and given him tit for tat? He might not like her sharp tongue, but he sure as hell had liked her fire and wanted to bed her. But that was then. Now his blood was as cold as an icy river. A frown began to pull at his brow. Maybe it was him. He decided to try again. After all, in his experience, which he had to admit was pretty vast, a hot-tempered woman was usually a very passionate woman, and there was nothing Traxton liked better than a passionate woman.

Taking a step forward, he reduced the distance between them to less than six inches, raised a hand, and slid one outstretched finger slowly, caressingly, along the line of her bare shoulder. "Are you sure you didn't realize I was out here, Belle?" he said, his tone seductively deep and drawling.

Lin gasped and yanked away from him, her eyes wide with indignation. "Mr. Braggette, please!"

Traxton's hand dropped from her shoulder and he stepped back out onto the gallery. "Sorry," he mumbled, turned, and sauntered insolently toward his own room. What in the hell was going on? He glanced back at her window just before entering his own room. Obviously his first impression of Belle St. Croix had been wrong. Dead wrong. She was no fiery vixen. No saucy spitfire. She was a lady. A damned, self-righteous, prim and proper, virtuous lady.

But the earlier surge of desire, though gone from his body, had left a very distinct memory in his mind. Traxton snapped close his own draperies as he prepared to bathe. He wondered if the girls at the Golden Fleece were still the prettiest ones in the Quarter. A smile curved his lips as he remembered his times at the brothel. Maybe he'd ride into town tonight.

Belle pressed herself against the door to Thomas Braggette's office and looked back down the steep set of stairs and the street. She was alone. No one had followed her. A sigh of relief left her lips, and she sagged against the door.

The office was less than a half-dozen blocks from the hotel. That afternoon when she'd walked there to locate the office and get her bearings, it had seemed such a pleasant, short walk. But the sun had been out, the casinos had been closed, the shops had been open, and she'd been one of many respectable people traversing the banquettes. Now it appeared she was the only respectable person out, and those few short blocks, shrouded by inky shadows, had seemed more like a half-dozen miles.

Twice that evening on her way to Braggette's office, she had been approached by men staggering out of the casinos, so drunk they could barely stand, but not so drunk that they hadn't tried to accost her. The first man had been dissuaded by a snap of her parasol to the side of his head. Luckily she had brought it along for just such an emergency. The second man who decided she was just what he needed to make his evening perfect had, in the end, needed no discouragement from her to desist. He had weaved his way toward her, slurring an invitation as he neared, but before he could finish his sentence, he reeled and fell face forward into the street and passed out.

Belle twisted the doorknob. It remained secure. She rattled it, pressed her weight against the door, and twisted again. It still held firm. "Damn." The lone curse seemed to hang in the night air.

She glanced back down at the street, relieved to see that she was still alone. Obviously the door was locked and wasn't going to open. Gathering up the folds of the heavy cape she'd draped over her shoulders, Belle bunched it around her hand, made a fist, and smashed it against one of the panes of glass in the door. It shattered instantly, several shards falling into the room and crashing loudly on the floor.

"Oh, double damn," Belle cursed. She hurriedly re-wrapped the dark cloak around her and tried to press herself into the shadow of the building.

"Hey, Charley, you heared somethin' back there in the alley?"

Belle held her breath.

"Nah."

"Sounded like glass breakin'. You think Mort's got a bottle back there and's holdin' out on us?"

"Nah. Mort's down at Sadie's." A man staggered past the stairs. "Le's go get our own bottle."

Belle released her breath and sagged against the door, but, realizing she had no time to dawdle, she reached through the broken window and unlatched the door. She slipped inside hurriedly and looked around. Moonlight filtered through the windows that faced the street and enabled her to make out the lay of the room. A huge desk was near the far wall, with two wing chairs placed before it. Several cabinets lined the north wall. She turned. A fireplace was set into the south wall. A table with several crystal decanters and glasses was sitting before the fireplace, along with two more chairs. A smaller desk had been pushed up against the streetside wall, along with more cabinets. A waist-high railing separated the area of the two desks.

Belle felt a surge of defeat as she looked at the cabinets. How in heaven's name was she going to search all of those tonight? She'd be here until dawn, and then most likely not be even halfway done. Removing her cloak, she draped it over a chair and pulled open a cabinet. Lord, it would take her forever to read by moonlight. And the files were a mess, shoved in the drawer haphazardly. Someone had obviously already searched the place, she reasoned, and evidently found nothing.

She heard a soft thud, like something hitting the wall, followed by a faint rustling sound, and then silence. Belle's heart lodged in her throat, and she nearly stopped breathing. Fighting to remain still and not fly out the door, she stood frozen, waiting.

No other sound was evident, and slowly Belle's heartbeat returned to normal, her ragged breath quieting and her hands ceasing their violent trembling. "Probably a rat," she mumbled. She pulled a handful of files out of the drawer, spread them on the desk, and rifled through them quickly. They were of no help.

An hour later the entire contents of Thomas Braggette's three filing cabinets were piled on his desk. Belle kicked the chair in frustration. "There has to be something here," she grumbled. "The man was a crook, or so everyone says." She stalked to the filing cabinets next to the smaller desk, which obviously belonged to Braggette's clerk. Yanking open the drawers, she began to thumb through the files. They were mostly deeds of trust, loan papers, and old shipment receipts. Nothing of interest. Halfway through the drawer of files, she stopped.

She folded her arms tightly across her chest and began to do the one thing she always did when she became either frustrated or angry or both: she paced. Back and forth across the room, ten strides north, ten strides south, her footfalls silenced by the Aubusson runner that covered the space of floor beside the railing.

On her twenty-first trip across the room, the toe of her shoe snagged the rug and Belle pitched forward, saving herself a nasty fall by grabbing hold of the railing. She straightened. "Damnation!" She glared accusingly at the moonlit rug, which was now rumpled where her toe had snagged it. "Dumb thing." She put her foot out and pressed the rug. There was a definite lump beneath the wrinkled nap. Suddenly she remembered tales from the penny books she'd read. White settlers who lived in Indian country dug root cellars beneath their homes and hid them with a door in the floor. They used them for storage, and also to hide in when the Indians attacked. Was it possible? On a second-story floor? Belle dropped to her knees and pushed the rug aside. The floor beneath the rug was planked cypress, stained dark. She squinted and ran her hand over the smooth surface. Her fingers felt a seam that ran horizontal to the vertical planks.

"Yes!" Belle slapped a hand quickly over her mouth and looked at the door, fully expecting to see someone run in. She lowered her hand and began to feel around the floor in search of the latch that would allow her to pull the door up. It took several more minutes, but she finally found it. Sitting down now, her legs framing the small door, her skirts bunched up around her legs, Belle made to reach down into the dark hole, but paused, her hand suspended over the dark cavern. What if Thomas Braggette hadn't used this little floor cabinet? What if an animal had found it and made it his home? What if there was a family of mice, or rats, snuggled down there? She said a quick prayer and reached into the cavern. Her fingers came into contact with something cold and smooth. A box. She flicked a finger against it. A metal box.

"This is it, Papa," she mumbled. "This has to be it." She slipped her hands around the edge of the box, wiggled her fingers beneath it, and lifted it from its hiding place. She slid the box onto the floor, quickly closed the small door, and put the rug back into place.

Belle struggled to her feet and carried the box to the desk by the window. A small lock hung from its latch. "Damn, damn, damn, and double damn." She looked around for something with which to break the lock. Her gaze came to rest on the fireplace poker. Belle grabbed it, then cringed. Hadn't Thomas Braggette been killed when someone hit him over the head with a fireplace poker? She looked at the poker, imagined it covered with blood, and nearly dropped it. "Stop it, Belle, for heaven's sake," she admonished herself, and tightened her grip on the metal rod. "You're acting like a ninny." She smashed the end of the poker down atop the tiny lock, and it broke open instantly.

Belle rifled hurriedly through the stack of papers piled neatly within the box but knew she didn't dare tarry and read them now. Too much time had already elapsed since she'd left the hotel, and that damned desk clerk seemed to know every move she made. She didn't need him wondering why she was out so late at night alone, the nosey busybody.

Belle stuffed the papers into the pocket of her cloak, along with the broken lock, and then set the empty box on one of the bookcase shelves. She began to turn away, stopped, and looked back at the box. No. If she left it there and anyone noticed, they'd know someone had been in Braggette's office and found something. She glanced at the mountain of files she'd left on Braggette's desk and the smashed window. They'd know she was there anyway.

Stepping from Braggette's office, Belle remained on the staircase landing for several seconds, looking down at the street and listening. Music filtered out onto the night air from one of the nearby casinos, but there was no sound of drunken revelers on the street. She scurried down the stairs and to the street.

"Hey, little lady, where ya goin' in such a hurry?"

A hand snaked out of the darkness. Its long, spindly fingers wrapped around her arm and nearly yanked her off her feet as they pulled her into the shadows of the roof that overhung the banquette.

Belle jerked her arm and tried to pull away from her assailant.

The man stumbled forward, nearly crushing Belle, who staggered backward under his weight.

As he fell forward, his face was illuminated by the light from one of the casino's windows. His countenance was a map of craggy lines and deep ruts, his features sharp, though too small for the wide berth of flesh in which they were set. A day's growth of dark whiskers covered a near nonexistent chin and deeply hollowed cheeks, a massive mustache obscured his upper lip, and scraggly eyebrows poked from a ridge of forehead that overhung eyes so small, and set so far into his skull, they could only be described as beady.

Belle shuddered with revulsion. "Let me go," she ordered, and yanked her arm back, again pulling the man off balance when he refused to release the grip he had on her arm.

"Damned whore, whatcha think you're doin' anyways?" His fingers tightened their hold on her.

"Whore? Why, you . . . you . . ." Outrage swept away her fear and blinded her to caution. Belle threw all of her weight into resisting the pull of his arms.

"Settle down, missy. I gots money ta pay you with," the man said.

Ignoring the pain she was inflicting on herself with her struggles, Belle yanked furiously on her arm in an effort to break his hold. "I am not a whore, you . . . you idiot." She tried again to twist away from him and managed little more than to snarl her legs within the voluminous folds of her cloak. "Damn it, let me go!" Belle lashed out with her other hand.

The man caught her by the wrist and twisted her arm backward, and a jolt of pain shot up her arm. He laughed as a startled shriek burst from Belle's lips. "That's good, girlie. I like my whores with a little spirit. Now," he brought his face closer to hers, "how's about a little kiss for ol' Jeeker before we go up to your room?"

Belle raised a leg and brought the heel of her shoe

crashing down on the man's toes. "How about that instead?"

"Owww, you little bitch!" He dragged Belle up against his chest and grasped her shoulders. "Now, I said I want a kiss."

His breath smelled of cheap whiskey and stale tobacco. Belle shuddered in disgust as it wafted around her. "I don't care what you want, you oaf," she spat as she struggled to free herself.

Belle readied to let loose with a bloodcurdling scream as his face neared hers.

Suddenly, a voice, its tone menacing and harsh, rumbled from the shadows. "Let her go."

Eleven

Belle felt a flash of hope and relief. Help. She tried to pull away again, but found the man had not loosened his grip.

Jeeker twisted to look over his shoulder. "This here one's mine, mister. Go on and find your own."

"I said, let her go."

The tiny hairs on the back of Belle's neck suddenly rose on end. No, it couldn't be. Fear and dread began to override her momentary sense of relief. She raised up on her tiptoes to peer over her assailant's shoulder. At the same time, Jeeker turned to face the man, pulling Belle as he moved and holding her roughly to his side.

"Oh, good lord," she muttered as her rescuer came into view.

"Obviously He was too busy to come to your aid," Traxton drawled. "Will I do?" His words were teasing, but his tone was hard and sheathed in anger.

She felt her already-racing pulse accelerate.

Before she had time to think of a response, the casino's frosted-and-etched glass door behind Traxton opened. For one brief second the sound of laughter, clinking glasses, and shuffling cards drifted out onto the night air. A man stepped through the doorway, glanced in Traxton's direction, and paused.

Belle felt her heart stop for the second time in the last minute. It was the gambler from the riverboat. The same gambler who had offered to carry her and Lin's bags.

"Need any help, Trax?" the gambler said.

A smile curved Traxton's lips, but there was no warmth in his deep gray-blue eyes as they stared at Jeeker. He cocked a hip and lay the heel of one hand impudently on the butt of the gun holstered there. "No thanks, Harlan, I think I can handle it."

The gambler glanced past Traxton to Belle. Smiling, he tipped his hat. "Ma'am," he said. "Nice to see you again."

Belle smiled weakly and chanced a quick look back at Traxton. He was still glaring at the man who held her.

"I believe I asked you to release the lady."

"I told ya," Jeeker snarled, "this here whore's mine. I saw her first."

"You clod!" Belle snapped. "I told you, I'm not a whore."

Jeeker growled and jerked her to his chest.

"The lady's telling the truth. You've made a mistake," Traxton drawled. He straightened slightly, his fingers sliding toward the trigger of his gun. "Now, for the last time, let her go."

Jeeker, his eyes suddenly riveted on the gun strapped to Traxton's thigh, snatched his hand away from Belle's arm as if it had suddenly turned to fire beneath his touch. He scurried several feet away, raising both hands toward Traxton. "Hey, I didn't know, mister. I mean," Jeeker laughed nervously, "how's I to know she wasn't no whore? R'spectable ladies don't usually go prancin' all over town alone after dark, you know?"

Traxton didn't bother to answer, but merely continued to stare at the man.

Jeeker quickly said, "Well, don't make no nevermind. You kin have her, mister. Too much sass for my blood anyways." With that he swung around and stalked off into the darkness of the alley.

"Are you all right?" Traxton asked, struggling to keep his voice calm. What he really wanted to know was what in the hell she was doing in town, alone, in the middle of the night. Belle's assailant had been right: no lady dared go out on the streets of the Quarter after dark, especially unescorted. Not if they wanted to continue to be regarded as a lady.

"I'm fine," Belle retorted sharply.

Traxton took a step toward her, ready to catch her should she suddenly spiral into a faint.

But instead of the simpering gush of gratitude he'd expected, Belle snatched the long folds of her cloak up and stormed past him.

"Hey, wait a minute." Startled, he spun around to follow her. "Just where in the hell do you think you're going?"

Without pausing, or looking back at him, Belle called over her shoulder, "Back to the hot—" Sudden realization of what she'd nearly said struck her. He thought she was Lin, who was at Shadows Noir pretending to be Belle, not at the hotel.

Traxton grabbed her arm and forced her to halt. "Better yet, what in the hell are you doing here in town so late? And unescorted?"

Belle jerked her arm free and stared up at him, her mind racing furiously in search of an answer. Her mind, however, balked and inexplicably began to wonder what it would feel like to be held in the cradle of his strong protective arms. She tried to force her mind back to where it belonged, on finding an excuse to get away from him, but it rebelled. What would it be like to be kissed by him?

"Oh, stop it," Belle snapped.

Traxton frowned. "Stop what?"

Her eyes widened and her heart thudded madly as she realized she'd spoken aloud. "Badgering me, that's what." Not knowing what else to do, Belle turned and began to walk away from him. With any luck at all, he'd return to his gambling and leave her to be on her way.

"Badgering?" He stepped in front of her. "I just saved your little hide from who knows what, and you accuse me of badgering you?"

"Yes. Now, if you would kindly get out of my way . . ." She darted past him.

"Damn it, Belle," Traxton cursed, grabbing her arm again and spinning her around. "Will you tell me what you're doing here?" She had more sauce and fire in her than a barrelful of rattlers, and though that might appeal to his more basic yearnings, he sure as hell couldn't figure why Trace was attracted to her. Traxton had noticed that this afternoon in the parlor. And he had a gut feeling that what his brother felt for Belle St. Croix was a hell of a lot more than just attraction.

"Poor fool," Traxton mumbled.

"What?" Belle snapped.

"Nothing." His face turned hard again. "Now, why are you in town, Belle? What's going on?"

"I . . . I had some business to attend to."

"At night?" he said, skepticism evident in both his voice and raised brows. He didn't know what kind of game Belle St. Croix was playing, but he was already tiring of it.

"Yes. So," she pulled away from him and began to fiddle with the pocket of her cloak, "you can just go on back to your gambling, or whatever it was you were doing in there, and I'll be on my way." She turned a cold eye to him. "I assure you, Mr. Braggette, I can take care of myself."

Traxton laughed, though the sound held no mirth. "Oh, I can see that, Belle. Yes, you can definitely take care of yourself."

Belle bristled. "I had the situation under control, Mr. Braggette, whether you choose to believe me or not."

"Then I guess I was just wasting my time."

"Yes, you were. Now, if you'll excuse me." Belle brushed past him again and began to walk down the banquette.

"I don't think so," Traxton said. Quickly untying Rogue, who stood at the hitching post before the casino, Traxton swung up into the saddle and maneuvered the horse beside the banquette and Belle. Swooping down upon her like a god from the sky, Traxton wrapped an arm around her waist and, lifting her from her feet, pulled her up beside him and onto his thighs.

"Traxton Braggette, put me down," Belle demanded, thrashing at his arm with clenched fists, her legs flailing.

"Watch where you're kicking or you'll hurt Rogue," Traxton ordered.

"I'll hurt you if you don't put me down," Belle threatened.

Traxton laughed, which only fed her fury.

Fear suddenly doused her anger and stilled her struggle. "Where are you taking me?"

"Back to the plantation, where did you think?"

"Shadows Noir?" Belle squeaked.

"That's what it was called last time I checked."

Panic filled her breast. "No, you can't. Uh, I mean . . . I don't want to put you out."

"I'm going back there anyway, remember?"

"Yes, but, uh, I mean, uh, you probably weren't finished with what you were doing in there . . . in the casino, and I don't want to take you away from—"

"I was finished."

Belle felt her heart plummet to the pit of her stomach. "Oh."

"Are you ready to behave now?"

"Behave?" Belle stiffened in defiance of his words.

"Quiet down?"

"Yes. I don't have anything to say to you anyway."

"Good. Just tell me where you left the buggy?"

"Buggy?" she echoed.

"Yes, buggy. I assume you didn't walk into town. And since you don't have on a riding habit, I figure you came in a carriage."

"I don't remember."

Traxton reined in. "You don't remember how you got into town?" he asked, clearly aghast.

Belle lifted her nose into the air and refused to meet his eyes. If she did, she was afraid he'd see that she was lying. "I don't remember where I left the carriage. All of these streets look the same to me."

"Lord save us from female drivers," Traxton muttered.

Belle smashed a fist against the arm that was still holding her securely around the waist. "Just put me down, Traxton Braggette," she demanded, and hit him again.

"Damned females," Traxton swore. But instead of putting her down, he flung her sideways and onto the back of the horse.

Belle, suddenly afraid she was being tossed into the middle of the street, grappled for his shirt as her legs swung through the air. One hand found a grip on the leather sleevehole of his vest, while the other clutched at folds of his muslin shirt sleeve. Surprisingly, rather than meeting the ground, she found herself straddling the rear end of his horse.

Traxton nudged his heels to Rogue's barrel, and the animal lunged forward.

"Traxton!" Belle shrieked; scooted her derriere forward, and clutched at his waist.

"We'll be at the plantation in less than half an hour," he said over his shoulder.

"Wonderful," Belle muttered grumpily. Begrudgingly she wrapped her arms around his waist as her rear end began to rhythmically bounce up and down on the horse's rump. Each collision of derriere against saddle jarred her spine, and she was forced to clench her teeth together for fear of biting down on her tongue. She had to think of something. Of some way to escape him before they got to Shadows Noir. She couldn't go there, not with Lin there. Her mind conjured up various plans of action with lightning speed, which she just as hastily rejected.

"Are you still alive back there?" Traxton asked fifteen minutes later. He shifted his position on the saddle, but it didn't help. He might not like Belle St. Croix, but that wasn't stopping his body from wanting her. And that was confusing him all the more. His initial opinion of her had been that she was one of the most ornery, outspoken, trouble-making females he'd ever encountered. Granted, he wasn't looking for a wife, and even if he was, it certainly wouldn't be one like that, but he'd never denied that her type of woman was exactly the kind he loved to bed. That is until she'd turned into a lady. And just like that. A prim and proper, cheek-blushing, eyelash-batting lady, which was definitely the type he *didn't* like, to bed or otherwise. And now she was the spitfire again. Why in the hell couldn't she make up her mind?

"I'm fine," Belle murmured. She adjusted her seat, felt herself begin to slide down the horse's rump, and grabbed hold of the curved back of Traxton's saddle. Five minutes ago she'd straightened away from him and scooted back so that her body was not in contact with his. Unfortunately because of the animal's sloping rear end, it didn't give her much of a seat, but that couldn't be helped. Being in physical contact with Traxton was beginning to wear on her nerves, for much as she tried to deny it, she couldn't ignore the fact that touching him sent a delicious shiver of heat rippling through her body, which in turn stoked a hunger for more, and more was definitely not in her plans. Anyway, he was a cowboy and a Braggette. Not exactly sterling attributes as far as Belle was concerned.

Traxton twisted around to look over his shoulder. "What in the hell are you doing now?"

Belle, not having the faintest idea what he was talking about, merely stared, wide-eyed.

"Get back up next to me. Do you want to ruin Rogue's spine?"

Belle scrambled forward. "I didn't mean to hurt the horse. I was just trying to give you some roo—"

His hand whipped around behind her, flattened against her back, and smashed her up against his. "Now stay there."

Belle closed her eyes and counted to ten. It didn't help. Her mind continued to wallow in fury as her body began to respond to being crushed up against his. She felt the sway of his back against her breasts with each step the horse took. What would it be like to be kissed by him?

"We'll be at the house in another ten minutes," Traxton said over his shoulder. And not one minute too soon, he thought. If he didn't get her to the house soon, he wouldn't get her there at all, and it wouldn't be the first time he'd made love to a woman outdoors. Though it would be the first time he'd made love to a woman he didn't even like.

With a barely perceptible movement, Traxton laid the reins against the left side of Rogue's neck. The horse instantly turned to the right and began walking down the curved entry of Shadows Noir. The crushed oyster shells that covered the drive crunched softly under his hooves.

Belle suddenly snapped out of her reverie. The house. They were nearing the house. And Lin was there. She had to do something. Get away somehow. She looked to each side and saw only moonlit pasture and trees. If she jumped off of the back of the horse and ran—no, that wouldn't work. He'd just chase her down. She could fall off and pretend to be hurt, then when he went up to the house for help, she could run—no, that wouldn't work either. He'd get to the house and see Lin there. She could pretend to be sick and—

Traxton reined up in front of the house. Lights shone from several of the upstairs windows. Downstairs only the foyer reflected any light; the rest of the house was settled into darkness. He swung a leg over Rogue's neck and slid to the ground, then turned and held his arms up to assist Belle down.

She stared at his hands.

"Are you going to get down or what?"

She scooted up onto his saddle. "No, I'm not sleepy. I think I'll ride your horse down to the stable."

Traxton grabbed Belle, his hands spanning her waist, and pulled her from the saddle.

"Traxton, damn it, let me go," Belle whispered harshly, her hands flailing at him. "Put me down."

"That's exactly what I'm trying to do."

"Leave me alone, do you hear me?" She kicked out at him. "Damn it, leave me alone."

"Believe me, lady, it would be a pleasure." Traxton uncinched his saddle, slid it from Rogue's back, and threw it, along with the animal's bridle, on the ground. The horse wandered toward the open pasture.

Belle glared at Traxton and suddenly realized if she didn't get out of sight, and quietly, everything might be ruined. She looked at the house again. All she could do was pray that everyone had retired for the night. Ignoring her fear, Belle turned and stalked up the pathway and across the gallery.

Traxton strode after her, catching the front door just before it shut in his face. "Damned women. The world would be better off if we could find a substitute for them."

"Try your horse," Belle whispered, just before she disappeared around the corner of the second-floor landing.

Traxton stomped up the stairs, a string of pithy oaths running rampant through his head as he envisioned hogtying Belle St. Croix and washing her mouth out with soap, an act, thanks to his father, that as a child he'd been well familiar with. Though he'd bet a hundred greenbacks Belle wasn't. He turned the corner of the landing just in time to see her disappear into her room and shut the door. Traxton figured it was a good guess that everytime Belle's parents had tried to reprimand or discipline her—if they'd tried at all, which he doubted—Belle had turned that simpering, prim and proper lady act on them, and that had been the end of any scolding.

Traxton scoffed. Well, he knew what "ladies" were really like beneath their false indignation and morals. Juliette had been a lady, and she'd taught him a lesson he wasn't likely to forget. Traxton shook his head and opened the door to his room. Ladies. He wanted no part of them—any of them—ever.

Belle stood with her back to the closed door, blinking furiously in an effort to get her vision accustomed to the shadowy darkness of the room. "Lin?" she whispered.

A soft moan came from the direction of the big four-poster bed directly opposite where Belle stood.

Belle made her way cautiously across the room. At the bed she slid her hand across the mattress and came into contact with a mound beneath the coverlet. "Lin?"

"Wha—"

Belle slapped her hand over Lin's mouth. "Sssssh. You want to wake the whole house?"

Lin yanked away from Belle's hand. "Belle! What are you doing here?"

"Sssssh."

"What are you doing here?" Lin again whispered fiercely.

"Traxton rescued me in town from some drunk and—"

"Oh, Belle," Lin gasped, "are you all right?"

"I'm fine, except that the idiot forced me to come back here with him. He thinks I'm you."

Lin frowned. "But he thinks I'm you."

Belle's temper was ready to explode. "You know what I mean."

Lin nodded. "What are you going to do?"

"I found some papers in Thomas Braggette's office, but I haven't had time to actually read them. I skimmed them, and it looks like we may have to include a few more people as suspects, but I won't know for sure until I go over them more carefully."

"I'll turn on the light," Lin said.

Belle grabbed her arm. "No. I can't stay here. I've got to go back to the hotel."

"But how?"

"Well," a devilish smile curved Belle's lips, "I'd love to take Traxton's horse. That would serve him right. But I can't do that or he'll get suspicious, so I guess I'll walk."

"It's an awfully long walk," Lin said. "I know, I've done it."

"What choice do I have?"

"Oh, dear, I guess you're right, but do be careful of the alligator."

"Alligator?" Belle's whisper rose a notch in surprise. "What alligator?"

"He crossed the road when I was walking back to town the other night." She smiled. "But he didn't come after me or anything, so I doubt you have to worry. Just be careful."

"Wonderful. Now, how do I get downstairs without being seen?"

"Well, there are outside stairs that lead off of the gallery. Or, if you don't want to use those, Teresa told me that her brothers used to sneak out of the house at night by climbing down the trellis so they wouldn't get caught by their father."

"A trellis." Belle looked down at the voluminous folds of her gown and dark cape. "I really don't think that's too practical while I'm dressed like this. I'll chance the outside stairs. Where are they?"

Lin slipped from the bed and walked to the window. Pulling back the heavy drapes, she slid the paned window up. "That way." She pointed.

"Do I have to pass anyone's room?"

"Traxton's," Lin whispered.

Belle nearly groaned. "Okay," she said weakly, and kissed Lin's cheek. "I'll contact you later."

Lin nodded and watched silently as Belle lifted her

skirts and climbed through the open window. She tiptoed across the gallery in the direction Lin had indicated.

Suddenly, as she passed Traxton's window, she heard a soft, sliding sound and turned to see the window being raised.

Belle froze, hardly daring to breathe.

A second later the sound of the jib door's latch being released echoed on the still night.

Belle sprang into action and scurried toward the stairs.

Traxton walked out onto the gallery and paused midway between his window and the railing. He cocked his head, as if listening, and a deep frown creased his brow. He could have sworn he'd heard something. Turning, he walked toward the outside stairs.

Twelve

"If I ever, ever, encounter Traxton Braggette again, I'll kill him," Belle spat, her voice wafting across the silent night air and disappearing within the bosk of trees through which the road weaved. In the distance a frog croaked as if in answer to Belle's comment. "Oh, shut up," she snapped. He croaked again, twice. Belle picked up a pebble from the road and threw it into the trees. "Men should be seen and not heard," she said, "so, shut up."

Normally she would have been nervous, walking on a deserted road in the dead of night. But she was too furious to be scared and too outraged to be nervous. "I'll kill him." She broke a twig off of a bush and began to twist it between her fingers. "Kill him, kill him, kill him."

The fact that while riding behind him she had begun to wonder what it would be like to be held within the circle of his arms, buoyed by their brawn, protected by their strength, that she had pondered how it would feel to be kissed by him, to experience the sensual caress of his lips on hers, didn't matter in the least anymore. He had forced her to ride with him, on the back of his horse no less, all the way to Shadows Noir, and now she had to walk all the way back to town—alone. "I'll teach him how to part his hair with a beam of lumber." She slapped the twig against the skirt of her gown. "No," she mumbled, "his head is probably too hard to take notice of that." She snapped the twig in half. "I'll tie him to his horse, belly down, and—"

The sound of a horse approaching caused Belle's jaws to immediately snap together, silencing her tongue. She stared into the darkness, momentarily stunned and trying to discern if she really heard the pounding of a horse's hooves on the ground or if her ears were just playing tricks on her.

The sound grew louder as the horse neared.

Belle's eyes darted around in search of a place to hide. This was no figment of her imagination. The prospect of encountering a highwayman out here in the middle of nowhere, while she was alone and unarmed, was not exactly an enticing one. She scooted toward the side of the road and a tree whose trunk looked wide enough for five people to hide behind.

Almost at the same moment she jumped from the road, horse and rider came around the curve. Dust, clods of dirt, and bits of gravel filled the air as a huge stallion sped past. The animal's black coat and the contours of his muscular body glistened in the moonlight, and the silken strands of his ebony mane and tail tangled in the wind while his long legs stretched outward and his hooves pounded the earth with incredible force and speed. The rider rode low in the saddle, his upper torso hunkered down over the animal's neck, a hat pulled low onto his forehead. His dark jacket and trousers blended well with the blackness of the night and the animal's shiny coat, causing them to appear more as a centaur than horse and rider. But as the rider's jacket flapped back in the wind, a quick glimpse of a brocade vest, its silver threads picking up a shaft of moonlight and reflecting it briefly, told Belle that the rider was Travis Braggette, obviously returning to Shadows Noir after a night at one of the Quarter's casinos.

Belle lifted her skirts and made to step back onto the road. The skirt of Lin's gray muslin gown, a color Belle hated but had chosen specifically for being out this night, caught on a jagged piece of protruding tree trunk. Not noticing, Belle stepped forward, and, as her weight pulled against it, the fabric ripped.

"Oh, fiddle." Belle yanked the cloak that hung from her shoulders and its copious folds swirled securely around the skirt of her gown. She stepped to the middle of the road, and as she did, the heel of one of her slippers twisted under her weight and she nearly stumbled, only catching her balance at the last minute and righting herself. A short, curt string of very unladylike oaths tumbled from her lips. She stared down the empty road in the direction Travis had disappeared. "I hope you gambled tonight and lost, Travis Braggette," she called out. "I hope you lost a lot." Stamping a foot on the ground, Belle whirled around and resumed her long trek toward town, grumbling and cursing with each step. It wasn't exactly the way she had planned to spend the rest of the night.

Trace lay stretched out on his bed and stared up at the canopy overhead. His room was steeped in darkness, the lamp extinguished, the drapes pulled tight to block out the moon's rays. He couldn't see the *ciel de lit* of midnight blue silk that was drawn into a sunburst pattern between the poster frames of his bed, but it didn't matter. Even though his gaze was directed upward, his mind was not on the silk canopy, but on a beautiful woman with platinum-gold hair.

One side of his mouth quirked upward in a small smile.

Not since Myra's death had he even thought of another woman in a serious way, in spite of his mother's promptings. But ever since dining with Belle in town, and then riding home with her in the carriage, he had thought of little else. The smile widened as he remembered that his first impression of Belle had been dislike. He nearly laughed aloud. She had seemed too forthright then, too outspoken, even a little brazen, but perhaps that had merely been nerves. At the hotel dining room the other evening, she had been a perfect lady. And when he'd assisted her into the carriage, his hands encircling her waist, he'd wanted desperately to pull her into his arms.

A long sigh slipped from his lips. And she was asleep just down the hallway. He closed his eyes and imagined her as she might be, her long hair spread across the white pillow like silver-gold threads atop a blanket of pristine snow, subtly curved lashes closed over eyes that were neither blue nor green, but a mesmerizing combination of both colors, and her lithe body covered by little more than a thin veil of gown or sheet.

Trace swung his legs over the side of the bed and pushed himself to his feet. His body was hard, hungry, and burning with desire. He walked to the window, threw back the drapes and lace panels underneath, draped both over a hook that protruded from the wainscoting, and shoved the window upward. The warmth of the day still hung heavy in the air, leaving it humid, but a faint breeze wafting toward the house from the bayou brought momentary relief to Trace's seething flesh. He inhaled deeply of the night's fragrance, immediately able to discern the familiar scents of jasmine, magnolia, and dogwood that permeated the air. Unlatching the jib door and pushing it open, he stepped out onto the gallery and crossed to stand at the railing. His eyes roamed the landscape, seeking nothing, but merely appreciating the moonlit scene.

The faint sound of a horse's hooves pounding against the earth drew his attention to the drive, and then to the main road that led to Shadows Noir. After several seconds he spotted the rider, then his attention was drawn to a spot of lightness on the road, a spot that moved in the opposite direction than that of the rider who was approaching the gates of the plantation. Trace frowned and squinted into the darkness, trying to ascertain just what it was he was looking at.

Lin looked up and smiled at Traxton as he entered the dining room, the last to come to the breakfast table.

"Hey, Trax, this what you guys do down in Texas, sleep half the day away?" Travis asked with a chuckle.

"Yeah," Traynor chimed in, "I thought you were supposed to get up and do a little something before you lay back down for a siesta."

Eugenia smiled at her sons' jesting, something she hadn't heard in a very long time.

"I had a little trouble sleeping last night," Traxton said, pointedly directing his gaze toward Lin, who quickly averted her eyes and began paying undue attention to the food on her plate.

Traxton walked directly to his mother, leaned over her shoulder, and pressed his lips to her cheek. "Good morning, Mama," he said softly.

Eugenia patted the hand he'd placed on her shoulder. "The food is on the sideboard, Traxton, as usual. Help yourself and then join us."

"I thought you might like to accompany me on rounds this morning," Trace said.

Traxton scooped scrambled eggs onto his plate from a silver server set on the sideboard and half-twisted around to look at his older brother. "Me?" he asked simply.

"All of you," Trace said. He had thought long into the night about Shadows Noir and the return of his brothers. By tradition it was the eldest son who inherited everything, but the plantation was over five thousand acres, and the Braggettes owned several more of equal size in Louisiana, enough for all of them. For all of the years they'd been gone, he'd brooded and remained angry at them for leaving, and at himself for staying. But now that they were back, now that he had to face what he'd always resented, sharing with them the plantations he alone had mastered for the past eight years, he knew he wanted them to stay. He hadn't realized it until they'd returned, but he had truly missed them.

"Yeah, I'd like that," Traxton said. He was used to being up early, before sunrise, and riding the range to check things out. But more important, he wanted to see what Trace had accomplished with Shadows Noir. He knew their father hadn't paid much attention to the plantation in years, leaving its management to his eldest son, though Traxton guessed the old man had never offered one hint of gratitude or appreciation.

"Count me in," Traynor said.

Travis took a long swallow of coffee, set his cup down, and settled comfortably back against his chair. "Not me," he said. "I got in late last night. A saddle is about the last place I want to put my—" He glanced at Lin and smiled. "Well, let's just say I don't feel like riding this morning."

Traxton slid onto a chair next to Lin and set his plate on the table. Turning from Trace, who sat to Traxton's left at the head of the table, with Eugenia at the opposite end, Traxton centered his attention on Lin. His gaze raked over her quickly, and he couldn't help but feel disappointment. The pale blue muslin day gown she wore was as modest as they came, its sleeves reaching from shoulder to wrist, its neckline high to her throat and trimmed with a short ruffle of lace.

Feeling his stare on her, Lin looked up, smiled demurely, and then quickly returned both her gaze and her attention to the food on her plate.

Traxton, in the few seconds her eyes had met his, looked for the fire that had been in her eyes last night, but it wasn't there. Instead, he met cool sea-green blue. They held warmth and a gleam of friendliness, but no fire. Puzzled, he leaned toward her and dropped his voice to a low, suggestive drawl. "So, Belle, since you love to ride so much, are you joining us this morning?"

Lin, confused by his statement, hesitated in answering. What did he mean, since she loved to ride so much? She really didn't care for riding at all. A frown pulled at her brows, and then she remembered that he had brought Belle to the plantation last night on the back of his horse! She looked at him quickly. Had something happened during that ride that Belle had neglected to tell her? She felt a flush begin to warm her cheeks.

"Belle, I'm going into the dressmaker's in town later this morning," Teresa interrupted. "If you'd like to join me, I'd love the company." She made a mocking face at Traxton. "My brothers will only start talking business while they're out riding anyway and most likely bore you half to death. You can help me choose some accessories and give me your opinion on my gown."

Lin felt a wash of relief. Accompanying the Braggette brothers, alone, on a ride around the plantation, was not a prospect she welcomed. She wouldn't have minded being with Trace. Far from it, she wished he would have asked her to go with him—alone. But three of them together? No, she couldn't risk that. Especially not with. . . . She chanced a glance at Traxton, found him looking at her, the gleam in his eyes definitely impudent and mocking, and quickly looked away.

Belle had been right. Traxton Braggette was an insufferable scoundrel with no manners whatsoever. Obviously he was used to turning on his charm whenever and on whomever he fancied, expecting the lady to just swoon right into his arms. She glanced at Trace. How could brothers who looked so much alike and were raised in the same family be so different?

Lin smiled at Teresa. "I'd love to go into town with you, Teresa, and I'd be honored to help you choose your accessories."

"Guess we'll just have to ride our horses alone, guys," Traxton said, not taking his eyes off of Lin.

She patted her lips with a linen serviette. Why did Traxton keep looking at her like that? She knew he'd forced Belle to accompany him back to the plantation last night, but why was he acting so strangely? And making such absurd comments? A shocking thought flashed into her mind. Had Belle kissed him? Was he looking at her like that, with that seductive, mocking smile on his lips, because Belle had kissed him?

"Don't you normally ride your horse alone, Trax?" Travis said, his brow furrowed in jesting skepticism.

"I've been known to share a ride on occasion," Traxton said.

His answer brought a surprised look to Travis's face.

Traxton turned his smile to Lin and continued, though she quickly looked away, "When the lady is pretty enough, and Rogue approves."

Everyone laughed except Lin, who merely smiled weakly. Who was Rogue?

Traxton glanced at Trace, who he noticed hadn't been able to look away from Belle for more than a few seconds at a time. Guilt washed over him, and he remembered the decision he'd come to hours before when he'd watched Belle tromp toward her room: if Trace wanted her, Trace could have her. So then why was he goading her now? Why in the hell hadn't he just said good morning to her and left it at that? Anger began to burn within him. So what if he was attracted to her? He'd been attracted to dozens of women, and he'd probably be attracted to dozens more before his number was up. So what if he had to forego the pleasure of bedding this one? It didn't really matter that much anyway. Belle St. Croix, in spite of her occasional outbursts of temper, was a lady, a very strait-laced and proper lady. He turned a brazenly assessing look on her. And ladies, most of whom had ice in their veins instead of red-hot blood, just weren't his cup of tea. Although when his gaze dropped to the snugly fitting bodice of her gown, he knew that, even though his mind had discarded her as a bed partner, his body had not.

Teresa transferred the reins of the carriage horse into one hand and adjusted her wide-brimmed pink straw hat with the other. "How long has it been since you've been to New Orleans, Belle?" she asked.

Lin's fingers twirled the parasol of white poplin and lace that rested on her shoulder as her gaze roamed over the passing landscape. Louisiana was so similar to Mississippi, and yet in so many ways she found it much different. Her home in Natchez was deeply forested in spots, and the land was made up of rolling hills and tall bluffs that dropped off sharply to the river below. This land was flat, with only an occasional knoll breaking the supine monotony.

"Belle? Did you hear me?" Teresa said.

Lin suddenly became aware that Teresa had spoken to her. "Hmm?" She whirled around, her eyes wide. "Did you say something to me?"

"Yes." Teresa laughed. "I asked how long it's been since you were in New Orleans."

"Oh, I'm sorry, I didn't hear you. I was so taken with the scenery." It was only half a lie. She was taken with the scenery, but she'd heard Teresa say Belle, not Lin, and hadn't realized the girl was directing the question at her, even though she was supposed to be Belle. In fact, she'd had that problem so much while at Shadows Noir, she was afraid the Braggettes were beginning to think she was slightly daft. "I haven't been to New Orleans in, oh, years. I came down with my father and sis—uh, cousin, just after my mother passed on. Papa needed to get away from the plantation for awhile, but that was so long ago I barely remember. And I'm sure things have changed considerably."

Teresa nodded. "I'm sorry about your mother. Were you close?"

"I don't remember her that well anymore," Lin said quietly, "though I know my father still misses her terribly."

"It must be wonderful." Teresa looked quickly at Lin. "Oh, I'm sorry, I meant it must have been wonderful to have parents that cared for one another. Mine didn't."

"Your parents weren't . . ." Lin hesitated. She'd never been good at wheedling information out of people. Belle was. She had a knack for it. And for getting her way, no matter what. Lin decided to try again. "Your parents didn't love each other?"

Teresa laughed. "Ha, that's actually funny. There was no love lost between my parents, Belle. I doubt there ever was. Their marriage was arranged."

"Did he . . . treat her badly?"

"Badly?" Teresa's dark brows soared upward. "He was a beast."

The carriage rounded a curve in the road and the city of New Orleans, sprawling endlessly over the landscape, came into sight.

"Well, we're almost there," Teresa said.

Lin wasn't sure whether Teresa's comment was merely an innocent one, or whether it was intended to change the subject, but she decided to allow for the latter. Anyway, she didn't like questioning Teresa. They passed a copse of dogwood, and her gaze moved toward the river as it came into sight. "Oh, I thought the docks of Natchez and Vicksburg were crowded, but this . . ." She laughed. "This is incredible. There must be several dozen packets docked out there."

"More like a hundred," Teresa said. "Not to mention the schooners anchored offshore, and the keelboats wedged in between the packets."

"However do they all get to the wharves?"

"Who knows? I hate boats."

Lin turned, surprised. "You do? Why?"

"My father made us take a trip with him once upriver. They served something I didn't like for breakfast and I wouldn't eat it. He got furious and decided to teach me a lesson."

Lin frowned, puzzled.

"He tied a rope around my waist and threw me overboard."

"What?" Lin couldn't believe what she'd heard. "Threw you overboard? For heaven's sake, why?"

Teresa shrugged. "The lesson was to eat your food or suffer the consequences."

"But to throw a child overboard?"

"That was my father," Teresa said bitterly. She suddenly smiled and turned eyes bright with happiness to Lin. "But he's gone now, and that's in the past."

"Yes," Lin said quietly, "that's in the past." She shuddered involuntarily. Could Teresa have been the one who. . . . She forced the thought away as ridiculous. Thomas Braggette had obviously been a very demented and cruel man, and Lin was finding it more and more difficult to harbor animosity toward the unknown person who had killed him. Not that she'd had a great deal to begin with. Only the driving desire to obtain her father's release from prison spurred her to cooperate with Belle's scheme, especially after meeting Belle's prime suspect, Trace Braggette.

The thought of Trace sent a warm rush through Lin's blood. He was like no man she had ever met before: gentle, sensitive, and caring, and in the few hours they had been alone together, he had sparked something within her she had felt for no other man. She sensed there was a quiet strength beneath his gentlemanly manner, an iron will that had served him well and would allow him to deal with whatever the world brought to his doorstep. That thought brought with it a shadow of doubt. Could that quiet strength and iron will have allowed him to finally rebel against his father? To the point of taking the man's life?

Lin didn't want to think so, didn't want to believe that, but she had no alternative except to consider it.

Teresa turned the carriage onto Levee. They passed the mint, its soldiers on guard at the door nodding as Teresa flashed them a glance. Another, in the process of dismounting, turned and waved, his smile wide.

"An old beau?" Lin asked, noticing Teresa's enthusiastic return of the man's greeting.

Teresa laughed. "No, that's Brett Forteaux, a friend of one of my brothers." She pulled the carriage to a halt as they came abreast of an open air market. "I promised to pick up a few things for Zanenne. I'll be right back." Teresa wrapped the reins of the carriage around the brake handle and began to climb down.

"No, wait, I'll come, too," Lin said. She looked around quickly, suddenly realizing how close they were to the St. Louis Hotel. What if Belle were out and about? She reached up to pull the veil of her hat down over her face but found nothing: she'd forgotten to wear a hat. Her gaze darted in every direction as she climbed from the carriage. Well, most likely it didn't matter anyway. Belle would stay in the hotel room. Lin followed Teresa under the canopy of canvas that roofed the vendors' stalls and found herself immediately surrounded by a bustle of activity. Vendors called out to each passerby, trying to lure them to their stalls with enticing chants and promises of the best vegetables, the tangiest fruits, the freshest fish while customers haggled over prices and children happily snuck samples of whatever they could reach while their parents shopped.

A plethora of scents immediately assailed Lin's nose, some sweet, some tangy, others stinging and tart. Over one vendor's stall a dozen snowy white geese hung suspended by ropes tied about their feet. Beneath them, on a long table lay dozens of brown eggs on a bed of Spanish moss. In another stall the glistening bodies of various fish were neatly on display in a row, the poor dead creatures' eyes staring glassily. Bright yellow plantains, green fuzzy-skinned okra, red apples, oranges, berries, and white onions decorated several more vendor areas and added a splash of color to the display. A huge tortoise slept beside another stall, and several squawking chickens were caged in still another.

While Teresa picked through a mountain of plantains, Lin began to wander down one of the aisles, fascinated by the various sights and the almost unintelligible dialect of many of the vendors.

As she came to another aisleway, she saw an Indian woman sitting on the ground. Her rounded back, draped with a colorful blanket, was settled up against one of the tent's support poles. Humidity hung heavy in the air, and there was not the slightest breeze wafting off of the river. Lin took a step toward the old woman. It was a hot day, yet this woman sat under a blanket and didn't even appear to be warm. Fascinated, Lin moved closer.

The woman's black hair was parted down the center of her head, pulled to just beneath her ears, and braided. The two braids hung down over her chest, and their full tails, tied by a string of leather, lay upon her ample breasts. She sat with her legs crossed beneath a skirt of dark muslin, feet hidden from view. Cradled in her lap was a bundle of straw. She didn't look up when Lin approached, but kept her concentration on what she was doing. Her stubby brown fingers worked deftly at several strands of the dyed straw, weaving them into a pattern and, as Lin watched, a basket began to take shape between the woman's hands.

"The missy be Belle St. Croix, yah?"

Startled at the deep voice that sounded just over her shoulder, Lin turned abruptly and was unnerved further to find herself staring up at a huge black man, his face so close to her own that she could feel his warm breath on her cheek. His black eyes swept over her hungrily, and she felt a wave of revulsion. Lin tried to take a step back from him and felt a vendor's wooden booth press against her skirt, impeding her retreat. "Who . . . who are you?" she managed finally.

The man smiled, revealing a slash of brilliant white teeth against a face so dark it could rival the night, except for the grotesque designs of pinkish scar tissue that covered his cheeks and forehead and circled his features. A turban of bright red cloth covered the top of his hair, secured in front by a large silver and diamond brooch. Two large white ostrich feathers stuck straight up from the pin. His chest was bare, his white pants barely reached his knees, and he wore a long flowing yellow cape.

"Don't matter, no. Brings you a message, me."

"A message?" Lin echoed.

"Stay away from Mr. Traxton, you." He grabbed Lin's hand, holding it palm up.

Lin felt a rush of fear. "What do you mean, stay away from Traxton?" She tried to pull away from him and found his hold on her too tight to break. Fear and panic burst to life within her breast. "Who are you?" she demanded, her voice weak and full of the terror that had begun to overwhelm her. "What . . . what do you want?"

He placed his other hand over hers. "Remember what Kayja say, yes?" He released her then. Lin looked down at her hand and saw a small red velvet bag in her palm.

"What's this?"

"Message. For you, Belle St. Croix."

Before she could question him further, or even look into the bag, he turned and disappeared into the crowd that milled throughout the market.

Regaining her composure now that she knew she was in no danger, Lin slowly walked back toward the carriage, untying the bag as she walked.

"What do you have?" Teresa asked, plopping the plantains in the rear of the carriage and coming around to her side in order to board.

"I don't know," Lin said. "A very large black man came up to me and said it was a message, then before I could question him, he disappeared back into the crowd."

"Ohhh, sounds mysterious." Teresa giggled. "From a secret admirer, perhaps?"

Lin looked up quickly. She hadn't thought of that. Could it be from Trace? Suddenly feeling foolish for having been so scared, she felt a burst of excitement at the prospect that Trace had sent her a gift. She smiled. And a warning to stay away from Traxton. She hurriedly untied the knot, picked the bag up by its end, and shook its contents into her open palm. A small, blood red wax heart, its center pierced by three silver sewing pens, dropped into her hand.

She heard Teresa gasp. "Oh, no."

"What?" Lin asked quickly, her eyes darting from the wax heart to Teresa. "What is it?"

"It's a *gris-gris*."

"A gree-gree? You mean a voodoo charm?" Lin stared down at the small ugly amulet. She knew some of the slaves on the Sorbonte plantation practiced voodoo, though she'd never seen any of their ceremonies. When she and Belle had been children, their old nanny had told them things, one of which was that when they heard the drums at night they were to stay in their rooms. Belle had wanted to sneak out and watch the clearing where the slaves held their meetings, but Lin had been too afraid and refused. Lin suddenly snatched her hand back and the amulet fell to the ground.

"Who gave it to you, Belle?" Teresa asked anxiously.

"And why? Did he say why?" Teresa grabbed Lin's hand. "Who was he?"

"I . . . I don't know who he was. He was big, and his face was covered with designs."

"Designs?" Teresa's eyes narrowed in suspicion and a hardness came over her pretty young face. "Like scars? Were they scars on his face?"

"Yes, but in the shape of designs, not like he'd been accidentally hurt or anything."

Teresa nodded.

"Who is he, Teresa?" Lin asked anxiously. "Do you know him?"

"I know who he is. What did he say to you?"

"Just that I was supposed to stay away from Traxton." Lin frowned. "Why would he say that? Who is he?"

"His name is Kayja, and my guess is that his message comes from Juliette Voucshon, though why he'd be delivering messages for her I have no idea. Unless she paid him to do it."

"Who's Juliette Voucshon?"

"Traxton's ex-fiancé."

"Traxton's ex-fiancé," Lin repeated, in nearly a gasp.

Teresa nodded. "Obviously she's back in town and has decided to pick up where she left off, though I rather doubt if my brother will be interested."

"Where they left off?"

"Uh-huh. Though I never did understand what Traxton saw in her." Teresa bent and picked the wax heart up, then took the velvet bag from Lin and dropped it inside. "We'll take this back to Zanenne; she'll know what to do with it."

"Why?" Lin asked, surprised. "Can't we just throw that," she wrinkled her face in disgust, "thing away?"

"No, you can't. A *gris-gris* is the symbol of a hex, and it's dangerous. If you throw it away, the hex could become worse." Teresa shook her head. "Damn that Juliette Voucshon." She forced a smile to her lips and looked at Lin. "Don't worry. We'll take it to Zanenne. She'll know what to do." Teresa stuffed the small velvet bag into her reticule and climbed into the carriage.

After Lin was situated, Teresa snapped the reins over the horse's rump, and the carriage lurched into motion. "Madame Carpentier's shop is only a few blocks from here. Just on the other side of the Square, actually. By the St. Louis."

Lin felt her heart plummet to the bottom of her stomach. "By the St. Louis?" She looked around quickly, hoping she wouldn't see Belle on the street.

"Uh-huh, on Chartres." Teresa's eyes brightened and, as if having already dismissed the incident with the *gris-gris* from her mind, she turned to Lin and smiled devilishly. "Oh, I have a marvelous idea. Have you ever been to the St. Louis Hotel?"

Thirteen

Lin stared at Teresa as if she'd just asked her if she'd ever been to Hell. She felt the breath lodge in her throat, choking her, and her heart tripped into a rampaging beat that threatened to engulf her in its thunderous sound.

"They hold auctions in the rotunda every day, and, oh, they're just marvelous. My father used to forbid me to go, and Trace wouldn't like it. . . ." She lowered her voice conspiratorially. "They have a slave auction there." Teresa pulled the reins to the left, the horse veered, and the carriage turned a corner onto Chartres. "But we don't have to pay attention to that auction. There are other more interesting ones, anyway. They have bolts of fabric from France. Jewelry. Millinery."

Panic had a firm grip on Lin, but she finally found her voice, though her fingers continued to frantically twist the beaded end of her reticule. "Oh, I don't think that would be a very good idea, Teresa." Her voice sounded strained even to her own ears. She struggled to bring a calmness to her tone. "I mean . . ." Oh, Lord, what did she mean? "I mean, it's already after noon, and we haven't even gone to the dressmaker's yet for your fitting, and, well, we were supposed to be looking for accessories for you, and with your brother not approving and all, I just think—"

"Oh, poo, Belle. I thought you were the daring sort. Listen, we'll go to the dressmaker's first. I'll get my fitting done while you look at the accessories she's got available, and then, on our way back out of town, we'll stop at the hotel." Teresa giggled. "How's that sound?"

Horrible, Lin thought. She smiled in spite of the sinking feeling in her stomach. "Well, let's see how it goes at the dressmaker. I wouldn't want to be riding home in the dark."

"Really? I'd have thought you wouldn't mind that."

Taken slightly aback by Teresa's words, Lin frowned. "Why?"

Teresa shrugged. "I saw you out walking the other night."

Lin gulped painfully. "You did?"

"On the drive. It was late, but I decided you probably couldn't sleep and just wanted to take a walk. So," she pulled the carriage to the side of the street, "I figured if we were late getting home, you wouldn't really mind."

Lin climbed carefully from the carriage. "Well, it's not that really, but, well, your mother would probably worry, and from what little I've seen of your brothers, I'm sure they're very protective. I wouldn't want a search party of Braggettes coming after me, especially if it was because I'd let you talk me into going to the hotel auction that you've been forbidden to attend."

Teresa laughed. "You're probably right; forming a search party sounds exactly like something they'd do. Especially Traxton." She walked around to where Lin stood. "Okay, we won't go to the hotel . . . at least not today. If we have time, there are other places we can go."

Lin didn't even want to venture a guess as to what other places Teresa had in mind. It was becoming obvious the girl liked to slight propriety as much as Belle did. Lin looked at the buildings that lined the street. They were all two-storied and stucco, with sloped roofs of slate shading tall windows adorned with shutters, and balconies edged with intricately designed balustrades of wrought iron. They passed an apothecary, a tobacco shop, and a millinery. Then Lin spotted a sign affixed to a wall over the door to one building, gold letters on a black background that proclaimed the shop *Madame Carpentier's Parisienne Modes*.

They walked to the corner where, both women holding their skirts well above their ankles, they carefully traversed the thick planks that led from the packed earth street, over the open canal, and to the bricked banquette.

"Why don't they cover those things over?" Lin asked. She wrinkled her nose in disgust at the putrid smell that drifted up from the stagnant river of waste.

At that precise moment, a man carrying a large bucket walked out from the shop that occupied the building next to the dressmaker's shop. At the edge of the banquette, he threw the bucket's contents into the canal.

"That's why," Teresa said as they neared the door to the dressmaker's shop. "How would people get rid of their waste if the canals were closed over?"

"Well, other cities don't have these horrid things."

"So what do they do?" Teresa asked innocently.

Lin looked at her, suddenly without an answer. She didn't know what they did. It wasn't something she'd ever given a moment's thought to. "I don't know, but whatever it is, it's better than this."

Teresa laughed and pushed the door of the dressmaker's shop open. A bell tinkled overhead. "Madame Lili, it's me, Teresa Braggette."

A tiny woman, no more than six inches over four feet and possessing the body of a child, swept out from behind a draping curtain that covered one of two interior door-ways. Her hair was dark and her face unlined, but a touch of gray at the temples attested that she was older than might be assumed at first glance.

"Mademoiselle Braggette, you are just in time," Lili Carpentier said. "I have just this moment finished the lining of your wedding gown and can go no farther on the alterations without another fitting."

"Madame, this is my friend, Belle St. Croix. May she look at your accessories while I change?"

"Mais oui," Lili said. "You go into the fitting room," she waved Teresa into the small curtained room and then turned back to Lin, "and you, mademoiselle, can look at those things over there." She pointed to the opposite end of the long room.

"Madame," Lin said, "is there a milliner nearby?"

"Oh, *oui,* mademoiselle. Just down the block. Jacqueline. She is excellent with the bonnets."

Lin smiled. "Good. I will visit her while you work with Teresa on her gown. I'll be back in no time, and then I'll peruse those accessories."

"Oui, mademoiselle, I will tell Miss Teresa."

"Oh, no," Lin said quickly, "you don't have to. She'll just worry about me. Please, I'll be right back."

The dressmaker nodded and disappeared behind the curtain.

Opening the door slowly, and careful not to let it touch the small bell, Lin slipped out of the dressmaker's shop. Once on the banquette, she turned and hurried toward the corner. The hotel was only two blocks away. Hopefully she could talk to Belle and get back to the shop before Teresa was done.

* * *

"So, now we have almost a half-dozen suspects instead of one," Belle said. She threw the papers she'd taken from Thomas Braggette's office onto the bed and began to pace the room.

Lin nodded but made no comment.

"Tell me about Shadows Noir. Have you found out anything while there?"

Lin looked pained. "I'm not as good at this as you are, Belle."

Belle paused in front of her. "Yes, you are. Now," she sat down on the settee next to Lin, "what have you found out?"

"Well, Teresa isn't at all bothered by the death of her father. In fact, it's as if none of them are. At times she seems almost happy about it."

"I knew that," Belle said. "What else?"

"Did you know that Traxton was betrothed to be married?"

Belle felt as if someone had just thrown a bucket of ice water into her face while someone else kicked her square in the stomach. "Be-betrothed?"

"Oh, I don't mean now," Lin hurried to correct. "He was bethrothed before, but he's not anymore. Teresa stopped at the open air market on our way into town, and while she was buying some fruit, I was looking at all the things the vendors have for sale there and then—"

"What has all that got to do with Traxton Braggette having been once bethrothed?" Belle interrupted impatiently. "And what does *that* have to do with his father's murder?"

Lin looked insulted. "Really, Belle, must you always be so churlish and interrupt? It's not very ladylike, you know, and it's very improper."

Belle felt her temper rising. "I don't care about being

ladylike at the moment, Lin, and I don't give a fig about being proper, as you're always so willing to remind me. Now, tell—"

"Well, you should care," Lin said, her voice full of sisterly concern. "Especially if you want to attract Trax—"

"Lin," Belle snapped. Her patience had been strained to the limit and now snapped like a barber's shaving strap.

Lin smiled sweetly. "Well, I don't know that it has anything to do with the murder, really. I just thought you ought to know, that's all. Especially since some huge, ugly black man with scars all over his face and a big red turban with a fancy brooch and feathers came up to me in the market and told me to stay away from Traxton Braggette. Then he handed me an amulet, a wax heart with pins in it, that Teresa said was like a curse and—"

"What?" Belle bounced off of the settee and stared at Lin in disbelief. "Are you telling me the truth?"

"Well, for heaven's sake, of course I am. Whatever reason would I have to lie?"

Belle began pacing again. "Why would anyone do that?" She stopped abruptly and whirled to face Lin. "Why would anyone try to warn you away from Traxton?"

"Well, most likely they thought I was you." Lin smiled again. "And you *are* taken with Traxton Braggette."

"I am not!"

Lin laughed softly and placed a hand over her chest. "A lady should never lie, Belle. It's not proper."

Belle decided to ignore Lin's comment. Anyway, her sister was such a romantic it would do no good to argue with her. "Someone thinks I'm getting too close to the truth. That's why they're trying to scare me away. Traxton knows something. Either that or he's the one we're after."

"But he was off buying horses somewhere. You said so."

"That's what *he* said." Suddenly an image of Traxton standing on a gallows popped into Belle's head and her stomach knotted.

"And Teresa said she thought the man was sent by Juliette Voucshon, Traxton's ex-fiancé. Teresa thinks the woman wants him back."

"Well, she can have him," Belle said, angry with herself for even thinking about Traxton Braggette in any way other then a suspect and a blackguard. "Have you managed to get any closer to Trace?"

"He didn't murder Mr. Braggette," Lin said.

Belle propped clenched fists on her hips and stared down at her sister. "And just how do you know that?"

A dreamy, faraway look came into Lin's eyes. "I just know, that's all. He's too nice, Belle. Trace is warm and kind and—"

"And he hated his father."

Lin sighed audibly. "How do you know he *hated* him? Hate is an awfully strong word, Belle. He disliked him, but I don't know if he—"

"They all hated him."

"Well, I agree they disliked him, but even if they did hate him, that doesn't mean they'd kill him," Lin said. "Anyway, Belle, the others weren't even in New Orleans when their father was murdered, and Trace didn't do it. We'll just have to look for other suspects. Trace just isn't the kind of man to murder anyone, and you're never going to get me to believe that he is."

Belle continued to stare at her sister. Lin was falling in love with Trace Braggette. It was written all over her face, engrained in each uttered word regarding the man. Belle nearly sighed but caught herself. It was obvious she couldn't send Lin back to Shadows Noir. It was too dangerous now, with her feeling the way she did about a man who might very well be a murderer. The alternative wasn't much better, Belle had to admit, but what other choice did she have? "All right, Lin, maybe you're right. I'm not saying Trace is innocent, or Traxton either, or any of them for that matter, but maybe we do have to look at other suspects, too, and there are plenty to look at. Aside from the others I mentioned who are suspect, I discovered that Thomas Braggette had a mistress."

Lin looked as if her sensibilities had been affronted. "Well, much as I don't approve of that sort of behavior, I've heard that it's a fairly common and accepted way of things down here, Belle."

"It is. In New Orleans, however, the wealthy men usually choose a very well-bred and refined quadroon for their paramour, and that is socially acceptable. Braggette's mistress, according to some papers he kept on her, is neither well-bred or socially acceptable. Not only does she own one of the gambling casinos in the Quarter, but she evidently acts as a madame for the women who work for her."

Lin gasped, "A madame?"

"Yes. Now here's what we're going to do." She resumed her seat next to Lin. "I need to talk to Eugenia again. I've got a couple of questions for her, if I can find a way to ask them without arousing suspicion. Anyway, we're going to switch places again. I—"

"Oh, Belle. I want to go back to Shadows Noir."

Belle smiled. "I know, but we have to do it this way, Lin. I'll question Eugenia and try to find out whatever I can from the others. I want you to go and visit Braggette's mistress and—"

"Are you touched in the head?" Lin jumped up from

the settee as if it had just burst into flames. "I am not going to go to a brothel."

"It's not a brothel, really; it's a casino."

"It's a brothel *and* a casino, and I'm not going to one of those either. It's scandalous, Belle, absolutely scandalous. No lady would go even near a place like that, let alone step foot inside of it."

Belle rose and glared at Lin. "Not even to save her father from hanging for a murder he didn't commit?"

"Oh, Belle," Lin wailed, and threw herself back down on the settee. "Why can't you go see this madame woman? You're so much better at making people talk about things they don't want to discuss. And you don't care about the impropriety of going into places like that, or what people would think of—"

"Thank you."

Lin blushed and waved a hand in front of her face. "Oh, you know what I mean."

"Lin, listen, I need to talk to Eugenia. And since you're so convinced Trace is innocent, I have a few questions for him, too. To convince myself. Anyway, you don't have to go to Mageline Toutant's place of business. She lives in a town house in the Quarter. The address was on Braggette's ledger. You can visit her there during the respectable hours of daylight."

"Wonderful. Someone will probably see me and think I'm asking her for a job."

"Oh, Melinda, for heaven's sake, don't be so ridiculous. Anyway, keep your face veiled and a parasol open on your shoulder when you're out on the street."

"I don't like this, Belle. I don't like this at all."

"Really? Well, I doubt Papa likes sitting in a jail cell either," Belle said.

"Oh, all right." Lin rose and started to remove her

gown. "Teresa's at a dressmaker's shop called Madame Carpentier's Parisienne Modes, on Chartres. Just go out of the hotel, turn left, then left again on Chartres. It's just two blocks down, but you'd better hurry and get back there before she misses me . . . er, I mean you." She handed the dress to Belle and took hers in return, tossing it on the settee.

Belle pulled Lin's blue muslin day gown over her head and turned to let her sister fasten the buttons that ran up its back. "There's one other thing I want you to do."

Lin sighed audibly. "What?"

"Visit the mayor."

"The mayor? Of the city?"

"Yes."

"Why?" Lin wailed. "He's not going to release Papa just because I ask him to."

"You're not going to ask him to release Papa. You're not even going to tell him your real name. You're Lin Bonnvivier, remember?"

"So what am I going to do?"

"I think he was a partner in some of Braggette's business ventures, which, according to some of those papers I found, don't appear to be legal. Either that or he covered up for Braggette. Oh, and I found this in Braggette's box along with the papers." She pulled a small bronze waxing seal from her reticule.

"A waxing seal?" Lin said. "So?"

"It has the initials *KG* surrounded by a circle."

"So?"

"Knights of the Golden Circle," Belle said impatiently.

"Who are they? A group from England?"

"Oh, Lin, for heaven's sake. If you'd pay attention to what goes on in the world, you'd know who they are."

"I know what I need to know," Lin answered indignantly.

"Obviously not." Belle dropped the seal back into her reticule.

"Just because I don't read the newspapers and sit for hours talking to Papa about politics doesn't mean I don't know anything."

Belle smiled. "You're right, but it wouldn't hurt you to know more about politics and less about dress patterns." She pulled the reticule's drawstring tight. "The Knights of the Golden Circle are a private organization. A few years ago they tried to persuade the government to take over Mexico and make it a permanent part of the United States."

"So?" Lin repeated.

"So they were considered a very dangerous group. Not only were they politically persuasive, though not enough to be successful with their plan, they were suspected of several instances of sabotage."

"What does all this have to do with the murder, Belle?"

"Thomas Braggette had their seal, Lin. I doubt he would have had it were he not a member of the Knights, and most likely, knowing his background, a very prominent member. And if he was a member, that would mean they didn't disband as everyone believes."

"So?"

"So maybe they're working on some secret plan, maybe something to do with the present problems between the North and South. Thomas Braggette, as a U.S. senator, would have been a valuable member to the Knights."

"So?"

"Will you stop saying *so?*" Belle snapped. She looked in the mirror and straightened the blue skirt. "All I'm saying is that this may be a clue as to why he was murdered."

"Then it wouldn't have been by a member of his family," Lin offered.

"Unless they're Knights, too."

"But you said yourself they all hated him," Lin argued. "So why would they get involved in an organization in which their father was an important member?"

"I don't know, but we can't rule it out. We can't rule anything out at this point."

"Belle, this is getting scary," Lin said. "Maybe we should hire someone else to do this. Someone who knows how to—"

"And they'd never find out a thing." Belle gave herself a quick once-over in the mirror and turned to face Lin. "Look, did the authorities find that cache of Braggette's papers when they searched his office? No. Did the authorities find out someone wants us to stay away from Traxton Braggette? No. Do the authorities even suspect that the Braggettes, any or all of them, could be behind this whole mess? No."

"But, Belle—"

"But Belle nothing," she snapped. Damn, she didn't really want to send Lin to question Braggette's mistress or the mayor. It could prove dangerous, but there really was no other way. She couldn't be two places at one time, and it was obvious she couldn't send Lin back to the plantation. Not with her swooning over Trace Braggette, who, as far as Belle was concerned, was still a very good suspect. Anyway, Belle knew that Lin could handle herself if she really had to. And she did have a few questions for Eugenia, and for that matter, Traxton Braggette.

* * *

As Belle stepped over the threshold of the dressmaker's shop, Teresa called for her from behind the curtained doorway.

Relieved that she'd found the right shop and had made it in time, Belle walked toward the curtain and drew it aside. Teresa stood on a small dais in the center of the tiny room, clad only in a lacy beribboned camisole and ruffled pantalettes. Her gaze pinned itself to Teresa's distended stomach, and the shock of what she saw left her speechless. Belle couldn't help herself; she gasped in surprise. It was obvious that Teresa and her fiancé had not waited until after the wedding to "enjoy each other's company."

Madame Carpentier ushered Belle into the room. "Come, come, mademoiselle, and look at the gown, please, there on the hook." She pointed to the wedding dress which Teresa had just taken off. "I will bring tea," Lili Carpentier said, and hurried from the room.

Belle moved to Teresa's side and helped her step into and fasten the large hoop around her waist. "Teresa, are you . . ." She didn't know exactly how to ask the question. Since it was a question she shouldn't be asking. Then again, she couldn't help herself. If Teresa was with child, which seemed evident, it would explain why Eugenia Braggette had refused to postpone her daughter's wedding. And if Thomas Braggette had known, perhaps . . .

"Yes, Belle, Jay and I are expecting a child," Teresa beamed. "Isn't it wonderful?" Then the smile left her face as abruptly as it had appeared, and she grabbed both of Belle's hands in hers. "But, please, please, don't tell Mama. She'd just die if she knew I was already with child and Jay and I weren't married yet."

"But, Teresa, she—"

Teresa's eyes filled with tears. "Please, Belle," she implored. "Please don't tell her." A look of fear came into her eyes. "Or my brothers. Oh, God, you can't tell my brothers. They'd kill Jay."

"Oh, Teresa, they would not. And I certainly—"

"Please?" Teresa nearly wailed.

Belle smiled and patted Teresa's hand. "Of course I won't tell; it's not my place. But judging from the way your stomach is protruding, I'd say you aren't going to be able to hide the fact much longer. Did your father know?"

Teresa frowned, as if puzzled by the question. "No. Why would you ask that?"

Belle feigned nonchalance. "Oh, I just thought that perhaps if your father knew, he would have already told your mother."

Teresa shook her head. "No, he didn't know. I'm certain."

Belle nodded. "Well, get dressed. We'll have tea with Miss Carpentier and then be on our way."

Teresa retrieved the pink-and-white checkered gown she'd worn into town from a nearby hook on the wall and slid it over her head. "Have you changed your mind about stopping at the St. Louis Hotel?"

Belle nearly choked. "The St. Louis?"

"Yes." Teresa slipped into the bolero-style jacket that matched her gown.

What in blazes was the girl talking about? "Well, I ah . . ." Lord, what was she supposed to say? Yes, I've changed my mind and I don't want to go? Or, no, I haven't changed my mind, I don't want to go? Why would Teresa want to go to the St. Louis? Belle's mind reeled. And why, in heaven's name, hadn't Lin told her about this?

Fourteen

Every muscle in Belle's body stiffened with tension as the carriage turned onto the entry drive of Shadows Noir. Somehow she had hoped they could solve the murder before she'd have to face Traxton again. Or that she wouldn't even have to face him again. She was attracted to him, she'd admit that, but it was only a physical attraction. There was no real emotion behind it, no true feelings. There couldn't be. They had absolutely nothing in common. And anyway, Traxton Braggette was a crude, arrogant, obnoxious Lothario who preferred to while his days away on the back of a horse, a gun tied to his hip, in that godforsaken territory they called Texas, than remain in a more civilized environment and behave like a gentleman.

Belle nearly sniffed aloud. Gentleman. That was a laugh. From the short time she'd been in Traxton's company, it had been obvious he wouldn't know how to act like a gentleman if his life depended on it.

Teresa looked at her. "Are you all right, Belle?"

She smiled. "Yes, I'm fine. Just a slight headache, that's all."

"Well, Zanenne can fix that. She makes a tea that does absolute wonders for a headache."

Belle decided to try and get a little information out of

Teresa while she still had the opportunity, but she'd have to form her questions subtly.

"Teresa, I was just wondering, how did your father feel about you getting married? I mean, you were his youngest child and his only daughter, and sometimes fathers can be very protective, you know."

"Protective? My father?" Teresa let loose a sardonic laugh. "Have you forgotten that little story I told you? About the riverboat?"

"Story?" Belle wanted to turn the carriage around, find her sister, and wring her neck.

"Yes. The one where he threw me overboard." She laughed again. "Now you can't tell me you find that the act of a protective father?"

Belle choked back a gasp. Thomas Braggette had thrown his own daughter overboard? "Oh, well, ah, of course not. I just mean, well, sometimes fathers are funny when their daughters finally decide to get married."

"Some, yes, but not mine. All my father was concerned with was whether I married a man he could control or not, and if he could, how it would benefit him."

"And would he have been able to control Jay?"

A look of pride came over her features. "No. Jay's his own man. There was bad blood between my father and Jay's, but that had nothing to do with us. We love each other, Belle, and as far as I'm concerned, that's all that matters."

"Yes, you're right." She looked beyond the oleanders that lined the drive out to the pasture where a half-dozen horses grazed, but her mind was not on the beautiful sight. There had been bad blood between Jay's father and Thomas Braggette. The papers in Braggette's box had indicated Harcourt Proschaud had given Braggette huge amounts of money. There had also been a bill of sale from

Proschaud to Braggette for a thousand acres of land at what seemed a ridiculously low price. She had been suspicious of these transfers, but in themselves they'd meant nothing. Teresa's words indicated she'd been right with her first impression. Belle felt a definite weight settle onto her chest. Harcourt Proschaud now had to be considered a serious suspect and added to her list. Belle nearly groaned. At this rate soon the entire town would be under suspicion.

She turned back to Teresa. Time to try one of the names from Thomas Braggette's papers. "Do you know a man named Anthony DeBrassea?"

Teresa fixed Belle with a puzzled stare. "Of course, everyone does. He's the leader of the Italians. Why?"

"Oh, no reason, really. I was just curious about him. When I was on the riverboat coming to New Orleans, I heard some people talking. He sounded like trouble to me."

The carriage turned a curve in the drive and the house came into view. Belle twined her fingers about one another. Maybe, if she was lucky, Traxton would be out.

"Yes. They claim they aren't being treated fairly, getting short wages and bad food from the warehouse managers. But Papa said they were lazy and just came to this country expecting too much. They tried to kill him when he said that."

"They what?" Belle jerked around to face Teresa.

She laughed. "Oh, not really. DeBrassea led a group of protesting Italians to my father's office a few months ago. They hurled a stone through the window, and when Papa went out onto the steps, one of them, most likely DeBrassea, took a shot at him."

"Was he hurt?"

"Papa? No." She pulled the carriage up in front of the

house. "The shot went way over his head. DeBrassea obviously isn't a marksman."

"So maybe he used a fireplace poker." Belle looked at Teresa. "Isn't that how your father was killed?"

"Yes."

"Do the authorities suspect DeBrassea?"

Teresa looped the reins around the brake handle and began to climb from the carriage. Once on the ground she smiled at Belle, who was still seated, and shrugged. "I really don't know."

And you really don't care, Belle thought. She climbed down from the carriage. "Teresa, can I see the amulet again?"

"Certainly, but why?" Teresa pulled the small velvet sack from her reticule and handed it to Belle, who untied it and, turning the sack upside down, dropped the wax heart into her palm.

She stared at it for a long moment. Three silver pins protruded from the center of the tiny crimson wax sculpture; one beneath each top curve of the heart, one in the center. Belle wasn't exactly sure, but she seemed to remember, from what their nanny had told them years before, that a wax heart with pins in it symbolized a curse against the recipient's feelings of love. Juliette Voucshon's message was clear: she wanted Traxton Braggette back, and she wanted Belle out of the way.

Belle slipped the heart back into its pouch and handed it back to Teresa. "I don't know this Juliette Voucshon, but I'd have to say, judging from her introduction, that I don't like her very much."

Teresa looked worried. "I don't either, and even though I was only a child when she and Traxton broke their engagement, I can remember how relieved I felt. Juliette Voucshon was very beautiful, but very cunning." She slipped the *gris-gris* back into her reticule. "I'll have Zanenne get rid of this. She'll know how to make up a powder to counteract whatever the curse is."

"Oh, I don't believe in that nonsense," Belle said.

Teresa stopped and stared at Belle, her face solemn. "I've seen it work, Belle. The voodoo is not something to take lightly."

"I don't take it lightly," Belle said. "I don't take it at all. Now, throw it away and let's forget about it."

She walked with Teresa into the house. It was quiet, everyone obviously in their rooms preparing for the evening meal. She started toward the stairs, then stopped. Lin was sweet on Trace, and Lin had never been any good at hiding her feelings, which most likely meant that Trace knew Lin was attracted to him. So, if she didn't want Trace suspecting she wasn't Lin, perhaps she should seek him out and let him know they were home. Yes, that was good. She turned to Teresa, who had already started up the stairs. "I'll see you at dinner, Teresa."

"All right."

Belle entered the dining room, and, as she'd hoped, Zanenne was in the process of setting the table.

"Zanenne, do you know where I might find Trace?"

The old housekeeper placed a fork atop a linen serviette and looked up at Belle. Her eyes narrowed, and she stared for a long minute before answering. "Why you want Michie Trace?"

Belle felt a start of surprise at the hardness in the old woman's tone. She suppressed an urge to repeat her question and instead smiled sweetly, as she imagined Lin would do. "I just want to let him know that Teresa and I are back from town, that's all."

"In the garden."

"Thank you, Zanenne," Belle said, and hurriedly left

the room. It was obvious from the cold glare in the old housekeeper's eyes that either she didn't like Belle or Lin very much, or she was suspicious of them. No matter which, Belle felt a shiver of apprehension. She exited the house through the front door and walked around to the garden.

The sun was just beginning to drop beneath the ragged line of treetops in the distance, its dying rays casting a shimmering golden haze over the landscape.

"Wonderful, he would go out into the garden at sunset," Belle grumbled to herself. Just the romantic environment Lin would desire, but exactly the opposite of Belle's wishes. But she had to go through with it. It's what Lin would do, blast her.

She entered the garden. In the daytime it was a panorama of color, but now, with only weak sunlight filtering through the oaks that grew at the edge of the manicured area, their gnarled and thickly leaved branches a heavy canopy, the garden had taken on an eerie presence. Dusk had transformed it to a place where leaves shimmered silver, gold, and bronze. Heady fragrances lingered on air that still held the warmth of the late afternoon, and shadows darkened the garden's edges.

Belle was just about to turn back to the house, having decided that either Zanenne had sent her on a wild goose chase or Trace had left the garden and gone elsewhere, when she spotted him. He was standing several yards away, his back to her. The soft rays of the setting sun shone on the black strands of his hair, catching the blue shadows that dwelt within its rich thickness. The sunlight spread across his shoulders like a golden mantle, accentuating the broad expanse of muscle and turning his already bronzed flesh to burnished sienna.

At that moment, Belle understood why Lin was so

drawn to Trace Braggette. Though he exuded virility, there seemed also a hint of sadness or pain, like that of a once-wounded animal whose body had healed, but whose mind and heart had never forgotten. Belle felt an overwhelming urge to approach him, to wrap her arms around him and kiss away the pain.

But she stood still, hardly daring to breathe. As she watched, his right hand reached out and touched a rose that grew on the bush next to him, its bloom closing for the night. His fingers gently cradled the delicate bud as he turned it slightly upward to get a better look at its folding silver-gold petals.

She continued to watch, enchanted by the tenderness she saw in his touch and the gentleness which she sensed dwelt within the lanky, yet well-honed length that made up Trace Braggette.

Belle smiled and unconsciously took a step toward him. Her gown brushed against a shrub. Its leaves rustled softly, breaking the silence of the dusk, and she paused.

He didn't turn but merely glanced briefly over his shoulder. "I was just admiring this rose," he said, his back still to her.

"It's beautiful."

"Yes, just like you." He snapped the stem of the rose and, holding it between his fingers, turned toward her, an imperious smile of deviltry on his lips, a spark of insolence in his eyes. "And just like you," he followed the curve of one wickedly sharp-looking thorn with the tip of his index finger, "its beauty can be quite deceiving."

"Traxton!"

One dark eyebrow quirked upward. "Whom did you expect?"

"I was looking for Trace."

"Were you now?" His tone held a note of disbelief. The

smile turned mocking as he closed the distance between them. "My brother and I look quite similar, I admit, but I believe you could tell us apart."

His warm breath wafted across her cheek, stirring a wisp of hair that curled just before her ear and sending a shiver rippling over her flesh. "Or did I give you too much credit, Belle?" The fragrance of rich tobacco and expensive brandy clung to him, as well as the smell of leather, even though he was dressed in evening clothes. The scents combined to form a redolence that Belle knew, in spite of herself, she would always associate with Traxton Braggette.

He regarded her steadily, those gray-blue eyes, so like the conflicting blend of a clear spring sky and a winter's fog, moving slowly over her face. "You did know it was me," he said, barely above a whisper, "didn't you?"

Belle swallowed hard. "No, I . . . the shadows," she said breathlessly, licking her abruptly dry lips. "You had your back turned to me . . . and I was expecting Trace to be out here . . . and the shadows. . . ." She suddenly yearned to reach out and touch him, to slide her hand over the sinewy length of his arms, across the mountainous path of muscle that made up his shoulders, to feel the silken black strands of hair at his nape. She felt her lips tremble in anticipation and the breath catch in her throat as Traxton's arms reached out to encircle her waist and draw her into his embrace.

No man had ever had the effect on her that Traxton Braggette seemed to have with merely a glance of his dark eyes, a curve of his lips, a touch of his hand. Though a part of her disliked his rawness and suspected him of murdering his father, another part of her longed for what he was about to offer. She knew she should resist him, should pull away from him and indignantly slap his face, but she couldn't. Instead, her gaze remained riveted to his, her body burned with a fire like none she'd ever known, and her heart pounded the frantic rhythm of excitement.

"Damn you, Belle," Traxton said under his breath, his voice a husky drawl of mingled anger and passion. His arms crushed her to him, a riata of strength from which she had no desire to escape. Her breasts pushed against his chest, and her hands rested upon the corded muscles of the arms that had wrapped around her waist.

She closed her eyes as his mouth moved to cover hers, his lips a fiery brand that touched not only her flesh, but her soul. His arms tightened around her, his hands, splayed against her back, crushed her up against him, pulling her closer and closer to his tall, hard length and molding the lithe, subtle curves of her body to the hard, rigid planes of his own.

He kissed her for a long time, but to Belle, at that moment, eternity would not have been long enough. Other men had drawn her into their arms and pressed their lips to hers, but none had ever ignited the fire that sparked to life within her at Traxton's touch. It threatened to devour her, to consume every fiber and cell of her being and turn them into a inferno of desire that had no hope of being assuaged except by Traxton's touch.

She gave a moan of pleasure at the unexpected ache that suddenly filled her loins and left her languid within the circle of his arms.

At the parting of her lips, Traxton's kiss deepened, the caress of his mouth on hers at once tender and savage, giving and demanding. His tongue slid into her mouth and filled it, urgently seeking the honeyed sweetness within.

Her hands slid upward, moving over the hills and valleys of muscle that made up both his arms and shoulders. Silky strands of his hair slid through her fingers, and feelings she had never known existed, never known she possessed or could experience, began to flood her being.

As his lips continued their hungry assault of both her mouth and her senses, Belle plunged farther and farther into an abyss of sensual pleasure. All thought of murder, treachery, and deceit, of her father and Lin, of everything but Traxton Braggette and the wonderful sensations he was causing to erupt within her body ceased to matter or even exist.

One of his hands moved from her back to cover her breast. His thumb rhythmically began to circle her nipple, taking from her what little sanity and reason she had left.

Suddenly the musical tinkle of the small silver dinner bell sounded upon the silent night air, drifting out through the open windows of the house. With the sound, reality came crashing down upon Traxton like the savage blow of a war ax to the center of his skull. Son of a—What in the hell was he doing? Dragging his lips from Belle's, he caught her wrists in his hands and forced them from around his neck.

Confused and still dazed from the passion he had sparked, Belle merely stared up at him. A curl of black hair fell rebelliously onto his forehead to give him a rakish mien, while his eyes, reflecting the same passion that burned in her, slowly began to cool.

She longed to move back into the circle of his arms, to press her lips to his again. But she remained still, for his eyes were narrowing in hardness and the full mouth that had just ravished hers with savage desire was pulling taut with anger.

Traxton set her away from him, his features settled into a hard grimace and his eyes as icy as winter's snow. "Damn you, Belle St. Croix," he said again, his voice ragged with emotion. "Damn you."

Startled, his words seemed to snap Belle from the haze of desire. "I don't—"

"What's your game, Belle?" He dropped her hands as if their touch suddenly repulsed him, and he fixed her with a riveting stare. "What the hell is it you want, lady?"

Instantly sobered by his harsh words, Belle bristled with indignation and hurt. "Game? What in blazes do you mean, *game?*"

Traxton scoffed, "Exactly what I said, Belle. Game. I don't know what you're up to, or after, but whatever it is, it isn't going to work."

Though her blood was still heated from the desire he had stirred within her, she was beginning to feel mortified that she had allowed him to kiss her in the first place, and so wantonly. "I haven't the faintest idea what you're talking about."

"Really?" The smile turned mocking. "Somehow I doubt that."

"I don't—"

"You've just about got my big brother wrapped around your little finger, and yet here you are throwing yourself at me."

"Throwing myself at—"

"I don't know if Trace is in love with you yet," Traxton said, overriding her spurt of indignation, "but he's damned well on his way, and you know it. Yet you're not satisfied with that, Belle, are you?"

Belle felt her temper begin to flare but made no effort to recapture her command of it. "I don't care what you know, Traxton Braggette, or what you think you kn—

"It isn't going to work, lady," Traxton roared, over-shouting her again. "I don't know what your game is, but I'm not playing. And," his eyes became shuttered and cold, "I would suggest you stop playing, too, before someone gets hurt."

Belle stiffened and thrust her chin out defiantly. "Is that a threat, *Mr.* Braggette?"

A cold smile curved his full lips. "So," he grated, "you do admit you're playing at something."

"No," she retorted, "I didn't admit anything. And I'm not 'playing at something.' "

Traxton looked at her through eyes that had become lifeless and empty. "We both know that's a lie, Belle."

She stared at him, suddenly afraid he knew exactly why she was at Shadows Noir and was merely toying with her until ready to denounce her. Did he know about her father? About her suspicions? But if so, then why didn't he say so? Not certain what to do next, or say, Belle let her gaze drop to the ground. If she continued to spar with him, she might say something she'd regret. And she couldn't tell him it was Lin who Trace was really attracted to, not her.

"Don't get coy with me now, Belle," Traxton said, taking her lowered gaze as an act of coquettishness. A sharp laugh followed the harsh words. "I'm not Trace, remember? That kind of thing doesn't work on me."

Fury filled her and swept away caution or guilt. "I am not being coy, you arrogant, self-righteous, lowlife beast."

"So then," Traxton said, not at all unnerved by her outburst, "what is it, Belle? What are you really after? Marriage? Money? Position?"

"No."

Traxton laughed, a mocking sound that held no warmth or humor. "Sounds more like that's exactly right. Come on, Belle, you want to get married?"

"Oh, I wouldn't marry you if you were the last man on earth, Traxton Braggette."

His face suddenly hardened, all trace of a smile, cold or otherwise, gone. "That wasn't a proposal."

"Well," Belle jerked her chin upward haughtily, the gesture sending blond curls flying from her shoulders to cascade down her back. "Thank heaven for that."

"My guess is you'd prefer a proposal of marriage from Trace. After all, he's the one with the plantation, right? The social position in New Orleans? The money?"

"That's a horrible thing to say," Belle protested.

"But my brother is such a gentleman that he doesn't spark your passion, is that it, Belle? You want his ring, but my bed."

"Why, you arrogant, egotistical, son of a—"

Traxton wagged a finger in her face. "Ah-ah-ah, Belle, that's not very ladylike. What would Trace say if he heard his delicate little flower cursing like a wharf-weary roustabout?"

"I don't care. If I had a gun right now, I think I'd blow your brains out." Belle whirled, then stopped and looked back at Traxton, who had raised a foot to a small marble bench and rested a forearm on his knee. The expression on his face was one of satisfied amusement. "I'm sorry, Traxton," she said sweetly, "that was a stupid thing to say. I forgot, you don't have a brain."

Traxton watched her leave the garden and swore softly under his breath. Earlier that day he had made a vow to himself that he would leave her alone, that he would ignore Belle St. Croix for the remainder of his stay at Shadows Noir. He'd also promised himself that he would do everything and anything to mend the torn relationship between himself and Trace, no matter what it took.

A bitter laugh escaped his lips. Seducing the woman Trace was obviously falling in love with was not exactly the best way to mend their relationship. He tugged at the inseam of his trousers. Belle St. Croix had lit a spark of interest within him that would be difficult to extinguish, but extinguish it he would, even if he had to visit every brothel in the Quarter to do it. Traxton sighed. He'd never been any good at keeping promises, even to himself, except for one: to stay as far away from ladies as he could get. Not women, just ladies. The marriage-expecting kind. They were off limits . . . for good. Once, long ago, when he'd been young and foolish, he had believed in love, but he'd been quickly shown the error of his ways. His gaze caught sight of the rose he had picked and then dropped when he'd pulled Belle into his arms. For more than seven and a half long years he had stayed away from Shadows Noir and New Orleans, building himself a life in Texas. He'd chosen his friends carefully and kept his distance from any woman who, because of a kiss or passionate caress, would then expect a promise of heart, home, and hearth.

Traxton ground the heel of his boot atop the rose. He had succeeded in keeping his heart safely locked away, his emotions under control, until now. But he hadn't counted on being betrayed by his own body, by his own passion. And he certainly hadn't counted on a breathtakingly beautiful and sassy little blonde named Belle St. Croix prancing her way into his life to complicate it further.

Fifteen

Lin stood before the tall door with its oval glass and forced herself to take a deep breath. Her pulse was racing crazily and her hands were trembling. She looked around furtively from behind the veil that covered her face. "Oh, if Trace sees me here, I'll just die," she murmured softly, looking back past the carriage that sat in the arched porte-cochere and which led to the street.

"I doubt there's any chance of that, *chère.*"

Not having heard the door open, and already as nervous as a frightened cat, Lin nearly jumped out of her skin. She turned to stare at the woman who had answered her knock. A smile curved the woman's heart-shaped lips, causing the outer corners of her blue eyes to raise slightly.

"Oh, excuse me, I am here to see Madame Toutant," Lin said, unable to stop wringing her hands.

The woman's eyes quickly moved over Lin's body in a blatant assessment. "Really?"

Lin drew back her shoulders and attempted to stand taller than her five foot two inches. "Yes, on a matter of business."

The woman's brow cocked upward in interest. "Business, is it? And just who might you be?"

"My name is Lin Bonnvivier, from Vicksburg."

"Well, Mademoiselle Bonnvivier," the woman extended a hand in a gesture of invitation and stepped back to allow Lin entrance into the house, "welcome to my home."

Lin paused with one foot on the threshold. *"You* are Madame Toutant?" she asked, slightly shocked. Thomas Braggette's mistress was not what Lin had expected. She had seen the prostitutes that walked the streets of Natchez's bawdy Under-the-Hill district, and the dozens who loitered upon the streets of the Vieux Carré, lazing before the saloons and casinos as they plied their trade. They were usually ill-kempt, disheveled, and garish in appearance. Mageline Toutant gave every impression of being a lady, and a very well-bred one at that. The amethyst-hued silk gown she wore was modest and of the highest quality, with ivory Valenciennes lace trimming her sleeves at the wrist and her high collar. Her dark brown hair was an arrangement of simplicity, swept back from her face and arranged in a neat chignon at her nape, and her features, flawless and with only a trace of lines, were aristocratic in shape and mien.

Lin glanced into a mirror that hung on the foyer wall. The lavender gown with its ivory lace trim that she had chosen to wear that day now seemed washed out and dull in comparison to the rich color of Mageline Toutant's gown.

"Oui, I am Mageline Toutant." She showed Lin into a very expensively appointed parlor, the furniture of cherrywood, the upholstery in gold-and-white brocade silk. "Please, mademoiselle, be seated."

Lin had a sudden disturbing thought. What if Belle was wrong? What if Mageline Toutant had not been Braggette's mistress? What if Belle had somehow misread the name and this woman wasn't even the one who had been partners with Braggette in the casino?

Mageline sat on a settee facing Lin. "Now, *ma petite,* what is this business you want to see Mageline about? A job at the casino perhaps?" She smiled warmly.

"A job?" Lin started. "Oh, no, madame, no. I don't want a job."

Belle had been right. At least about this being the woman from the casino.

"Then what is it you want of Mageline?"

"I wanted to talk to you about Thomas Braggette," Lin blurted before she could lose her nerve and dash for the door. She twisted the silk cord of her beaded reticule.

"Thomas Braggette? Ha!" Mageline shot to her feet and began to pace the room. Her features hardened and her eyes turned cold. "That man should be lucky enough to rot in Hell. But even the devil may have turned him away, and I would not be surprised. Or sorry. *Non,* not sorry at all."

Taken aback at Mageline's words, Lin stuttered, "B-but, ah, didn't, I mean, weren't the two of you . . . ?"

"Wasn't I his mistress?" Mageline offered. She laughed, the sound laced with bitterness. "Yes, I was. Monsieur Braggette owned half of the Golden Slipper, my casino."

"So you were lovers and business partners," Lin ventured, feeling a slight swell of courage.

"No," Mageline said, the word curt and abrupt. "I was his mistress, not his lover. Thomas Braggette did not offer love to anyone, nor did he make love. He used me to relieve his sexual urges, that is all."

"Oh." Lin felt her cheeks flame with embarrassment. Why had she ever allowed Belle to coerce her into coming here? She offered what she knew was a rather insincere smile and forced herself to continue. "I don't understand, madame. You seem obviously to have disliked Mr. Braggette, so why were you associated with him?"

"Ha, I see you do not know the ways of business, *ma petite,* or of love either, for that matter." Mageline stopped her pacing and turned to stare down at Lin, her eyes narrowing. "But what is this to you? Why do you want to know about Thomas and me?"

Lin prayed she could remember the story she'd made up. She tried to look sad. "Mr. Braggette owed my father a great deal of money, Madame Toutant. My father would have come himself, but he is very sick." She dabbed at her eyes with a lace handkerchief quickly retrieved from her reticule. "Papa heard of Mr. Braggette's death, and, since he was too weak to come himself," she dabbed at her eyes again, "he implored me to come to New Orleans and lay claim upon Mr. Braggette's estate."

"So why do you come to me?" Mageline asked.

Lin felt a thrill. The woman believed her. She was actually being convincing. Oh, she wished Belle could see her. She'd be so proud. Lin kept a sorrowful expression on her face. "Well, I tried to see Mrs. Braggette, but they said she was not receiving. Too distraught, I imagine. But Papa said that Mr. Braggette told him about his dealings with you, so I, well, I thought I'd come here while I waited to see Mrs. Braggette."

Mageline clamped fisted hands on her slim hips. "To lay claim to the Golden Slipper?"

"Oh, no, madame, no," Lin said quickly. "I was merely hoping you could give me some insight into Mr. Braggette's other holdings, information, as it were."

Mageline poured herself a drink from a sideboard, gulped it down, and turned back toward Lin. "Thomas Braggette was a blackguard of the worst kind. As far as I am concerned, Hell is too good a place for him." She sat again. "I cannot help you, mademoiselle."

"Oh, please, Madame Toutant," Lin said. "There must

be something. Perhaps if you could tell me what Mr. Braggette was like, that will help when I have to see his widow."

Mageline frowned as memories assailed her, memories she normally refused to recall for the pain they still brought. "All right," she said. "Perhaps I can do that." She sighed and sat back in the chair. "Ten years ago my protector—" She paused and looked at Lin. "You do know what a protector is?"

Lin shook her head and Mageline sighed again.

"Ah, so young and innocent, but then you are not from New Orleans, so it is understandable. I am a quadroon, mademoiselle, which means I have black blood in my veins. My mother was a mulatto, my father was white."

Lin nodded.

"In New Orleans the young men of the wealthy are allowed to choose a free woman of color, or a quadroon, as their mistress. Many times this is a union for life, even when the young man marries another. Other times it is not. I had been with my protector for five years when he became betrothed to a young lady from Boston. She did not understand or accept our ways and demanded he sever our relationship. Jacques complied with her wishes, naturally. He was very generous to me and I bought a half interest in the Golden Slipper. My business partner then was a man I considered a very good friend and whom I had loved for a very long time, Eric Richards."

"So how did . . . ?"

"Thomas managed to maneuver Eric into a, shall we say, situation. A very unhealthy situation. Then, in return for his help in clearing up the matter, Thomas forced Eric to sign over his half of the casino to him."

"And he couldn't get it back?"

"Perhaps he might have, but Eric was killed the next night."

Lin gasped.

"A gambler accused him of cheating at cards. Eric rose from his seat and was shot by the gambler before he had a chance to even deny the accusation."

Lin could see the pain of loss that still shone in Mageline Toutant's eyes when she talked of Eric Richards. "How horrible."

"Yes, it was." Mageline straightened and threw off the shroud of sadness that had momentarily enveloped her. "I have already sent a message to Shadows Noir, *ma petite,* with an offer to purchase Thomas's interest in the Golden Slipper."

Lin dabbed the lace handkerchief to her nose. "I'm sorry, Madame Toutant, for your loss."

"My loss of Eric was a devastating one. My loss of Thomas Braggette was a thankful one." Mageline laughed, a heartwarming sound that filled the room with merriment. "And I imagine the widow Braggette feels exactly the same way. Perhaps now she, too, can get on with her life in peace."

"Really?" Lin gasped.

"Yes, really," Mageline said. "Thomas Braggette was not a good man, *ma petite.* The world is a better place for his passing. I doubt the widow would admit it, but if you don't believe me, try asking Anthony DeBrassea or Edward Mourdaine. Or even Harcourt Proschaud. All must be not only relieved that Thomas is dead, but elated."

Lin felt her heart soar and sink at the same time. Mageline had just confirmed what Belle had deduced from Thomas Braggette's papers, that these three men also had motives for wanting to see Braggette dead. But were they the same motives Belle suspected? "Why would they be happy Mr. Braggette is dead?"

"Ah, not only them, *ma petite*. Many in New Orleans silently cheered at news of Thomas's death. But these three, yes," she nodded. "They, I suspect, cheered the loudest."

"But why?"

Mageline shook her head. "I have a business to run. It is better if I do not repeat such things."

"Please, Madame Toutant, it might help my father to know what other creditors he's up against in settling his claim with Mrs. Braggette. I swear I won't reveal to anyone that we have even talked."

"No, *chère,* I don't imagine you would," Mageline said. She smiled then, and the gesture rid her face of the last vestiges of grief that had appeared at the memory of Eric Richards. She reached for a silver ewer that sat on a table between them and poured two cups of coffee, handing one to Lin, then settling back on the settee with her own. "Anthony DeBrassea is the leader of the Italians who came to New Orleans in search of a better life. Poor things." She shook her head. "They come to this country, to this city, with high hopes, and what they find is squalor and poverty. But they work hard, and with pride. All they ask is to be treated fairly, something Thomas did not know how or care to do. Thomas was a senator and as such was able to wield much power. Anthony is a good man. He stood up to Thomas, challenged some of the things he did, and nearly got himself killed for doing so." She shook her head. "But Thomas was smart. He knew if Anthony died everyone would know who caused it, so he merely made the man's life miserable, as he did every other Italian in the city."

Mageline took a slow sip of her coffee before continuing. "Anthony announced only days before Thomas's death that he would challenge him legally. Of course, no one took him seriously, including Thomas, but," she shrugged, "one never knows."

"And Edward Mourdaine?"

"Ah, Edward. He comes to the Golden Slipper quite frequently, but he no longer has much to lose, thanks to Thomas. Edward is a descendant of one of the oldest Creole families in New-Orleans, and at one time was bethrothed to Eugenia Braggette—before she married Thomas, of course. I don't know what happened . . ." Mageline suddenly grew quiet, as if not wanting to continue.

"Please, madame, go on."

She shook her head. "I shouldn't. Even though Thomas was," a fire of hatred burned in her dark eyes, "a horror in my life, his widow and children have never done me any harm, and I should not repeat the things Thomas told me." She shrugged. "They may not even be true."

"Please, madame, I promise you I mean the Braggettes no harm. I only want what is rightfully due my father, and if some sliver of information you can provide me will accomplish that, then I beg of you to tell me."

"Once, in a pique of anger, Thomas said that Eugenia had not been a virgin when they married. She had already given herself to another man, Edward Mourdaine, and was carrying his child."

Lin gasped. "Then Trace Braggette is . . . ?"

Mageline shook her head. "No. Trace is Thomas's son."

"Then what happened to the child Eugenia bore Edward?"

"Thomas sold off the slave who'd helped with the birthing and told Eugenia the baby had died."

"But it hadn't?" Lin said.

"No. Thomas gave the boy away."

"Gave him away?" Lin echoed.

"Yes. To a band of Gypsies that, at that time, had been camped in the swamps of Shadows Noir."

Lin felt her head spinning. Could this child have grown, found out what had been done, returned to New Orleans, and killed Thomas Braggette for what he'd done?

"Eugenia evidently never came to love Thomas and never got over her love for Edward. Thomas came to hate her for that. He knew he couldn't destroy her without making himself look bad, so he turned his vengeance on Edward. He set out to rob him of everything and leave him in ruin. Last year he finally managed to do it."

Lin felt as if her senses were whirling. The more she learned about Thomas Braggette, the more she wondered how he had managed to live as long as he did.

"And of course there is Harcourt Proschaud," Mageline said. "Dear, quiet little Harcourt."

"Proschaud?" Lin said, feigning surprise. "Didn't I hear that a Jay Proschaud was bethrothed to Teresa Braggette?"

"Yes, Jay is Harcourt's son," Mageline said. "Ten years ago Harcourt made an effort to get elected as U.S. senator. He ran against Thomas, a bad idea in itself, and of course he lost. In the years following that foolhardy venture, Harcourt also lost over half of his fortune and his wife."

"And Thomas Braggette was going to allow his daughter to marry Harcourt Proschaud's son?"

Mageline laughed. "Thomas loved to control people. He believed Jay to be no stronger or smarter than Harcourt. Therefore, he was convinced he would have no problem with the boy and eventually end up with whatever he hadn't already swindled from the Proschauds."

Lin nodded. "Yes, I see." She stood. "Thank you very much, Madame Toutant, for being so candid with me. I'm sorry I troubled you, but your words have helped me immensely, in, ah, understanding how to deal with Mrs. Braggette."

Mageline bowed her head and walked Lin to the door. "Then I am glad we spoke."

On the threshold, Lin paused. "It seems a sorry thing to say about a man, but was there anyone in the city of New Orleans who liked Mr. Braggette?"

"Only those who did not know him," Mageline said.

Lin pulled the veil of her hat down before her face.

"Do not fear that anyone will misinterpret your visit to my home, Miss Bonnvivier," Mageline said. "You see, most believe I live in the rooms above the casino. Its back door is adjacent to this town house, so I never use the banquettes to get here."

"How clever," Lin said.

"Yes. It was Eric's doing. This was his home and meant to be ours, but . . ." She shrugged. "His mother lives here now with me. She is old and ailing. Most believe she lives here alone."

"Thank you," Lin said. "For everything."

She hurried back through the shadowed porte-cochere and onto the banquette, snapped open her parasol, and settled it on her shoulder as Belle had suggested. Between the veil and the parasol, she did feel a little more hidden and not quite so easy to recognize, although she wouldn't actually feel safe until she was back in her room at the hotel.

But that was going to have to wait. She had one more stop to make before she could retreat to the seclusion of the hotel room. She had learned, from one of the stewards in the hotel, that the city's mayor maintained an office in one of the government buildings that flanked the St. Louis Cathedral. The boy had said the building was called the Cabildo. He had then gone on in lengthy detail about its origin, explaining, among other things, that it had been built by the Spaniards when they ruled the city.

Following his directions, Lin approached Jackson Square, looked about, and located the Cabildo, situated toward one corner of the Square. She approached the squat two-storied building casually.

Its main floor was a series of archways covering a wide gallery. Beyond this were double doors. Its second-story windows were all arched to match the first-floor entries, and its roof was a sloping expanse of gray slate, the color matching the exterior walls of the building.

Lin walked up the wide flight of stairs to the second floor and almost at once spotted the tall door to the mayor's office. A brass plaque with both his name and title engraved on it was affixed to the door's panel. She opened it and stepped into a spacious chamber.

Several men stood on the opposite side of the room near a wide mahogany desk, their voices raised in argument.

Lin closed the door soundly, and the men abruptly stopped speaking and turned toward her, all obviously surprised to find themselves in the company of a lady.

A short, rather portly man with a head of curly gray hair and a bulbous nose straightened his jacket and strutted around the desk toward her. Muttonchop whiskers adorned his face and were connected by a thick mustache. He cleared his throat. "Mademoiselle, please allow me to introduce myself. I am Mayor Davianneau." He swept her hand up into his in a flourish, bowed, and pressed his lips to her fingers. Straightening he smiled, but did not release her hand. "Now, how can I assist you?"

"I . . ." Lin looked over the mayor's shoulder to the

others, who were staring, blatantly curious to hear her response. "I am seeking information about Mr. Thomas Braggette," she said quietly.

A hum of whispers immediately broke out in the group.

"Thomas Braggette," the mayor repeated, and seemed to pale. "What, ah, what type of information, my dear?"

"Well, I have come to understand he was involved in some, shall we say, illegal business transactions before his death, and that you might possibly kno—"

"Ahem, I beg your pardon, young lady," the mayor interrupted quickly. He took her arm and ushered her toward the door. "But this is quite absurd. I don't know where you got your information, but let me assure you, it is wrong. Mr. Braggette's dealings were all very respectable." He opened the door and practically pushed her through it. "Now, I really must get back to my meeting. Good day."

The door slammed in Lin's face.

"Well! So much for your good manners." Whirling around, she walked back to the staircase and began to descend.

"Frederick, I didn't know you were back from Washington. How are things going there?" a familiar voice called out.

Lin clutched the railing and lurched to a sudden stop. Panic filled her breast. What was *he* doing here? She bent down to get a view of the downstairs area.

Trace stood near the entry door, hat in hand, and had obviously just arrived. He shook hands with a man and turned toward the staircase.

Lin, halfway down, stared at him as if hypnotized. She wanted suddenly to run to him, to throw her arms around his neck and lose herself within his embrace. Longing filled her breast as tears filled her eyes. Forcing herself to move, she gathered up her skirts and fled up the stairs, the only direction open to her. She glanced toward the mayor's door. No. She couldn't go back in there. That rude little man would just usher her right back out again. Anyway, maybe that's where Trace was headed. She heard his footsteps on the stairs behind her.

"Oh, good lord, help me." She hurried along the wide hallway, her gaze darting about frantically in search of a place she could hide. Finally, at the opposite end of the hallway, she spotted a partially open door. Lin peeked in, saw that it was some sort of storage room, and slipped in, closing the door softly behind her.

The curtains on the window were drawn, so that once she closed the door she plunged herself into total gloom.

"Oh, poo."

Sixteen

"I don't want to ride an old nag," Belle said, presenting Traxton with her best glare.

"Queenie is not an old nag," Traxton shot back, "and she's the only horse available right now, so you either ride her or you don't ride at all."

"Only horse?" Belle's head turned, her gaze taking in the ten other horses in the stable. "What do you call those," she asked, "elephants?"

Traxton made a concerted effort to hang on to his temper, but she was trying it sorely. "No, Miss St. Croix, I call them studs," he retorted, but if he'd thought he was going to embarrass her with his frankness, he'd been sorely mistaken. Not even a blush colored Belle's cheeks.

"Well, I've ridden studs before," Belle said, her tone as sarcastic as his, "and I most certainly will do so again in the future, so you needn't worry about it, *Mr.* Braggette."

Traxton tried his hardest to keep a wicked smile from curving his lips, but he just couldn't help it. He crossed sinewy arms across his chest, leaned a hip insolently against one of the stall rails, and crossed one booted foot over the other. "Well," he drawled, "there aren't too many *ladies* who would admit a thing like that."

Belle tossed her head defiantly. "What's wrong with a lady riding a stud?" She paused as she recognized the roguish gleam in his eyes and realized how her words sounded.

Traxton laughed aloud at her surprised expression.

"Oh, you cur." Hurtling herself toward him, Belle raised a gloved hand.

Traxton caught her by the wrist as her arm swung toward his face. "Now that wouldn't be a very nice thing to do, Belle," he said, his voice a husky blend of amusement and passion.

"Nice?" Belle echoed incredulously. She yanked at her arm in an effort to free herself from his grasp. "Who said I was trying to be nice?" He released her arm and she stumbled backward, cursing.

"Belle, for a lady," Traxton said, "you know the most unladylike words." He chuckled softly and walked from the stable, leaving her to fume alone. As heated as it was, he had enjoyed their exchange, but now he had to leave. Spending more than a few minutes in Belle's company wasn't doing his libido a whole lot of favors. Why she had that effect on him, he didn't know. He'd never met a woman quite like her, and, God help him, he hoped he would never meet another one. At least not unless he could just bed her, say adieu, and ride off into the sunset.

Belle whirled around and walked toward the rear of the stable. She paused before one of the stall gates and looked down at the word on the plaque attached to its top rail: *Lightning.* She grabbed a lead rope from a hook on one of the support pillars, threw up the latch, and swung the gate open. "All right, Lightning, let's go."

The huge black stallion turned and followed Belle from the stall, nudging her arm a couple of times with his soft muzzle. Belle laughed and slipped a bridle over his head. "Well, I like you, too, boy," she said. "And, contrary to what Mr. Traxton Braggette said, I think we're going to get along just fine." Looping the reins around a stall rail to prevent the horse from wandering off, Belle glanced around for help, but there was no one else in the stable. Walking to the opposite side of the barn Belle inspected the numerous saddles set on a long, rounded rail. She picked up a sidesaddle and walked back toward the horse. Within minutes she had blanket, saddle, and bit in place. "Okay, boy," she said, "now it's my turn."

The horse nickered and tossed his head.

"Good, I'm glad you like the idea." Picking up a small mounting step she had noticed by the saddles, Belle took hold of the horse's reins and led him out into the sunshine.

Traxton had made it into the house and had even poured himself a cup of coffee from a server on the dining-room sideboard. Then he'd experienced a rush of guilt and an almost dead certainty that Belle was going to do exactly as he'd warned her not to do. "Damn stubborn hellion," he mumbled, slamming the china cup down on its saucer and sending hot coffee spraying all over the sideboard.

"What's the matter?" Trace asked, walking into the room just as Traxton was walking out.

"Nothing," Traxton barked, and strode through the front door. He marched down the path toward the stable, a different curse slipping from his lips with each step. Life had been a hell of a lot simpler before Belle St. Croix had sashayed her little body into his line of vision, and now all he wanted was for her to sashay it out again and leave him in peace. Trace didn't know what he was getting himself into, falling for that spitfire, but if that's what he wanted, then so be it. Traxton sure as hell wasn't going to stand in his way.

He rounded the garden and came into sight of the stable. "Belle, no!" he yelled.

Belle heaved her weight onto the sidesaddle, but her derriere had no sooner met the curved leather than she felt it rise beneath her. A shriek of surprise tore from her throat. Losing her grip on the reins, she flew upward.

Lightning let loose with a loud whinny, and the earth thudded as his rear hooves slammed back down on the ground.

"Belle!" Traxton yelled again. His anger with her was forgotten as he watched her fall to the ground.

The horse, satisfied now that he was once again rider-less, slowly shuffled a few yards away and began to graze on the grass that bordered the garden.

Traxton ran to where Belle lay stunned on the ground. He hunkered down beside her. "Are you okay? Anything broken?"

Belle jerked away from the arm he'd wrapped around her shoulders, and scrambled to her feet. "I'm fine," she said, her voice a whiplash of curtness. "It would have been nice of you, however, to have warned me about that horse."

"I did."

Belle stamped her foot. "No, you didn't. You never once said those horses weren't broken for riding."

"I told you none of them could be ridden."

"Only by me, you said," Belle snapped. "You didn't say not at all, you said only by me."

Traxton laughed. "Well, that was the truth."

Belle raised a hand to slap him, but as before, Traxton caught her wrist to prevent the blow. "I warned you about that, Belle."

Too angry to be thwarted, Belle slammed her other hand, fist closed, against his arm.

Traxton grabbed her arm as it began to pull away, locked steely fingers around her wrist, and brought both of her hands to his chest. "Stop playing your games, Belle," he said from between clenched teeth. Dragging her up against him was not the smartest thing he'd ever done. The sweet scent of the violet powder she'd used in her morning bath filled his nostrils, her breasts were thrust tantalizingly against the broad wall of his chest, and, with his head lowered threateningly and hers lifted to face him, her lips, so full, soft, and inviting, hovered only inches from his. Traxton felt his body tremble from the fierce onslaught of desire. The hunger that had dwelt within him ever since he'd first set eyes on Belle St. Croix, that had simmered in his loins and given him no peace, intensified with her nearness.

The need to join his body with the supple one before him became almost overwhelming. He knew he should release her, should get as far from her as he could. Yet it was the last thing in the world he wanted to do. Cursing himself, Traxton brought his mouth down hard on hers.

As his head lowered toward her, Belle saw the fire in his eyes change from one of anger to desire. She watched helplessly, filled with both anticipation and dread, as his lips neared and then covered hers. And much as she tried to deny it, to squelch the sensations his touch had aroused, her traitorous body responded to him immediately. Her lips parted beneath his, and his tongue dueled with hers; his strokes enticed, excited, and teased her senses.

It was Traxton who, as he had the first time he'd drawn her into his arms, tore himself away from Belle, the silent battle waging within him having finally broken to the forefront of his consciousness. For a long moment he continued to hold her in his arms and look down into her eyes, his gaze roaming slowly over the lovely curves of her face, as if imprinting each feature to memory. Never again, he knew, would he be able to look at a rolling meadow of grassland beneath a brilliant blue sky and not think of her eyes. He would never again be able to turn his gaze upon the setting sun and watch its pinkish rays sweep over the land, without it reminding him of the soft hue of her full lips, and every time he happened to touch a satin thread, he knew he would remember the silken strands of her silver-gold hair sliding between his fingers.

The ache in his loins deepened, and he pushed her away from him. Long ago he had hurt his brother by deserting him, by running away from the cruelty of their father and leaving Trace to face it, counter it, and protect the rest of the family from it. He would not hurt him again. The idea of bedding the woman Trace was falling in love with, no matter how much he wanted her, no matter how much the need was tearing him apart inside, was more than even Traxton could stomach. A twisted smile curved his lips. "Forget it, Belle."

Belle merely stared at him, too stunned by her own reaction to him to comprehend his words or their meaning.

Traxton, summoning every ounce of self-control he could muster, turned and walked away from her, not slackening his stride until he was well out of sight of the house. Trace was in love with Belle; that was evident in his eyes every time he looked at her. But was Belle in love with Trace? Traxton laughed bitterly. Obviously not. There had been a few times he could have sworn she returned his brother's feelings, that he had seen a look of deep love for Trace in Belle's eyes. But if that were so, then what of the passion that surfaced between them when Traxton kissed her? He slammed a gloved fist against a fence railing. It didn't make sense. A woman couldn't love two men . . . or could she? He turned and began to walk back toward the house. It didn't matter anyway. Trace wanted a wife. Traxton didn't. "So I'll stay away from her," he mumbled angrily. "Damn, good, and far away."

Belle stood in front of a cheval mirror that was set in one corner of her bedchamber and stared at her image. "No," she muttered. "No, no, no." Turning back toward the tall armoire in which her gowns hung, she began rummaging through them again, pushing aside skirt after skirt. She yanked a sea green gown of Florence satin from its hook and tossed it onto the settee, then began to unfasten the hooks of the gown she wore. As soon as she'd pulled the dress over her head, she threw it toward a ladies chair upon which she'd already discarded five other gowns.

She picked up the sea green gown, pawing through the voluminous folds of cloth in search of its interior. A groan spewed forth from her lips. "Why did I ever trade places with Lin? Why didn't I just stay in town and talk to that woman and let Lin come back here like she wanted?" Belle slipped the gown over her head. She'd uncovered nothing useful from her conversations with Eugenia or Teresa, and the situation between she, Trace, and Traxton was becoming difficult. "Why in blazes did I come up with this ridiculous scheme in the first place?" She righted the bodice over her breasts.

Because your father is in jail, a nagging little voice at the back of her mind whispered.

"Oh, I know that," she snapped, feeling an instant flash of guilt. "But for once couldn't everyone involved just cooperate and let my plan work the way it's supposed to?" Moving quickly, she fumbled with the bodice hooks that fastened beneath one arm, straightened the skirt over the hoop and petticoats, and turned back to the mirror. She ran a critical eye over every line of the gown. "Okay, this is the one," she said to herself, finally satisfied. Dressing for dinner had turned into quite a task. First she had decided to dress for Trace. After all, Lin was sweet on him, and since he thought she was Lin, it made sense. But then she had decided to dress for Traxton. Not that she cared about him, the lout. But he evidently was attracted to her, and if she could play him along and get close to him, without falling into his arms again, she might perhaps learn something that would further her plan.

But then she realized that dressing for Traxton was not the same as dressing for Trace, and had changed again. The demure gown she'd chosen for Trace seemed much too innocent for Traxton, and made her feel foolishly chaste. But the dark blue moire had too plunging a neckline for either man.

She moved to the cherry- and lemon-wood dressing table that was set against the wall between the two windows. Pulling a half-dozen dresses over her head hadn't done much for the mound of curls she'd pinned to her crown. Half of them were now dangling about her ears. Belle quickly pulled out the pins and brushed her hair, turning the tight sausage curls into lustrously rich and loose waves that fanned across her shoulders and cascaded down her back. A touch of rose petal to her lips and cheeks added a dash of color, and rice powder took the shine from her nose.

Belle gave herself one final assessing glance in the cheval mirror before leaving the room. The green of her gown brought out the green in her eyes, and the thick, dripping ruche of lace that adorned both the deeply scooped neckline and the highly puffed pagoda sleeves was almost the exact color of her hair. She fluffed the flounced satin that draped over both hips, straightened the velvet sash at her waist, and, taking a deep breath to calm her nerves, headed downstairs.

As she descended the staircase into the foyer, she heard voices from the dining room. "Wonderful, I'm late," she murmured, realizing she'd missed having sherry in the parlor with the family before dinner, as was Eugenia's custom. Belle hurried her pace.

"Belle," Trace said, leaving his chair at the end of the table and coming toward her. His gaze moved over her, appreciation sparkling in his gray eyes. He offered her his arm. "Traxton told us about the fall you took this afternoon. I was beginning to worry that you weren't feeling well enough to join us for dinner."

Belle smiled up at him, though she felt more like glaring at Traxton. What else had he told them? "It wasn't a bad fall, Trace, really. In fact, I'd almost forgotten about it." All except for the ugly bruise on her hip and the fact that her derriere was as sore as blazes.

"Well, next time you want to ride, you let me know." He placed a protective hand over hers, squeezed gently, and lowered his voice. "And perhaps we can find the time to take that ride we missed, just the two of us."

Belle looked at him quickly. Just the two of them. Though she'd like nothing better than to get him alone and question him, "just the two of us" suddenly made her uncomfortable. She looked into his eyes, recognized the passion swirling there, and knew her discomfort had nothing to do with the fact that she suspected he might be a killer. Oh, lord. She glanced toward Traxton, met his gaze, and quickly looked away again. Was Trace more like Traxton than she'd thought?

"I'll arrange for a nice, gentle mare to be at your disposal." He brought her hand to his mouth, allowed his lips

MORE PASSION AND ADVENTURE AWAIT... YOUR TRIP TO A BIG ADVENTUROUS WORLD BEGINS WHEN YOU ACCEPT YOUR FIRST 4 NOVELS ABSOLUTELY *FREE* (AN $18.00 VALUE)

Accept your Free gift and start to experience more of the passion and adventure you like in a historical romance novel. Each Zebra novel is filled with proud men, spirited women and tempestuous love that you'll remember long after you turn the last page.

Zebra Historical Romances are the finest novels of their kind. They are written by authors who really know how to weave tales of romance and adventure in the historical settings you love. You'll feel like you've actually gone back in time with the thrilling stories that each Zebra novel offers.

GET YOUR FREE GIFT WITH THE START OF YOUR HOME SUBSCRIPTION

Our readers tell us that these books sell out very fast in book stores and often they miss the newest titles. So Zebra has made arrangements for you to receive the four newest novels published each month.

You'll be guaranteed that you'll never miss a title, and home delivery is so convenient. And to show you just how easy it is to get Zebra Historical Romances, we'll send you your first 4 books absolutely FREE! Our gift to you just for trying our home subscription service.

BIG SAVINGS AND FREE HOME DELIVERY

Each month, you'll receive the four newest titles as soon as they are published. You'll probably receive them even before the bookstores do. What's more, you may preview these exciting novels free for 10 days. If you like them as much as we think you will, just pay the low preferred subscriber's price of just $3.75 each. *You'll save $3.00 each month off the publisher's price.* AND, your savings are even greater because there are never any shipping, handling or other hidden charges—FREE Home Delivery. Of course you can return any shipment within 10 days for full credit, no questions asked. There is no minimum number of books you must buy.

4 FREE BOOKS

TO GET YOUR 4 FREE BOOKS WORTH $18.00 — MAIL IN THE FREE BOOK CERTIFICATE T O D A Y

Fill in the Free Book Certificate below, and we'll send your FREE BOOKS to you as soon as we receive it.

If the certificate is missing below, write to: Zebra Home Subscription Service, Inc., P.O. Box 5214, 120 Brighton Road, Clifton, New Jersey 07015-5214.

FREE BOOK CERTIFICATE

4 FREE BOOKS

ZEBRA HOME SUBSCRIPTION SERVICE, INC.

YES! Please start my subscription to Zebra Historical Romances and send me my first 4 books absolutely FREE. I understand that each month I may preview four new Zebra Historical Romances free for 10 days. If I'm not satisfied with them, I may return the four books within 10 days and owe nothing. Otherwise, I will pay the low preferred subscriber's price of just $3.75 each; a total of $15.00, *a savings off the publisher's price of $3.00.* I may return any shipment and I may cancel this subscription at any time. There is no obligation to buy any shipment and there are no shipping, handling or other hidden charges. Regardless of what I decide, the four free books are mine to keep.

NAME

ADDRESS _____ APT _____

CITY _____ STATE _____ ZIP _____

TELEPHONE ( )

SIGNATURE _____ (if under 18, parent or guardian must sign)

Terms, offer and prices subject to change without notice. Subscription subject to acceptance by Zebra Books. Zebra Books reserves the right to reject any order or cancel any subscription.

ZB0594

to linger on her fingers for several seconds, and then pulled her chair from the table.

"Oh, that's very sweet of you, Trace," Belle said, bristling inside and settling herself onto the chair. A nice, gentle mare. Just like something Lin would ride. But then, to Belle's way of thinking, Lin didn't really ride. She and the horse *strolled*. Belle recalled her own horse, Diablo. Beautiful, spirited, and as fleet as the wind, yet he was as loving as a horse could be. She smiled a greeting to everyone at the table, except Traxton, of course, and noticed that all were present except Travis.

"Maybe you could bring Genghis in out of the pasture," Traxton offered with a smirk. "Or did he pass away while I was gone?" He shot a devilish look at Belle. Damn, but she looked beautiful tonight. The green fabric of her gown brought out the emerald shade of her eyes. His gaze moved over the flowing waves of her hair, each strand glistening beneath the glow of the overhead chandelier and resembling threads of white gold. What he wouldn't give to reach out and run his fingers through that silky mane. His eyes dropped to the scooped neckline of her gown, settling on the barely perceptible shadow of cleavage. If her kiss that afternoon had been any indication at all, he had no doubt Belle St. Croix would be a tigress in bed, unless she was overcome by a surge of propriety at feeling a man's hands on her body.

Belle's eyes narrowed as she stared at him. If it wasn't obvious to everyone else what indecent thoughts were tripping through Traxton's head, it certainly was to her. She felt her hand ache to reach out and slap him.

Trace laughed softly at Traxton's suggestion and looked at Belle. "Genghis is a stallion who's almost twenty-eight years old. In his prime he had the energy of ten horses; now he's just a gentle old man who spends his days graz-

ing. My father bought him just after Traxton was born—
that's how we keep track of his age. Whatever Trax is,
Genghis is right behind. We retired him eight years ago."

"Perhaps that means we should retire you, too, Traxton," Teresa said, a smile of mischief on her lips. "Are you
beyond your prime?"

"I think I've got a ways to go before I need to worry
about that, Tessie."

"That all depends on what you'd be retiring, doesn't
it?" Belle countered.

His dark brows rose in amusement. "Well, now, Belle,
just what did you have in mind that I should retire?"

Your lips, your arms, your attitude, she thought, but
said coyly, "Why, whichever part of you needs the rest, of
course."

Teresa giggled, Eugenia looked slightly shocked, and
Traynor just smiled.

Traxton leaned slightly forward and pinned Belle with
a challenging stare. "And just what would you suggest,
Belle?"

Zanenne walked in and set a huge bowl of fried okra
and tomatoes on the table, while another maid followed
with a platter of baked fish.

Belle ignored Traxton and instead turned her gaze to
Trace. She smiled but received only a cool nod of acknowledgement in response. Now what was wrong? He'd
been the epitome of warmth just a minute ago.

Trace concentrated on his meal as he felt his mood
grow steadily darker. He didn't understand how she could
change so drastically. During their dinner in town and the
ride home that evening, she had been so sweet and demure. And basically she was still like that much of the
time, but then there were her flashes of—he glanced at

her—impudence and outspokenness. He had never liked that in a woman.

Then that sweet voice interrupted his thoughts again. "Trace," Belle said seductively, "I would truly appreciate it if you would join me for a walk around the gallery after dinner." She smiled. "Just for a breath of fresh air?"

The frown that already creased his forehead deepened as he stared at her. Ladies didn't invite gentlemen on walks, especially alone and at night. It wasn't proper. He was about to decline, then changed his mind. He was being foolish. Wasn't being alone with her again exactly what he wanted? "It would be my pleasure, Belle," Trace said, and hoped that would be true.

A few minutes later Trace escorted Belle out through one of the open jib windows of the dining room and onto the gallery. The sun had settled beyond the horizon, leaving the earth cradled within the blackness of night with only a slice of moon to light her rolling landscape. The warmth of the day still clung to the air and heightened the sweet scent of the jasmine blossoms whose veins twined their way around several of the house's massive pillars.

"You have a very beautiful plantation," Belle said as they strolled slowly.

"It's one of the largest in Louisiana," Trace answered proudly.

"Your father bought it?"

"Yes." The word snapped from his lips curtly.

Belle did not fail to catch the hardness in the lone word. "But you run it?"

"Yes. My father was more interested in politics and power than in Shadows Noir."

"Well, I suppose many men are taken with politics now, with the way things are going with the North and all." Her gaze swept over the moonlit landscape. "I mean,

Lincoln ran on a platform of states' rights and promised to leave the issue of slavery to the people and governing body of each state, and now it appears he is attempting to retract that stand and—"

Trace paused and glanced down at her curiously.

Belle sensed immediately she'd blundered again. Damn. She'd forgotten to act simple about politics. It wasn't accepted for women to be interested in the subject, and she knew Lin certainly wasn't. Turning her lips upward in a simpering smile, Belle said, "Well, that's what my father and cousins say, anyway." She saw the disturbed shadow leave his eyes, and she breathed a sigh of relief.

They continued their stroll about the gallery. Belle wanted to ask him questions, about his whereabouts at the time of his father's murder and if the rumors she'd heard of Thomas Braggette being responsible for the collapse of Trace's own political career were true, but she was having trouble finding words that wouldn't arouse his suspicions. At the corner of the house they turned and moved onto a portion of the gallery lit only by moonlight.

Trace turned and drew Belle into his arms. "I've been wanting to get you alone again ever since I brought you back here the other night," he said, his voice a husky blend of velvet and honey. "You've stirred something within me, Belle, that I thought I'd never feel again, that I thought had died with . . ." He let the words fade on his lips. Now was not the time to think of Myra or remember the past.

Belle stood in the circle of his arms and stared up at him. Good grief, he was going to kiss her! He thought she was Lin, and he was going to kiss her. What was she supposed to do? What would Lin do? She felt her heart accelerate to a maddening pace. Lin would not have allowed herself to be in this situation. She wouldn't have invited a man to escort her into the darkness. She wouldn't have wandered into the shadows with him. And she certainly wouldn't have allowed him to draw her into his arms. But then, Belle thought, if the man was Trace, maybe she would, regardless of the fact that he was one of their suspects, that he might very well be a murderer. Belle's mind spun in confusion. Had Lin already kissed him?

"I think I'm falling in love with you, Belle," Trace said. His head lowered toward hers.

No, not with me, Belle's mind screamed. With Lin. With Lin. She watched his face draw closer to hers. What should she do?

His arms tightened around her waist and crushed her body against his. She felt his hands move to press against the bare flesh of her back.

"Trace, I . . ."

His mouth covered hers in a gentle kiss that offered tenderness and deep love, a kiss meant to tempt her senses and woo her heart and which did neither. She sensed within him, now more than at any other moment, an aching loneliness, and felt a momentary wave of compassion for him. His hands moved slowly over her back, caressing her.

Belle made to pull away from him, to utter a protest. His arms tightened around her, and, as he felt her lips part, his tongue slipped between them and filled her mouth, seeking the sweetness of promise there.

Imprisoned within his embrace, forced to endure his kiss, Belle could not help but remember the feel of Traxton's arms around her, of the passion that he had sparked within her, the fire and hunger that his touch, his kiss, had brought to life within every cell and fiber of her being. Traxton Braggette was a scoundrel, a rake, and blackguard who delighted in mocking her, who, she knew, would seduce her into his bed, have his way with her, and then arrogantly say thank you and goodbye. But she also knew, though she hated to admit it, that he had made her feel again, made her feel something she had thought died when John died.

Belle felt tears sting the back of her eyes, but why they were there, what unconscious thought had brought them, she didn't know.

If from nothing more than his kiss, Belle sensed that Trace was a man who would offer marriage, who would love and honor a woman, give her his name, his home, his children. Exactly the kind of man Lin needed, and if he proved not to be the murderer they sought, then she would be happy to see her sister marry him. Placing her hands on his upper arms, Belle pulled away from him. "Trace, please," she whispered raggedly, and moved from the circle of his arms.

She saw the hurt that flashed in his eyes and knew she couldn't let it remain there. Belle closed her eyes and tried to think of her sister, of what Lin would do, of what she'd want. She looked back at Trace. "It's just that this is all so sudden," she said breathlessly. He smiled, and Belle felt a flood of relief.

"You're right," Trace said, his voice still heavy with the desire that having her in his arms had brought to his veins. He closed the distance between them, took Belle's hand in his, and smiled. "Forgive me?" he asked lightly.

"Why, what'd you do?" Traxton asked, sauntering onto the gallery.

Seventeen

Belle looked at a china statuette that sat on the etagere in one corner of her room. "Where were you when I needed something to bash Traxton over the head with?" she fumed. Flinging off the green gown and dropping both her petticoats and hoop to the floor, Belle began to pace the room.

On the gallery outside, obscured from sight by the darkness of night and a shadow cast by the wide pillar opposite his room and upon which he leaned, Traxton inhaled deeply of the whiskey-soaked cheroot he held in one hand. He watched its end simmer, the brilliant orange glow of the burning tobacco like a small sun against the darkness of night. Not until that moment, when he'd heard her mutter his name, had he realized Belle was in her room. If he had thought about it, he might have assumed it, but he'd been doing his best not to think about her at all. Yet obviously she was thinking about him and in spite of his better intentions, a smile pulled at his lips.

"Obnoxious lout, that's what he is," Belle muttered. "Arrogant, egotistical, self-centered, outspoken lout." She tripped over the petticoat she'd left on the floor, regained her balance, and glared down at the mound of ruffles and lace as if it had purposely moved into her path. "Stupid." She kicked the petticoat aside and resumed pacing, her anger mounting rather than subsiding with each step. "Never, ever, have I met such an impossible, infuriating rake."

Amused by her tirade, Traxton dropped the cheroot to the gallery floor and crushed the burning tip with the heel of his boot. Well, if she wanted to curse him, he might as well give her the pleasure of doing it in person.

Not willing to examine his actions or his motives, Traxton ignored the fact that only moments before he had been reaffirming his vow to himself to stay as far away from Belle St. Croix as he could get.

He walked across the gallery toward her open window. She hadn't heard his approach or sensed his presence and continued her pacing, though now her mutterings were under her breath. Delighted at the sight before him, Traxton watched silently as Belle stalked from one end of the room to the other in nothing more than her camisole and pantalettes. On the opposite side of the room, a lamp sat on a small table by the door, the flame within its glass chimney casting a golden glow over the room. Each time she passed it, the light from the flame penetrated the sheer threads of the camisole and pantalettes so that the muslin was little more than a diaphanous veil, revealing every line and curve of her body to him. Belle reached the end of the room, stamped her foot as if to emphasize something she'd muttered, and swung around to pace back in the opposite direction. As she did, the long strands of her hair flew across her shoulders, a tangled mane that glistened beneath the lamplight.

She paused as she neared the fireplace and reached to unlace the pale blue ribbon that held the front of her camisole closed. The movement seemed to pull Traxton from the spell that had come over him.

"Run out of curses to hurl on my head?" he said, leaning insolently against the window's wainscoting.

Belle whirled, throwing her arms across her breasts. "What . . . what are you doing in here?"

"I heard you say my name and thought you were calling me." He smiled, a devilish grin that sent her heart skipping merrily in spite of the anger roiling in her breast.

"Liar."

He shrugged. "But you were talking about me."

"I was not."

"It's not nice to lie."

Her shoulders stiffened slightly, and without looking away, Belle reached to a chair that stood beside her, grabbed a wrapper that lay over its back, and clutched it loosely to her breast. "Did you enjoy the show, Mr. Braggette?" she asked impudently.

He laughed, and the sound sent a delicious trail of shivers racing over her. "Very much."

Belle's fingers tightened on the thin fabric of her wrapper. "Good, I'm glad. But now, if you'll excuse me, I think I'd like to retire."

"Alone?" Traxton asked, one brow cocked impishly.

Belle glared at him. "Yes, alone."

"You're sure you wouldn't like some company?" A smile drew one corner of his mouth upward.

"Quite sure."

Traxton pushed away from the wainscoting. "Too bad." He reached up and released the draperies from the hooks that held them back from the window. "You know, a lady would keep her curtains closed while undressing," he said, and chuckled softly. He stepped out onto the gallery and dropped the draperies into place before she could respond.

Filled with an abrupt flash of indignation, Belle screwed

her face up and stuck her tongue out toward the window through which he'd disappeared. That was the second time in two days a man had implied that she wasn't a lady, and she didn't like it one bit. She especially didn't like it coming from Traxton Braggette. After all, it wasn't as if he were a gentleman. Belle tossed the wrapper back onto the chair, walked to the bed, and threw herself down on the high mattress. Imagine, spying on her like that. She stared up at the pale blue canopy. Well, Traxton certainly wasn't a gentlemen, but then from what little information she'd gathered on Thomas Braggette, that was no surprise. Like father like son.

Travis pushed open one of the elegant doors of the Beaujolais casino, stepped out onto the banquette, and inhaled deeply of the sultry night air. The sun was just setting, but the Quarter was already well-settled into shadow. A patron from the casino next door, L'etoile, stepped through its swinging entry doors, followed instantly by several more men, all grumbling over their losses. Travis smiled, remembering what he always told his own customers: if you can't afford to lose, don't play the game.

His gaze moved assessingly over L'etoile. The establishments in New Orleans were certainly different than what he had become used to in the few years since he'd left. His own Mountain Queen Saloon in Virginia City was nice enough, ten times more comfortable and sumptuous than any other in Nevada Territory—some even called it luxurious—but it was nothing compared to the Beaujolais, L'etoile, Golden Slipper, or a dozen others in the Quarter. Then again, the saloons in Virginia City catered to miners and ranchers, not plantation genteel and city rich. He drew a cheroot from the pocket of his cut-away jacket, snipped the end with a pair of silver clippers from the same pocket, and slashed a lucifer against the rough wall of the casino. Lounging with his back against the wall, Travis drew one foot up and hooked the heel of his boot on the edge of the windowsill behind him. He cupped the lucifer's flame with his hands and lifted it to the tip of his cheroot. As he did, his gaze was drawn by a movement on the street, and he looked up.

"What the hell is Belle doing in town this late?" Travis murmured to himself, watching her hurry along the ban-quette on the opposite side of the street. She had been at Shadows Noir when he'd left, and that had been only minutes before dinner was to be served. Tossing the che-root to the ground, he pushed away from the wall. He should at least offer to escort her back to the plantation. It was dark, and a lady shouldn't be out at night alone, though obviously Belle, as a stranger to New Orleans, didn't realize how dangerous the streets of the Vieux Carré could be once the sun went down. At the corner Travis stepped from the banquette, walked over the con-crete slab that bridged the canal, and crossed the street. He stood looking down Rue de la St. Louis in puzzle-ment. In the center of the street a lantern hung suspended on a rope that spanned the distance between the roofs of the two corner buildings. Its flame illuminated the center of the street but left the banquettes in shadow. In the center of the block the doorman for the St. Louis Hotel stepped back from a carriage just pulling away from the hotel's entry. "Where in the hell did she go?" Travis mut-tered to himself, then looked at the carriage. He couldn't tell if it was one from Shadows Noir, but it didn't matter. Obviously Belle was either in that carriage and headed back to the plantation, or had boarded another. Either way,

he was no longer obligated to see her home. He had
friends to see and money to win. Turning on his heel, he
walked back to the Beaujolais.

Lin hurried along the banquette, throwing a series of
furtive glances over her shoulder as she walked. She
didn't like being out alone after dark, especially not in the
Vieux Carré. People disappeared from the French Quarter, shanghaied, her father had told her once, men forced
to work on ships, women taken to be sold as slaves in the
Orient. Lin shuddered, drew her pelisse cloak about her
shoulders, and quickened her pace. She should never have
gone back to Mageline Toutant's so late. Her fingers tightened on the reticule she carried as a tall man in a long
coat passed her. In fact, she shouldn't have gone back to
Mageline Toutant's house at all. It had been a ridiculous
idea. After nearly being caught by Trace at the Cabildo,
she had raced back to the St. Louis and hibernated in her
room for nearly the remainder of the afternoon. But then
she'd remembered that she hadn't asked Mageline if she
knew anything about any dealings between the city's
mayor and Thomas Braggette. During her earlier visit
Mageline had seemed friendly, even helpful. And she had
again upon Lin's return, until Lin got another brainstorm
and mentioned that her father had received a letter from
Braggette with an unusual wax seal on it. She was looking
for Mr. Braggette's attorney, Lin fibbed, but didn't know
the man's name and wondered if that was his seal. When
she'd described the seal Belle had found in Braggette's
hidden box, the letters *KG* within a circle, Mageline had
become tense and nervous. She obviously knew what the
seal meant, and she wasn't willing to talk about it.

"Piddle, piddle, piddle," Lin said, turning the corner

and breathing a sigh of relief to see the familiar entrance to the hotel. She was just about to hurry through the lobby when she noticed one of the stewards attaching a sign to the wall near the front desk. Curious, she approached. A thrill of excitement coursed through Lin as she read the announcement attached to the wall. Angelina Miles was coming to New Orleans. She would be performing at the French Opera House the following night. "Oh, I just have to go," Lin murmured, staring at the poster. She adored the opera and attended every chance she could. Lin felt a shiver of anticipation. Angelina Miles was the brightest star of the opera. She just couldn't miss a chance to hear her sing.

Forgetting to glance around the lobby to make sure there was no one there who would recognize her, Lin hurried across it, raced up the wide staircase, and entered her room. She threw open the door to the armoire and began to rifle through the gowns she'd hung there. Had she brought one suitable for the opera? Pink. Blue. Green. Apricot. Lavender. "Oh, no," Lin moaned. Red. Black. Yellow. "Ah!" She pulled out a gown of white Caledonian silk. "Thank goodness." White was the only appropriate color for the opera. She lay the gown over a nearby chair, then paused. Belle would be furious if she found out Lin had gone out. Especially to the opera.

Lin smiled. Well, she'd just have to pray Belle didn't find out. Anyway, Belle was at Shadows Noir. As long as they didn't both appear at the same place at the same time, what would be the harm? That thought wiped the smile from her face. What if Belle went to the opera?

"No, Belle hates the opera," Lin said, making up her mind to go. "She'd rather die than go to the opera."

* * *

"The opera?" Belle stared at Eugenia Braggette as if the woman had just informed her they were going to the gallows.

"Yes, dear. Angelina Miles is performing tonight, and I thought it would be nice if we all went." She smiled at Belle. "Have you ever attended one of her performances?"

Angelina Miles. Belle's mind raced. Who was Angelina Miles? Lin would know. Lin loved the opera. Belle hated it. She smiled at Eugenia, quickly glancing around the table at the others. They were all staring at her. If she could get out of accompanying them into town and if they all went, it could prove a perfect opportunity to search their rooms without fear of being caught. Except by the servants, of course, but she could handle that. Belle made up her mind. "No, actually, I haven't, but I think you'll have to excuse me this evening, Eugenia. I'm afraid I'm not really feeling too well today." Thank heaven Trace and Traxton hadn't returned to the house for the noonday meal. The last thing she needed at the moment was Traxton's sarcasm or Trace's concern.

"Oh, I'm sorry to hear that," Eugenia said.

"Would you like me to stay home and keep you company?" Teresa offered.

"Oh, no, thank you, Teresa. I'll be fine and probably just retire early."

"Speaking of town, I saw you last night," Travis said, "though I guess I should apologize for not offering to escort you back to the plantation."

"Saw me?" Belle said, her voice a squeak.

"Yeah. I was at one of the casinos. Stepped out for a breath of air and a smoke. You walked by on the other side of the street."

Belle twisted the napkin that lay in her lap. Lin! She

smiled sweetly. "No, I'm afraid it wasn't me, Travis. I was right here all evening."

"Really?" Travis drawled, rolling the word slowly off his tongue, his gaze fusing with hers.

"So, what time do we leave?" Traynor asked his mother.

"Seven," Eugenia said, "assuming your brothers are back and can be ready by then."

"Count me out," Travis said. "I have a little unfinished business in town."

"More gambling?" Eugenia's brow cocked in amused disapproval.

"Call it collecting on a loan, Mama," Travis answered, and laughed.

Belle studied Travis from beneath lowered lashes. She didn't like the idea that he wouldn't be with the others. What if he came back early?

"Belle, you do look a little peaked," Eugenia said, breaking into her thoughts. "Why don't you go up to your room now? I'll have Zanenne make you a nice glass of iced tea and bring it up to you."

Belle felt as if she'd just been punished and relegated to her room. She smiled, thanked her hostess, and went upstairs. Well, it was her own fault. She'd said she didn't feel well. Belle closed the door behind her. So now she would have to spend the remainder of the day in bed. Wonderful. Well, there was nothing else to do except go ahead with her plan and pretend she was sick. Removing her gown, petticoats, and hoop, she drew a wrapper of embroidered batiste around her, tied the sash at her waist, and plopped down on the bed.

"Let's see," she mumbled angrily, "I can stare up at the canopy, count my fingers and toes, try to sleep, or . . ." She sighed in frustration. "Or continue to talk to myself."

Surprisingly, she slept.

Several hours later a soft knock on her door brought her awake.

"Come in."

Trace entered carrying a tray. "I thought you might want some soup." He set the tray down on a marble-topped table near the bed, then settled a hip on the mattress. "We're going to be leaving soon. Are you all right?"

Belle nodded. The smell of the soup teased her near-empty stomach.

"I was disappointed to hear you wouldn't be going with us." He touched her cheeks with the tip of his fingers, a featherlight touch meant more as a caress than a stroke of concern.

Belle smiled. "I'll be fine in the morning, I'm sure. You go on and enjoy the opera."

He leaned over and brushed his lips lightly across hers. "I could stay here with you."

"No."

Trace straightened and looked down at her.

"I mean," she took his hand in hers and smiled, "I want you to go and enjoy yourself. Anyway, I'll probably just go back to sleep."

Five minutes after Trace left her room and Belle had gobbled up not only the soup, but the two biscuits that had accompanied it, Traxton sauntered casually into her room through the open jib window that led to the gallery.

"I see being sick hasn't done anything to your appetite," he said, glancing at the tray.

Belle, startled at his sudden and unannounced appearance, jerked around to confront him. He was dressed in evening clothes and was one of the most beautiful sights she had ever seen. A black cutaway coat of broadcloth hugged his upper torso, its lines accentuating his broad shoulders and narrow waist, its velvet lapel framing a white silk shirt that complimented his bronzed face. Thigh-hugging trousers were held taut to his long, lean legs by leather *sous pieds* looped under the arch of each highly polished black dress boot. The sight of him nearly took her breath away, but Belle struggled to remember, and hold on to, her anger at his rude entry. "Knocking is always nice, Mr. Braggette," she snapped.

He shrugged. "If you're at a door, I guess." His gaze moved over her outstretched body. "I hear you're not feeling too well."

Belle let her head drop back against the pillows and closed her eyes. "Yes, that's right," she said, trying to sound weak and tired.

"Stay out too late in town last night?"

She looked up at him again. He'd moved nearer the bed and now towered over her. "I wasn't in town last night."

"Travis said he saw you."

Belle felt a horde of butterflies flutter within her stomach. "Travis was wrong."

She felt the hungry caress of his gaze move over her length just as much as if it had been his hand, inciting her own desires. Memory of his kiss, of how it had made her feel, suddenly turned her blood to flowing rivers of lava, burning her from the inside. She longed to draw him down to the bed beside her. Belle clenched her hands into fists at her sides. Why did he have such a potent effect on her? It was maddening. He was handsome, yes, she'd admit that. And he was charismatic. But that was all. She certainly wouldn't consent to be courted by anyone like him. After all, it wasn't as though he was a gentleman anymore, if he'd ever been one. He was a cowboy.

"Was he?" Traxton drawled, his tone holding more

than a hint of disbelief. He didn't know what the hell Belle St. Croix was up to, but he knew damned well she was up to something. His eyes came to rest on the swell of her breasts. He watched them rise with each breath, then fall as she exhaled, and felt his body growing hard with need, taut with hunger, hot with fire.

Belle closed her eyes again, hoping that would urge him to leave. "Yes, he was."

His brother was in love with her. Traxton had to keep reminding himself of that. Even if Trace didn't realize it yet, Traxton did. It was written all over his brother's face, blazing from his eyes whenever he looked at her. Trace was in love with Belle, but Traxton was not. He wanted her, yes. Damn, how he wanted her. He wanted to strip the clothes from the lithe length that lay before him so enticingly, wanted to cover her naked body with his and join them together, to thrust himself inside of her and taste her passion. But that's all he wanted. He did not, and never would, want more than that with a woman.

Eighteen

Lin felt a wave of disappointment when a gold tassle-trimmed white silk curtain came down before the stage and a young man appeared to announce a fifteen-minute intermission. But her disappointment was instantly replaced by a sense of dismay as the gas chandeliers overhead suddenly blazed with light. She looked quickly around the huge theatre. It was the most magnificent thing she had ever seen. Spacious viewing boxes covered the entire first floor, those in the center being portable, enabling them to be moved when the opera house was used for a soiree. Second and third floor balconies held yet more boxes. The ceiling was a huge mural from which dangled several very ornate, and very large, crystal chandeliers. But it was the sea of faces she was looking at rather than the scenery. Hopefully there was no one present who would recognize her.

Lin felt her pulses race. Everyone seemed to be rising from their seats, if not to adjourn to the lobby, then to saunter between boxes and visit their neighbors. She had planned to slip out before the intermission and return to the hotel, but she'd been so mesmerized by Angelina Miles's performance that she had forgotten, and now it was too late.

She snapped open the feather-trimmed fan she had

brought with her and fluttered it in front of her face. If she remained seated, she would look conspicuous. Intermission was a time for chatting with friends and being seen, and only elderly people, usually those who had dozed off, remained in their boxes. But if she got up and moved around, she might run into someone who would recognize her as Belle. The sight of a tall gentleman moving down the aisle and heading directly toward her box helped make Lin's decision an abrupt one. She didn't know him, and she didn't want to. Standing, she opened the gate of her box, slipped out, and hurried toward the opposite aisle. She continued to flutter the fan in front of her face as she moved between the other patrons. Suddenly her idea of coming to the opera, no matter how much she'd wanted to see Angelina Miles, didn't seem like such a good one. She hadn't known the opera house was so large, hadn't thought there would be so many people.

"Belle."

Lin froze at the familiar voice. Unable to help herself she paused and her head whipped around, her eyes searching the crowd for him. She spotted him almost immediately. He was a good head taller than most of the other men in the room, his hair glistening beneath the glow of the chandeliers, black evening coat stretched taut across broad shoulders, white shirt accentuating the richness of both his dark hair and bronzed face. Trace. Her eyes met his and her fingers tightened convulsively on the spine of the small fan. She wanted to go to him so badly she nearly moved in his direction, then caught herself. She couldn't. Belle must be here somewhere. What if he saw both of them? "Oh, Lord."

Suddenly another dark head appeared above the crowd a few yards to the left of Trace. Lin's gaze darted from one to the other. The second was in profile to her, and he hadn't seen her yet. She realized almost instantly, unaware of even how she knew, that the first brother she'd spotted hadn't been Trace after all, but Traxton. This was Trace. To her horror, she watched as yet another Braggette moved up to stand beside Trace. She nearly groaned. "My God, are they *all* here?" Lifting her skirts, Lin turned and pushed her way through a crowd of people milling before one of the exit doors. "Please get me out of here," she murmured in prayer. "Please, please, *please,* get me out of here."

Traxton tried to push his way through the crowd toward her. Damn it all, what in blazes was that woman up to? Why had she pretended to be sick, then shown up here, and now was running away from him as if he were Satan himself? "Belle," he called again toward her fleeing form.

Trace heard his brother's voice, heard him say Belle's name, and looked around in confusion. Why was Traxton calling out to Belle when she was back at Shadows Noir in bed? He pushed through the crowd in the same direction he'd seen Traxton disappear and caught up with him at one of the exit doors to the street. "What are you doing?"

"I was trying to catch Belle," Traxton nearly bellowed, his anger getting the better of him.

"Belle's back at the plantation," Trace said calmly.

"No, she's not. I just saw her here."

Trace urged Traxton away from the door and back toward their box. "Come on, Trax, you probably saw someone who looked like Belle at a glance, but it wasn't her. She was sick in bed when we left. Now, come on, forget it. Enjoy the rest of the performance."

"It was her," Traxton grumbled. He slumped down into his chair and glared toward the stage. It was her, damn it, and if she knew what was good for her, when he got back to the plantation she blasted well was going to tell him just what she was up to.

"Traxton?"

The voice, a light musical sound that he had hoped never to hear again, swirled around him and jangled his nerves further. Traxton wished he could slink further into his seat and disappear, but instead he swung around to locate the voice's owner. His dark gaze found hers instantly. "Juliette," he said, his tone holding no enthusiasm at seeing the woman with whom he had once thought himself in love. She was still as beautiful as ever, her black hair piled high in a mound of curls, her skin the rich hue of cream, and her body curvaceous and enticing. But Traxton, to his relief, found himself uninterested.

She laughed lightly and moved closer. "Well, I might have hoped for a warmer welcome, darling, but I guess I should allot you time to get over the surprise of seeing me again."

Juliette Voucshon bent forward, the calculated movement lending him an unobstructed view of her cleavage, which was nearly fully exposed by the scandalously low cut of her white moire gown. She brushed her lips over his. "We have a lot to talk over, Traxton," she murmured softly. "And I've missed you, *chère*." She smiled seductively. "I'm staying with the Caloites, just down the street, and I'm not really interested in the opera."

He knew it was an invitation to leave with her, but if he'd had any doubt at all about the way he felt about her, the cold disgust the touch of her lips on his had aroused within him erased it. "Thank you, Juliette, but I am."

"Oh, Trax," she purred, "you never cared for the opera." A playful pout pursed her lips. "Are you still mad at me?"

He smiled, but the gesture was just as artificial as her

feigned innocence. "No, Juliette, I'm not mad at you. I just don't have anything to say to you."

She leaned forward again and smiled. "Oh, Trax," she cooed, "are you sure?" Her eyes issued the invitation again. "Really sure, *chère?*"

"I'm sure, Juliette," he said, and rose. "Now, if you'll excuse me, I think I'd best locate my mother before the lights go out again."

Lin scurried down the banquette, throwing furtive glances over her shoulder with every other step and clutching a pelerine cloak around her shoulders. Why, oh why, had she gone to that opera? Why couldn't she just do what Belle had told her to do? It was almost as if someone was manipulating it so that whenever she stepped a foot from the hotel, a Braggette was there.

Practically flying through the lobby, up the stairs, and into her room, Lin slammed the door behind her and slumped against it. Long moments later, both her breathing and heartbeat having returned to normal, and finally confident neither Traxton or Trace had followed her and were going to bash down the door, Lin walked across the room and drew the drapes closed over the window. She sighed in relief.

A knock at the door almost sent her jumping out the window. Lin whirled around. Dare she ask who it was?

"Mademoiselle Bonnvivier," Pierre Loushei called, "I saw you return to the hotel and have taken the liberty of bringing you some coffee."

Lin sighed, a combination of relief that it wasn't a Braggette at her door and frustration over the fact that Pierre Loushei was not taking the hint that she wasn't interested in his continuing attentions.

"I'm indisposed at the moment, Mr. Loushei," Lin called out. "Could you please leave the tray at my door and I'll retrieve it shortly?"

"Oh, certainly," Pierre said, disappointment thick in his tone.

Lin tiptoed toward the door and pressed her ear to the panel.

Pierre placed the tray on the floor, then, since he was already hunched down, positioned his eye in front of the keyhole and looked through. He frowned. Something was in front of the hole on the opposite side. He couldn't see anything.

Belle sat at the writing desk in Eugenia's room, facing the window so that she had a clear view of the moonlit drive. She had already searched all the others' rooms and uncovered nothing. She had searched Eugenia's room last and found it offered the most. Belle cursed herself for not having started there in the first place. Glancing at the drive and reassuring herself that the Braggettes were not yet returning from town, she turned her attention back to the diary that lay open on the desk before her and flipped the page.

Thomas Braggette had been a monster, at least in the opinion of his wife, and after reading only a portion of Eugenia's diary, Belle had to agree with her. With every disappointment or failure in his life, with every business deal that didn't go exactly the way he'd wanted, or for every associate who made him angry, Thomas Braggette had come home to the plantation and taken his frustrations and rage out on his wife. Several times he had beaten her so badly she had been unable to go out in public for weeks. Once, when Trace had traveled to Baton

Rouge on business, Eugenia sent Teresa to stay with friends and then told her husband she wanted a divorce. He'd flown into a rage and beat her. The next day she packed her bags and attempted to leave Shadows Noir. Thomas Braggette had caught her before she'd even gotten off the property. Only because of his threats against Teresa, threats she knew he would carry out and that her sons could not prevent, had Eugenia returned to the plantation. For several days after her return Thomas had kept Eugenia locked in the attic, refusing to let her out until she swore she would never try to leave again and would not tell Trace what had happened while he was gone.

Belle gasped. "The man was an absolute monster," she muttered, hardly able to believe the words Eugenia had written. "A beast." She turned to an earlier entry in the diary and found a passage about Travis. Eugenia's delicate handwriting seemed filled with anger.

Travis left New Orleans today, but then, what else could he do? Thomas provided him no choice. An arranged marriage with Suzanne Forteaux was politically beneficial to Thomas, but it wasn't what Travis wanted. He tried to reject it, but Thomas then let it "slip" to his friends, who quickly told others, that Suzanne was heavy with Travis's child. Of course, Bernadette terminated her relationship with Travis immediately and refused to even talk to him. That nearly broke his heart, and would have, if it hadn't been filled with so much hate for his father.

Belle sat back in the chair and released a long breath. "Travis definitely had a reason to want to kill his father," she mumbled. A movement near the moonlit drive caught her eye and she looked out the window, but it was only a squirrel skittering across the lawn. She returned her attention to the diary, moving ahead several dozen pages.

> *My youngest son said goodbye to me tonight and left home. I prayed he wouldn't go, but I couldn't ask him to stay, not after what Thomas did to him. Traynor loved that girl—why couldn't Thomas see that? Did it matter that her parents were not wealthy? That they were Italians? Thomas had no reason to call her those vile names. And then to buy off her family in return for their word they would never come back to New Orleans, that was cruel enough, but why did he have to tell Traynor? Why did he have to tell him that the girl he loved had accepted money to leave him?*

Belle found what she was reading almost incomprehensible. How could anyone treat his children so terribly? She flipped back toward the beginning of the diary.

> *Trace is almost helpless with grief and guilt over Myra's death. I truly believe the only thing that keeps him going is his loathing for his father. And God forgive me, but I don't blame him. Poor Myra's death was a direct result of Thomas's irresponsible actions; that cannot be denied. Except by Thomas, of course. If only he hadn't lambasted Trace in public that way, tried to humiliate him and ruin his political ambitions, none of this would have happened. But he did. He wielded his power and got that man out of jail just to prove that Trace was wrong in prosecuting him, and because of that, because of Thomas's ego and jealousy, Myra is dead.*

Traxton, Belle thought. Since Eugenia had written about the other three sons, she must have also written about Traxton. Belle flipped the pages quickly, her eyes skimming over the flourish of Eugenia's handwriting until finally spotting his name.

I'll never forget how proud and happy I was for Traxton. He was so handsome standing there at the altar waiting for his bride. But after what he'd done to Trace, I should have known Thomas would never let it happen. It was cruel, though, to let his own son stand there in the church, in front of his friends and family, while all the while Thomas knew the bride was not coming.

Belle felt her eyes fill with tears as a wave of compassion swept over her. My God, she thought, is that why he acts so arrogant and brazen: to cover up the hurt he still feels at experiencing such a humiliating rejection? She blinked the tears back and read on.

Six months have passed since that day, but now finally we know the truth of the matter, horrible as it is. I can't blame Traxton for leaving New Orleans. It was probably best. Especially after we heard reports that Juliette was in London, much richer than when she'd left and heavy with child. Traxton swears he never bedded Juliette, and I believe him. It is not his child. Thomas proudly admits he paid Juliette to leave Traxton, but when I questioned him about the child, he merely laughed. I shudder to think there might be a possibility the child is . . .

Belle reread the unfinished sentence several times, unable to believe what the words insinuated. Thomas had bedded his own son's fiancée? "The fiend!" Belle said. "How could any man be so vile? So rotten? And to his own son?"

Belle felt herself reel from the words she had read. Was it any wonder they had hated him? That his wife did not grieve his passing? That his daughter could continue to merrily plan her wedding? A shiver rippled over Belle's body. She had never really considered that there were people like Thomas Braggette in this world. Her parents had always been so kind and loving, both toward each other and to their daughters.

She closed the book and stared unseeingly out of the window. Thomas Braggette had been an evil man. Perhaps he had deserved to be killed. Belle stood and began to pace the room. Yes, perhaps he had deserved to be killed, she thought again, but Henri Sorbonte hadn't done it, and he didn't deserve to be hanged for it.

Picking up the diary again, Belle flipped toward the back and found the page Eugenia had written just after the murder.

I saw Edward today when I was in town. He looks just as handsome and debonair to me now as he did that day so long ago when he asked my father for permission to marry me. If only my father had said yes, how different things might have been. But Papa, like Thomas, was more interested in the financial standing of my husband-to-be and his political connections than he was in whether there was any love in the marriage. Even after I begged him to reconsider. Edward has never married, and has now asked to call on me. I consented happily. There

will be talk, I know, but I do not care. Perhaps it is
not too late for us.

Eugenia's diary confirmed what Braggette's papers and
rumor had intimated: Edward Mourdaine had a motive to
kill Thomas. Lord, how many suspects were there?

The sound of carriage wheels brought Belle whirling
around to face the window.

They were home.

She jammed Eugenia's diary back into the drawer of
the writing desk, hurriedly extinguished the oil lamp, and
dashed for the door. Scurrying down the hallway, Belle
darted into her own room, ran a brush through her hair,
straightened the scooped collar of the embroidered batiste
wrapper she wore over her nightgown, grabbed a glass of
cold milk she'd left sitting on the table earlier, and hastened back to the staircase. She was halfway down, taking
her time now, when the family entered the foyer.

"Belle," Eugenia said, "I expected you'd be asleep."
She handed her wrap to Traynor and met Belle at the
bottom of the stairs. "How are you feeling, dear? Better,
I hope?"

"Yes, much," Belle said, and smiled. "I was just going
to the warming kitchen to heat up my milk." She laughed,
though the sound echoed nervously even to her ears. "I
can't seem to get to sleep."

"I would assume you haven't had much time to try,"
Traxton said. He moved forward, grabbed Belle none too
gently by the arm, and ushered her into the parlor.

Tripping on tiptoe after him, her temper immediately
flaring, Belle jerked her arm free and glowered up at him.
"What in blazes are you doing?"

"Why did you pretend to be sick?" Traxton demanded.
The others, who had followed, stared in shock.

"Pretend?" Belle said. "I don't know what you're talking about. I didn't pretend."

"You were in town."

Belle's brows shot upward in surprise. "What?"

"You heard me."

"Trax, you're being ridiculous," Trace said. "It obviously wasn't Belle."

Traxton didn't take his eyes off her, piercing her with his stare. "Yes, it was."

"Traxton, please," Eugenia said quietly. "You've made a mistake."

"What the hell are you up to, Belle?" Traxton growled, ignoring the interjections of his family. "You were at the opera, Belle. You know it and I know it. So why'd you pretend to be sick?"

"I didn't."

"And why'd you run off when I called to you?"

Belle opened her mouth, a sharp retort ready on her tongue, when sudden realization hit her. She clamped her mouth closed. Lin. Damn, blast, and tarnation. She'd gone out again. And she'd been seen again. Damn, damn, damn.

Belle tried to smile, though she knew it wasn't too convincing, at least to Traxton. "You know, I heard about a case like this once, where someone spotted someone they thought looked just like another person they knew and—"

"It was you," Traxton snapped.

"It was not me." Belle felt her temper reaching the conflagration point, but whether she was angrier at Traxton for his persistence or at Lin for her stupidity, she wasn't sure.

"Traxton, you were obviously mistaken," Trace said. "It seems evident Belle was here while we were gone."

He chuckled. "How could she have dressed and gotten to the opera before it started when we were nearly late? We obviously left before she did."

"Maybe she was late, too."

"Then you would have seen her come in."

"Not necessarily."

"Traxton, this is ridiculous," Eugenia cut in. "Now," she smiled, "let's all have a brandy. Belle, you can have your milk, and then we'll retire."

Belle moved to stand by the window. A moment later, Traxton moved up beside her. "I know it was you," he said, his voice a deep, whispered growl. "I don't know what the hell you're up to, and I don't know how you did it or why, but I know damned well that was you I saw in the opera house tonight."

Belle rose early the next morning and slipped out of the house before, she hoped, anyone else was up and about. Of course, there was no way she could be sure, but the only one she really worried about was Trace. He liked to rise early and do his morning rounds before breakfast. Traxton and Traynor both liked to sleep in, having said more than once at the breakfast table that it was the first time in longer than either remembered that they'd had the opportunity. Teresa and Eugenia would most likely be rising within a half an hour. Travis was another unknown. Several times he'd gone into town in the evening and hadn't returned till morning, and she wasn't sure now if he was fast asleep in his room or hadn't returned to the house yet.

"Lord, don't let me run into him on the road." She entered the stable.

Nineteen

Lin looked at the sign sitting in one corner of the milliner's window. The store wouldn't open for another ten minutes. A reflection of the auctioneers setting up their individual spaces and wares for the afternoon auctions on the main floor of the hotel lobby was clear within the huge pane of glass, and the cavernous rotunda hummed with the soft buzz of conversation as guests moved in and out of the dining rooms, the bar, and the lobby.

The evening before, nervous and unable to sleep, Lin had meandered along the gallery, looking into the windows of each shop. A bonnet of pale green silk and velvet had caught her eye, and she'd fallen in love with it. Of course the shop had been closed, so Lin had decided to return the next morning and buy the hat. It would be both a salve to her nerves at almost being caught by both Trace and Traxton at the opera and a reward for summoning the courage to go to Mageline Toutant's.

She refused to think anymore on her close call at the opera house, and if she were lucky, Belle would never hear of it. Instead, she remembered Braggette's mistress and shuddered again at the realization that she'd actually gone to a madame's house.

"Miss Bonnvivier?"

Lynn spun around to stare at the man who had ap-

proached her. Her first impression was that he was square
and dark, and rather handsome in an exotic, foreign way.

"Excusa," he whipped a bowler style hat from his head,
"you are Miss Bonnvivier?"

"Yes," Lin answered without thinking, and was immediately sorry. Ladies did not talk to gentlemen to whom
they were not properly introduced.

His build was one of mass, his arms, legs, and chest all
thick yet well-proportioned for his height, which was only
a few inches taller than Lin. His hair was black, straight,
and combed away from his face, which was blunt, yet
somehow attractive. Sky blue eyes peered out from below
thick black lashes. He bowed. "Please, I am Peter Marconi."

Since the name meant nothing to her, Lin remained
silent and merely stared.

"I am, how you say, a representative of the Italian peo-
ples in New Orleans."

"How do you do," Lin said stiffly, still not sure she
should be talking to him or why he had approached her.
She looked about her quickly. Other people were now on
the gallery and the stores were starting to open. Well, at
least he couldn't abduct her without being seen.

"Please, Miss Bonnvivier," he lowered his voice to a
conspiratorial level, "we must talk. You see, I saw you
break into Mr. Braggette's office the other night."

Lin stiffened. "I most certainly did not." Too late she
remembered that Belle had.

"Ah, Miss Bonnvivier, please, I saw you," Marconi repeated, "because I was there to do the same."

Lin remained quiet, not knowing what else to do.

"You see, Mr. Braggette was holding some papers for
me. I, uh, how you say, borrowed some money from him,
but he insist on having the deed to my mama's house until

I pay him back. I pay him, but he no give me back the papers, then when I go to his office to demand them, he is, ah, what is your word?" A frown creased his brow as he tried to think of what he wanted to say, "Ah, murdered. Yes, he was murdered." His fingers played with the brim of his hat and his gaze darted nervously about the gallery. "My mama, she lose her house if I no get those papers back. You see, Mr. Braggette, he no give me receipt."

"Oh, that's terrible. But what does that have to do with me, Mr. Marconi?"

"I saw you take the box from the floor, Miss Bonnvivier, the one Mr. Braggette kept his secret papers in."

"The box," Lin repeated.

"Yes. Please, you give me the paper on my mama's house?"

"Well, of course, if I have it. I'll check. How can I get in touch with you?"

"Oh, that is difficult. I mean, the Italian neighborhood, it is not one for such a lady as yourself. I will come back to the hotel. Perhaps this afternoon?"

"Oh, well, I don't know, I mean . . ."

Before she could say more, he bowed his way toward the stairs, turned, and descended into the crowded lobby.

Lin shrugged and walked into the milliner's. She would have to ask Belle about Mr. Marconi's deed, but that would have to wait until Belle came into town. She went straight to the hat she'd seen the night before, took it from its display rack, and walked toward a clerk who stood behind the counter.

"Go back to your room," a whispered voice ordered.

Lin swung around, startled at the harsh words. A woman stood directly behind her, dressed in an ill-fitting black gown, a black and gray bonnet hiding her hair, and its wide silk ribbon pulled around the woman's chin and tied in a big bow. Her face was screwed into a comical pucker, and she glared at Lin from behind a pair of spectacles propped on the end of her nose.

Lin started to turn away and ignore the woman, but something made her turn back and look again. She took a step closer. "Belle?"

"Shhh, you want to ruin everything?"

Lin immediately straightened and stepped away, trying to stifle a giggle. "But you look like an old lady."

"I borrowed these things from Eugenia's closet. Now go to your room. We have to talk."

"But I want this hat," Lin whispered.

Belle groaned in frustration. "Fine. Pay for it and then go. I'll be there in a minute."

Lin hurried to the counter, pulled several coins from her reticule, and waited while the clerk boxed her hat. When he handed it to her, she turned to signal Belle, but her sister was nowhere in sight. Curious to know what Belle had to tell her, Lin left the shop and hastily walked down the hall to her room.

She had no sooner stepped into the room than a sharp rap sounded on the door.

"Have you learned anything?" Belle swept into the room, yanking the spectacles from her face.

Lin placed the reticule and her new hat on the bed and breathed a sigh of relief. Belle hadn't asked about the opera. That must mean she didn't know. Lin turned toward her and smiled. "Well, I went to see Mageline Toutant. She's very nice."

"That's wonderful, but did you learn anything from her?"

"She wasn't Braggette's business partner or his mistress by choice."

Belle waited, but Lin was silent. "Well?" she demanded finally. "Are you going to tell me what that means?"

"Oh, certainly," Lin said cheerfully. She quickly explained the shady maneuvers that led up to Thomas Braggette's coming into part ownership of Mageline's casino, and how, with the threat of running her out of business, he had forced her to become his mistress.

"I also suspect, though she didn't really accuse him, merely insinuated, that he had the man she loved killed."

Belle shook her head. "The more we find out about Thomas Braggette, the worse he sounds."

"Yes, and Mageline told me that Eugenia had been in love with Edward Mourdaine before her betrothal to Thomas Braggette."

Belle nodded.

"And that she was with child when she married Braggette, but it was Edward's child."

Belle stared in shock. "Edward's?"

Lin nodded.

"Then Trace is . . . ?"

"No, that's what I assumed, but Mageline said no. Evidently Thomas Braggette told Eugenia that the child died, but it didn't."

"So?" Belle nudged. "What happened to it?"

"Thomas gave it away to a band of Gypsies that had camped in the swamps of Shadows Noir."

"Lord," Belle muttered. "But Eugenia doesn't know this?"

Lin shook her head. "Not according to Mageline."

"And that gives us another suspect," Belle said.

"Yes."

Belle sighed. "I doubt there was one person in this city who liked that man."

"Or didn't want to kill him," Lin added.

"What about the mayor, Lin? Did you find out anything about him?"

Lin began to fidget, not at all eager to admit she hadn't succeeded in even talking to the mayor. "Well, I did go to his office."

"And?"

"And I did see him."

"And?" Belle coaxed, holding a tight rein on her impatience.

"Well, he wouldn't listen and he ushered me out. And then I was almost spotted by Trace."

Belle looked shocked. "But you did manage to hide?"

"Yes, in a cleaning closet."

"Well, at least you did better that time than you did last night at the opera."

Lin stared at Belle, flabbergasted.

"Oh, don't go getting all upset and defensive," Belle said. "I handled it."

"What happened?" Lin asked weakly.

"Traxton came back to plantation in an uproar and wanted to know why I'd faked being sick and then went to the opera alone, and then ran away when he called to me."

"Oh dear. What'd you say?"

"I told him I hadn't left the house."

"Oh dear."

"It's all right; no one saw you but him. All you have to do if he brings it up is keep denying it was you."

Lin nodded.

"Okay, anything else?" Belle asked.

"Well, I did go back to Mageline Toutant's."

"Why?" Having a conversation with Lin was a lot like pulling teeth, and no matter how much practice Belle had at it, she always found that whatever she did or said, it always went the same, slow way.

Lin looked rather sheepish. "I started to think and figured she might know something about that waxing seal you found. So I went back to her house and described it to her. I said the seal had been on a letter sent to my father from Mr. Braggette's attorney."

"Oh, that's wonderful," Belle said, sounding exasperated. "Just wonderful. Now you've gone and implicated Papa in the Knights of the Golden Circle."

"I have not. Mageline doesn't know who I really am." A pout shadowed Lin's pretty face. "And anyway, you said they were only interested in making Mexico part of the United States. What's that got to do with Papa? He doesn't care about Mexico. Does he?"

"No, but the Knights might care about the South if this slave issue isn't resolved soon."

"What slave issue?"

Belle groaned. "Honestly, Lin, do you ever pay attention to anything that's going on in the world besides new fashion patterns and who's marrying whom?"

"A lady doesn't engage in talk of politics and such."

"I know, I know," Belle said, waving dismissively, "it's not proper." She began to take off the clothes she'd secretly borrowed from Eugenia's closet. "We have to trade places."

Lin tried to squelch her excitement. She'd be able to see Trace again. "You want me to go back to Shadows Noir?"

"Yes."

Lin frowned at Belle's getup. "In that?"

"No one saw me leave, and I came in a carriage, so I imagine you can wear your own gown. I changed into this stuff on the road so no one would see or recognize me in the hotel. Good thing, too, since you were out gadding about."

"I was not gadding about, as you call it. I was merely purchasing a hat."

"You were supposed to stay in the room."

Lin took the hat from its box and walked to the mirror on the dressing table. She secured the hat to her crown with a long pin, then gave an assessing look as to how it accessorized her white poplin gown with its bodice of embroided green leaves. "What am I supposed to do at Shadows Noir?"

"Nothing. Just stay there, be nice to them, and find out what you can."

"And what are you going to be doing?"

"I want to look into Braggette's dealings with some of the other people mentioned in his papers." For the next half-hour Belle explained to her sister about what she'd read in Eugenia's diary. "We keep accumulating suspects, Lin," she said, "and until we're certain of the murderer, we can't discount any of them."

That reminded Lin of Peter Marconi. She turned back to Belle. "Oh, I met a man in the hotel just before I went into the milliner's shop."

"You talked to a stranger?" Belle asked, shocked.

"Yes." Lin ignored her sister's look of feigned outrage. "He said his name was Peter Marconi and he had borrowed money from Mr. Braggette. But when he paid it back, Braggette didn't return the deed papers on his mother's house, and now he's afraid, with Braggette dead, that his mother's house is in jeopardy. Can you give him the papers? He seems worried."

"Marconi?" Belle's eyes narrowed in suspicion. "There were no papers on a Marconi. Anyway, why would he think you had them if they were Braggette's?"

"Oh, he saw you break into Braggette's office," Lin chuckled. "Said he was there to do the same thing, but you beat him to it."

Belle felt a chill trip over her at the thought that someone had been standing in the shadows, watching her rifle Braggette's office. "What did he look like?"

"Well," Lin pursed her lips while she conjured up an image of Peter Marconi. "Kind of dark, swarthy. Oh, and he said he was a representative of the Italians."

"DeBrassea," Belle said.

"Dee-what?"

Belle ripped Eugenia's bonnet from her head and threw it on the bed. "Lin, I swear, you're going to get us both tossed in jail alongside Father, if you don't get us killed first. How could you talk to that man? And I suppose you told him you'd look for his papers?"

"Well, yes," Lin said slowly.

"Lin, damn it, now he *knows* it was me that broke into Braggette's office."

"He already knew, and he said if he didn't get those papers, they'd take his mother's house away from her."

"There were no loan papers to Mr. DeBrassea in Braggette's box, and—"

"He said his name was Marconi."

"Trust me," Belle snapped, "it's DeBrassea, and he is a suspect, though not a great one. He opposed Braggette politically and made a lot of public speeches about it, especially where it concerned the Italians and how they were treated."

"I don't understand," Lin said. "What did Braggette have to do with the Italians? And why did Mr. DeBrassea lie about his name to me?"

Belle flopped down on the settee. "During his political career, Mr. Braggette seems to have ignored the immigrants, and when he wasn't ignoring them, he was finding ways to cheat them. DeBrassea was trying to expose him and force him to do right by the Italians."

"But how?"

"It seems Braggette's had a lot of influence with the local businessmen about who got hired and who didn't. My suspicion is that if the Italians didn't pay Braggette some kind of bribe or percentage, they didn't get work."

"That's terrible."

"It's also a motive for murder."

Lin turned and picked up her reticule. "That Mr. Marconi, I mean DeBrassea, he was too nice to be a murderer, Belle."

"Even a murderer can be nice, Lin, when he wants to be."

Lin arrived at Shadows Noir and entered the house just as the noonday meal was being served.

"Belle," Eugenia called from the dining room, "we were starting to worry about you. Come join us, please."

"Yes, Belle," Traxton drawled, lazing back on his chair and pinning her with a suspicious gaze as she walked into the room. "Why not tell us what took you out so early this morning?"

"Traxton," Eugenia admonished, throwing him a scolding look, "Belle is our guest, not our prisoner."

He shrugged and threw his mother a mischievous smile. "Just want to make sure our guest is enjoying her stay," he said.

Lin smiled at him. "Why, that's very sweet of you, Traxton. Thank you." She felt a stab of disappointment that Trace was not in the room.

"So, where did you run off to so early?" Traxton persisted. He watched her carefully, sensing immediately that she'd reverted to her other self, the "lady."

Lin slipped into a chair near Eugenia, held out for her by Traynor, and poured herself a glass of iced tea. "Oh, I went for a little drive. Nowhere in particular, really."

A knock on the front door drew everyone's attention, and they remained silent while Zanenne hurried through the room and into the foyer to answer it. A few seconds later the housekeeper reappeared. "Mr. Mourdaine to see you, missus," she said to Eugenia.

Not waiting for an invitation, Edward Mourdaine entered and approached Eugenia.

Lin's gaze darted from Eugenia to Edward as she tried to remember everything Belle had told her about the man. Between Braggette's papers, Eugenia's diary, and Mageline Toutant, they had learned a great deal, and all of it pointed to an excellent motive for Edward wanting Thomas Braggette dead. Lin sipped at her iced tea. Yet, in spite of logic telling her Edward could be the murderer, it was hard to think ill of the man when she knew what Thomas Braggette had been like and with Eugenia staring up at Mourdaine with love in her eyes.

Eugenia stood and allowed Edward to kiss her cheek. She laughed lightly. "Edward, I'd like you to meet our guest. Belle St. Croix, this is an old, and very dear friend of mine, Edward Mourdaine. Edward, Miss Belle St. Croix of Vicksburg."

In one fluidly graceful sweep, Edward bowed, lifted Lin's hand to his lips, kissed it, and released his hold on her. "Mademoiselle St. Croix, it is an honor," he said, his deep voice as smooth as his bow.

He was a tall, slender man, his dark brown hair combed neatly from his face, his features a blend of patrician handsomeness and aristocratic elegance. Lin noted that for a man whose fortunes had gone the way of the wind, or more accurately, the way of Thomas Braggette's pocket, he was well turned out. His brown suit looked of the finest broadcloth, his shirt of a quality silk, and both the diamond stickpin nestled within the pale blue cravat at his neck and the gold and diamond ring upon his finger appeared expensive.

"Ah, *je t'aime*," he said, turning back to Eugenia. "I cannot stay, but as I was passing on my way to Barataria I just had to stop. Can you join me for the opera tomorrow night?"

Eugenia smiled. "Most definitely," she said softly.

Edward brought her hand to his lips. "Good. Then I will call for you tomorrow evening at seven."

"Edward," Eugenia said, "have the authorities questioned you anymore?" A shadow of worry darkened her face.

Edward laughed softly and patted her hand. "No, my dear. As I told them the first time they asked, when your dearly departed husband was being handed his ticket to Hell, I was busily engaged in a game of poker at L'etoile."

"And the others verified that?" Traxton asked, breaking into their conversation.

Edward glanced at Traxton. "I'm sorry, I should not have spoken so harshly of Senator Braggette, but, yes, they have verified my story."

Traxton nodded. "Good."

"Well, my dear, I must go," Edward said, wrapping Eugenia's arm around his and urging her toward the foyer with him.

At that moment, Trace walked into the dining room. "Sorry, guess I'm late for dinner," he said.

Lin felt a surge of joy. Trace was here. She smiled up

at him as he slid into a chair at the head of the table, opposite the end Eugenia occupied. Her body began to tingle with warmth just at his nearness, and she blushed.

"Belle," he said, looking at her for several long seconds, "I was going to invite you to join me on my rounds this morning, but when Zanenne went to your room, you were already gone." He began piling food onto his plate.

"Oh." The word echoed despair. "I would have loved to go." A look of excitement came into her eyes. "Could we do it tomorrow?"

Traxton watched her closely, scowling.

"Of course," Trace said. "My pleasure."

Travis entered the room from the doorway that led to the warming kitchen and immediately stopped in his tracks. He stared at Lin. "How in the hell did you beat me here?"

Lin looked at him blankly. "Pardon me?"

He moved toward the table. "I could have sworn I saw you in town just before I left to come home."

While her heart slammed against her chest in panic, Lin tried to smile complacently. "No, I went out for a little ride, but not to town." She glanced over at Traxton and smiled sweetly. "There must be someone in town who looks an awful lot like me. At least at first glance." She laughed nervously and began to fiddle with the napkin that lay on her lap. "It's rather intriguing, don't you think? Having someone who everyone mistakes for being you?"

"Yes," Traxton answered, though his tone was one of skepticism, "it is."

Twenty

Belle stood on the gallery and looked down at the auctions being conducted in the center of the lobby. They were just about to close down for the night, each auctioneer having only one or two more articles to offer the waning crowd.

"Excusa, Miss Bonnvivier?" Anthony DeBrassea said, tapping her lightly on the shoulder.

Belle turned and, from his swarthy appearance and accent, recognized him instantly. "Mr. DeBrassea," she said. "Or would you rather I call you Mr. Marconi?"

He smiled sheepishly. "You have uncovered my lie."

"Yes, but I don't understand why you offered it." She looked about quickly, confirming once more that the stores had all closed and no one else was about on the gallery. "You knew there would be no papers in Thomas Braggette's box with the name Marconi on them."

"But I needed to know whether you would even look, if you were willing to help me."

"I see." Belle turned back to the railing and looked down into the lobby. "Well, I didn't find any papers for Mr. Marconi, but I did find yours, Mr. DeBrassea. You are not in this country legally. Mr. Braggette threatened to reveal that, didn't he?"

"Yes. I have a, how you say? physical ailment. Your, ah,

officials in New York turned me away, shipped me back to Italy, but . . ."

"But you managed to find a way back."

"Yes, but only to help my people here. My ailment is not, ah, not something others need fear. It is my heart. I have little time, Signorina Bonnvivier, and much to do for my people here. Please, you will help?"

"Perhaps."

"You will give the papers to me?"

"Yes, Mr. DeBrassea, but I want something in exchange."

"I am not a wealthy man, Signorina Bonnvivier."

"I do not want your money, Mr. DeBrassea. You've lived in New Orleans a number of years, correct?"

He nodded. Belle continued, "I need information. Specifically, I want to know what you can tell me about Edward Mourdaine and Harcourt Proschaud. For starters?" she added, and smiled.

He moved to stand beside her, neither looking at the other. "They were both wealthy men at one time, until Thomas Braggette cheated them of their fortunes."

"Cheated them," Belle repeated. "So they hated Braggette?"

"I would assume so."

"Anything else?"

He shrugged. "I have heard they are members of a secret society."

Belle felt a surge of elation. She turned toward him. "The Knights of the Golden Circle?"

"Yes, the Knights." He looked around quickly as if afraid someone might hear and did not continue until satisfied no one lurked close by. "Many powerful men in New Orleans belong to the Knights, Signorina

Bonnvivier, though it is not a good thing for one to talk of."

"And was Braggette a member?"

"I have heard so, yes. Signor Mourdaine, he is a General. Signor Proschaud, I am not sure. Braggette also had a high ranking." He shrugged again. "General, Colonel, I do not know."

"And both Mourdaine and Proschaud wanted revenge against Thomas Braggette?"

"Didn't everyone?" DeBrassea said, more as if it were a matter of fact than a question.

"And what about you, Mr. DeBrassea?" Belle said.

He smiled. "I cannot say that I am sorry he no longer walks this earth, Signorina Bonnvivier. But I did not kill him."

"Do you know who did?" She was playing a dangerous game, she knew, but there was no other way. He could be the killer, or he could be the source of information that would lead her to the killer. Either way, she had to proceed.

DeBrassea shook his head. "No, and even if I did, Signorina Bonnvivier, I would make sure and forget. Signor Braggette was a dangerous man, but whoever killed him is obviously much more dangerous."

Belle looked at him sharply out of the corner of her eye. Was that a subtle threat?

Lin fidgeted with the jacket of her riding habit, straightening it over her breasts, tugging at the cuffed sleeves, and hooking and then unhooking the silk frog at her neck. She wanted to look perfect for her ride with Trace this morning and so had risen early to prepare her toilette. The habit was a soft sky blue percale, the jacket, bolero style, barely reached her waist, which was swathed in a sash of darker blue velvet. Her blouse was a soft ivory silk, and she had arranged her hair in a mound of curls atop her crown. Butterflies fluttered in her stomach. There was no way she would be able to eat breakfast.

Deciding not to wear the small hat that matched her habit, Lin left her bedchamber and proceeded downstairs. The tangy aroma of chicory-laced coffee wafted through the foyer to tease her tastebuds as she descended the stairs.

Trace met her at the door to the dining room. "I've already eaten, Belle, but you go on ahead. I'll wait for you down at the stable."

"Oh, no," Lin said. "I'd really rather not. I mean, I hardly ever eat breakfast anyway." She looped a hand around his offered arm and accompanied him from the house. The last thing she wanted to do was encounter Traxton or Travis in the dining room. She stood silently in the shadows of the stable as Trace and a groom saddled the horses, and she felt a thrill of warmth sweep through her as, taking her hand, Trace helped her mount.

They rode side by side, he astride a huge dapple gray stallion, she mounted sidesaddle atop a delicately beautiful golden mare, the animal's flaxen mane and tail almost the exact color of Lin's own tresses.

Trace led her through fields of cotton, the endless expanse of blooming plants resembling, at first glance, an infinite plane of pristine snow, broken only by the occasional form of a worker edging between the plants. The tobacco fields were nearly ready for harvest, their tall spearlike stalks reaching toward the heavens, the thick abundance of the plants creating an almost impenetrable forest.

She gave no thought to where they were going or how far they had already gone, content merely to ride beside him, and hard-put to keep her mind on the scenery as Trace described the plants and talked of his plans for future crops. Both her mind and body were overwhelmingly conscious of his nearness, of the broad shoulders beneath the white silk shirt whose flowing sleeves masked the muscular, well-honed arms she so longed to feel wrap her in their embrace. A silken tangle of hair, glistening ebony beneath the sunlight, was evident within the plunging vee of his shirt's collar, and steel gray trousers hugged his legs, the fabric molding itself to the sinewy curves and disappearing within the knee-high black boots he wore.

As Trace talked, pointing to a mill house in the distance, Lin studied his profile, her gaze drinking in the high cheekbones that dipped to lean hollows which in turn swooped to embrace a strong jawline. Black brows arched above gray eyes which she knew, without seeing, held both warmth and past pain. She remembered the passage Belle had related to her from Eugenia's diary about Trace. Tears stung her eyes as she felt an almost overwhelming urge to reach out to him, to allow her fingertips to soothe away the lines of anguish that framed his mouth and had left a crease between his brows.

"There's a small grove of pine and oaks over there," Trace said, cutting into Lin's thoughts, "bordering a creek. It's one of my favorite spots." He chuckled softly. "Especially on a hot day. Would you like to stop and rest a moment?"

His eyes met hers, misty gray melding with blue-green, and Lin felt her heart contract.

"Yes," she said, her voice so full of emotion the lone word broke forth as little more than a whisper.

Trace led the way, and within minutes they were beside

the small creek, surrounded by a lush copse of sweet-smelling pine trees, majestically tall oaks, and a profusion of colorful wildflowers.

"Let me help you dismount," Trace said. He encircled her waist with his hands and lifted her easily from the saddle. But, even as her feet touched the earth, he failed to release her. Instead, he drew her into his arms and crushed her petite form against his, her breasts to his chest.

Lin longed to slip her arms around his neck, to embrace him as he embraced her, but her arms were pinioned between their bodies, her hands splayed atop the wall of his chest. She stared mutely up into his eyes, and though she knew the liberties she had already allowed him to take were improper, and the further liberties she knew she would allow were scandalous, she made no effort to move from his arms. She had never before allowed a man to embrace her or kiss her. She had never felt desire or the need to know that a man loved her, but she felt them now with Trace Braggette. She felt them, needed them, and wanted them.

His head lowered toward hers, and for one seemingly eternal moment, his lips hovered a hairsbreadth from hers as if he were unsure of whether to proceed. Then, as her heart slammed madly against her breast, as her breath caught in her throat and her pulse raced, she felt his mouth capture hers, and her world spun madly out of control. For the first time in her life, she felt passion fill her body, felt it sweep through her limbs, invade her blood, and conquer her senses. And also for the first time in her life, nothing else mattered, nothing but this handsome stranger who had haunted her dreams and conquered her every waking thought since the moment she'd met him.

His lips were a touch of flame that cajoled, caressed, and demanded her acquiescence; yet at the same time, it was a strangely gentle kiss, a kiss that offered tenderness and promise.

Lin moaned at the ache of unexpected pleasure that swept through her, simmered within her veins, and coiled with hungry intensity just below her stomach. At the slight parting of her lips, she felt the invading fire of his tongue slip into her mouth, and his kiss turned to a demanding caress, an exotic stroke of intimacy like none she had ever experienced. She pushed herself tighter against him, needing his closeness, her fingers curling around the open collar of his shirt. Each move of his lips on hers, of his tongue within her mouth, of his hands on her back induced a wave of unbelievable pleasure and stirred her passion to ever-increasing heights until soon she was incapable of rational thought. Only Trace and the glorious, mounting ache of pleasure in her body made up her world, her reality.

He was unable to let her go. He knew that with a certainty beyond anything he had ever known. Whatever control Trace may have had over his senses and emotions before, he had lost it the moment his lips covered hers, and with each passing second, as his tongue continued to slowly explore the velvet warmth of her mouth, any shred of reality still left to him dissipated.

For days now she had teased him with just her presence, and he had thought he'd go mad with longing. Not once since Myra's death had a woman affected him so deeply or so quickly.

He was unaware of just when her arms had slipped to encircle his shoulders, of when her fingers had buried themselves within the curls of his hair, or when her kiss, so innocent and soft, had begun to evidence the same hunger as his. Suddenly Trace felt a rending deep within his heart as if the years of barriers, the walls he had erected around his emotions and the ice he had instilled within his veins, were breaking away, crumbling, and dissolving beneath her touch.

His hand moved to cup her breast, and his thumb began to move in a rhythmic circle across the nipple that had already grown taut beneath the thin layers of fabric. He heard the moan that left her throat at his caress and felt a surging of need flash hot within his loins, so intense it nearly sent him to his knees.

Beyond the edge of the grove, in the distant cotton fields, the overseer called out to one of the field workers, his voice echoing on the still morning air. The sound roused Lin from the haze of passion into which Trace had led her. She pulled her lips from his, the fires of passion that had overtaken her body leaving her struggling for breath, her hands trembling. "Please, Trace, no," she whispered, her tone one of deep anguish and regret. "I . . . I can't do this."

Though still standing within the circle of his arms, she turned to look away from him, not wanting him to see the tears that filled her eyes. She knew if she had allowed the kiss to go on, had allowed him to continue with the liberties he had already taken, she would lose complete control of herself. Gladly and wantonly, she would have given herself up to the swirling ache of desire his touch evoked.

Later that day, Lin sat on the settee across from Teresa, who was diligently working at a petit point and cursing at her poor progress.

Eugenia had gone riding with Edward, and the men

were all out and about somewhere, so Lin thought it the perfect opportunity to talk with Teresa.

"Is Jay getting nervous about the wedding, Teresa?" Lin asked. "I've been told men usually do—when the date draws near, that is."

Teresa laughed. "Well, now that you mention it, he has been awfully touchy lately, like something is bothering him, but I guess you're right. He's just nervous about the wedding."

"What's his family like?"

"Oh, Mr. Proschaud is nice enough, and I'm sure he'll win the election, now that my father's gone."

"Election?" Lin echoed, all of her attention suddenly riveted on that one word.

Teresa pricked her finger with the needle, cursed, and then continued. "Oh, I forgot. You live out of the state. Well, anyway, Mr. Proschaud ran for Senator against my father some years ago. Poor man, after that he lost almost everything, most of it to my father."

Lin remained silent, hoping she would continue.

"Well, with all the things Lincoln's doing about the slaves and all, Jay says Mr. Proschaud has been planning to run again. Of course, if the South goes to war against the North, Mr. Proschaud would naturally change his allegiance to the Southern government." Teresa held up her petit point, examined it with a critical eye, and then went back to her stitching and talking. "And Jay tells me his father has received strong backing and support, which I can only assume infuriated my father. But now, with Papa dead, Mr. Proschaud will most likely have no problem."

Lin stared at Teresa, unable to believe what the girl had just told her. Didn't she realize what a solid motive for murder her fiancé's father had? Lin bit her bottom lip. Of course, Teresa had given every indication that she really didn't care who had killed her father, so why could she even think about things like motive?

"Does Mr. Proschaud think there will be a war?" Lin asked.

"Oh, yes, though not a long one. Jay says it will most likely be very short, just long enough to show the Yankees we're not going to be pushed around."

Lin nodded. There obviously hadn't been any papers in Braggette's box about this election or Belle would have mentioned it. Lin stared out the window, her mind churning over the information Teresa had just provided. She had to get to town and tell Belle.

Belle knew exactly what she had to do. She was only glad that Lin had been able to get away from Shadows Noir undetected and bring her the information on Harcourt Proschaud. It might be exactly what they needed to uncover the killer of Thomas Braggette and get their father out of jail. She only hoped Lin could stay out of Trace's arms—and Traxton's suspicions—until they made sure neither of them were involved with the murder. It hadn't done anything for her nerves or her confidence when Lin had blithely informed her that Travis had mentioned, in front of everyone, that he had seen her in town that morning before he'd left. Belle bit her bottom lip. She'd have to more be careful and more watchful.

She looked into the mirror, giving herself one final assessing glance before departing the hotel. Blue and green were her best colors, but the green silk she'd brought was not right for a morning outing, and the pale mint percale was just a tad too plain for what she had to do this morning. She ran a hand over the sky blue chintz hip flounces that overlapped the gown's skirt of ruffles, fluffed the short puffed sleeves, which left most of her arms bare, and straightened the lace-trimmed neckline, scooped just low enough to tantalize but not scandalize.

Belle smiled. She was ready for Harcourt Proschaud. Retrieving a small reticule adorned with royal blue and white beads, Belle left the room. At the desk in the lobby, she breathed a sigh of relief to see that Pierre Loushei was not on duty, and then discreetly asked the young man who was there where the gentlemen of New Orleans usually congregated to talk business.

"Mademoiselle," he said, his tone one of both shock and admonishment, "ladies do not go to the Napoleon House."

Belle sniffed. "I didn't say *I* wanted to go there, I just asked where the men go." Turning on her heel, Belle flounced her way out of the lobby. "Ladies do not go to the Napoleon House," Belle mocked under her breath. "Silly twit." Once out on the banquette she approached the doorman and asked again. He, obviously not so propriety-minded as the desk clerk, pointed toward the western corner of the hotel.

Directly across the street was a sprawling three-story building, dormer windows protruding from its sloped roof attesting to yet another floor and crowned by an octagonal cupola. The windows were all shuttered, and the second-story was lined with a very plain balcony. As she neared, Belle could see, nailed over the Chartres Street entrance, a very small sign that proclaimed the building the Napoleon House. The doors of the coffeehouse were open, as were all of its windows.

Belle approached the door and peered in. A small boy, standing just inside the door, pulled on a rope that was attached to a large punka fan that hung from the ceiling. With each pull the boy gave, the fan swished back and forth, creating a subtle breeze over the patrons who sat at the small round tables scattered around the room.

"Is Harcourt Proschaud here?" she whispered to the boy.

He nodded and pointed to a rather short, portly man on the opposite side of the room who was just exiting through a door that led to St. Louis Street. Belle quickly dropped a coin into the boy's hand and stepped back out onto the banquette. She hurried around the corner, saw Harcourt walking toward her, and deliberately stepped into his path. But Harcourt, obviously more agile than his healthy girth made him appear, sidestepped her, tipped his hat, smiled widely, and continued on his way.

"Damn," Belle said under her breath, and spun to glare after Harcourt. She followed him along the banquette, across the street, and directly back into the St. Louis Hotel where he joined a group of other men gathered before an ongoing auction. Harcourt, however, did not seem interested in the auction, rather he was intent on conversing with one of the men in attendance. He looked absolutely nothing like his son, and Belle could only assume that Jay had inherited his tall, sinewy body from his mother's side of the family. She couldn't tell about his hair. Jay's was dark brown. Harcourt's was silver-gray, as was the bushy mustache that covered his upper lip. His face was ruddy, and his features were not quite coarse, yet not refined either.

Snapping open the silk fan that dangled from her wrist, Belle sauntered slowly and casually across the lobby, squeezed her way past several men, weaved around several more, and finally stepped up beside Harcourt, who took no notice of her.

Piqued, Belle bumped into him. "Oh, pardon me, sir," she drawled, lacing her voice with as much sugar as she could and batting her eyelashes at him seductively. "How clumsy of me." She fluttered the fan just below her chin.

"Au contraire, mademoiselle," Harcourt said, removing his hat and bowing with a wide sweep of his hand. "A young lady possessing beauty such as yours could never be deemed clumsy." As he bent before her, a small balding spot on his crown caught the light.

Belle half-turned toward the auctioneer as he called out for bids and looked coyly over her shoulder at Harcourt. "Well, I'm sorry if I interrupted your bidding, sir. Please, do not let me bother you further."

Harcourt laughed. "Bother? Oh, no. In fact, I was just preparing to leave, but . . ." He paused and then smiled. "I would be most honored if you would consent to join me in the atrium for a glass of refreshment?"

"Oh, that's sounds delicious but . . ." Belle forced a pout, "we really haven't been properly introduced and I'm afraid I . . ."

He clasped her hand in his, lifted it, and pressed his lips to her fingers. "Harcourt Proschaud, mademoiselle, of Cypress Grove Plantation, New Orleans, at your service."

"Ohhh," Belle said, drawing the sound out slowly and inflecting it with delight. "A plantation. Why, I just love plantations." She fluttered the fan and slipped her arm around Harcourt's offered one. "I am Be . . . Lin Bonnvivier, Mr. Proschaud. My daddy has a plantation up in Vicksburg and another near Natchez. Have you ever been to Vicksburg, Mr. Proschaud?"

They walked into the atrium that adjoined the rotunda. Sunlight streamed in through its tall windows and glass roof to gleam brilliantly off the white marble floor. A profusion of lush ferns, blooming azaleas, and dripping fuchsias decorated the room.

"No, my dear, I have never had occasion to visit your fair city, but perhaps now I do."

Belle giggled. "Why, sir; I believe you just might be right."

Travis stood in the center of the rotunda and looked around at the milling crowd. He could have sworn he'd seen her enter the hotel. A frown tugged at his brow. He'd been in the Napoleon House trying to rid himself of a hangover by having another drink when he had looked up and spotted her standing in the doorway. At least he thought he'd spotted her standing in the doorway. By the time he'd managed to rise from his seat, she had left. In the amount of time it had taken him to weave his way past the multitude of tables that crowded the room, normally an easy feat but this morning made difficult by the crash of thunder that went off in his head every time he moved, she'd been gone. The only thing that had led him to the hotel was the fleeting glimpse of a blue skirt, the same color as the gown he thought she'd been wearing, disappearing inside of the hotel's entry.

Travis walked slowly around the rotunda, looked up at the few people strolling the galleries overhead, and poked his head past the open door to the hotel's atrium.

Belle, feeling suddenly as if someone were staring at her, glanced furtively over her shoulder and nearly screamed. Travis was standing in the doorway to the atrium. She scrunched down in her chair, trying her damnedest to make herself as small as she could. Invisible would have been better, but she couldn't manage that. She snapped the fan open again, raised it before her face, and began to flutter it madly.

Twenty-one

Belle turned the key in the door of her hotel room, twisted the knob to make certain it was locked, and, dropping the key into her reticule, proceeded toward the stairs. Just before reaching the landing, she pulled down the apricot tulle veil of her straw hat. No sense taking any unnecessary chances. The close call with Travis two days before had been more than enough, and she'd only escaped being discovered because one of his friends had spotted him and steered him toward the hotel's bar.

"You look lovely today, my dear," Harcourt said as Belle descended the wide staircase toward him. His gaze moved over her apricot silk gown, a simple dress whose hem was trimmed with crocheted ivory edging to match that which trimmed both her cuffs and scooped collar. He took her hand in his and, lifting it to his mouth, pressed his lips upon it. "So, what would you like to do this afternoon?"

"Would you mind terribly if we just ride through the countryside again, Harcourt?" Belle said coquettishly. "I do so love riding in the country with you." They had gone for leisurely afternoon rides in his carriage during the past two afternoons, and it had proven both the easiest way to be with him and the least worrisome about being seen.

"Of course not, *chère*," Harcourt said. He assisted her

into his carriage, a very well-appointed brougham, which had at first surprised Belle, since DeBrassea claimed Braggette hàd forced Harcourt into near financial ruin. Questioning Harcourt, Belle had discovered that several years before Harcourt had allowed Jay to sell off part of the plantation. The younger Proschaud invested the monies into warehouses and had managed to recoup at least part of what his father had lost to Braggette.

As Harcourt directed the carriage horses through the narrow streets of the Quarter, Belle made sure to keep her veil down and a fan fluttering before her face. There were only a few days left now before Henri Sorbonte's trial was scheduled to begin. She couldn't take the risk of being seen in town again by a Braggette and having everything ruined. Not now. Not when her every move was so important.

Once out of the city, Harcourt allowed the horses to saunter casually along the curving path of the River Road, an old trail that followed alongside the wide meandering river. They passed sprawling plantations, small farms, and open pastureland, stopping every once in awhile to climb to the ground and stretch their legs.

"I had a feeling you'd want to take another ride today, Lin," Harcourt said, giving her a sly smile as they walked into the shadows created by the overhanging limbs of a live oak.

"Oh, you did, did you?" Belle laughed, giving him her best flirtatious smile.

"Yes. So I brought a picnic lunch with me today."

"Oh, how wonderful." She clapped her hands together. "Harcourt, you are such a dear." She tapped him on the shoulder with her fan. "And such a rascal, too." He was about to open up to her, she could feel it. In the past two days, she'd asked him several personal questions. At first he'd merely brushed them off or given her a noncommittal answer, but lately he'd been a little more forthright, a little more willing to talk about himself.

"How can I help it when I am around you?" Harcourt said, and joined in her laughter. He hurried back to the carriage and retrieved a basket from beneath the seat. "Here we are," he said, approaching Belle again and tossing a blanket out onto the ground.

A short while later, after enjoying a lunch of fried chicken, sliced tomatoes, crawfish salad, and butter bread, Belle leaned back against the tree's trunk and looked over at Harcourt. He sat directly opposite her on the blanket, his legs crossed Indian style. "Harcourt," she said slowly, "I heard a rather interesting tidbit about you while I was breakfasting at the hotel this morning."

"Eavesdropping, Lin?" Harcourt said, and chuckled, his round stomach shaking with mirth.

"Well, yes, but I couldn't help it." Her lips curved in a sly smile. "I mean, these two gentlemen were sitting at the table next to mine and, well, they were talking in a normal tone and all, and—"

"And you just couldn't help but overhear," Harcourt said teasingly.

"Well, yes." Belle smiled sweetly at him. "So, anyway, one of them said that Senator Braggette, the politician who got killed a few weeks ago . . ." She paused and looked at him, as if questioning whether he knew this.

"Yes?" Harcourt said, both his tone and face having become serious.

"Well, this man said that this Thomas Braggette belonged to something called the Knights of the Golden Circle and—"

"What does that have to do with me?" Harcourt interrupted.

Belle giggled and waved a hand at him. "Well, I was just getting to that, silly. One of the men said that Senator Braggette probably got himself killed because of something he did for the Knights, or . . ." she screwed her face into a thoughtful frown, "or was it something he didn't do?" She shrugged. "Oh, well, whichever. Anyway, then the other man said he knew you and that you were a Knight, too, and maybe you knew why this Braggette man had been killed but weren't telling."

"That's preposterous," Harcourt said, his face turning a brilliant shade of purple. Jumping to his feet, he began to throw the remains of their picnic into the basket. "I think it's time to go, Lin," he said curtly, and held out a hand to help her to her feet.

"Why, Harcourt," Belle said, feigning hurt feelings, "did I say something wrong? I was only telling you what these two men said. I don't believe it, of course."

He hustled her back up into the carriage. "I know, I know," he said. "But rumors like that can have a very unhealthy effect on my business," Harcourt said. "And my career. Imagine, me, a Knight? Ha!"

Belle looked at him out of the corner of her eye as he whipped the horses into motion. He had disclaimed the rumor that he was a Knight. She frowned. But he hadn't disclaimed the implication that he'd had something to do with Thomas Braggette's death.

She also did not neglect to notice how quickly Harcourt wanted to get them back to town. Belle clutched the thin railing and watched the scenery whip by. As they swerved dangerously fast around a curve in the road, a horse and rider suddenly appeared.

Belle screamed and covered her eyes with one hand.

Harcourt slammed a foot down on the brake pedal, pulled back on the reins, and swerved to the right, narrowly missing the rider, who had jerked his horse to a halt.

"Cripes, Harcourt, you heading for a hanging or what?"

The carriage had slid to a stop just a few feet from the horse and rider.

Belle cringed at the familiar voice and realized too late she had neither her veil pulled down or her fan in her hand.

"I . . . I just realized I have to get back to town for a meeting, that's all," Harcourt stammered. He pulled a handkerchief from his pocket and began to mop his brow.

Traxton's eyes moved from Harcourt to the female sitting next to him. "Belle," he said, the word more an accusation than a greeting.

Belle whipped the veil down over her face.

"Sorry, Trax, but you've got the lady confused with someone else, and I'm not going to introduce you because I remember exactly how unscrupulous you always were about another man's—" Harcourt flushed. "I mean, not that Lin and I are . . . I mean, she's not my . . ." Harcourt snapped the reins. "Oh, never mind," he muttered loudly. The carriage jerked into motion.

Traxton stared after them as they sped down the road. Her silver-blond hair had come loose of its ribbon and was flying out behind her like a delicate flaxen shawl whipping in the wind. His eyes narrowed. If that wasn't Belle St. Croix, he'd eat his damned hat.

Belle could feel his eyes boring into her back, but she refused to turn around. That would only confirm for him that it was indeed her sitting next to Harcourt Proschaud. Drat, why did it have to be Traxton they ran into? What was he doing out on this road in the middle of the day anyway? He usually stayed pretty close to the plantation. At least that had been his habit while she'd been there.

She suddenly realized her heart was pounding rapidly. She reached a hand to her cheek. It was warm. And why were her eyes filled with tears? She stiffened her spine. It was merely because she was upset at having run into him, that's all. She would have had the same reaction if it had been any of the Braggettes.

Traxton tossed Rogue's reins over the hitching post and took the shallow steps to the gallery two at a time. He pushed the front door open and walked into the foyer, his wedge-heeled boots creating a hollow echo throughout the large room, the sound accompanied by a musical tinkle as his spurs jangled with each step he took. He didn't have to wear the spurs while at the plantation, he knew, nor the leather chaps or the gun holstered to his hip, but they were comfortable, and he was used to them. So used to them, in fact, that without them he felt sort of unfinished or naked.

Standing in the center of the foyer, legs spread wide, gloved hands resting on his hips and hat pushed back from his forehead, he called out loudly, "Anybody here?"

Lin appeared at the top of the stairs. "Why, Traxton," she exclaimed, putting a hand to her breast, "you fairly frightened me half to death." She began to descend. "I was just on my way downstairs. Whatever is the matter?"

She wore a percale gown of sunshine yellow, its snow white yoke gathered at her neck by a circle of velvet above which rose a short ruche of lace. Her hair was pulled to her crown and arranged in a mound of sausage curls that cascaded down and over her left shoulder.

Traxton stared as if he'd just been confronted by a ghost, and his bottom jaw dropped open, his voice momentarily paralyzed by shock. There was no way she could have beaten him here. Yet here she was. In a different gown, with a different coiffure, and looking refreshed, rested, and not at all nervous.

"Traxton? What's wrong?" Eugenia said, hurrying to the landing. She wore a wrapper, obviously having been awakened from an afternoon nap by Traxton's bellowing. Her eyes were wide with alarm, her tiny hands trembling. She clutched the railing and stared down at him. "What's happened? Is one of your brothers hurt?"

Traxton, overcoming his momentary shock, shook himself and glared at Lin, who was now standing only a few feet from him, her hands entwined before her.

"How in the hell did you get here?" he growled. His eyes flashed the fury he felt at not being able to comprehend what was going on.

Lin looked taken aback. She stared up at him in confusion, but registered in her eyes was also a spark of fear. Traxton saw it immediately and pounced on it. He grabbed her by the shoulders and dragged her close to him.

"Traxton!" Eugenia yelled, startled by her son's action. She hurried down the stairs.

"How in the hell did you get here, Belle?" Traxton snarled again.

"I . . . I came by packet, and then carriage a few days ago."

"I mean now: how did you beat me back to the plantation?"

"Traxton," Eugenia snapped, hurrying up beside him, "whatever are you talking about? Belle hasn't been anywhere."

Traxton ignored his mother and continued to glare down at Lin. "You were with Harcourt just a little while ago. In his carriage. But I rode directly back here, across the fields. So, how in the hell did you beat me?"

Lin felt a sudden swell of panic invade her breast. He'd run into Belle. Oh, good lord, what was she supposed to say? What could she say?

"Belle, what's going on?" Traxton demanded again. He released her abruptly, and she watched in fear as a shadow of suspicion darkened his eyes. "Has your being here, at Shadows Noir, got anything to do with my father's death?"

"Oh, Traxton, for heaven's sake," Eugenia said, "stop being so ridiculous."

Traxton stared at Lin. Fifteen minutes ago he had seen her on the old road that ran alongside the river and which bordered the western boundary of Shadows Noir. It had been her; he'd known that beyond any question. But how she had gotten back to the plantation before him, how she could have changed her gown, styled her hair. . . . His mind whirled with the impossibility of it all. But more than that was the confusion he felt at his own reaction to her. On the road, for those few brief seconds when their eyes had met, he'd felt that same damned spark of attraction she'd ignited within him the first moment they'd met and which had been nagging at him with each encounter since. He'd felt the gnawing ache of desire coil tight within his groin, felt his blood turn to fire, needing her touch to assuage the heat and hunger building within him.

He looked down at her closely, his gaze piercing hers, searching deep, delving further, as if trying to penetrate her soul, to invade her secrets and leave nothing of her unrevealed.

Lin's eyes nervously flitted away from his.

So, why now, he asked himself, when she stood before him, when his hands had held her so close only a moment before, was his blood cold, his passion unstirred? "Look at me, Belle," he demanded, rationalizing that it was remembrance that Trace was in love with her, that his brother wanted to marry her, that had cooled his ardor.

Lin jumped and her gaze jerked back to meet his.

Traxton stared long and hard into her eyes, blue-gray fusing with blue-green, melding, scrutinizing, assessing. "I don't know how you did it," he said, his voice a guttural whisper that sent a chill of alarm racing up her spine, "and I don't know what the hell you're up to, but I'm going to find out."

Spinning on his heel, Traxton stalked past the open front door. Harcourt Proschaud had been both a political and personal enemy of his father's for years. He didn't know what had started their bad feelings toward one another, and frankly he didn't care. And if truth be known, he didn't give a tinker's damn who had killed his father. Whoever it was had probably done the world one hell of a favor. But he had to know if Harcourt was involved. If Belle was involved.

"Whatever is the matter with that boy?" Eugenia murmured.

Lin looked after Traxton, uncertainty swimming in her eyes.

"So what are you two looking so worried about?" Trace said, entering the foyer from the warming kitchen.

Lin turned, both surprised and pleased to see him. Her gaze swept over him quickly, and she saw he was no longer in the worn brown trousers and chambray shirt he had worn when he'd left the house earlier to ride out into the fields. He had changed, his knee-high black boots glistening as richly as newly mined coal. His beige trousers hugged well muscled-legs while a tightly cinched black leather belt emphasized the narrow waist that broadened to a wide, well-honed wall of chest.

"I didn't know you were home," Eugenia said.

"I wasn't. I mean, I just got here a few minutes ago. Zanenne said she hadn't served the noonday meal yet and that Belle was here, so I had her pack a picnic for us." He looked at Belle, his gray eyes caressing hers with their soft gaze. "You will join me, won't you?" he asked softly.

Lin felt a thrill of warmth sweep through her. "I'd love to join you."

Trace glanced at his mother, who was smiling. "You're welcome, too, Mama," he said, though it was evident Trace was nearly holding his breath as he waited for her response.

"No," Eugenia said, and laughed. "You two go ahead. I have a dozen and one things yet to do for the wedding, as well as overseeing the preparation of the bedchambers in the *garçonnière* for some of our expected male guests."

"Oh, did you want me to stay and help?" Lin said. An unconscious frown of disappointment tugged at her brow.

"Of course not," Eugenia said. "Go on now and enjoy yourselves."

"Do you know how many times I've dreamed of holding you like this?" Trace said.

"Not as many as I have," Lin whispered against the lips that were brushing teasingly over hers. She knew she shouldn't have come out alone with him again, shouldn't have let him pull her into his arms again, but she couldn't help herself. Never before had she wanted to kiss a man so desperately, wanted to be held in the cradle of his arms and feel the steely length of his body pressed to hers. Propriety demanded that she pull away from him, that she slap his face for the liberties he was taking with her, but for the first time in her life, Lin did not care about propriety. The only things that mattered were Trace Braggette and his love for her.

His velvet lips descended on hers, a touch of fire that both soothed her hunger and stoked it to new heights. His arms enveloped her, drawing her to him and crushing her breasts against his chest where their heartbeats seemed to meld into one. She felt his hands upon her back, wings of flame that skipped over her skin to leave behind fiery paths that ached to be touched again. His tongue slid between her lips, filled her mouth, and dueled with her own tongue, exploring, tantalizing, and teasing, until Lin felt her senses reel, her world spin on its axis, tilt crazily, plummet out of control.

In what was most likely the greatest effort he had ever exerted, Trace pulled his lips from hers.

Caught in a swirl of passion, Lin looked up at him. Seeing the feelings of her own heart mirrored within his eyes, she felt the breath nearly pull from her lungs and the beat of her heart nearly stop. Whatever happened from this day forth, she would remember him like this always, the dark, lean face that bespoke of both aristocracy and infinite strength, the gray-blue eyes that were at once the color of a clear spring sky and an English fog, and the dimples that were more deep creases carved within each cheek whenever he smiled.

"I want to make love to you, Belle," Trace said. His voice was like a blanket of warmth that wrapped around her.

She was incapable of answering, every muscle languid within his arms, her mind and heart swelling with such happiness she was almost afraid to breathe dare he disappear like a dream.

Holding her within the circle of his arms, Trace looked down at her for a long minute, a minute he knew was only a flash of the eternity he wanted to spend with Belle St. Croix. His eyes drank in her beauty, impressing every curve of her delicate features, every plane and line upon his memory for all time. He let himself nearly drown within the blue-green sea of her eyes, and he brushed a fingertip across one faintly flushed cheek. His body was as hard as a rod of steel, every muscle, every cell responding to her nearness, to her response to his kiss, to the hunger coiled tight and burning within him.

Trace slowly released the buttons at the back of her gown, his eyes never leaving hers. His fingers slipped beneath the fabric and gently, slowly, pulled the fabric away from her. He saw her cheeks flame, but she did not move, did not pull away from him.

Lin watched his head lower and felt his lips brush tenderly across the swollen mound of one breast, revealed above the lacy bodice of her camisole. A moan, unbidden, slipped from her lips and she sagged against him, her legs buckling as a languor invaded them and an ache of pleasure hit her loins.

In spite of the hunger gnawing at his body, a starving sensation that both imperiled his sanity and control, Trace moved slowly. He removed each piece of clothing she wore with infinite tenderness, pausing as each dropped to the ground lest she change her mind and beg him to stop. But Lin made no move to stop him. She couldn't. All her life she had waited for Trace Braggette to love her, and now that he was here her body, her mind, and her heart were his without question, without hesitation, without doubt. Her breasts, bare now, begged for the feel of his hands upon them as the flesh between her legs burned for his touch.

But rather than touch her, than assuage the desperate ache that all but overwhelmed them both, Trace eased away from her and stepped back.

Suddenly embarrassed, Lin's arms raised to cover her breasts.

"No," he said softly, his voice husky with the emotion roiling within him, "don't hide yourself from me. You are too beautiful for that, and I want to see all of you, love all of you." He felt his body tighten further as she dropped her arms to her sides. Trace raised a hand toward her and she placed her smaller one within it. He pulled her toward him again, took both her hands in his and placed them on his chest.

She instinctively knew what he wanted and began to unbutton his shirt, her fingers sliding beneath the white material to move slowly, hesitatingly, over the contours of his shoulders and arms as she pushed the shirt from him. Its ends caught within the belt at his waist, and Lin fumbled with the buckle, her fingers trembling slightly. A thrill coursed through her as, when the belt popped open and broke from his waist, he chuckled softly, the deep sound like a wash of honey over her flesh.

As she worked to release the buttons of his trousers, Trace bent forward, unable to wait any longer to taste the beautiful body displayed so tantalizingly before him. His mouth found a pink nipple. Warm lips enveloped it and pulled it into his mouth while his tongue curled around it to caress the pebbled peak. She felt a hand on her other breast, cupping it, a finger moving rhythmically across its nipple, sending a series of pleasure-filled shudders through her body and bringing a gasp of surprise and delight to her lips. Her hands pushed his trousers to the ground, and Trace stepped from them, kicking them toward his boots, which had been removed earlier.

Lin's arms encircled his neck, and she pressed her naked body to his, feeling his warmth, needing his strength. Trace trapped her mouth with his again, and, his arms around her waist, he urged her down on the blanket.

His hands explored her body, caressed each curve intimately, possessively, branded it his and his alone, forever. She felt his mouth everywhere, his hands everywhere, and trembled with the onslaught of passion he evoked within her, the hunger his touch created. Fear of the unknown was forgotten, thoughts of impropriety and virtue were all but vanquished from her mind. The feelings Trace was bringing to life in her were frightening, yes, but so intoxicating, so delicious, that nothing else mattered, nothing else would ever matter.

She felt his hand slide lightly over one hip, teasingly caress the length of her thigh, then move to the inside, toward that hungry ache that simmered between her legs. His fingers moved through the triangular patch of silver-gold hairs between her thighs, and a jolt of desire, so devastating, so intense, ripped a moan from her lips and brought her body rising to meet his hand, pleading silently with him not to stop the sweet torture, not to deny her whatever it was his touch promised to bring.

Traxton turned Rogue toward the small copse of trees in the distance. He'd been riding for two hours, first hard out, then at an easy lope, usually just the thing to calm him when something had piqued his anger, but this time it hadn't worked. Every cell in his body was still seething with fury. He knew damned well Belle was lying, that she was up to something, but he just didn't know what the hell it was. She was playing up to both he and Trace, playing the lady for his older brother, acting the vixen for him, yet she all but ignored Travis and Traynor. Why, damn it? Why? That was the question that nagged at him. What was she after? And now she was riding with Harcourt Proschaud, and lying about it. Traxton pulled up on the reins and brought Rogue to a slow walk as they approached the shade of a grove.

Whatever Belle's scheme, as far as the Braggettes were concerned, it had only to do with him and Trace. He was confident of that now. But he couldn't ascertain how Harcourt figured into the picture. Traxton pulled a cheroot from his shirt pocket and slipped it into the corner of his mouth, then struck a lucifer against the laced leather edge of his saddle horn. The match burst into flame, and holding it to the tip of the cheroot, he puffed on the rolled tobacco.

Rogue shuffled across the small patch of unplanted ground that separated the copse from a cotton field and into the shadows the thick-growing pine and oaks cast within the small grove.

Could it be as simple as marriage? Traxton wondered. Could that be what she was after? But then why ignore Travis and Traynor? Why not play up to them, too? And again, what did Harcourt have to do with it? She couldn't be interested in him that way. . . . he was old enough to be her father. Traxton inhaled deeply from the cheroot, and as he exhaled and the smoke left his lips, a contemptuous smile drew his lips upward. It wouldn't be the first time a young woman had come visiting Shadows Noir with the intention of procuring a proposal of marriage. When the four brothers had all still lived there, it had been an almost constant occurrence. He sometimes suspected that his mother had even had a hand in arranging the visits. Somehow though, he didn't think his mother had arranged this one.

A noise off to his right interrupted Traxton's musing and brought his attention back to his surroundings. He reined Rogue up short and peered into the sun-hazed shadows of the grove. Another sound, faint and weak but resembling a soft moan, wafted to him upon the otherwise silent afternoon air.

Curious now and worried that an animal might be lying hurt within the copse, Traxton nudged his heels to Rogue's barrel and, laying the reins ever so lightly against the big stallion's neck, urged him in the direction of the sound.

The center of the copse was a small natural clearing, the ground covered with a matting of pine needles and a profusion of colorful wildflowers. To one edge of the clearing a small creek meandered past, its shallow water rippling softly as it moved westward toward the Mississippi, glistening silver beneath the sun.

Rogue's head broke from the shadow of the trees into the sunlight of the clearing. The sound of his hoof settling on a brittle branch startled both Trace and Lin. At the same moment that they, lying together on the blanket, their naked bodies entwined, looked up, Traxton saw them and jerked the horse to a stop. Shocked, he stared openly, his emotions swirling in too many conflicting directions to allow him the power of speech.

Lin seemed the first to recoup at least part of her senses. "Traxton," she muttered, looking at him over Trace's shoulder and instantly realizing the possibly dire consequences of this confrontation.

His dark eyes bore into her, his gaze unwavering.

Embarrassed, even though her body was mostly hidden from his view by that of Trace's, Lin grabbed for her gown.

Trace looked over his shoulder at his brother. "Traxton," he said finally, "I don't—"

Traxton didn't care what Trace had to say, what either of them had to say. Just like Juliette, his mind screamed. Just like Juliette. He yanked on Rogue's reins. The stallion wheeled around abruptly and, feeling Traxton's spurred heels dig into his barrel, lunged for the trees.

Twenty-two

Travis stepped from the dusky interior of L'etoile and out onto the sun-shrouded banquette. His eyelids immediately and instinctively narrowed against the harsh light of the late day sun as he struggled to adjust to the brightness. He tossed a half-smoked cheroot across the open canal that lay between the banquette and the cobblestoned street, and as he idly watched it arc through the air, a carriage moved into his line of vision. His gaze rose to the driver: Harcourt Proschaud.

Travis nodded, lifting a hand to the brim of his hat to acknowledge the woman sitting beside Harcourt. His hand froze in mid-rise. "Belle?" he muttered stupidly, staring at her in disbelief.

Belle snapped the fan up before her thinly veiled face and turned her head away. Damn, damn, damn, she swore silently. Obviously the gods were not on her side this day. First Traxton, and now Travis. She wished she could warn Lin, but there was just no way to do that.

Travis thought about the last time he'd spotted Belle in town, or at least he'd thought it had been her, but she'd denied it and insisted he had mistaken someone else for her. Was this woman the someone else? Because if she was, and she wasn't related to Belle, it was the weirdest thing he'd ever seen. He watched the carriage move on down the street. Well, he wouldn't intrude on Harcourt's time with the lady, but he'd damn sure talk to the man some other time and find out who she was, if for no other reason than to assuage his curiosity.

Lin had never experienced a more uncomfortable dinner in her life. Eugenia and Teresa chattered almost nonstop about wedding arrangements, which was only natural since the event was nearly upon them. Traynor and Trace were engaged in a conversation relating to establishing a partnership in the import business, specifically Trace setting up a warehouse and outlet facility while Traynor brought in the goods from Europe. But neither conversation included Lin, nor interested her. At least not at the moment. Instead she was painfully aware of Traxton practically staring a hole through her. His eyes were dark, hard, and so cold she nearly shivered each time her gaze met his. She knew what he was thinking and wanted desperately to tell him he was wrong, but she couldn't. How could she without revealing the truth?

Though she sensed both would deny it vehemently, Lin felt certain that Traxton cared as deeply for her sister as Belle did for him. But in spite of the anguish she saw etched in his features and shining from within the dark depths of his eyes, she didn't dare tell him that she wasn't Belle. A swell of compassion and regret filled her breast. Farsadoodle, she cursed silently, why did she always allow Belle to get her into these impossible situations?

Lin sighed and began to push the food on her plate with her fork. It wouldn't do any good to try and talk to Traxton anyway. She'd tried, and it had proven impossible. Not only wouldn't he talk to her, he wouldn't even stand still in her company long enough for her to get a complete sentence out of her mouth.

She picked at the food on her dinner plate and glanced at the only other person at the table, Travis. She realized too late it was another mistake. He, too, was staring at her, but instead of anger an intense puzzlement seemed to reflect from his eyes.

Now what? Lin nearly groaned aloud. Why was he staring at her like she was some sort of unexplainable oddity?

"Well, if you'll all excuse me," Lin said finally, pushing away from the table and rising, "I really don't feel very well this evening. I thought I'd retire early."

Trace immediately rose to his feet, a deep frown of concern creasing his forehead. He took her hand in his. "Can I get you anything, Belle? Have something brought up to your room?"

Lin smiled, wanting nothing more than to slip into his arms again. "No, I'm fine, thank you. Just overly tired, I think."

"I'm not surprised," Traxton drawled.

Lin felt Trace's fingers tighten around hers, but she spoke up before he could. "Yes, it has been a long day, hasn't it?" She turned from the table. "Good night, everyone."

Traxton watched her walk from the room. He still didn't have a clue as to what she was up to, but he was more suspicious now that Travis had mentioned seeing her in town several times. Travis's latest sighting had her with Harcourt Proschaud, and just about the same time Traxton had walked into the house to find her there, when only a short time before he, too, had thought he'd seen her with Harcourt.

Of course, Travis could be mistaken, gotten his days mixed up, or the time of day he'd seen her. An easy thing to do when one spent most of his time in a gambling casino sipping on whiskey. But somehow Traxton found that just as hard to believe as the fact that Belle had been seen in two places at the same time. He felt certain that it had been Belle he'd seen in the carriage with Harcourt earlier that day, even though he couldn't figure how she could have gotten back to the plantation so quickly. But how?

He took a long sip of his wine. Well, since Belle seemed so fond of sneaking away from Shadows Noir and then denying it, he'd made a decision. If she wanted to go out tonight, she'd have a little ol' shadow following after her.

Excusing himself from the table, Traxton sauntered up to his room, grabbed a pillow from the bed, and walked out onto the gallery. He looked at the window of Belle's bedchamber. Light shone through the curtains. He moved to a corner of the gallery, opposite the one with the stairs that led to the ground floor. Tossing the pillow down on the ground and propping it up against a massive pillar, Traxton settled down for the night, or however long he'd be there.

Lin paced the room. Should she try and sneak out tonight? She needed to get to Belle as quickly as possible, to tell her what had happened. Oh, Lord, she wasn't looking forward to that. How in heaven's name was she going to tell Belle that she'd allowed herself to be seduced by Trace Braggette? Lin's heart began to thump madly in reaction to her memory of their lovemaking and fear of what Belle would say.

It could wait until morning, she decided. She turned down the lamp that sat on the table next to her bed and snuggled beneath the covers. Maybe a good night's sleep would give her a little more courage.

Traxton saw the light go out in Belle's room and smiled to himself. It wouldn't be much longer now.

Lin glanced toward the window. It was no longer night and not yet dawn. The sun was just barely peeking over the horizon, its brilliant gold light turning the darkness to a shroud of hazy grayish mist. She slipped a rose percale and white lace cape around her shoulders and secured it at her throat. A last assessing glance in the mirror confirmed that she was ready to go, whether she really was or not. The skirt of her gown was of rose-and-white vertical stripes, the bodice was white and a mass of tiny ruffles, her sleeves pagoda style. A sash of dark rose silk encircled her waist. She took a deep breath, more to summon her courage than to fill her lungs, and quietly opened the jib door beneath her window and stepped out on the gallery.

Lin stood still for a long moment, then took a step and immediately stopped, her eyes catching the form of a man hunkered down at the far end of the gallery. Her heart nearly jumped into her throat until, staring intently, she realized it was Traxton.

He'd been watching for her! That was the only explanation. What other reason could there be for him sleeping on the gallery all night? Lin tiptoed quietly to the outside stairs and descended quickly. She avoided walking on the drive, certain that the crunch of oyster shells beneath her shoes would wake someone and alert them to her departure. In the stable she hurriedly bridled one of the horses and made to hook him to the carriage rigging. She suddenly realized that was a bad idea. There was no way that she knew of to leave Shadows Noir in a carriage except down the main drive. She saddled the horse instead, and then another realization hit her. "Oh, double drat," Lin cursed. Why hadn't she worn a riding habit? Now she'd most likely ruin her new dress. Moving a mounting box up beside the horse, Lin lifted her skirts, slipped a foot into the stirrup and hoisted herself onto the animal's back. It took a few minutes of maneuvering to get her legs secured around the horn of the sidesaddle and her petticoats and skirts settled into place.

Horse and rider emerged from the barn into the morning sunlight and turned toward the open pasture rather than the drive. Lin urged the tall bay gelding into a quick trot. Somewhere farther down the pasture they would find a gate or an opening to the road, she felt certain. In the meantime she prayed no one was watching her departure.

She made good time, arriving in town less than half an hour later, though once in the Vieux Carré she managed to get herself momentarily turned around and wasted ten minutes trying to find the hotel. Tying the horse to a hitching rack, she walked purposely through the lobby of the St. Louis, praying that the desk clerk Pierre was off duty that morning so that she would not have to see him.

"Oh, Mademoiselle Bonnvivier," Pierre called out from behind the desk.

Lin cringed, forced a smile to her face, and glanced toward him. "Sorry, Mr. Loushei," she called out, "I really am in a terrible hurry." She made for the stairs.

"But I have a message for you."

"Piddle," Lin muttered under her breath, and hurried toward the desk. She reached out to take the message from Pierre's hand and found he wasn't quite ready to let it go. One long finger snaked out to touch hers as both their hands held the note.

Pierre, oblivious to her annoyance, smiled widely. "I've been wanting to ask you, mademoiselle," he said, his eyes roaming her body hungrily, "if you would care to have lunch with me?"

"No," Lin said, and yanked the note from his hand. She smiled as she turned away. "But thank you."

Dashing up the stairs, Lin went directly to Belle's door and knocked. No one answered. She leaned close to the panel. "Belle?" she called softly. "Belle?"

There was no sound from the other side of the door.

"Piddle." Now what was she going to do? She looked at the note in her hand. It was from Harcourt Proschaud inviting Belle to dine with him that evening. If she'd had a quill and inkwell, she could have written her sister a message on the back of Harcourt's. But she didn't. She slid the paper under the door and hurried back downstairs and out to where she'd left her horse. What to do? What to do? She looked in both directions of the banquette, hoping to see Belle strolling toward the hotel.

Mounting the gelding again, Lin was just about to head back to the plantation when she remembered Teresa's dress was supposed to be ready that morning. If she stopped at the dressmaker's and picked it up, she could use that as her excuse for being away from the house so early. She rode the two blocks to Madame Carpentier's and was just edging her horse up to the hitching post when she heard the tinkling sound of the bell over the dressmaker's door and looked up.

"Oh, heavens," Lin said, jerking the reins around and kicking the horse into motion.

Belle froze on the threshold of the dressmaker's shop and stared at Lin as she rode down the street. What in blazes was she doing here in town? She felt a chill of alarm. Something had happened. That had to be it. Something had gone wrong and Lin had come to warn her. Belle practically flew down the banquette toward the hotel.

"You did what?" Belle said, unable to believe what her sister had just said. She had never believed Lin could shock her, not dear, sweet, prim and proper Lin. But she just had.

"I made love with Trace, but that's not what I—"

"I don't believe this," Belle said. She began to pace the room, her steps hurried. "My sister, my propriety-minded sister made love to a suspected murderer."

"*I* don't suspect him of murder, Belle," Lin interrupted.

Her sister ignored her. "She made love to a suspected murderer." Belle laughed sarcastically. "Of all the men she could have allowed to seduce her, my sister picks a man suspected of murder."

"Belle, damn it, will you shut up and listen to me?"

Startled by Lin's unusual outburst and use of profanity, Belle paused and stared at her. Obviously she'd heard wrong. "What did you say?"

"You heard me," Lin snapped. "Now just be quiet and let me finish."

"There's more?"

"Yes."

"You're heavy with child?"

"Belle."

"Oh, all right. What?"

"Traxton saw us."

"Traxton saw you what?" Belle said.

"He saw Trace and I making love."

"What?" Belle flew across the room to stand in front of Lin, leaving little more than two inches between their faces.

"He saw us making love, and of course he thinks it was you."

Belle felt as if her entire world had just popped and was fizzling into a small puddle of nothingness on the floor. She forced herself to take a deep breath and remain calm. Anyway, what did she care if Traxton saw Lin and Trace making love and thought it was her? He didn't love her, and she certainly didn't have any warm feelings toward him. Well, not sincere ones anyway. Not the kind that last for a lifetime. And this would definitely cool that arrogant spark of lust that was always in his eyes whenever he looked at her. She turned a hard gaze on her sister. "You are crazy, you know that?"

"I'm fine."

"Lin, we haven't proven that Trace didn't kill his father. It's still possible, you know?"

"No, it's not," Lin insisted stubbornly. "He didn't do it, Belle, and that's that."

"You're impossible."

Lin smiled. "Maybe we're more alike than we ever thought."

"*I* would never allow myself to be seduced by a man I suspected of murder."

"But I told you I don't suspect him," Lin said simply.

"You're impossible," Belle repeated.

"There's more."

"More? What else have you done? Promised to marry him?"

"No, but I will if he asks. Traxton is suspicious."

"I guessed he would be. He saw me with Harcourt yesterday afternoon."

"I know. When he got back to the plantation, he wanted to know how I'd beaten him there and what I was doing with Harcourt Proschaud."

"I figured that would happen. What about Travis?"

"What about him?" Lin echoed.

"He saw me with Harcourt, too, just as we were returning to town."

"He didn't say anything."

"Good. Maybe he's convinced he's seeing things."

Lin giggled. "Traxton slept on the gallery outside my room last night. Waiting, I suppose, to see if I snuck out."

"Did he see you leave?"

Lin beamed proudly. "No, he was asleep, but it doesn't matter. If anyone asks, I'll just say I couldn't sleep and went for an early ride." She rose from her seat on the bed. "Well, I'd best get back. I want to ride with Trace this morning."

"If I didn't have this dinner with Harcourt tonight," Belle held up the invitation, "and if it wasn't so damned important, I'd make you stay here."

"Ha, you think you would," Lin said, and laughed lightly as she slipped into the hallway. "Have fun tonight," she called out, just before closing the door.

Belle threw herself upon the bed, crossed her arms over her chest, and glared up at the canopy. "Have fun tonight," she mimicked. Tears suddenly smarted her eyes and she blinked them back. He thought she'd made love to Trace. She clenched one hand into a fist and smashed it down atop the mattress.

Harcourt held both her hands in his. "I had a wonderful time tonight, Lin," he said, "and I know we haven't known each other for very long, but . . ."

She slipped her hands from his. Whatever he was going to ask, she didn't want to hear. And she had the horrible feeling he was also going to try and kiss her good night.

"So did I, Harcourt, and I feel as if I've known you for years." She laughed softly and patted his cheek teasingly with her fingertips. "But now you really must excuse me. I think I had just a tiny bit too much wine with dinner this evening, and it's not agreeing with me."

He looked suddenly crushed, as if it was his fault she didn't feel well. "Oh, Lin, I'm sorry. If I'd known, I would—"

"It's not your fault, silly." She turned and opened the door, then slipped past it and turned back before he could follow her into the room. "Now, you just let me get some rest tonight, and I'll be good as new in the morning."

"All right. Will you be up to the ride we planned tomorrow?"

"Of course." She kissed the tip of her index finger and then touched it to his lips. "Good night." She shut the door before he could say anything further, then leaned back against it. Not until she heard his footsteps retreating down the hall did Belle release her breath. So far so good.

Hurrying to the armoire, she rummaged through the gowns hung there until she found what she sought: the riding habit of gray wool and black velvet trim. Perfect for what she had in mind. Taking off the peach silk gown she'd worn to dinner with Harcourt, she struggled her way into the riding habit, tied her hair back with a ribbon, and, throwing a long black cloak over her shoulders, slipped from the room. Rather than chance being seen by descending the main staircase into the lobby, she slipped down the rear stairs and out onto Rue Royal. It was late, and everything was closed in the Quarter except the casinos. Thankfully Harcourt's town house was only a few blocks away and not in the direction of the casinos, but if she didn't find anything there, she would be forced to find a way to search his plantation house. She hadn't been able to get him to talk about the Knights of the Golden Circle again, but she was convinced that if he wasn't the killer, he at least knew more about Braggette's involvement with the Knights than he'd admitted.

Belle stayed close to the buildings lining the banquette, out of the glow of both the streetlights and the moon, and hurried down the street toward Harcourt's town house. She slipped beneath the shadowed porte-cochere, skirted around the carriage parked there, and paused in the small courtyard that was the surrounded by the house. The windows were all dark and there was no sound. It had been a little over an hour since he'd dropped her at the hotel, more than enough time for him to return to the town house and retire for the night.

Belle moved to the French doors of his study. Earlier that afternoon Harcourt had brought her here on the pretense that he'd forgotten his billfold. She guessed, since he'd been hinting strongly of his desire to marry again, that it had been his way of getting her reaction to his home in the Quarter, and she hadn't disappointed him. She had oohed and ahed over everything, and while he was off supposedly collecting his wallet, she'd raced back to his study and unlocked one of the doors.

She found it easily now. Slipping inside, she quietly closed it behind her. "Thank heaven for moonlight," she murmured, and went directly to Harcourt's desk.

The contents of the first two drawers she opened proved of little value: writing paper, household journals, inkwells, a box of cheroots, and several pairs of spectacles. The third held a large journal. She flipped it open without removing it from the drawer. It was Harcourt's household and plantation expense diary. Opening the fourth drawer, she found a packet of letters bound together by a ribbon. She slipped the top letter from the pack, unfolded it, and held it up, straining in the moonlight to read the writing. But it wasn't that difficult. Imprinted at the top of the paper was the same sign that had been on the waxing seal she'd found in Thomas Braggette's office: the letters *KG,* surrounded by a circle. Excitement bubbled within her breast, and Belle shoved the letter into the pocket of her cloak. She was about to open the fifth drawer of the desk when a movement at the French doors, across the room, drew her eye. Belle watched, breath lodged in her throat, as the door swung open and a tall figure, indistinguishable in silhouette, suddenly filled the space between room and courtyard.

Her heart thumped madly in her breast, the sound roaring in her ears.

"What the hell are you doing here?" Traxton hissed.

A brief flash of relief that he wasn't some unsavory character come to rob or kill the occupants of the Proschaud house was quickly replaced with a surge of anger. "I could ask you the same thing," Belle shot back in a harsh whisper.

He strode into the room, not stopping until he stood before her, little space left between their bodies. "You've tried to play us all for fools, Belle, but the game's over, you hear me? Whatever it is you're up to, it's over. I don't know who you really are, or what—"

"Shhh." Belle looked toward the door. "Will you please lower your voice?"

One black brow arched insolently. "What's the matter, Belle? Afraid I'll wake your lover?"

"Lover?" she spat, taken back.

"What's your game, Belle? Robbery?" He looked at the open drawers of the desk, the cloak that draped her shoulders. "I don't really care about Proschaud, Belle, but I do care about my brother. Trace may have fallen for your little act like a fool, but that's as far as you're going with it. And where I'm concerned—"

Belle glanced at the door again, petrified that he was going to wake Harcourt.

Traxton suddenly stopped talking. Why the hell was he being so pious? Hadn't he been wanting to bed her since the moment he'd laid eyes on her? He'd held off because of Trace, but that didn't matter anymore. She'd not only given her body to his brother, she'd also evidently given it to Harcourt Proschaud. Why else would she be in his house after midnight? The old man was probably up in his room right now lolling in an exhausted sleep. Traxton wanted her more than anything he'd ever wanted in his life, and he knew she wanted him, too.

"Ah, what the hell," Traxton mumbled. He grabbed Belle by the shoulders and dragged her up against his chest, crushing her breasts to his wall of strength, curling steel-strong fingers around her arms in an unbreakable clasp.

Her attention having been riveted on the door, his grasp of her came as a shock. Belle jerked her head around to face him, ready to demand that he release her. His mouth came down on hers, trapping her lips. As she tried to utter a protest, his tongue plunged into her mouth.

Belle felt fire instantly erupt within her body, fill her veins, her muscles, every fiber and tissue. His lips ravaged hers, moved to caress her neck and nuzzle her ear as his hands roamed her back, her waist, her shoulders. His caresses robbed her of her senses while his kisses stripped her of her inhibitions and chased away the doubts and suspicions that still lingered deep in her mind. Nothing in life had prepared her for Traxton Braggette, and nothing in life would ever allow her to forget him.

"I knew you were a vixen, Belle," Traxton muttered

against her flesh as his lips moved from hers and traveled down the length of her neck. "Hot, passionate, wanting. Just like I thought." His mouth covered hers again, his tongue assaulting hers, and then moving away again. "I knew you weren't the untouched little magnolia you pretend to be for Trace." His lips trailed along the line of her jaw, leaving burning flesh behind wherever they touched.

His words broke the spell that had bewitched her the moment his mouth had captured hers. She pushed against him, twisting to break his hold on her. Instead she felt Traxton's embrace deepen, pull her ever closer to him, until her body was pressed so tightly to his length that even through the jacket of her habit, through her petticoats and skirt, she could feel every line and muscle of his body.

His lips moved over hers again, and the fire returned.

No. She beat a fist against his shoulder. She wasn't what he thought she was. She wasn't like that. Tears stung the back of her eyes. She didn't want him to kiss her anymore, yet she did. She didn't want him to touch her anymore, but she was helpless to resist him, to deny the fire, the need, the passion he aroused within her.

As his hands roamed her back, his tongue moved through the sweet recesses of her mouth, inciting, teasing a hunger within her she was powerless to deny any longer. And, as a dove spreads its wing and quietly soars into flight, resistance slipped away from her, unnoticed and unhampered. This was where she belonged, where she wanted to be: in his arms, being held by him, loved by him. She was only dimly aware of his hands sliding the cloak from her shoulders, pushing the jacket of her habit from her arms, and releasing the small hook that held her skirt secure about her waist.

Her own arms slipped around his neck. Her fingers

buried themselves within the thick curls of his hair, slid over the corded muscles of his shoulders, down the length of his arms and back again, exploring, filling her with a sense of wonder at his strength.

His body raged with fiery need, a need intensified by her caresses. Without taking his lips from hers, and holding her secure to him with one arm, Traxton kicked her clothes aside, shrugged out of his own shirt, and dropped his gun and holster to the cushion of a nearby chair. As his lips moved over the curve of her neck, he released the buttons of his trousers and, his mouth returning to claim hers, lowered them both to the floor.

Not until she lay beneath him did Traxton pull his lips away and look down at her. She was beautiful, he had never denied that, but now the sight of her beneath him, her silver-gold hair spread out on the floor, the rosy peaks of her breasts touching his chest, was a breathtaking sight. He wanted to look further, to drink in every inch of her beauty, but he couldn't. His hunger for her was too great; it pounded within his body, screaming for release.

With a growl deep in his throat, Traxton covered her mouth with his in a kiss that was a savage ravishment of her senses. His hands moved over her, exploring every inch, sliding over every curve, and dipping into every hollow.

His touch inflamed her and turned her into exactly what he thought she was, a woman filled with passion, a woman who craved a man's touch. And Belle kissed him back, her hunger matching his, her naked body arching toward him, pleading with him to give her more of the pleasure his caresses had instilled within her. Her arms held him to her, her legs entwined with his, and her tongue boldly moved inside his mouth, dueling with his, unconsciously stoking the same fire, the same burning need in him as he had awakened in her.

She felt his hand slip over the taut plane of her stomach, his fingers move amid the curls of blond hair that grew at the apex of her thighs, and then slide between her legs. Startled at the jolt of raw desire that wracked her body at the intimate touch of his fingertips to the small nub of hidden flesh, Belle stiffened within his arms, frightened by the unknown, hesitant to allow his continued theft of her innocence, his trespass of the most private parts of her body, of her very spirit.

"Let me love you, Belle," Traxton whispered in her ear. His lips caressed the shell-like curve of flesh as he spoke, and his hot breath sent a tingle of shivers rippling over her skin. He pressed his lips to her neck. "Let me love you like you were meant to be loved, Belle. Like you want to be loved."

Belle relaxed beneath him, turning her face to receive his kiss. Yes, her heart cried, yes, she wanted to be loved by him. There was no longer any will left in her to deny that.

His finger delved inside of her, plunging into the cavern of femininity that no other man had been allowed to touch, that was the core of her being, of her passion. He felt her writhe beneath him, her arms tighten around his neck, and deepened his kiss as his leg urged her to open for him. "God, you're so beautiful," Traxton whispered harshly.

She felt him rise slightly above her, his back arched, and then something was between her legs, something hot and hard, pushing at her, moving inside her.

"No, don't," Traxton said, his voice thick with emotion as he felt her stiffen again. "Don't be afraid, Belle. I only want to love you." His hand caressed the curve of her cheek as his lips spread kisses across her face. "Don't deny me, Belle. Don't deny yourself."

Traxton felt the veil of her virginity like a barricade, and paused. Not a barricade, his mind reminded him through a haze of passion, a last chance to draw back, to escape the reins that could bind him to her if he continued.

Belle, following his example, moved her tongue into his mouth, and a new wave of passion, of hunger, swept over him. He wanted her, damn it, and she wanted him. Rising slightly on his knees, he thrust into her, pushing his body against hers. He felt her stiffen with the shot of pain that his action had caused and heard the soft, startled shriek that escaped her throat and was swallowed by his mouth on hers. His hands moved over her breasts, his lips ravished her mouth, as he began a steady, rhythmic movement with his hips, entering her slowly, pulling back, and entering again. He felt the passion rise in her again, mounting with each thrust of his hips, each caress of his hands, each touch of his fingers to her breasts.

She began to move beneath him, her body gripped in the throes of desire. Her hands moved over his length, sliding across the long curve of his back, following the trail of his spine to the round, hard swells of his buttocks. He felt her fingers knead his flesh, felt her body arch against his, asking, pleading, begging for more, and giving him all she had to give.

"More, Traxton," she whispered against his shoulder, nipping at it with her teeth. Belle threw her head to each side, writhing as the gnawing ache of pleasure within her grew fiercer, hungrier. "More," she cried softly. Tears slipped from the corners of her eyes at the joy she felt at their merging. "Love me more, Traxton."

Her words tore at him, intensified his passion a hundredfold, twisted the knot of desire that was coiled hard and tight in his groin, and caused him to nearly spill his seed within her at that very moment. He had made love to dozens of women, from ladies to whores; he'd paid for it and he'd gotten it free, but never had he found it as sweet, as touching, as passionate as he was finding it with Belle.

Slipping his arms around her, Traxton rolled them both over, pulled Belle on top of him, and held her there. He slowly sat up, holding her hips to him and pulled one taut nipple into his mouth, laving the pink pebbled nipple with his tongue.

Belle threw her head back and a moan of pleasure escaped her lips as her arms wrapped around his neck and she clung to him. She felt his hands push her up, then pull her down, the hard, turgid rod that he'd plunged inside of her filling her with even more pleasure, more hunger until she thought she'd go mad with it. Their movements became more rapid, more frenzied, as their need of each other grew.

Suddenly Belle felt an explosion of satisfaction deep inside her. It rolled outward, like the swells of a tidal wave, washing over her, moving through each limb with searing heat, filling her with a tempest of pleasure that routed her senses and left the imprint of his touch, of his love, on her soul forever.

She clutched at him, her hands pressing into his flesh, her body arcing up to his, a low moan of ecstasy spilling from her throat. Feeling her release, Traxton ripped away the last reins of control he held over his own passion, letting it sweep over him, engulf him, and pull him into its fathomless abyss of pleasure.

For long moments afterward Traxton held her in his arms, both his mind and body spent. Reality came back to him slowly, and as the realization of just who it was he held in his arms and what they had just done pierced the fog of passion, Traxton began to feel a hardening of his heart and a self-loathing that overshadowed everything else.

Twenty-three

Traxton looked down at Belle, whose head was snuggled against the curve of his shoulder. This was the woman his brother was in love with, the woman Trace most likely wanted to marry, and Traxton had just seduced her. He closed his eyes tightly. God, how could he have done that? Then his eyes shot open and his features hardened further as a frown pulled at his brow. He'd seen Trace making love to her. He'd seen it, damn it, yet here, tonight, she'd been a virgin. How was that possible? How?

But even as he silently asked the question, she shifted position, her thigh moved against him, and he felt himself begin to grow hard again as his hunger flamed anew. A wave of self-revulsion washed over him. With more discipline than he'd ever exerted, Traxton's fingers encircled her waist, and sitting up, he set her away from him.

Belle, still languishing in the hazy aura of passion, looked startled.

Traxton got quickly to his feet and began to pull on his clothes with jerking, angry movements. She watched him, dazed and confused, as he rebuckled the leather chaps over the trousers he had yanked on. He grabbed his shirt from the floor and shoved his arms into it. "Get dressed," he ordered, his voice a harsh whisper that was a cold slap to her senses.

Belle stared stupidly up at him. She'd just made love to Traxton Braggette! The realization exploded in her brain and left her trembling. She looked around the moonlit room as she hurriedly pulled on her clothes, trying to ignore the flush of heat warming her face. They'd made love, and in Harcourt Proschaud's study.

"No better than a goddamn dog in heat," Traxton muttered to himself. He should have known better, should have controlled himself and stepped right back out that damned door the moment he'd encountered her, but no, he'd let his pants rule his brains.

Belle, heard Traxton's angry words and assumed they were directed at her. "Dog in heat?" she spat. "Why, you arrogant bastard." Her hand flew out and connected with his cheek.

Traxton saw a split second of stars swirl through his brain before the world righted itself again.

"How dare you," Belle riled. "How dare you, you bastard. You take advantage of me and then . . . and then . . ."

"Take advantage of you?" Traxton ground out. "Who the hell took advantage of whom? Seems to me like you were more than willing to be seduced." He laughed nastily. "Hell, lady, you were doing half the seducing."

"Ohhh." Belle raised her hand again, but Traxton grabbed it in mid-swing.

"Not again you don't."

Footsteps on the stairs in the hallway suddenly brought them both up short. Belle jerked around to look at the door, her blouse still unbuttoned, her fingers on the hook of her skirt. Traxton grabbed his hat.

"I think it's time for me to go," he said, and moved toward the window. "Say good night to Harcourt for me."

"Say it yourself," Belle said, grabbing both her jacket and cloak, and pushing past him.

The door behind them flew open, crashing against the wall with a resounding thud. "Who the hell's in here?" Harcourt called out. Not waiting for a reply, and seeing shadows before the French doors, Harcourt pulled the trigger of his gun, and an explosion of gunfire filled the room.

Belle screamed as a bullet tore through her flesh.

With a writhing, moaning Belle in his arms, Traxton hurried through the Square, making sure to stay off the moonlit path and well within the shadows. He looked over his shoulder with every other step. Just before reaching the eastern boundary of the Square, he spotted a small marble bench set beneath a live oak. Moving to it, Traxton settled Belle onto the cool stone. Blood from her wound covered his hand as he pulled it away.

"Jesus, Belle," he said, "you're really hurt."

A wince of pain tightened her features as he pushed her skirt away, causing her leg to move. "Will you be careful?" she grumbled.

He ripped a ruffle from her petticoat, wrapped it around her thigh, and tied it tightly, causing her again to groan. "Damn it, Traxton, what are you, a sadist?"

He stood up. "So where'd you leave your horse?"

Wide-eyed and suddenly speechless, Belle stared up at him.

"Well?"

"I don't remember."

"You don't remember where you left your horse?" he repeated derisively.

"No, I don't remember," she mimicked.

"Didn't we have the same conversation once before?"
She threw him a nasty look.

Traxton whistled loudly, and Belle heard Rogue's hoofs
upon the cobbled walkway outside the Square. "Then I
guess we'll just have to ride double again," Traxton said.

Belle nearly groaned. Obviously her punishment for
the night was not over, but what was she going to do this
time? If he took her all the way back to Shadows Noir,
which obviously was what he intended to do, and if she
were lucky enough, again, to get away from him before
they encountered Lin, she couldn't walk back to town
with a bullet in her leg. She'd probably bleed to death
before she was halfway there. Then she remembered the
alligator on the road and shuddered. Did alligators attack
at the scent of blood?

Without warning, Traxton swept her into his arms and
carried her, cradled to his chest, back across the Square.
Pausing beside Rogue, he set her down on the ground but
held her tight against his side as she balanced on one foot.

"Can you stand while I mount?" he asked.

Belle nodded, though she wasn't at all sure she wouldn't
collapse on the ground in a heap the moment his solid
length left her side.

"Here, hold onto this." He placed her hands on the
front seam of his stirrup strap, and she curled her fingers
around it.

Once mounted, Traxton bent down, slipped his hands
under her arms, and pulled her up and onto his lap.

"We're . . . we're going to ride like this?" Belle asked.
She turned to look at him and found his face only a hairsbreadth from her own.

"I thought you'd be more comfortable this way. And
bleed less."

Belle turned away and for the next hour tried to ignore

both Traxton and her throbbing leg. She was successful at neither. Her leg felt as if it had been stung by a hundred angry bees, and her body was doing its damnedest not to let her forget just how much it had enjoyed its fusing with Traxton's. She held herself stiffly, trying not to lean into him, but it didn't help.

"Relax," Traxton muttered, as if able to read her thoughts, or at least feel her intentions. "It'll take us at least another hour to get home at this rate."

"Why don't we go faster?" Belle asked, keeping her face turned from his.

"Because I don't feel like trying to explain how you bled to death because I wanted to get home sooner, that's why."

Belle's eyelids were getting heavy. Several times she'd caught herself just before nodding off. She felt so weak. So tired.

Traxton knew the moment she fell asleep. Her body seemed to finally release the tight hold it had on itself and sag against him, her curves fitting naturally into the hollows of his body as it sought support and strength. He could still smell the scent of violets on her hair and skin, teasing his senses mercilessly as he struggled to maintain control over his faculties.

"Love me, Traxton," Belle murmured against his chest.

Traxton nearly swallowed his tongue as he fought the surge of desire her words had brought. He looked down sharply, saw that she was asleep, and cursed silently. As soon as Teresa's wedding was over, he was leaving New Orleans. He'd head back to Texas, away from Belle St Croix, away from the temptation that would always exist if he was anywhere near her. He may have seduced her and he'd hate himself for the rest of his life for doing it but he wasn't about to take her away from Trace. He couldn't do that.

An hour later he reined Rogue to a halt before the entry steps of Shadows Noir. "Mama," he called loudly. "Mama."

Every light on the second floor seemed to flame to life at once.

Lin scrambled from bed and rushed out onto the gallery, instinct telling her something was wrong. She leaned over the railing and nearly gasped. "Belle," she muttered.

Waking as Traxton pulled her from the saddle and yelled, Belle looked quickly up toward Lin's room and met her sister's startled gaze. She smiled weakly.

Racing back into her room, Lin threw a heavy cloak around her shoulders, grabbed a gown, her shoes, and a hat, and returned to the gallery, intent on taking the outside stairs to the ground as soon as everyone else reentered the house. She peeked over the gallery railing again. But this time she wasn't about to walk to town. Once had been enough. No, this time she would take Traxton's horse and just hope the animal could wander back to the plantation on its own when she was through with him.

Traxton carried Belle into the parlor and set her on a settee. "She's been hurt," he said by way of explanation as everyone gathered around.

Eugenia immediately took charge, ordering Teresa and Traynor to get hot water and bandages, sending Travis to the pantry for liniment, and ordering Trace, who was reluctant to leave Belle's side, to get bandages.

"What happened, Traxton?" Eugenia demanded, once Trace was out of the room.

He shrugged. "I think her horse threw her. I came across her on the road when I was coming home."

Eugenia pulled Belle's skirt back. "Looks more like gunshot to me."

"Someone did shoot at me," Belle said quickly, taking up the story Traxton had begun to weave. "A highwayman. He wanted my reticule, but I wouldn't give it to him. I kicked my horse to get away, and he shot me." She lowered her gaze, afraid Eugenia would be able to see the lie in her eyes. "I fell off the horse then, and I guess I fainted because I don't really remember anything else."

Eugenia looked at her sharply, then glanced at Traxton but said no more.

Belle managed to sleep the next day away, waking only to take a few bites of food, a sip or two of water, and a spoonful of laudanum. Her dreams were filled with Traxton, the way his lips had felt pressed to hers, the sensations his hands on her naked body had aroused within her, the pinnacle of ecstasy to which he had taken her. When awake she could deny she had any true feelings for him, could curse herself for being a fool, for allowing him the liberties no man other than a husband had the right to take. But when she closed her eyes, when sleep lulled her into that velvety cocoon of warmth and fantasy, he was always there waiting for her, and she could deny him nothing.

The next morning Eugenia came to her room just after Zanenne had brought coffee and biscuits. "Are you up to coming downstairs today, Belle? We'll miss you at the wedding if you don't, but if you don't feel up to it . . ."

Belle's eyes widened. "The wedding's today?"

Eugenia nodded.

"But what happened to yesterday?"

"You slept through it. The doctor said you might."

Belle closed her eyes. A day. She had lost a whole day. And what had happened to Lin? Was she all right?

"Belle, are you all right, dear?" Eugenia said. "Should I call the doctor? He's here, you know, for the wedding."

"Oh, no," Belle said, "I'm all right. Just let me get myself ready." With those words, Belle struggled her way out of the bed. The room instantly turned to a blur and she reached out to grab for the bedpost.

"Are you all right?" Eugenia asked in concern.

"Oh, I'll be fine. I just need to wait for the room to stop spinning around," Belle responded with a weak laugh.

"Oh dear, it must be the effects of the laudanum the doctor gave you." Eugenia moved forward to take Belle's arm and lead her back to the bed. "Rest here awhile. You can come down to the wedding later."

After seeing Belle comfortably settled, Eugenia turned to leave the room. "Now, you must excuse me. I've still got a hundred and one things to do and barely enough time left to do a half-dozen." She left the room, and Belle dropped her head back on the pillow.

Her eyes had been closed several minutes when she heard footsteps. She looked up to see Traxton standing in the open doorway. "Oh damn," she muttered.

"Tsk-tsk, is that anyway to talk to the man who carried you, wounded, to safety?"

"I wouldn't have been wounded if it hadn't been for you," Belle said sharply.

"Me?" Traxton feigned a look of innocence.

"Yes, you. I wasn't the one who raised my voice and woke Harcourt up. And I wasn't the one who pushed you out of the way to get to the window first." She turned her head away. "Some gentleman."

"Well, I didn't expect you to flee since you were his guest. But I wasn't."

"I wasn't his guest."

"Then what were you doing there?" He stared at her long and hard, and Belle suddenly realized she'd just done exactly what she was always accusing Lin of doing: talking without thinking. "I . . . I left my reticule there and went back to get it. Harcourt was asleep, so I let myself in and . . ." She suddenly remembered the letter she'd taken from Harcourt's desk, which she'd hidden in the pocket of her cloak.

"And you just thought you'd ransack his study while you were there," Traxton sneered.

Belle bolted upright and winced at the abrupt movement. "I was not ransacking his study."

"Uh-huh."

"Anyway, what were *you* doing there?" she asked pointedly, suddenly realizing his eyes weren't on her face but on her breasts, which were clearly evident beneath the thin veil of her batiste gown. Belle grabbed at the coverlet and pulled it up before her.

His devilish smile drooped into a slant of disappointment, but when his gaze met hers, there was still a spark of mischief in their depths. "I thought we were a little past that," he said, dropping his gaze to her breasts again.

Belle felt her cheeks flame. "You're right, we are," she said seductively. She let the coverlet fall back to her lap, then grabbed the sugar bowl that sat on her breakfast tray and threw it at Traxton.

The china bowl smashed against the doorjamb and shattered. The lid, however, slashed across Traxton's cheekbone. The shock of the blow, rather than the blow itself, stunned him and pushed him back a step. His hand flew to his cheek as a thin rivulet of blood snaked its way down his cheek. Fire blazed in his eyes. "Why you little . . ." He took a threatening step toward her.

"Don't you dare come near me, Traxton, or I'll scream," Belle threatened. "And I'll hit you again." She hurriedly picked up the creamer.

Muttering a string of curses, Traxton spun around and stalked from the room.

Belle lay back down and closed her eyes. She drifted in and out of sleep for the next several hours. Unable to rest any longer, she finally sat up and swung her legs over the side of the bed. Pain thudded through her. "Oh, drat," she groaned. This was going to be more difficult than she thought.

As she hobbled to the armoire, the sounds of music and gaiety reached her. The ceremony must be over, she reasoned, removing from the wardrobe an emerald moire gown trimmed with ivory lace.

A half-hour later, with much cursing from the pain, she stood dressed. As she was about to leave the room, she remembered the letter she had stolen from Harcourt. Limping back to the armoire, she pulled out her cloak and found the missive.

Her gaze moved first to the emblem at the top of the page. The emblem of the Knights. Her eyes swept rapidly over the flourish of writing that covered less than half the page. The note was neither addressed nor signed, and merely stated that there was a meeting that very day at the "usual place." The last line indicated a vote would be taken to replace "TB."

So, Belle thought, DeBrassea was right. Harcourt was a member of the Knights. A galvanizing realization hit her. Harcourt! As father of the groom, he was most likely downstairs at that very moment. There was no way she could possibly leave her room now. He only knew her as Lin Bonnvivier. "Double drat," she muttered.

She sat down. As the minutes passed, the room grew

stuffy with the afternoon heat. "Maybe if I just stand on the gallery for a bit to catch a breeze," she mused aloud, "Harcourt won't see me."

Poking her head out the jib door, she looked to both sides. The coast was clear. As she stepped onto the gallery, she took a deep breath of fresh air. "Heaven," she murmured.

In the distance on the lawn, several guests strolled in their finery. Belle stood enjoying the scene. Soon she should probably get back inside, she told herself. She wouldn't want to be recognized by—

A creak on the gallery stairs had her head whipping around. A man stood at the end of the aisle smiling at her. Joshua! The name fairly screamed from her mind. Belle clung to the railing, her legs feeling weak. "Joshua," she called, "we must talk."

"But of course, cousin." He strolled toward her, then gave her a peck on the cheek. "I didn't expect to see you here. This really is a pleasure. I mean, weddings are usually such tedious affairs, it is good to have someone—"

"Joshua, will you please shut up and listen to me?" Belle said.

Joshua Kindall looked slightly startled at her command. With a brush of a hand through his sandy blond hair and a fluttering of the other over the wide collar of his brown lapel, he stared at her.

"Joshua," she said abruptly, "you don't know me."

"Well, of course I do, silly," he said and laughed. "You're my second cousin, on my mother's side, Belinda Sorbonte. Or are you Melinda?' "

"No, Joshua, you don't know me," Belle repeated, not bothering to edify him. "Papa's in jail." She looked around furtively to make certain they were still alone. "For killing Senator Braggette."

"Well, I know that. I guess that's why I was so surprised to see you here and all."

"But he didn't do it, Joshua. Someone else did, and I'm going to prove it."

"So, why are you at the Braggettes' plantation?"

"Because I suspect they may be involved."

"Oh, cousin, really," Joshua scoffed. "Did you actually tell them that?"

"Of course not, silly. I told them my name is Belle St. Croix, and I got the invitation from Helene."

"Helene's not here? Oh, dear, I so wanted to see her."

"Will you pay attention to me, Joshua?" Belle squelched an urge to grab him by the lapels. "This is important. If they knew I was Belle Sorbonte, they'd make me leave, and then I wouldn't be able to find out anything and get Papa out of jail."

"Well, you shouldn't be doing this, you know," Joshua said, shaking his head piously. "I doubt your papa would approve."

"Joshua, all I want you to do is pretend you don't know me. That's all. And don't say a word about Lin or Papa or anything. Now can you do that?"

His thin lips pursed in a haughty curve. "Well, of course I can do that, for heaven's sake. What do you think I am, a silly twit?"

Belle didn't think she should answer that, so she remained silent and merely looked at him.

"Oh, all right. I don't know you. I don't know Lin, and I don't know your father. In fact, I don't know anything. How's that?"

"Perfect." Turning, she began to limp her way back into her room, but after taking only several steps she paused and looked back at her cousin. "Joshua, do you know anything about the Knights of the Golden Circle?"

"Are they like the Knights of the Round Table?" Joshua asked.

"Never mind." She whirled back and hobbled into her bedchamber.

With a deep frown cutting into his otherwise lineless forehead, Joshua pulled a folded piece of paper from his breast pocket, unfolded it, and stared at the writing. *Meeting tonight. Usual place. Vote needed to replace TB.*

Twenty-four

"Who is it?" Lin called hesitantly. She stared at the door as if trying to see through it, twisting her hands nervously. It was five o'clock on the day of the Braggette-Proschaud wedding.

"Hotel steward, Mademoiselle Bonnvivier," a voice called back.

She hadn't rung for a steward. Puzzled, Lin opened the door a crack. "Yes?"

The steward held a silver tray toward her. "Message, mademoiselle."

Lying on the tray's gleaming surface was a card. Lin picked it up and read the signature scrawled in flourishing script across the paper. Harcourt Proschaud. She felt her heart accelerate. Harcourt Proschaud. Lin looked at the steward, praying this didn't mean what she thought it meant. "He's here?" she said, her voice little more than a surprised squeak.

"Yes, mademoiselle. Monsieur Proschaud is waiting in the lobby and requests your company. Shall I tell him you will come down?"

Come down? Lin felt a spurt of hysteria. Come down? She fought to control the panic erupting within her. What was she supposed to do? She couldn't go downstairs. This was Belle's affair. Belle had been handling Harcourt Pro-

schaud. How would Lin recognize him? She hadn't the
faintest idea what the man looked like. And what would
she say to him? "Oh, dear," she muttered.

"Mademoiselle?"

Lin stared stupidly at the steward. She wanted to decline, to refuse Harcourt Proschaud her company, but she
knew she couldn't do that. There was nothing else to do
but accept. "Oh, ah, yes. Tell Mr. Proschaud I shall come
down, ah, in a few minutes."

She slammed the door and leaned her forehead against
its panel. What was she doing? He'd know immediately
she wasn't Belle. By some slip of the tongue, she'd fail in
her impersonation of her sister. She pushed away from the
door and went to the dressing table. Why hadn't she asked
more questions about what conversations had taken place
between her sister and Harcourt Proschaud? Why hadn't
she insisted that Belle tell her everything? Lin sighed.
Why hadn't she just refused to go along with this ridiculous scheme? She looked into the mirror of the dressing
table. It was too late to chastise herself for allowing Belle
to lure her into yet another intrigue. There was nothing
else to do now but go downstairs and hope that Harcourt
approached her before she walked past him.

After tucking a few ends of hair back into the ribbon at
her nape and straightening the gigot sleeves of the yellow-
and-white checked gingham day gown she'd slipped on
that morning, Lin left her room and proceeded downstairs. She descended the wide staircase slowly, her gaze
darting over the thinning crowd that had been gathered
around the auction blocks in the rotunda. Lin fought to
suppress her panic at the multitude of male faces. Good
heavens, there must be more than a seventy-five men
standing about the rotunda area alone. She let her eyes
move over the people who milled about the lobby near the

front desk. What if she walked right past him? What if he were watching her at this very moment and realized she didn't know who he was?

"Belle, my dear," Harcourt said, moving to stand at the bottom of the stairs as she descended. "You look lovely as always."

She stared at him. Silver thinning hair, a slight flush to his complexion, bushy mustache, muttonchop sideburns, and a stomach that had obviously, over the years, been stuffed with too much good food and drink. But, Lin mused, it was still evident when one looked close, that before age, tragedy, and hardship had been etched on his features, Harcourt Proschaud had been a handsome man. And he dressed well: his formal suit was cut to complement his generous girth rather than accentuate it.

"I know you weren't expecting me this afternoon," Harcourt said, "what with the wedding and all," he smiled and his puffy cheeks became puffier, "but I've been thinking and, well, I just had to leave Shadows Noir and come talk to you about something very important."

"Talk?" Lin repeated, and stared at him while her mind buzzed in panic. Of course she had expected to talk, but only lightly, and of nothing of importance. What would he want to talk to Belle about that could be important? Had she discussed the Knights with him?

"Yes. My carriage is right outside. Do you have time for a short ride? Perhaps just out to the Oaks and back?"

"Ride?" Lin looked down at him, feeling much like a mouse caught in a trap. Belle would go. She knew Belle would go. She'd been trying to get information from Harcourt Proschaud, and this could prove the opportunity, so there really was no choice. Even as she felt a sinking sensation in the pit of her stomach, she forced a smile to her lips. "Well, yes, Harcourt, of course I'll go. But only a short ride."

She had no idea where "the Oaks" were and could only hope he was being truthful in saying a short ride. But to make sure, she decided to use a ploy of her own. "I've . . ." she touched a hand to her temple and let her eyelids flutter close for a second, "I've had a touch of headache all day, Harcourt, and have decided to retire early this evening."

Harcourt beamed. "I understand, my dear, but perhaps the fresh air will do you good." He took her hand and settled it snugly in the crook of his arm, then led her through the lobby.

Fresh air? Lin thought immediately of the open sewage canals in the Quarter and nearly laughed. They would have to travel miles outside of the city if they wanted fresh air, and she wasn't about to go any great distance with Harcourt Proschaud if she could help it. The longer she was in his company, the more chance there was that he would begin to suspect that she wasn't Belle.

True to his word they didn't travel far from the Quarter. Ten minutes after leaving the hotel, Harcourt ordered his driver to stop the carriage. They were on a dirt road that wound its way through a large tract of undeveloped land, though the city was still within sight. The ground was covered with a thick mat of wild grass and shaded by several tall live oaks that spotted the landscape.

Lin felt suddenly more uncomfortable than ever. What was he going to say that was so important? Her mind nearly quivered with anticipation. When Harcourt turned toward her and placed a proprietary arm around her shoulders, she felt her stomach churn with both fright and nausea.

"My dear, I must tell you, these past few days with

you, well," his free hand groped to hold hers, "they've just been the best I've had in a long time, Belle."

Lin smiled. "Well, I'm glad, Harcourt."

"And I don't want them to end."

Lin felt the smile freeze on her face. What was he saying? Oh, please, dear Lord, don't let him be saying what it sounded like he was saying. She felt his overly warm moist fingers twine around hers, and revulsion washed over her. Lin struggled against the temptation to jerk her hand from his. How did Belle always get her into these messes?

Before she knew what he'd intended, Harcourt leaned forward and brushed his lips over hers, a featherlight kiss intended to kindle a flame of passion within her, but which did exactly the opposite. The arm he'd wrapped around Lin's shoulders suddenly contracted, pulling her toward him and holding her tightly pressed to his round form.

"I want you to marry me, Belle," Harcourt said. His mouth moved to press against her neck as she turned her head away. "I want you to be my wife."

Marry him? Lin would have screamed if she hadn't been too busy fighting the queasiness that had swept over her when Harcourt's lips had touched hers. It was now threatening to engulf her.

"Say yes, Belle," Harcourt urged, and crushed her against him. "Please say yes. I never thought I'd want to marry again, but since meeting you . . . oh, Belle, please marry me."

"No," Lin finally blurted. She pushed against his shoulders and tried to pull her way out of his embrace.

His arms tightened around her and held her in place, refusing to allow her escape. "Oh, please, Belle. I'll make you happy, I promise," Harcourt pleaded, desperation lacing his tone. "I'll give you anything, take you anywhere you want to go."

Lin felt compassion for him, and more than a little guilt. "Harcourt, you're a very nice man, but . . ." Lin turned slightly and was startled when his lips came down on hers. Compassion, pity, and guilt were instantly replaced with anger and repugnance. She jerked away from the wet mouth whose touch sent a shudder of distaste snaking up her spine. "Harcourt, stop." She put all of her strength behind one solid push and broke the embrace.

"You'll marry me?" he said hopefully.

"No."

"You won't marry me?" He stared at her in disbelief.

"No." Lin edged across the seat, away from him, and busied herself straightening her skirt and tucking in a few loose curls of hair. For the moment, her mind seething in outrage at his lack of propriety, she completely forgot that she was supposed to be Belle, that Belle had been playing up to Harcourt, and that she should have been doing the same.

Harcourt stood and stiffly climbed from the carriage. "Edgar, take Miss Bonnvivier back to the hotel," he ordered curtly.

The sharp words jerked Lin back to reality and swept her indignation and anger away. Oh, now she'd really done it.

"Sir?" the driver said, clearly surprised.

"Harcourt, wait, we can—"

"Take Miss Bonnvivier back to the hotel," Harcourt repeated to the driver, ignoring Lin completely. "Now, be off with you, Edgar."

Lin jerked around to stare at Harcourt just as the carriage driver snapped his whip over the horses' rumps and the carriage rolled into motion. Oh, goodness, what had she done? Belle would be angry. She had to find a way to appease him somehow. "Harcourt, I . . ."

But he had already stormed away.

"Oh, piddle," Lin mumbled, and flopped back in her seat. "Now Belle will really be mad."

Once back at the hotel, Lin tried to put the episode with Harcourt Proschaud from her mind, but it seemed that the more she tried to vanquish it from her thoughts, the more it worried her. By mid-evening she had worked herself into a complete and utter dither, and knew there was no recourse but to try and contact Belle and explain what had happened. She grimaced at the prospect, but it had to be done. Anyway, she did want to make certain that Belle was all right.

Since she had no idea how she was going to get to Belle, Lin dressed in a riding habit of gray barege, its fitted jacket offering her warmth against the night air, its skirt allowing her to forego a hoop, and its color enabling her to blend with the darkness, if that should prove necessary. At the hotel entry, the doorman looked at her curiously when she requested a carriage, but he eventually acceded to her wish.

Twenty-five minutes later the carriage neared the entry gate of Shadows Noir.

Lin leaned forward toward the driver, who was little more than a bulky shadow on the seat before her. "Stop here, please."

He pulled back on the reins and the carriage stopped.

Lin handed him a five-dollar gold piece and climbed from the carriage. Once on the ground she turned to receive her change for the fare. She was met instead by a faceful of dust as the driver snapped the reins and the carriage moved on down the road.

"Well, I never!" Lin sputtered, and glared after him.

Brushing herself off, she began to walk down the drive toward the house, careful to stay toward the side of the road and in the shadows. The moon hung low in the sky, a thousand stars dotted the vast blackness, and the silence was broken only by the occasional hooting of an owl.

Suddenly a faint rustling met her ears, followed instantly by the soft whinny of a horse. Lin scurried behind a live oak and flattened herself against the tree's massive trunk. She hardly dared to breathe as she prayed that whoever was approaching hadn't seen her.

"Quiet boy," the figure whispered, leaning over and stroking the horse's neck.

The horse nickered.

"That's good. Just a little farther and we'll be out of here."

Recognizing the voice, Lin peered around the tree trunk, puzzled. Teresa and Jay had just been married this afternoon. So why was the bridegroom sneaking off, alone, on their wedding night?

Once Jay was out of sight, Lin turned and continued her way toward the house. She put the question of Jay's seemingly stealthy departure from her mind. There were too many other things to worry about. Like how she was going to get to Belle once she neared the house. As it came into sight, she stopped again and stared at the second story. The jib windows to Traxton's bedchamber were open.

Lin nearly groaned. She couldn't chance going up the side stairs and passing his room with the doors open, but there was no other way to get to Belle's room. "Piddle, piddle, piddle," Lin muttered, stamping her foot on the soft, grass-covered earth. She couldn't exactly go through the front door. Or even the rear for that matter. So how was she supposed to get up there?

She stared at the lighted window of Belle's room and then her gaze dropped to the jasmine-covered trellis that reached from the ground to the second-story gallery, just opposite Belle's windows. "Oh, no," Lin groaned, "I can't climb that thing." She shook her head. "No. It's too ridiculous to even think about, let alone consider." She looked back at Traxton's open windows and a long sigh left her lips. There really was no other choice.

Lin tiptoed up to the vine-covered lattice, wrapped her fingers around one of the horizontal beams, slipped a foot into another, and began her ascent. The small thorns of the vine pricked at her flesh through the soft kid gloves she'd worn and tore at the skirt of her dress, bringing her to a precarious halt midway up her climb as she tried to free the fabric and nearly lost her handhold on the trellis. Almost to the top and beginning to feel a swell of self-confidence, she heard the wood crack and felt it give beneath her weight. A shriek burst from her lips as she dangled in midair, saved from a fall only by the death grip her hands had on the latticework above her.

She heard the front door of the house open, followed by the soft shuffle of footsteps on the gallery below. "What the hell was that?" a deep voice asked.

Lin closed her eyes, clung to the trellis, and said a prayer.

There was the sound of more footsteps. "Did you hear a woman scream?" Lin thought she recognized Traynor's voice

"Yeah. We'd better make a search and find out what's going on," the first voice answered.

Lin pushed herself up, caught the railing of the gallery, and scrambled over it. Not waiting to catch her breath, she darted on tiptoe toward the open jib window of Belle's room.

"What in blazes?" Belle whirled around. Lin whipped the drapes closed behind her. "What are you doing here?"

"Harcourt proposed," Lin gasped, trying to talk and catch her breath at the same time.

"What?"

"Harcourt Proschaud," Lin whispered. "He asked me—you—to marry him."

Belle laughed softly. "Well, I hope you told him you—I—needed time to think about it."

"I told him no, and he got mad."

"Well, what'd you go and do that for, Lin? You knew I was trying to butter him up."

"Well, you certainly did that. He was an old lech. The man practically turned into an octopus."

Belle limped toward the bed and sat down.

"Oh, your injury!" Lin said, suddenly reminded of their hasty exchange of roles two days before. "What happened?"

"Harcourt shot me."

"He did *what?*" Lin exclaimed, her mouth agape.

"Ssssh." Belle glanced toward the window. "Keep your voice down."

"So what happened?" Lin whispered.

"I went back to Harcourt's town house after he dropped me at the hotel and . . ." Memory of Traxton making love to her on the floor of Harcourt's study suddenly made Belle's blood simmer and gave her cheeks a rosy hue. She forced the memory away. "I haven't been able to get him to talk much about the Knights, not at all, in fact, so I thought I'd see what I could find in his papers. I broke into his desk, and while I was leaving, he came in and shot me."

"But he just asked me—you—to marry him."

"It was dark. He didn't know it was me."

Lin remained silent for a moment, digesting what Belle had said, but the conversation was arousing more questions in her mind than it was answering. "But Traxton brought you to the plantation. How did that happen? Did he find you wounded on the street?"

"No. He was at Harcourt's, too."

Lin threw up her hands and walked toward the settee. "I don't understand. You were both at Harcourt's?"

"Belle, are you all right?" Trace's voice came through the drawn draperies only a split second before he did.

Lin dived behind the settee and huddled in a ball on the floor, her eyes scrunched closed, her lips tightly pressed together, the breath she had just taken caught in her lungs. She said a quick prayer, promising God that if He got her through this one, she'd be good from now on, regardless of what schemes Belle tried to drag her into. Oh yes, and, of course, if He let her have Trace. She pulled her legs in tighter to her body.

Trace drew Belle from the bed and into his arms, crushing her against his tall length. "Are you all right?" he asked, his deep voice threaded with concern.

"Yes, I'm fine," Belle answered. "Why? Is something wrong?"

He exhaled slowly, as if in relief, then hugged her to him and brushed his lips lightly over hers. "We heard someone scream earlier and made a search thinking there might be an intruder, but we found no one. Then I thought perhaps you had fallen, because of your leg, I mean."

Belle smiled. "I'm fine, really," she said, purposely forcing her voice to be soft and lilting, like she figured Lin's would be if Trace were embracing her.

He pressed his mouth to hers, his tongue slipping between her lips.

Rather than close her eyes, Belle watched him as he

kissed her, unable to prevent the slight wrinkling of her nose at the intimate touch of his mouth on hers. His lips slid to the curve of her neck.

"Sleep tight, beautiful," Trace whispered. He released her and, touching his lips lightly to hers again, stepped back onto the gallery and strode toward the outside stairs.

Lin made to rise. How could Belle kiss Trace like that? It wasn't right. Lin had never tried to steal one of Belle's beaux, and here Belle was simpering up at Trace like she was in love with him. For the first time in her life, Lin felt like throttling Belle. Outrage coursed through her veins. She pushed to her feet.

"Very touching," Traxton said.

Lin hastily slumped back down on the floor, then chanced a peek around one side of the settee.

Traxton leaned against the jamb of the door to the hallway. "But, Belle, don't you think you ought to just give it up now and tell him about us?"

Belle glared at him. "There is no *us.*"

"Oh?" He smiled lazily. "Then I was just imagining what happened between us at Proschaud's house, is that it?"

Happened between them? Lin scooted to the opposite end of the settee and chanced another peek, this time toward her sister.

"Traxton, I'm tired," Belle said, settling back down on the bed. "Could we discuss this in the morning?"

"There's nothing to discuss, Belle. I mean, I agree, there is no *us* in any kind of permanent way, regardless of what happened."

What happened? Lin's curiosity fairly screamed.

"But," he smiled slyly, "there is an us *now*. So, tell Trace there's nothing between you two. He wants a wife,

Belle. A good wife. One who loves him. And you obviously don't."

But I do, Lin wanted to shout. She felt tears sting the back of her eyes. She wanted to yell at Traxton that he was wrong, that she loved Trace with all her heart, but she forced herself to remain scrunched on the floor.

"Stop the games, Belle," Traxton drawled. "Whatever their purpose, forget it, and stop them. Now." With that he wheeled around and disappeared.

Lin rose to her feet the minute she heard the door close. "How could you?" she demanded, whirling on Belle.

"It just happened," Belle said, thinking Lin had figured out from her conversation with Traxton that she'd stupidly allowed the man to have his way with her. "I didn't mean for it to happen."

Lin felt a surge of temper like none she'd ever experienced. "You did, too, Belle, don't lie. I saw. You let him take you into his arms and kiss you, and you kissed him back. Even though you know how I feel about him. How could you do that? How could you?"

Belle laughed to cover her relief. "Lin, will you listen to yourself? For heaven's sake, Trace wasn't kissing me, he was kissing you, silly. Or at least he thought he was."

"Oh."

"And I was only trying to respond to him the way I thought you would, so he'd know you cared about him."

"Oh. Then I guess I should say thank you," Lin said, feeling abashed.

"You're welcome. Now, come sit over here with me; we need to—"

"So what happened between you and Traxton?"

"Nothing."

Lin smiled slyly. "It didn't sound like nothing to me."

"The man just has an ego the size of a horse, that's all.

Nothing happened. Now," she patted the bed, "come sit down and let's discuss this Harcourt business."

Lin sat on the bed. "I'm sorry, Belle. I didn't mean to ruin things, but he was so," she shuddered, "repugnant. When he kissed me, I couldn't help it. I just cringed inside."

"It's all right. I can fix it if I have to." She pulled open the drawer of the night table near the bed and removed the note she'd stolen from Harcourt. "Close the window, would you?"

Belle waited while Lin complied, then unfolded the note. "Look at this."

Lin took the piece of paper and quickly read it. "It has the same insignia on it as that waxing seal you took from Braggette's office."

"Right. Knights of the Golden Circle," Belle said. "Obviously Harcourt is also a member, in spite of his denial. And I suspect, from what Anthony DeBrassea has to say, that Eugenia's friend, Edward Mourdaine, is also a member."

Lin put the paper down on the bed. "But it really doesn't tell us anything, Belle. I mean, so what if they're members of that club? It doesn't prove they killed Braggette or that the Knights even had anything to do with the murder."

"I know that, Lin, but the Knights have a reputation for sabotage, and with the Southern states seceding from the Union, I can't help but believe there's going to be a war. If that happens, I'm sure the Knights will be involved. Remember, most of their members, so I understand, are Southerners, and what better way to insure that Thomas Braggette did not serve in a Southern cabinet if the South goes to war, than to be permanently rid of him?"

"But that's so drastic."

"Yes, but possible. Obviously the rumors that Harcourt had a strong backing for office have some basis in truth. My guess is there were quite a few powerful people around who did not want to see Thomas Braggette in office if the time comes to form a Southern government."

"But we're not at war yet, Belle, and we might not go to war at all."

"True, but the possibility that we will is a strong one. Especially if Lincoln doesn't order his troops out of Fort Sumter. We have to consider that the Knights had something to do with Braggette's murder, Lin, unless you'd rather we go back to concentrating primarily on Trace and Traxton." Belle expected a curt refusal from Lin, but instead her sister remained quiet, her eyes averted. "What is it, Lin? What's wrong?"

Lin sighed. "Well, I haven't had a chance to tell you before now, but the same day you were shot, I did a little snooping around while everyone was out riding."

"And?" Belle prodded.

A tear slipped from the corner of Lin's eye. "And I found this." She pulled a folded piece of paper, much like the one Belle had discovered in Harcourt's desk, from the pocket of her skirt and handed it to Belle.

Meeting two days hence. Urgent you attend. Usual place and time. Need vote on replacing TB.

Belle gasped and looked at her sister. "Where'd you find this?"

"In the desk downstairs." Lin straightened her shoulders and blinked away her tears.

"In Trace's study?"

Lin nodded. "But everyone uses that desk, Belle, not just Trace."

"You're right. It could belong to any of them." She looked back at Lin. "Or all of them."

Twenty-five

"I want you to stay here tonight," Belle said.

Lin nodded, more than happy to comply. Returning to town on foot at night was not something she wanted to do again. "I'll see what I can find out here tomorrow and come into town the next day."

"No, I'm staying here too, at least for tonight," Belle said. "Papa's trial date is getting too close, and we haven't come up with anything that will help. We're going to search Thomas Braggette's bedchamber tonight, and his plantation office, too."

"What?" Lin nearly shrieked. She glanced quickly at the door and dropped her voice to a whisper. "Are you crazy? Everyone's here. We'll get caught."

"Not if we're careful. Anyway, we'll split up. You take his bedchamber, and I'll go down to the office. That way, if either of us gets caught, we won't be together, so they'll only see one of us."

"And what do I say if someone finds me in his bedchamber?"

Belle chuckled. "That you were looking for a good book to read."

"Oh, Belle, honestly," Lin moaned, and shook her head. "I must be touched in the head to let you talk me into things like this."

"Here, change into a nightgown like mine, then lie
down and get some rest. We'll wait until we know everyone is asleep, then we'll start."

Lin hated snooping. She hated it even more when she
had to do it by moonlight in a room with which she was
unfamiliar. She especially hated doing it in Thomas Braggette's bedchamber, with Trace Braggette sleeping right
down the hall. At least she hoped he was sleeping. And,
of course, that was not mentioning Traxton, Traynor,
Travis, Teresa, and Eugenia being nearby.

The man's writing desk offered nothing. Neither did his
dressing table, the drawer of his shaving stand, his night-
stand, the bookcase, the armoire, or the etagere. Lin
looked around. Where else should she look? She slipped
her hands beneath the mattress as far as she could, felt his
pillows, looked under the throw rug and behind the pic-
tures on the wall. Vases and jars were either empty, or
held what they were supposed to hold—creams, spices,
tobacco. There were no notes tucked into his shoes, nothing in the pockets of his suits, nothing crammed between
furniture and walls. "I give up," she said finally, wiping
perspiration from her forehead. Then her gaze fell on the
armoire again and its scalloped top. Dragging a chair to
the front of the huge wardrobe, Lin climbed onto the
chair, reached over the edge and began to feel along its
flat roof. Her fingers immediately felt something smooth
and hard. She lifted it toward her and felt a burst of joy.
It was a journal, a small, bound, leather journal.

Excited at her find, Lin scrambled to step down from
the chair. Her foot caught on the ruffle of her nightgown,
and suddenly she was falling backward. She made a lung-
ing grab for the doorknob of the armoire. Her shoulder hit

the paneled door, made a loud thud, and the chair flew from under her and directly into the dressing table.

Lin cringed at the loud crash that seemed to reverberate through the room.

"Oh, God," she muttered, and scurried to her feet. She crammed the journal into the pocket of her robe and made a mad dash for the door. Maybe, just maybe, she could get back to her own room before anyone came in to shoot her as an intruder. She swung open the door to the hall.

"And just what are you doing now, may I ask?" Traxton demanded, standing in the doorway and blocking her path. He held his gun in one hand and wore nothing but a pair of trousers. Moonlight from the window across the room fell on him, turning his bare chest into a wall of bronze muscle, his hair to a field of glistening ebony curls.

Lin stared at him, her mind frozen in a state of utter panic.

A sardonic grin pulled at the corners of his mouth and a gleam of deviltry sparked his eyes as he rested a bent arm against the doorjamb and leaned toward her. "Belle, my sweet," he drawled, his voice a deep roll of black velvet, "if you don't tell me what the hell you were doing in there, I'm going to do to you now exactly what I did to you at the Proschaud house."

"I . . . I was . . ." Lin didn't know what to say. What had he done to Belle at the Proschaud house? And what possible excuse could she offer as to what she was doing in his father's room? She came to get a book? Lin nearly groaned.

"Yes?" he said, drawing the word out slowly. He tucked the gun into the waist of his trousers.

Lin swallowed hard. "I, ah, I thought I heard a noise,

and, ah, I came in here to make sure no one was breaking in and, ah, I thought I heard someone on the gallery . . ."

"The only noise I heard, Belle, my sweet, was you." His arm dropped from the doorjamb and slipped quickly around her waist. He dragged her up against him, her breasts crushed against his bare, hot chest. "I've been thinking about you, Belle," he said, his voice seductive and low. "In fact, try as I might, I can't seem to get you out of my mind." His head swooped down, and he pressed his lips to the curve of her neck. "Were you thinking about me, too, Belle?" Traxton's other hand moved to cover Lin's breast, and she gasped in shock. "Maybe looking for my room?"

"No, Traxton, please don't," Lin pleaded, pushing against his shoulders.

Traxton chuckled softly as his lips pressed a trail of kisses down the column of her neck and his fingers began to undo her robe. "It's too late to be coy, Belle," he said. "And I'm not in the mood for games. But I am in the mood for you."

Belle tiptoed stealthily around the corner of the staircase landing. Hearing Traxton's voice, she stopped dead. She flattened herself instantly against the wall and hardly dared to breathe. What in blazes was he doing? Then she heard Lin's frantic plea for Traxton to stop. Stop? Belle's mind screamed. Stop what? Hugging the wall, she crept closer. Traxton's next words told her all she needed to know. *In the mood for you.* Oh, Lord. Memory of his naked body lying atop hers, the feel of his hot flesh, so sensuously smooth, so muscle-hard, danced through her mind and ignited a knot of need deep within her.

She pushed the memory away and ignored the gnawing ache his words had aroused. This was not the time.

"Traxton, please," Lin pleaded.

Belle moved up behind him. She had to do something. But what? She looked about frantically, her gaze searching the dimly lit hallway for some type of aid, something. . . . Her fingers closed around a very thin, very delicately shaped brass candleholder.

"Belle, I can't help it. I want you again," Traxton said, his deep voice soft and low, conveying seduction and just a hint of anger.

Belle moved up behind him just as his lips captured Lin's. She raised the candlestick and, putting all her force behind her swinging arm, brought it down toward his head.

But the same sense of survival that had gotten him through childhood as Thomas Braggette's son and kept him alive during his first years on the Indian-infested plains of Texas warned him that peril was imminent.

He heard the soft rustle of fabric behind him, felt the cool brush of air as something was lifted in the air, and smelled the faint fragrance of violets. Traxton jerked his mouth from Lin's. One hand moved toward the gun in his waistband, and he began to turn.

The candleholder grazed the side of his head and then smashed into his collarbone, his movement having deflected the full force of the blow.

Stunned, Traxton reeled, staggered, and grabbed for the doorjamb, clutching it as everything around him spun crazily and his knees threatened to buckle.

"Run," Belle whispered to Lin.

Snapping his eyes closed, Traxton sucked in a deep breath and leaned into the wall as blackness threatened to overtake him. "Son of a bitch," he muttered, holding the side of his head with one hand, the other still gripped tight to the jamb.

Lin bolted around him and dashed into her bedchamber, but Belle hesitated. She stared at the thin stream of blood trickling from Traxton's dark hair onto his hand and arm. She knew she should run, should get away from him before he regained enough sense to turn on her, to figure out what had just happened, but she couldn't. What if she'd really hurt him? Anxiety filled her breast and nearly stopped her heart.

The hand that had been gripping the doorjamb suddenly reached out, fast as lightning, and curled around her wrist.

Belle tried to jerk away and lost her grip on the candleholder. It fell to the floor, making a dull thud as it landed on the thick carpet that covered the floor of the hallway.

"What the . . ." Traxton shook his head, trying to clear it of the stars still swirling around in his brain. "What the hell did you just do?" he asked, his voice ragged.

Belle's mind raced to find an answer that would seem plausible, and found none. There was only one way to make him forget his question. Slipping her arms around his neck and pressing her body suggestively against his, Belle said, "I'm sorry, Traxton." Her lips trailed a path of kisses across his bare chest. "Are you all right?" Her hands slipped within the curls of hair at his nape and moved sensuously, slowly, through the dark strands. "I didn't mean to do that. Honest, I didn't. I thought you were an intruder." She pressed her lips to the hollow at the base of his throat, and then filled it with her tongue. "Forgive me, sugar?" she whispered, and began to urge him toward the open doorway to his own bedchamber. "Please?"

Traxton wanted an answer as to why she'd clobbered him, wanted to know what the hell she had been doing in his father's room in the first place, but at the moment those things were seeming less and less important. His body was on fire and hard with need. He'd had dozens of women in the past, but none had ever stirred his hunger like Belle St. Croix, igniting it by just a look or a fleeting touch, stoking it to unbelievable depths with a caress, teasing him toward madness with a kiss.

He had taken her once and had thought that would be the end of it, that the need to taste her passion would be out of his system. That's how it had always been with him. He'd see a beautiful woman, seduce her first with flattery, then with his body, and once his passion for her was satisfied, so was his hunger for her. He had made love to very few women more than once, and he'd figured it would be the same with Belle St. Croix. But he'd been wrong.

With a growl deep in his throat, Traxton swept her up into his arms. So with Belle St. Croix it would take two times to satisfy the hunger of desire he felt for her.

He carried her into his bedchamber, slammed the door shut with the heel of his boot, and walked across the room. What did it matter anymore? He wanted her again, so he'd have her again. And if Trace asked her to marry him and Belle dared to accept, Traxton would, to protect his brother, make certain that Trace found out everything there was to know about Miss Belle St. Croix before he actually married her. He looked down at her long and hard as he stood beside the rumpled canopy bed he had vacated only moments before. "You're a witch, Belle St. Croix," he said finally, his words husky with emotion.

"And you're a blackguard, Traxton Braggette," she said breathlessly.

His lips descended on hers, his kiss hard, demanding, and savage. He lowered them both to the bed, his long length stretched beside her. Releasing the thin ribbons that secured the front of her gown, Traxton's fingers swept the cloth of her nightgown from her body and moved to caress the taut flesh. His tongue plunged deeply into her mouth, ruthlessly exploring, mercilessly teasing, taking everything she had to offer and anything she might think to hold back.

But Belle had no desire to hold back from Traxton, to deny him anything. She reveled in the conquering claim of his lips and welcomed the flames of desire his touch awoke within her veins. She had vowed to refuse him, to deny even the possibility that he had touched her heart and awakened desires in her like none she had ever felt before, but now, with his hands on her body, his caresses like a cool touch to her burning flesh, she could no longer deny him anything.

Lin turned the page of Thomas Braggette's journal and continued to read. It had been hours since her encounter with Traxton, and Belle had yet to return to their room, but once Lin had begun to read the journal, she had forgotten everything else. A yawn overtook her. Lin stifled it, rubbed her eyes, and turned up the wick of the lamp that sat only inches away. She immediately turned her attention back to the journal. Thomas Braggette had written down everything: all of his business transactions, both legal and illegal, all of the schemes he had pulled in the past and planned for the future, his feelings toward his family and business associates, and, most interesting, his involvement with the Knights of the Golden Circle.

But it was the last entry in the journal that brought Lin up from her chair, shock and disbelief rippling through her body. She began pacing the floor in anxious anticipation of Belle's return.

* * *

Traxton opened his eyes and felt an instant chorus of drums erupt inside of his head. He snapped his eyes closed and hissed in pain. The pounding lessened somewhat, and he slowly reopened his eyes as memory of he and Belle making love swept back over him. He turned slowly and reached out for her. His hand came down on the empty space of bed beside him.

Surprised, he remained still for several long minutes, willing the headache to go away and staring at the empty spot next to him that, at least to his recollection, shouldn't be empty. Had he dreamed it? His gaze fell on a long strand of blond hair lying atop the pillow next to his and he smiled. No, she had been there. He rolled back over, feeling content and relaxed, and stared up at the sunburst pattern of his canopy. For a split second he had begun to wonder if last night had been merely a fantasy his sleeping mind had conjured up, if he had wanted her so badly that his mind had brought her to him while he'd slept. He raised his arms and slipped his hands, fingers twined together, under his head.

But with the memory of their lovemaking came the realization that his brother was in love with Belle, haunting Traxton and turning his serene mood turbulent.

He never had gotten an answer out of Belle as to how or why she'd hit him. Or what she'd been doing in his father's bedchamber. A moment of disgust filled him. If Thomas Braggette had still been alive, there would have been no reason to wonder what Belle was doing coming from his room. As it was, the man was dead, so why had she been in there? In the middle of the night?

* * *

"Lin? Lin, wake up," Belle said. She shook Lin's shoulder again.

Using Thomas Braggette's journal as a pillow, her arms folded atop it, Lin groaned but did not move.

"Lin," Belle said again. "Wake up."

Lin raised her head from her arms and looked up groggily. "Belle? Are you all right?"

"I'm fine. Did you find anything?"

The question served to immediately chase the fog from Lin's brain and pull her into full wakefulness. She grabbed the journal and thrust it at her sister. "Last night, before Traxton attacked me, I found this. It's Braggette's diary."

Belle took the book and began leafing through its pages.

"I fell asleep reading it, but it looks like he wrote down everything, Belle."

"So I see," Belle murmured, having come to one of the sections devoted to Braggette's intended schemes involving the Knights.

"He only joined the Knights to use them as a cover if the South went to war. He was going to swindle people, Belle, and say he was doing it for the South, for the war."

Belle flipped several pages, her eyes fairly glued to the scribbled writing. "He was in charge of getting munitions from England in case we went to war," Belle murmured.

"Yes, and he'd already starting buying them, but he bought substandard weapons so that he could make a profit off the Knights," Lin said. "They agreed to pay a certain price for the munitions, but he bought them cheaper and kept the difference."

Belle finished reading the page, then looked at Lin, her eyes full of hope. "Harcourt was supposed to bring

Thomas the money for the arms. Their appointment was on March 12th, the same night Braggette was murdered."

She snapped the diary closed. "We have to get this to the authorities, Lin." She moved to the armoire and swung the doors open, pulling out the first gown her hand found, a soft pink muslin.

Lin stood quickly. "Belle, it doesn't exactly clear Papa. It only says Harcourt had an appointment. There's no proof he even showed up. And I forgot to tell you—"

"But it proves Harcourt was supposed to be there."

"So was Papa," Lin said softly.

Belle whirled around, the gown dropping from her hands. "What?"

"Look at the last entry in the book, Belle," Lin said. "Papa was supposed to meet Braggette that night, too."

Belle picked up the diary again and quickly thumbed to the back in search of the last entry. She read it quickly.

March 12, 8 P.M. Appointment with Henri Sorbonte, General of the Western Division, KGC. His note said he wasn't happy with last shipment of arms. Could be trouble.

"Oh, lord," Belle murmured, and looked at Lin. "Papa's in the Knights of the Golden Circle?"

Lin nodded.

Belle quickly tore out the last page of Braggette's diary and ripped it into tiny pieces. "We know Papa didn't kill anyone, but if the authorities see that, they'll just use it against him and ignore the fact that Harcourt Proschaud also had an appointment to see Braggette that night."

"But that doesn't prove Harcourt's the murderer either," Lin said.

"No, but it raises a few questions."

Belle finished dressing and tucked the diary into the pocket of her cloak. "I'm going to have to sneak out of the house and get this journal into town, Lin. You stay here. This isn't cleared up yet, and we still don't really know who the killer is, so be careful."

"I don't think I'm in any danger here," Lin said.

Belle smiled. "If you run into Traxton, you might be."

Lin's eyes narrowed in suspicion as she remembered that Belle hadn't returned to their room the night before. "Just what is that supposed to mean?" she asked.

Belle laughed softly. "Just stay clear of him, and you'll be all right. I'll get word to you as soon as I can."

Using extreme caution and moving slowly, Traxton rose from the bed, the little demons inside his head having started a drumroll the moment he'd lifted it from the pillow.

Damn, but that woman had about split his skull. And then she'd said she hadn't meant to hit him. He cursed softly. He'd hate to feel what it would be like if she'd intended to hit him. Not that he believed she hadn't intended it. But he sure as hell didn't understand. Bash a guy on the head, then seduce him. A rainbow of color burst to life behind his eyes as he bent to pull on his trousers and chaps. Though he'd liked the second part of her scheme, it was the first part he wasn't fond of.

Slipping into his shirt brought a fresh wave of agony. He gritted his teeth and ignored it. Pouring water from the washstand pitcher into the bowl, he dipped a wash cloth into it and held it to the swollen lump on the side of his skull. He began to feel better immediately.

Now it was time for Belle to do a little explaining. No, he amended, a *lot* of explaining. Traxton walked to her room and rapped on her door. Impatient, he waited only a few seconds. When she didn't answer, he turned the knob and pushed the door open. "Belle," he said as he stepped into the room, "we have to ta—"

Traxton stopped and looked around. The room was empty. "Damned woman," he cursed.

Twenty-six

The echo of gunshots and shouting reached Belle's ears long before she came into view of the city. Her horse pranced nervously, but she fought to hold him on a tight rein and continue onward. From the sound of things, she wasn't certain she wanted to venture into the city either, but she had no choice. There was no way she could go back to Shadows Noir now. She had been lucky just to get a horse saddled and get out of there before anyone saw her. And she had to get Braggette's diary to the authorities.

A wagon careened around a curve in the road, and Belle jerked the reins to the right, forcing her mount to jump to the side of the road. Three men, two in the seat and one sprawled on the wagon's bed, and all obviously drunk, howled with glee and paid her no mind as they passed. The man sitting in the back of the wagon tossed an empty whiskey bottle onto the road.

"Lord, what's happened?" Belle muttered under her breath. A sudden thought filled her with almost-paralyzing fright. Had they hanged her father? She had seen a mob in Boston once when they'd executed a man for murder. Some of the spectators had gone crazy, shooting off guns, laughing, and howling in drunkenness. "Just like this," Belle said. She rammed a heel against the horse's barrel, and he instantly broke into a gallop.

The streets of the entire city were mobbed, those of the Vieux Carré near impassable. People were everywhere, some cheering and shouting, others standing in the shadows, their expressions somber, tears glistening in their eyes. Roustabouts from the wharves crowded the banquettes before the saloons, drinking, yelling, and fighting with one another. Drays fought for right of way on the streets with carriages, horsemen, vendors, and carts. Prostitutes were pulling at some of the men, urging them to their rooms, while others were busy picking pockets.

Belle drew her horse to the side of the street and stared at the melee. Everyone had gone crazy. But why?

A roustabout staggered toward Belle, a half-empty bottle of cheap whiskey dangling from the fingers of his calloused and dirty hand. Whiskers covered his cheeks. "Hey, come on and celebrate wit' me, beautiful." He fell against Belle's horse and tried to pull her from the saddle.

Belle slipped a foot from the stirrup and kicked out at him. "Get away from me."

The man stumbled back a few steps. "Aw, that wasn't very nice. I was only inviting you to a party." He held the whiskey bottle to his lips, threw back his head, and took a long swig.

"What's happened?" Belle asked. "Why has everyone gone crazy?"

"Crazy?" He laughed. "Hell, we're celebrating, missy, 'cause we just whupped them damn Yankees." He took another swallow of whiskey. "Yup," he said, wiping his mouth across the sleeve of his shirt, "we showed 'em. Damn right."

"Yankees? What are you talking about?"

"War, missy, war," the man said. His legs suddenly

gave out beneath him, and he flopped down on the ground. "They wouldn't leave our fort, so we done run 'em out." He giggled childishly. "Damn Yankees."

"Fort? You mean Fort Sumter?" Belle remembered the newspapers she'd read while at the hotel, describing the stand-off in South Carolina. "We fired on Fort Sumter?"

"Sho enuff," the man said, smiling proudly. "Whupped 'em bad, too. Skidaddle, they did." He rolled over in laughter.

Belle felt a sudden heaviness in her heart. It had happened. The South was at war with the North. She urged her horse forward, weaving through the chaos of the streets. Ten minutes later she reined up in front of the city's jailhouse. Alarm filled her as she stepped inside the building. There was no desk clerk and no sign of the guards. Belle didn't know which cell had been her father's, but it really didn't matter now. All of the doors hung open, and every cell was empty.

She whirled around and ran back out onto the banquette, fearful now that the authorities had not waited for a trial but had taken the law into their own hands. "Papa!" she shouted, looking about frantically. "Papa!"

"Who you calling for?" a man's voice said behind her.

Belle spun around and came face to face with a city policeman. His jacket hung open, his shirt was torn, and he smelled of beer. Belle took a deep breath and tried to remain calm. "My father. He was in jail. Where are the prisoners?" She clenched her hands into tight fists in an attempt to stop their trembling. "What's been done with them?"

"They're gone," the man said simply.

"Gone? What do you mean gone?" She felt like shaking him to make him answer her sensibly.

"Gone. Walked off. Gone," he repeated.

"Gone where?" Belle all but shrieked, fear getting the better of her now.

The man shrugged. "I don't know. Everybody went crazy when word came about the fort. One of the other guards said we were going to need all the help we could get and opened the cells. Let everyone out. Crazy fool."

"Out?" Belle echoed.

"Captain's going to be madder than hell, but it wasn't me." He shook his head. "No, sir, wasn't me. I didn't let them out." He laughed then. " 'Course I didn't stop them either."

"Henri Sorbonte, the man they said killed Senator Braggette, did you see which way he went?"

"Nope. Didn't see nothing." He smiled slyly. "Can't get in no trouble if you didn't see nothing, so that's what I'm telling you and that's what I'm telling the Captain. Didn't see nothing."

"But *did* you see where my father went?"

"Nope. Didn't see nothing," the man repeated.

Belle felt a flash of rage. The man was an idiot. Whirling on her heel, she grabbed the reins of her horse and, not bothering to mount, pushed and weaved her way down the center of the street toward the St. Louis Hotel. At its entry she handed the reins to the doorman, seemingly the only calm person in sight, and ran into the lobby.

It was a sea of humanity. Some women were wailing, bemoaning the war that would soon spread over the land, while others were smiling gaily, proudly. Men lifted their glasses in toast after toast, while others climbed to the auctioneer boxes and rattled off impromptu speeches of patriotism to the newly formed Confederacy, damnation to the Yankees, and allegiance to England.

Belle pushed and shoved her way through the crowd until she finally reached the front desk.

"Oh, Mademoiselle Bonnvivier," Pierre Loushei said. "I was worried about you. Are you all right?"

"I'm fine," Belle said, jostling for a position at the crowded desk.

"I had coffee sent up to your room last night, and when you didn't answer, well, I was quite concerned and used my passkey. I—"

"You went into my room?" Belle said, her voice suddenly hard. She had tried to remain polite toward the busybody clerk, but this was the last straw.

"Well, yes. As I said, I was concerned and thought maybe something—"

"Mr. Loushei," Belle said, "I would appreciate it if you would kindly mind your own business."

Pierre's brows soared upward in shock. "Well, really, Mademoiselle Bonnvivier, I—"

"I need to send a note to Shadows Noir. Can you arrange that?" Belle snapped curtly.

"Of course." Pierre waved to Markus.

Belle scribbled a note to Lin summoning her to the hotel and signed their cousin Joshua Kindall's name to it. She decided against mentioning their father's escape, knowing Lin would panic if she knew what had happened. No, she'd tell Lin when she arrived. Belle folded the note and handed it to Pierre, who stiffly handed it to Markus.

"Take this to Shadows Noir and deliver it to . . . ?" He looked at Belle. "To whom should the boy deliver it to, Mademoiselle Bonnvivier?" he asked, his tone curtly formal.

"Belle St. Croix," she said. "Deliver it to Belle St. Croix." She looked at Markus steadily. "Make sure you only give it to Miss St. Croix, Markus."

He nodded, stuffed the note into his pocket, and made for the door.

Two blocks from the hotel, Markus found himself surrounded by three very drunk roustabouts.

"Hey, Charley, lookee here. The kid's got on one of them Frenchie soldier suits."

"I'm a steward at the St. Louis," Markus said. He tried to dart past the man who had spoken.

The burly roustabout lifted Markus from the ground by the collar of his jacket. "A steward, huh?" The man laughed, his whiskey-laced breath making Markus gag. "What's a steward do, boy? Stew things?" He guffawed loudly and shook Markus up and down.

"I . . . I do errands for the customers."

"Hey, he does errands for the cust'mers, Mac," one of the other men said. "Maybe he's doing one now. See if he's got any money in them fancy pockets of his."

The huge roustabout, his' fist still closed around Markus's collar, rammed a finger into first one, then the other of the boy's jacket pockets. Belle's note dropped to the ground and Mac left it there as it wasn't money.

"This gold stuff on your jacket real?" Charley said, running a gnarled hand over the corded trim of Markus's uniform.

"N-no," Markus said, his eyes wide with fright.

Mac released his hold on the collar of Markus' jacket, and the boy stumbled to catch his balance. Charley ripped one of the gold epaulets from the jacket and began to dance around, holding it over his own shoulder. "Hey, lookee here, Mac, lookee me. I'm N'poleon."

The other two men started to laugh. Markus edged away, then dashed toward Canal Street. It wasn't safe in the Quarter, and it wouldn't be until things quieted down.

He'd be better off at home. Markus ran around a corner and disappeared into an alley.

Belle sat before the window of her room and looked down at the street. The crowd had all but dispersed. The celebrating and wailing had long been quieted and been taken indoors to saloons, casinos, and homes. She looked at the small pocket watch that had once been her grandfather's and which her mother had given her before she died. Lin should have been at the hotel by now. Belle knew her sister, knew that she'd come immediately upon receipt of the note. Yet she hadn't come, and she'd had more than enough time to get to town from Shadows Noir . . . unless something was wrong.

Worry began to nibble at Belle's nerves. What if Lin had tried to come to the hotel and been waylaid by some ruffians, men celebrating the South's attack on the North and out for a little fun? What if her horse had been scared by the gunshots and reared, maybe throwing Lin to the ground? Or overturning her carriage?

Belle stood and began to pace the room. Maybe she should take the chance and ride back out to the plantation. Perhaps Lin just hadn't been able to get away. She walked to the window again and looked out. The sun had nearly slipped from the sky, its last faint rays settling a golden pink haze over the Quarter and filling the alleys and archways with inky shadows. A figure walking along the banquette across the street caught her attention. Harcourt Proschaud. Belle stepped back from the window, just enough so that she could see him.

Suddenly someone stepped from the shadows of the arched porte-cochere that led to the town house which Harcourt was about to pass. The man greeted Harcourt.

Edward Mourdaine. The two conversed for several long minutes, their conversation appearing heated, both men waving their arms and shaking their heads vigorously.

Belle wondered what they were yelling about. Could their argument have something to do with Braggette's death? Or his swindle of the Knights? Or maybe even her father's escape?

The sleek gelding stiffened as the silver bit in his mouth was pulled back. His black body was slick with perspiration from the hard ride from town to the plantation. He threw his head to one side and whinnied loudly as Travis yanked back on the reins. His hooves dug into the earth, and bits and pieces of crushed oyster shell flew in every direction.

Travis jumped to the ground. "Trace!" Travis jumped over the small boxwood hedge that trimmed the front pathway, took the shallow entry steps two at a time, and crossed the gallery in only three running strides. "Trace!" he yelled again, slamming open the front door and darting into the foyer. "Traxton! Traynor!" His voice boomed through the house, reverberating off the walls, echoing down the hallways as he ran into the parlor, found it empty, and dashed to the study. "Damn it, where the hell is everybody?" He ran to the dining room. "Trace? Mama? Where are you?" He slammed open the door to the warming kitchen. "Anyone?" he yelled again.

Eugenia appeared from within the pantry, her arms full of canned fruits. "Travis, whatever are you shouting about?"

"It's started, Mama. The war."

Eugenia's arms dropped to her sides, and the jars fell to the floor with a clatter. "War?" she echoed softly. Her fingers clutched at the gray-and-white checkered fabric of her percale skirt, and she stared up at Travis.

"Where is everyone, Mama?"

Eugenia swallowed hard, fighting the tears that filled her eyes. "Your brothers should be back anytime now. They rode out to check the tobacco fields. Teresa and Belle are upstairs looking at patterns."

"I've got to get back to Virginia City, Mama, and see what's going on there."

A sound at the rear gallery drew their attention, and both turned toward the door.

Trace walked in first, laughing and brushing a hand over his shirt to rid it of trail dust. "Mama, your other sons are crazy," he said, and kissed her cheek.

"You've just gotten too staid in your old age, that's all," Traxton retorted, entering on Trace's heels.

Traynor was the last through the door. "Yeah, I second that, old man."

The three laughed heartily until they noticed that neither Travis or their mother had joined in.

Trace was the first to stop. He looked from Eugenia to Travis. "What's the matter?" Alarm filled his breast, and a flash of fear flickered in his gray eyes. "What's wrong? Has something happened to Belle?" He looked toward the foyer. "To Teresa?"

Eugenia shook her head.

"They fired on Fort Sumter," Travis said.

Traxton threw down his gloves. "Shit. I was hoping it wouldn't come to that."

"Let's go into the parlor," Eugenia said. She picked up the jars of canned fruit she'd dropped and, with trembling hands, placed them on the counter, then turned and walked from the room.

"She's scared," Trace said.

"Scared?" Traynor echoed. "Of the war?" A scoffing laugh escaped his lips. "Hell, those fool Yankees will never get to New Orleans."

"She's scared we'll get killed," Traxton said, staring at the empty doorway through which Eugenia had disappeared.

For several long seconds a somber silence fell over the Braggette brothers. Trace was the first to speak. "Come on. She's waiting for us."

The others nodded and followed him into the parlor. Eugenia had already settled herself on a green and white silk tête-à-tête that was set near the fireplace. Her face was pale.

Travis settled on the seat next to her and reached across the small round table that connected the two round seats of the tête-à-tête.

"I'm going to be leaving in the morning, Mama," he said. "I think, under the circumstances, I'd best get back to Virginia City as soon as possible."

"Why?" Teresa asked, walking into the room.

They all turned toward her.

"Beauregard fired on Fort Sumter," Travis said.

Teresa's eyes grew large. "Fired on . . . ? Then we're at war?"

"I doubt Lincoln will ignore the attack."

"We're at war," Traxton said.

Teresa moved to sit on a ladies' chair near her mother.

"Where's Jay?" Trace asked.

Teresa stared at him for several long minutes before answering, a confused look in her eyes. "He . . . he left last night. Something about some business he had to attend to that couldn't wait."

"Business? On his wedding night?" Eugenia said.

"It's fine, Mama. He said it was important and couldn't wait."

"Will this mess affect you all out there much, Travis?" Traxton asked, changing the subject. Jay Proschaud was twenty-four, so Traxton hadn't really known him before he'd left for Texas. He hadn't really cared for him when they'd met upon Traxton's return to Shadows Noir, something about Jay just not striking him right, but he'd shrugged the feeling off, something he normally didn't do. His opinion of the man hadn't changed over the last couple of days, but he figured Teresa didn't need them to dwell on the fact he'd left his new bride on their wedding night. Damn, the man had rotten timing. Traxton moved to stand before the fireplace, rested one arm along the mantel, and hooked the heel of one boot over the brass fender.

"You wouldn't think we'd be troubled by things happening here much, would you, Trax, with Nevada Territory being so far west?" Travis said. "But, yes, it's had an impact on the folks on the mountain more than you can imagine. Damned city's been split right down the middle ever since the brouhaha started, half for the Union, half for the South."

"I hear there's a big following of the Knights in California," Trace said.

Travis nodded. "Yeah. Real big, the way I hear it. Bakersfield and San Francisco both. They're in Virginia City, too."

Eugenia looked at Travis. "You're not involved with them, are you?" Fear glistened from her dark eyes. "Don't be mixed up with them, Travis. They can't do you anything but harm."

He smiled. "I'm not mixed up with the Knights, Mama." He squeezed her hand. "Don't worry so much."

"I can't help it," Eugenia said, and shook her head. "I can't help it. They're dangerous men, like your . . ." She let the sentence trail off, but everyone in the room knew she'd been about to say "like your father."

"I guess I'll put my ships to good use and bring in supplies," Traynor said. He lounged on a brocade-covered settee, one long leg dangling over the settee's curved arm.

"Yeah, you do such a good job eluding the naval authorities now, you should have no problem eluding the Yankees," Traxton said, and winked at Trace.

Traynor narrowed his eyes and sat up. "You calling me a pirate, big brother?"

"Pirate?" Traxton laughed. "No, *little* brother, not a pirate. An entrepreneur."

"I like that," Traynor said, and beamed. He puffed his chest out. "An entrepreneur. Yeah, I like that. I'll entrepreneur my way right through the Yankee Navy."

"They'll throw up blockades," Trace said.

Traynor shrugged. "They can't block every port, and they sure as hell can't stop every incoming ship. Especially mine."

The men chuckled. Eugenia remained silent, her face a mask of concern.

Travis looked at Traxton. "So what about you, Trax?"

"I'll be pushing out in the morning, too. I've got to make sure everything's taken care of at the ranch. When I've got that squared away, I'll join a unit there, if it comes to that."

"Texas will swing to the Confederacy?" Traynor asked.

"The people there have never had a great love for Washington, D.C.," Traxton said. "Or its politicians."

Eugenia turned her gaze to Trace, her eldest son, as did the others. In the past the others had left, and he had stayed. She prayed he would stay this time, too.

Trace met his mother's eyes. "If Louisiana secedes,

Mama, which I have no doubt she will, and there's a call for troops, I'll have to go. You know that."

She closed her eyes and settled back, her shoulders sagging in defeat.

Lin paused on the last step of the staircase. Her fingers tightened their grip on the railing as Trace's words echoed in her mind over and over.

Call for troops, I'll have to go. . . . Call for troops, I'll have to go. . . . Call for troops, I'll have to go.

She felt the breath catch in her throat, felt her heart stop its steady beating and stand still, frozen by fear. Her legs began to tremble, threatening to buckle beneath her, and tears stung the back of her eyes. Forcing herself to move, she walked into the parlor. "What's happened?" Lin asked, her voice breathless with anxiety, her hands clutched together before her in an effort to control their shaking.

"The war's started," Trace said. His gaze moved over her, and he knew, in that moment, that he could never love anyone as much as he loved Belle St. Croix. The midnight blue of her gown brought out the blueness of her eyes, turning them into infinite pools of promise.

She looked long and deep into his eyes as they rose to meet hers. The fear in her breast began to grow deeper. She had found him, the man she wanted to spend the rest of her life with, the man she loved with all of her heart, and now she was going to lose him . . . to war.

"No," she whispered, the lone word filled with agony. Tears fell from her eyes, and she felt a deep rending within her chest, as if her heart were being torn in two. "No," she said again and, giving no heed to the others, ran across the room and threw herself into Trace's arms. "I can't bear to lose you now," Lin cried softly, her head buried against his chest. "I can't."

Wrapping her in his embrace, Trace pressed his lips to the top of her head. "You won't, Belle, you won't," he said huskily, overcome by her show of concern for him. "I promise."

Tears streamed down her cheeks as she lifted her head and looked up at him. He had become her world, her heart, and at the moment nothing else mattered to her: not the murder of his father, not the cloud of suspicion that still hung over his head, not even the fact that she and Belle were no closer to discovering who the real killer was than they had been when they'd arrived in New Orleans.

Turning toward the open jib window and still holding her tightly against his side, Trace led Lin out onto the gallery and into the dusky gardens.

"I have to go, Belle," he said, his strong arms holding her crushed against his chest. "You know that."

She laid her hands on his chest. "I couldn't bear it if anything happened to you, Trace."

His lips covered hers, a tender, featherlight kiss that turned deep and demanding as they clung to one another. Her arms slipped around his neck, and his circled her waist, dragging her up against his body, melding her to his form, fusing her to his tall length.

When he finally tore his lips from hers, he found it the most difficult thing he had ever done, but he had to say what was on his mind. "Belle," he whispered, his lips moving against her neck as he kissed her there, "marry me, Belle. I love you more than anything in the world." He straightened and looked down at her. "Will you marry me?"

A surge of happiness rose in her breast, overriding all other emotions. Lin smiled through her tears. "Yes," she said softly, and pulled his head back down toward hers.

* * *

Standing in the shadows of the gallery, Traxton watched Lin move into Trace's embrace. He felt an aching emptiness in the pit of his stomach and a seething rage in his chest. His eyes burned, his throat constricted, and he knew he had to get the hell out of there. Turning on his heel, he strode back into the parlor. Eugenia was alone in the room.

"I gotta go pack," Traxton said, his voice little more than a hoarse grumble. He began to walk past her.

"Trace needs her more than you do, Traxton," Eugenia said.

He stopped and looked down at her. "I know, Mama," he said. "I know. And it's all right. Trace wants a wife. He needs a wife. I don't."

"You're wrong, Traxton," Eugenia said, and reached out to take his hand. "You need love in your life, too, but you're stronger than Trace. You can find it again." She glanced toward the open doorway and the gardens beyond. "Ever since Myra died, Trace has been so distant with everyone. So cold and unfeeling. It was like he pulled into himself and shut everyone else out. Belle changed that, brought him out of himself, and I don't know if he could have stood it if she'd turned away from him." Eugenia smiled and glanced back up at Traxton.

Looking at her then, Traxton suddenly realized how weary his mother looked, how frail and tired. "Mama," he said, moving to sit beside her, "are you all right?"

She smiled, but the gleam in her eye was one of sadness rather than joy. "I'm fine, son," Eugenia said, and patted his hand. "This war has me worried, though. I don't want to lose any of my boys."

"You won't, Mama," Traxton said, and smiled wryly. "We survived our father; we can survive a war. Anyway, it won't last that long. It can't. I doubt Lincoln thought we'd fight back, but now that he knows we will," Traxton shrugged, "hell, there might not be a war, or at least not more than one battle. And England and France will most likely stand behind the South. They get too much of our cotton not to."

Eugenia turned to look out into the gardens "I hope you're right, son." She sighed softly. "I truly hope you're right."

Traxton stood. "I've got to go get my things together, Mama. I'll be back down in awhile." He took the stairs two at a time and strode purposefully down the hallway to his room. If it wasn't for his mother, he'd be out of here within minutes, but he couldn't do that, no matter how badly he wanted to. Belle would have what she wanted now: a husband. A rich husband. He only prayed she could be faithful to Trace. The thought brought a searing hunger to his groin and the image of Belle naked, lying beneath him, her body moving with his, welcoming him into her. Damn it. He should have stayed away from her. Far away. Traxton retrieved his shirts from the bureau and stuffed them into his saddlebags. Maybe when he got home, he'd ride into town and visit Rosie's place. She was always glad to see him as long as he had a gold eagle for her.

He rammed a fist down on the bureau. He wasn't going to wait until morning to leave. He couldn't. He had to go now, before his damned desire for Belle got the better of him and he did something he'd be sorry for. Not that he already hadn't. His mother wouldn't understand, or maybe she would, he didn't know. He'd say goodbye to everyone, use the excuse that it was cooler riding at night, and get the hell out of there.

When he was done packing, he looked around the

room. Most likely he'd never see it again. He didn't want to come back to Shadows Noir with Belle here. It wouldn't be good for either of them. Traxton buckled his holster, tied the thin leather thong around his thigh, and settled his gun securely in place. Belle St. Croix was the most frustrating, bullheaded, self-righteous, and outspoken female he'd ever had the misfortune to come across. She was ill-tempered, stubborn, and—he threw his saddlebag over his shoulder—and passionate as all hell.

In almost eight years, Belle was the first, the only, woman who had made him feel things he'd thought he'd never feel again, emotions he had been sure Juliette had effectively killed. And she was going to marry his brother, which was exactly why he wouldn't come back with her here. He didn't trust himself around her. Not now, not ever. All he wanted to do whenever she was around was drag her into his arms, conquer her lips with his, strip the clothes from her body, and brand her with his love.

A hot burning coil of need seared through his groin, and Traxton cursed under his breath and threw open the door. It slammed against the wall with a resounding crash. He stalked down the hallway toward the stairs.

Damn it. He didn't need this kind of torment. Didn't need it, didn't want it, and sure as hell wasn't going to put up with it. His mother could visit him in Texas, or he'd come and stay at the St. Louis, but he wouldn't come back here. He would never again return to Shadows Noir. He couldn't do that to Trace.

Twenty-seven

Fear for her sister finally galvanized Belle into action. She grabbed her cloak from the hook behind the door, threw it around her shoulders, and fled her hotel room. Why had she waited so long?

Belle hurried down the hotel's wide, curving staircase. Crowds of men were everywhere in the lobby, their voices raised in discussion or argument about the war they were certain was coming and how it should be fought. Clouds of cigar smoke floated just below the domed stained-glass ceiling overhead, and the smell of alcohol hung heavy in the air. Belle made her way through the crowd, weaving, pushing, and darting, and was relieved to find the doorman at his post.

"I need a carriage," she said breathlessly.

The man nodded and looked around, but there wasn't a carriage for hire anywhere in sight. He looked back at Belle. "I'll have one of the boys hitch you up the hotel carriage, miss," he said. "If'n you can wait?"

"That'll be fine," Belle said. She began to pace the banquette.

Ten minutes later a carriage rolled to a stop before the hotel, and a steward jumped down from its box. Belle looked up hopefully, and the doorman motioned her toward it.

"I ain't got no one I can have drive you, ma'am," he said, his tone apologetic.

Belle nodded. "I can do it." She leaned her weight on his arm as he helped her ascend the carriage. "Thank you." She picked up the reins and snapped them over the horse's rump. He broke into an instant trot. Since the streets were practically deserted, they were out of town in mere minutes and traveling down the River Road at a brisk pace, their way lit only by the pale glow of moonlight.

Where had her father gone? She'd been asking herself that question since her arrival at the jail, and she had yet to figure out an answer. He wouldn't return to Natchez, she was confident of that. If the authorities decided to go after him and bring him back to jail, Natchez and the Sorbonte plantation would most likely be the first place they'd look, and he'd know that. A frown tugged at her brow. So where would he go?

Suddenly she thought she knew the answer. The Knights. Could they be the ones hiding him? The ones who helped him escape? Her father was a general in the Knights, that much she'd found out from Braggette's diary. He'd obviously come to New Orleans on business for their organization, but she'd never believe his business was murder.

The entrance gate to Shadows Noir came into view, and Belle pulled on the reins to urge the horse to turn onto the drive. She would drive partway down the drive, then pull the carriage beneath one of the giant oaks and walk the rest of the way to the house. If she was lucky, she would be able to get up to Lin's room without being observed, though she wasn't sure it made any difference anymore.

Traxton suddenly appeared out of the darkness, his horse moving at a slow lope. As the carriage loomed before him, he jerked on Rogue's reins. "What in tarnation?"

Startled, Belle slammed a foot against the wooden front fender of the buggy and threw all of her weight into pulling back the reins. "Whoa!" she yelled at the carriage horse as his weight pulled against the reins. "Stop there, damn you, horse. Whoa."

"Belle?" Traxton said. Swinging a leg over his mount, he jumped to the ground and stalked around to the side of the carriage. "Belle, goddamn it, what are you doing out here?"

Not more than ten minutes ago he'd said goodbye to her, along with everyone else, in the parlor. He rammed a booted foot on the mounting step, and the carriage swayed under his weight. So how in the hell did she get out here? He leaned forward, grabbed her upper arm, and hauled her toward him until their faces were less than an inch apart.

"Let go of me," Belle ordered, and tried to jerk free of him.

"You," he whispered, the lone word rushing from his lips in a breath of shock. The truth of the matter struck him like a bolt of lightning. He had just said goodbye to Belle, and yet here she was sitting in front of him. It was impossible, and yet . . . Realization pulled the line of his mouth tighter as anger turned the gray of his eyes to dark rage. They weren't the same. The Belle he had just left, the Belle who was in love with Trace, was the one whose ladylike decorum always ended up turning his blood to ice. But the Belle whose arm was now held tightly in his grip, whose eyes were spitting fire at him, was the Belle who had turned his blood to flame, the same Belle whose body, whose spirit, whose passion wouldn't let him forget her.

There were two of them! He felt a growl of fury roil within his chest. All this time when he'd thought he was going crazy, when he'd felt so damned guilty about seducing the woman his older brother loved, all this time there had been two of them, trading places and laughing at their deceit. Playing Trace for a fool. Playing him for a fool. He nearly groaned. She was just like Juliette. Cut from the same mold. Betrayal and deceit. And he had fallen for it again.

The mere thought turned his blood to boiling flame, his anger to raging fury. "There's two of you."

"Well, yes, but—"

"What the hell are you up to, Belle?" Traxton demanded at last. "Or isn't Belle your name?"

Jerking her arm free of his grasp, Belle pushed him back and scrambled from the carriage. He was leaving. His saddlebags were on his horse, and he was dressed exactly the way he had been the day he'd arrived. Belle glanced at the saddlebags again, then back at Traxton, who was glaring down at her, waiting for an answer. But she didn't want to think of she and Lin's plan at the moment, of their scheme to free their father, to clear his name. That didn't matter now. All that mattered now was Traxton and the fact that he was leaving.

Belle reached out to grip the side of the carriage to steady herself, and closed her eyes. When John had died, she'd thought that she would never love another man. But she'd been wrong. Traxton was not the type of man she had always pictured spending her life with: he was rugged, bullheaded, ill-tempered, and ornery. She opened her eyes and looked up at him, and the corners of her lips turned upward just slightly. He was also gentle, sensitive, and loving. He was strong, virile, and protective, and she couldn't lose him. No matter what happened, no matter what she had to do, she couldn't lose him.

The smile left her lips and her features turned hard. Belle

rammed clenched fists on her hips and thrust her face nearly into his. "Where are you going?" she demanded.

"At the moment, back to the house," he growled. His hands circled her waist and lifted her from the ground.

Belle felt her derriere thump upon the seat of the carriage. She felt the jarring impact rattle every bone in her spine, and her skirt and crinolines flew up and settled in a mound on her lap. "What the—?" She quickly brushed her gown back into place.

Traxton looped the reins of his mount over the carriage's back railing and climbed into the seat beside her.

Belle remained silent, though confused. He was taking her to the house instead of leaving, but he was obviously upset to have discovered there were two Belles. Well, she couldn't blame him for being angry. She chanced a quick glance at him. No, he wasn't angry, he was furious. Her heart nearly plummeted to her toes. Oh, God, she was going to lose him. How could she make him understand why she'd deceived him? Why she had felt she had to lie to him? To all of them? Tears stung the back of her eyes, and she fought to stave them off.

Traxton snapped the reins over the carriage horse's rump. They rode to the house in silence, Belle feeling as if she were taking the last few steps toward a guillotine, Traxton wallowing in self-loathing at having allowed himself to be duped—again—by a scheming, conniving, uncaring woman.

Belle turned to him. "Traxton, I was coming to tell you—"

He jerked the carriage to an abrupt halt before the front door and jumped down. A second later he was standing at her side, but rather than assist her in stepping down, he practically dragged her from her seat. "You can tell us all," he snarled, and pulled her by the arm toward the front door.

Belle jerked free of his grasp. "I can walk on my own, thank you very much," she snapped.

"I just want to make sure that you walk in the right direction," Traxton said.

"I was coming here, wasn't I?" Belle stomped away from him before he could respond, her nose held high in the air.

Voices coming from the parlor met them as Traxton pushed the front door open. Belle didn't wait for him. She stalked across the foyer and swept through the open doorway leading to the parlor.

"Belle? But I thought—" Eugenia started. An expression of puzzlement crossed her face as she turned to look through the open jib window toward the gardens. She looked back at Belle. "I don't understand, I thought . . ." Her gaze moved to Traxton, who stepped into view behind Belle. Eugenia glanced back over her shoulder again.

At that same moment, Trace and Lin walked through the window and into the parlor.

"Well, I'll be damned," Travis said, and laughed. "There's two of them."

Traynor's head swiveled from one couple to the other. "Two?" he echoed.

"And there'd better be a damned good explanation for their little charade," Traxton growled.

"There is," Belle said.

Ignoring her, Traxton walked across the room to stand before the fireplace. Laying an arm along the mantel, he propped a foot on the ornate brass fender railing. He threw Belle a hard glance. "So then explain," he said, his tone as cold and hard as the marble before which he stood.

Trace settled Lin onto a settee, then took the seat beside her. "There are two of you," he said softly, as if in a daze.

"I didn't want to lie to you," she said softly, "but . . ." Tears filled her eyes.

"Let me tell them," Belle said.

"Yes, why don't *you* tell us, *Belle,*" Traxton ground out.

Belle refused to rise to the sarcasm so evident in his voice. She couldn't blame him for being angry, and fighting with him wouldn't do any good, not if she wanted him to understand. And she desperately wanted that. Belle took a deep breath and turned toward her sister. "It's all over, Lin. Papa's gone."

"Gone?" Lin repeated. Her face turned ashen. "You mean they—"

"No," Belle said quickly, realizing Lin had misunderstood. "They let him go."

"Thank God," Lin whispered, and seemed to droop in relief. Trace, who obviously didn't understand what was being said, slipped an arm around Lin's shoulders and pulled her to his side, the silent gesture meant to comfort her and let her know that whatever was to come, whatever they'd done, nothing could change what was in his heart.

Belle looked at Trace and smiled to herself. Lin would be fine. She turned then and let her gaze meet that of each Braggette for several seconds before moving on to the next, all, that is, except Traxton. She couldn't look at him, not yet. "First, I think my sister and I owe you all an apology. You offered us your hospitality and friendship, and in return we lied and deceived you. But I assure you, we thought it necessary."

Everyone remained silent.

She took a deep breath and summoned every ounce of courage she could muster. "I guess if there is any hope you'll understand and forgive us, I should start at the beginning." Belle glanced at Lin, who smiled in support. "My name is Belinda Sorbonte. My sister's name is Melinda. We are obviously identical twins. Our father, Henri, is the man who was arrested for the murder of—"

"Thomas," Eugenia said softly.

Belle looked at her hostess. "Yes. Your husband, Thomas Braggette."

"But Papa didn't do it," Lin offered.

"We came here to clear our father's name," Belle said. She looked at Eugenia. "Your cousin Helene was a close friend of my mother's before she died, and is now a good friend to both my sister and I. She offered me the invitation to Teresa's wedding. Lin and I decided that, since we weren't known in New Orleans or to your family, we might find out more if no one knew our true identities or that there were two of us. So when we arrived in town, I came here and Lin checked into the St. Louis. We . . . I . . ." She paused again and looked at Lin. "Because of rumors I'd heard, I suspected that Trace had killed Senator Braggette and framed my father."

"Trace?" Travis said. His jaw nearly dropped to the floor. "Are you crazy?"

"Has to be," Traynor added.

"Maybe I was, a little," Belle said, "but I was desperate to prove my father innocent and get him out of jail, and Trace seemed like a better suspect than my father."

"And Traxton," Lin said. She smiled slyly at Belle.

Belle kept her back turned to Traxton. "Yes. We didn't suspect Traxton at first, but when he said he'd been in Louisiana looking at horses at the time Senator Braggette was killed, I knew we couldn't ignore the possibility he had done it, so we added him to our growing list of suspects."

"I'm flattered," Traxton drawled from behind her.

Belle took a deep breath and continued. "I didn't want to suspect Traxton, and Lin was insistent that Trace was not guilty either, so we had to begin looking elsewhere."

Twenty-eight

For the next thirty minutes, Belle talked to a captivated audience, ignoring Traxton's sarcastic remarks and attempting to explain everything. And with each word she said, each question she answered, she prayed that somehow Traxton would come to understand, and forgive her for deceiving him.

"Edward Mourdaine would never commit murder," Eugenia said, interrupting Belle.

Belle sighed. "Maybe not, but he did have reason."

"You mean his money? Thomas cheating him out of his money and his home?"

"And his fiancée," Belle said.

Eugenia closed her eyes briefly, then snapped them open again. "Yes, that's all true, but if Edward were going to seek revenge, if he were going to murder Thomas, why wait all these years? Why wouldn't he have done it long ago?"

Belle shook her head. "I don't know, Eugenia, I really don't. But ever since I read Mr. Braggette's diary, I have felt certain about one thing: the Knights of the Golden Circle are involved in his death somehow."

"The Knights?" Travis echoed.

Eugenia's head dropped forward, and she pressed a finger to the bridge of her nose as she closed her eyes. "I suspected Thomas was involved with them," she said softly.

"But so was your father," Traxton said, and stared at Belle with eyes gone dark.

She turned to him then and felt her heart contract in fear at the look of disdain in his eyes. "Yes, but I know my father. He is not a murderer," Belle insisted. "No matter what his involvement in the Knights or how important he thought their cause, he is not the kind of man either to commit or condone murder."

"Well," Traynor said, "if you've discounted both Trace and Traxton, then whom do you suspect?"

Belle turned toward the youngest Braggette son. "I honestly don't know, Traynor. Anthony DeBrassea had reason for wanting your father out of the way, but I doubt it was strong enough that he would commit murder." She glanced back at Eugenia. "Your mother is convinced that Edward Mourdaine is innocent of any wrongdoing." She sighed. "There are several others who feel they were cheated by Thomas Braggette. Harcourt Proschaud, for one, and his son Jay."

Everyone's eyes turned toward Teresa.

"He wouldn't murder my own father," she said, though her words echoed the same doubt that shone in her eyes.

"Anyway," Travis said, "why would he stick around and marry Teresa, and then run off?"

"To give his child a name," Lin said.

"His child?" Eugenia stared at her daughter.

"He was called away on business," Teresa said staunchly, her chin lifted in defiance, daring anyone to challenge her statement.

Eugenia sighed. "I agree with Travis. Jay is a good young man, and he's worked hard to help his father rebuild their fortunes. Murder is something . . ." She shook her head. "It's not something the Proschauds or anyone else we know would do."

Belle moved to stand before Eugenia. "I'm sorry we had to deceive you like this, but it was something," she glanced over her shoulder at Lin, "*I* felt was necessary. But now our father is free and even though we don't know where he is, his freedom is all that matters. Our sleuthing is finished. Can you forgive us?"

Eugenia smiled. "Of course." She reached out and patted Belle's hand.

Traxton inhaled deeply and stormed from the room.

Belle watched him. She felt her heart clench up. He was walking away from her, out of her life, and she didn't know what to do.

Go after him, a little voice within her said.

Lifting her skirts, Belle raced for the door. On the gallery she was forced to pause long enough for her eyes to become accustomed to the dark. The moon was only a golden crescent suspended in the midst of a black velvet sky, its pale light a weak illumination of the night-enshrouded earth.

"Traxton?" Belle called. She peered into the dense shadows that filled the garden area, but only silence answered her call. "Traxton?" she tried again. The chirping of a bird somewhere off to her left startled her, and she jumped, scraping the skirt of her gown against a rose bush and catching the material on a thorn. She yanked it free and began to wander down the narrow moonlit path. At the opposite edge of the garden, she stopped. Open pastureland spread to her right and the stables to her left. Before her was a grove of moss-shrouded live oaks, and beyond them fields of cotton.

She looked about frantically. Where could he have gone? He wouldn't have left, would he? Have gotten his horse and headed out for Texas without saying goodbye to anyone? To his mother?

Then a flash of silver caught her eye. Belle squinted into the shadow-cloaked landscape beneath one of the tall oaks. Its branches were spread wide: gnarled, twisting limbs heavily laden with both its own foliage and draping curtains of Spanish moss that allowed only the faintest streams of moonlight through them. She took a step closer and was able to discern the shape of a man leaning against the tree's massive trunk. He stood with his back to the tree, one foot propped up against it, his arms crossed tightly over his chest.

"Traxton?" Belle said softly. She approached slowly, afraid that he would leave or denounce her, or both. Tears threatened at the back of her eyes, her hands trembled, and her heart was racing madly out of control.

He looked up at her then. Moonlight fell across his features, and Belle saw that they were as hard as granite, as unyielding as steel. Anger had replaced every vestige of warmth.

"More games, Belle?" His icy tone, more than the harsh words, cut through her like a knife.

She paused while still several feet from him. "I never wanted to play games with you, Traxton."

"What's the matter, was I too easy to fool?"

She heard the hurt in his voice. Suddenly, remembering what she had read in Eugenia's diary, Belle knew why Traxton was so angry. Long ago Juliette Voucshon had told him she loved him, then had betrayed him, and now he thought Belle had done the same thing. "I'm not Juliette, Traxton," she said softly.

"No, but you're just like her."

Belle felt his words like a blow to her heart. "No," she whispered, "you're wrong. She didn't love you. I do."

"Then I guess you lose," Traxton said, and pushed away from the tree. "Goodbye, Belle." He walked past her without another glance in her direction.

She whirled around. "Damn it, Traxton Braggette, you can't leave me."

He paused and looked back at her. "Oh, can't I?"

"No, you can't, because if you try, I'll follow you. I don't care where you go, or how far, or how long it takes, but I'll follow you."

He shrugged. "Be my guest."

"Where are you going?" Belle called after him, her voice edged with panic.

He didn't answer but instead turned away from her and began to walk toward the stable.

Belle suddenly felt more afraid than she ever had in her entire life. He was leaving her. She ran after him. "Where are you going?"

He didn't answer but kept walking, the light jingle of his spurs tinkling merrily with each step he took.

Belle grabbed his shirt sleeve with both hands. "Damn it, Traxton, where are you going?"

"Home," he growled, the response slipping from his lips before he even thought about it.

"Texas?" she persisted.

"Yes, Texas," he grumbled, his tone now as harsh as hers. He tried to jerk free of her. "Let go of my shirt, Belle."

"No."

He glared down at her. "There's nothing more to talk about, Belle. It's done. You did what you came here to do."

Tears sprang to Belle's eyes, but she didn't release his shirt. "You're not going anywhere without me, Traxton," she said.

"I'm going to Texas, Belle, and then I'm going to war, most likely to die. If you want to follow, fine. It's a free trail." He spun away from her, jerking his shirt sleeve from her grasp.

"Fine, then that's what I'll do. Which horse would you suggest I saddle?" She stalked into the stable after him. "I suppose since it's a long ride to Texas and we don't know how long we'll be on the trail once you join the army, a good saddle horse would be best, right?"

He glowered at her and caught Rogue's loose reins as the horse contentedly munched his oats. "Take whichever one you want. Isn't that what you usually do?"

She ignored his sarcasm and walked to the gate of a tall bay gelding. The horse whinnied at her approach and hung his head over the gate.

"He seems friendly enough." Belle gave the horse a quick once-over. "Big and strong, too."

"You can stop with your games now, Belle."

She smiled sweetly, but her eyes, riveted upon his, were hard and determined. "I'm not playing any games, Traxton. I told you: where you go, I go. I would appreciate it, though, if you'd wait just a few minutes so that I can run back to the house and pack a few things."

Traxton stared at her for several long, seemingly eternal seconds, his eyes hard and searching. "Just what the hell do you think you're doing?"

"Exactly what I said I'd do: I'm going with you," Belle snapped.

"No, you're not."

She moved to stand in front of him, fists propped on her hips, a scowl of anger etched on her brow. Less than a hairsbreadth of space separated their bodies. "In case you don't realize it, you pigheaded idiot, I happen to be in love with you, and I'm going with you whether you like it or not." Her chin rose higher into the air. "And you can't stop me."

Logic and passion warred within his soul, each battling for victory. His mind told him to leave her; his heart told him he couldn't. Traxton's hands closed around Belle's forearms, his fingers like steel bands around her flesh. "I won't have a woman who lies to me, Belle, for any reason."

She felt a spark of hope. "I'll never lie to you again, Traxton," she said softly. "I promise."

Traxton felt the last barriers around his heart begin to crumble and fall away. He was still afraid to love her, afraid to trust her, but he knew he really didn't have a choice—not anymore. "Damn you, Belle," he whispered, his voice husky with emotion. His hands slipped to her waist, and he pulled her up against him, crushing her to his length, reveling in the feel of her in his arms again. "Damn you," he said again as his lips swooped down to claim hers.

Guilt had overshadowed his passion before. The shame of desiring the woman his brother loved had tempered his emotions and left him feeling remorse rather than satisfaction, self-loathing rather than joy. But that was all forgotten now.

She had captured his heart with an unspoken promise to cherish it forever; she had etched her love upon his being, branding him hers; and she had touched his soul and melded it with her own, so that they would always be one, together. Rapture filled his veins, and love his heart. She was a fiery vixen, a bewitching enchantress, a wanton seductress, and he loved her. God help him, but he loved her more than he'd ever thought he could love again, more than life itself.

Traxton felt Belle's arms slip around his neck, felt her pull him toward her and cling to him. His own arms tightened around her, crushing her to him, two silhouettes melding into one in the shadows, soft curves filling hard planes. His tongue moved against hers, exploring the dark promises of her mouth, tasting the honeyed sweetness of her lips. A moan of desire filled his throat as he pulled his mouth from her and pressed a trail of kisses along her neck.

"I love you, Traxton," Belle said, sweeping her lips across the strong line of his jaw. She laughed softly, filled with more happiness than she ever thought possible. "I love you so much."

Traxton felt a torrent of joy wash over him. His lips moved to claim hers again, but she turned her face away.

"What's wrong?"

Belle turned back and smiled. "I love you, Traxton."

His head lowered toward hers, but again she turned her face away.

"Belle?"

"I love you, Traxton," she repeated.

He stared down at her, a frown pulling at his brow.

"I love you, Traxton," Belle said again.

His eyes bored into hers.

Belle sighed. "Do you love me, Traxton?"

"Do I have a choice?"

"Yes," she whispered, suddenly afraid again, "you do."

He smiled, that same devilish smile she remembered he graced her with that first day they'd met. "Then I guess I'll choose to love you."

Belle's eyes once again shone with happiness.

"I love you, Belle Sorbonte," Traxton growled as his head lowered toward hers. "God help me, I love you."

Epilogue

June, 1861

Belle stood beside Lin and looked at their reflections in the cheval mirror. "You look beautiful," she said.

Lin laughed happily.

Teresa walked around to stand in front of them, her stomach protruding out in front of her. "Since you both look identical," she said, "I'd say it's safe to say you both look beautiful. Oh, and Belle, I almost forgot." Teresa reached into a pocket of her skirt. "This was delivered for you a few minutes ago." She handed Belle a folded piece of paper.

Belle's first thought was that it was a message from her father, but upon opening the note and seeing the delicate flourish of handwriting, she realized it was not. Her eyes moved over the words quickly.

He will always belong to me.

She crumpled the paper into a small ball and threw it to the floor.

Lin frowned. "What was that?" She stopped to retrieve the paper.

"Nothing," Belle snapped, her tone one of anger.

Lin unfolded the note, read it, and handed it to Teresa.

"Juliette," Teresa said. "This is just the type of thing she'd do to try and ruin your wedding."

"Well, she can't," Belle said, and smiled widely. "Nothing can ruin this day. Anyway, she's wrong. Traxton doesn't belong to her, he never did, and as long as I'm around, he never will."

Teresa suddenly reached out for a chair and slowly lowered herself into it.

Belle frowned and went to her side. "Are you all right, Tess?"

"What's wrong?" Lin added.

"I'm fine." She held a hand to her stomach. "Junior here is just feeling a little rambunctious, that's all." Teresa struggled to her feet. "I'd best get downstairs now and see if Mama needs any help. Most of the guests have already arrived, and my guess is that your bridegrooms are starting to get fidgety."

Lin and Belle exchanged glances as Teresa waddled toward the door. It had been two months since Teresa and Jay Proschaud had married, and two months since he'd left, stealing from the house in the night—their wedding night. He hadn't returned, nor had anyone heard even one word from him.

The door to Belle's room opened and Eugenia entered. "Girls, are you ready?" she asked. "Everyone's waiting."

Belle clasped Lin's hand, forcing every thought out of her mind except one, that within minutes she would be Traxton's wife, and smiled. "We're ready," she said.

"I wish Papa was here," Lin murmured softly, and wiped a tear from the corner of her eye.

They paused at the door. "Papa will always be with us, Lin," Belle said, "even if it's only in our hearts."

* * *

The small quartet of musicians which were seated on a dais in the garden began to play as Lin and Belle stepped onto the gallery.

White ribbons of satin were draped from one rose bush to another, creating a pathway from the gallery steps, past the assembled guests, to a clearing beneath one tall oak. A makeshift altar had been set within the shadows of the tree's gnarled, widespreading limbs, its heavy foliage creating a lattice ceiling through which sunbeams shone in soft, hazy streams.

Lin descended the steps first, and a hush of whispers swept over those present.

In spite of her words of bravado, Belle's gaze moved over the crowd in search of Juliette Voucshon. A small sigh of relief escaped Belle's lips when she failed to find anyone fitting the description Teresa had given her of Traxton's ex-fiancée.

At the far edge of the garden, Trace and Traxton stood on either side of the priest from the St. Louis Cathedral. At the sound of the music, both men, each proudly dressed in the gray uniforms of the newly formed Confederate Army, turned to watch Lin and Belle approach, as did the hundred guests standing nearby.

The white Caledonian silk of their gowns shimmered beneath the bright rays of the late morning sun as they descended the steps, the pale green threads that were woven beneath the white lending the fabric an almost iridescent quality.

Traxton watched Belle move toward him, a fiery temptress clothed in swirls of white, and felt a wave of emotion wash over him. She would give him hell for the rest of his life, run him in circles, and tease his patience constantly. A smile pulled at the corners of his mouth. But he wouldn't have it any other way.

And he would never forget the way she looked today.

Eugenia stood only a few feet from Traxton. For the moment all thoughts of the impending war, of its possible horrors and consequences, were put aside. Trace and Traxton had found love again, and her heart filled with happiness and relief.

"You didn't win, Thomas," she whispered softly, and turned to watch her future daughters-in-law approach.

Their skirts were full, with cascading flounces, each trimmed with a ruche of snow-white Valenciennes lace to match that which dripped from the gowns' plunging necklines. The sleeves were pagoda style, puffed and full, and ending just above the elbows. Green velvet ribbon trimmed the necklines and the sleeves.

Both sisters had pinned their silver-gold hair in a mound of curls atop their crown, then allowed one side to cascade down over a shoulder, the left for Lin, the right for Belle. Thin green velvet ribbon had been woven in amongst the curls, and each bride wore earrings shaped like teardrops, a gift from their late mother: crystal blue for Lin, emerald green for Belle.

Trace stepped forward, took Lin's hand in his, and tucked it into the crook of his arm as they moved to one side of the priest. He looked down at her, and as their eyes met, he felt his heart swell with the love she had awakened within him. He had been so lonely for so long, but he would never feel that way again.

Traxton felt his eyes burn with tears as he watched Belle walk toward him. She was so beautiful he was almost afraid to breathe for fear she would disappear and prove to be nothing more than a dream. His gaze moved over her slowly, appreciatively, lovingly. Her silver-gold hair seemed to pick up the light of the sun and reflect it in shining brilliance, each curl, each wave, each tress turning to a thread of silver, a swirl of gold, a strand of platinum. Her eyes were pools of joy, swirling mists the rich color of both the lush grass beneath their feet and the clear sweep of blue sky over their heads. The plunging neckline of her gown revealed just enough of the swell of her bosom to tantalize and tease his senses, and the fullness of the gown's sleeves accentuated both the delicate curve of her shoulders and the narrow breadth of her waist.

Traxton felt his body fill with desire, as it always did whenever she was around, and his heart with love.

As she approached him, Belle reached out a hand. Traxton's strong fingers closed around hers, and as always happened when they touched, she felt a delicious shiver of warmth trickle its way up her arm.

She smiled up at him, her gaze meeting his, and the breath in her throat caught as her heart seemed to skip a beat. He was her life and her love. He was all she ever wanted from this world and all she would ever need.

Traxton turned to face her and took her other hand in his.

She heard the priest talking, heard Trace and Lin say something, but her world was too filled with Traxton to allow her to pay any real attention. His eyes held hers as his love held her his willing captive. She saw the faint hint of a smile curve his lips, a spark of happiness shine from his eyes, and felt the warmth of love in the secure clasp of his hands.

"And do you, Traxton Braggette, take this woman, Belinda Ann Sorbonte, to be your wife, to love her, to honor her, and cherish her until death do you part?" the priest said.

Belle smiled up at Traxton. How could she have ever thought *not* to love this man?

"I do," Traxton said, his voice a rich drawl that reached out to caress her heart.

The priest turned to Belle. "And do you, Belinda Ann Sorbonte, take this man, Traxton Braggette, to be your lawfully wedded husband, to love him, to honor him, and to obey him until death do you part?"

Belle opened her mouth to respond, and paused. She pulled her gaze from Traxton's and stared at the priest.

He frowned and nodded his head in encouragement for her to answer.

"Obey?" she whispered.

Traxton bit his bottom lip to keep from laughing.

"Belle!" Lin said under her breath.

The priest stared at Belle.

Her gaze pierced his. "Obey?" she whispered again.

Traxton leaned toward the priest. "Change it, Father," he said softly into the man's ear.

The priest straightened, shook his head in curiosity, and repeated his question. "And do you, Belinda Ann Sorbonte, take this man, Traxton Braggette, to be your lawfully wedded husband, to love him, to honor him, and to *cherish* him until death do you part?"

Belle turned back to Traxton and smiled. "I do."

From beneath one of the tall live oaks that dotted the vast landscape of Shadows Noir, Henri Sorbonte watched his daughters take their wedding vows. The gray of his uniform melded with the inky shadows within which he stood, giving him the advantage of seeing without being seen. As his daughters kissed their new husbands, Henri's gaze traveled over the guests who had assembled for the ceremony and a frown tugged at his brow. His daughters were happy now, but neither he nor they were safe, for within their midsts still lurked a murderer.

Turn the page for a sneak preview of the second book about the Braggette family, **HEARTS DENIED,** *a December 1994 release.*

One

Virginia City, Nevada
Spring, 1862

"I told you, Charley, I'm not a joiner," Travis said. He pulled a gold watch from the pocket of his silver-threaded black vest, flipped its cover open with a flick of his thumb, and glanced down at the roman numerals painted on the face of the timepiece.

Charles Mellroy glanced over both shoulders nervously, then downed the last of the whiskey in his shot glass. "Judge Terry's not too happy that you keep turning down his invitation to join the Knights, Travis."

"Then maybe he should stop asking." Travis snapped the lid of the watch closed and returned it to the pocket of his vest. He tugged on the lapels of his black cutaway jacket, straightened the cuffs of the white silk shirt he wore, and glanced into the mirror set over the bar to straighten the string tie at his throat and run a hand over the dark waves of his hair. He was ready. "The South has my support, Charley, and David knows that. I just don't do it his way. Now, if you'll excuse me, I have to meet a stage."

Travis pushed through the swinging doors of the Mountain Queen and walked out onto the raised and shaded boardwalk that fronted the saloon. "Where the hell is that stage?" He stepped to the edge of the walk and stared down C Street. It was a sea of activity: miners coming off their shifts flooding into the dozen or more saloons that dotted Virginia City's narrow main street while those miners going on shift were just leaving the breakfast houses, hotels, and boarding houses and trudging down to the mines whose tunnels bore directly beneath the streets they lived on. Heavy ore-laden drays, buckboards, carriages, and saddle horses were tied up to hitching racks, pillars, and water troughs while still others moved along the street.

A flicker of red on the boardwalk directly across the street caught Travis's attention. A smile drew his lips upward as he watched her move from the shadows of the overhanging roof, the bright color of her satin gown intensifying as she stepped into the sunlight. The long strands of her chestnut mane had been piled high on her crown and then allowed to cascade loosely down her back and over her shoulders, drawing the spectator's gaze to the daringly low cut neckline of her gown and the swell of her bosom. But then, that was Magnolia's intent.

She blew him a kiss and laughed. The rough, almost bawdy sound drifted to him above the din of street noise.

Travis chuckled and waved to her. Magnolia Rochelle's saloon was one of his fiercest competitors, yet they had managed to remain friends . . . good friends. It helped that they were both from New Orleans, their sympathies in the war were the same, and in spite of the fact she was at least seven or eight years older than him, she had one of the most delicious bodies in Virginia City.

"So, *cher,*" Magnolia called out, "where is this little songbird you are supposedly importing to put my Silver Lady out of business?"

Travis shrugged. "The stage is late." He glanced down C Street again. A cloud of dust could be seen rising from the curve of the mountain road in the distance. "But I think it's about to arrive," he added.

Magnolia followed his gaze. "Well, *cher,* if you find that your little canary has changed her mind and flown elsewhere, perhaps you will still consider my offer, hey?" Her lips curved in a seductive and rather suggestive smile.

Travis laughed. "We're both too headstrong and stubborn to ever be partners, Magnolia."

"Ah, a pity," Magnolia said, "but then, one never knows what the future may bring, hey *cher?"*

The stagecoach from Sacramento came into view at the end of C Street.

"I'll wager my future is bringing Georgette Lindsay to the Mountain Queen right this minute, Magnolia, and I'll have all the customers tonight."

Magnolia feigned a pout. "Then I will be all alone."

"You're never alone, Maggie," Travis said, "but if you get lonely," he winked, "you know where my room is."

The stage driver, a grizzled old man in buckskins sitting high in his seat, slammed a foot down on the brake pedal and pulled back on the reins. "Whoa, there, you bone-headed beasts!" he yelled gruffly.

Six well-muscled horses, their brown bodies sleek with perspiration, snorted and pranced to a halt. The huge stagecoach swayed on its leather shocks as its wheels ground to a standstill in the dirt street.

An agent ran from the express office to greet the driver, who had already climbed down from his seat to open the passenger door.

Travis ambled forward. Several months ago, looking for ways to increase the Mountain Queen's profits, he had contracted a two-week engagement with Georgette Lindsay. Though he had never personally witnessed her performance, or even seen her, he felt confident in her abilities. Georgette Lindsay had come highly recommended, and Travis had lofty hopes that she would bring in the kind of money his brother Trace had asked for on behalf of the Confederacy.

"Good luck, *cher*," Magnolia called out.

Travis waved to her, but his attention was on the door of the stagecoach, which was just swinging open. The driver's gnarled, weather-beaten hand held to the door's knob, but just above it, resting lightly on the bottom of the door's window frame, was a graceful hand, its body encased in a black lace glovelette, its long slim fingers bare.

Months ago, when last in San Francisco, Travis had seen a poster of Georgette Lindsay and had found her not only beautiful, but hauntingly familiar. But he knew those announcement posters never did a person justice and had shrugged off the feeling that he'd seen her somewhere before.

The coach swayed slightly as she placed a dainty foot, only momentarily visible beneath a mound of ruffled crinolines and the percale hem of her cocoa-colored traveling suit, onto its boarding step and emerged. Beneath a small-brimmed straw hat adorned with a trail of yellow-and-brown feathers and ribbon, her dark hair had been pulled to her crown, and a fall of sausage curls draped one shoulder. As the sunlight touched them, the darkness of the curls suddenly shone with red-gold highlights.

Travis caught a glimpse of her profile and knew instantly the poster he had seen of her had indeed not done her justice. Her cheekbones were exquisitely carved curves of grace, her nose pert, yet aristocratic, and the creamy richness of her skin reminded him of a day-old gardenia, magnificent in its whiteness, yet touched by just the softest hint of gold.

Travis paused on the boardwalk directly in front of her and bent to offer his hand. Thickly ruched dark lashes fluttered as she raised her head to look up at him.

"Why, thank you, Travis," she said, and smiled.

Travis froze. He felt her fingers come to rest lightly upon his hand, heard the soft, almost musical quality of her voice, and was faintly aware of the fragrance of jasmine that seemed to surround her. His voice was caught somewhere deep in his throat, paralyzed by shock and disbelief, while his eyes met hers.

It had been six years since he'd seen Suzanne Forteaux, since he had refused to marry her and left New Orleans.

Author's Note

Hearts Deceived is the first of a four-book series on the Braggette family and spans the entire period of the Civil War, each story taking place in a different locale, with a different romance, but all held together not only by family ties, but by murder and conspiracy.

This series is very close to my heart as I have a passionate love for the Civil War and cowboys, murder mysteries, and intrigue, and delightedly was able to weave aspects of each into this series.

The Knights of the Golden Circle truly did exist. They were formed before the Civil War by Americans who wanted to see Mexico annexed into the United States. When the War Between the States broke out, the Knights turned their attentions to helping the Confederacy. They were a widespread organization, having chapters all through the South, some in the North, and many in the West. The KGC was a secret organization with the reputed penalty of a member's betrayal being death. Their efforts to help the Confederacy were mainly cloaked in secrecy and ranged in everything from the passing of information to sabotage.

I hope you enjoy reading about the Braggettes as much as I've enjoyed writing about them. *Hearts Denied,* The Braggettes, Book Two, is scheduled as a December 1994 release. *Hearts Defiant,* The Braggettes, Book Three, and the finale, *Hearts Divided* will follow shortly thereafter.

I am always happy to hear from my readers and will respond with any promotional materials I have if you include an SASE. Write to me at POB 6557, Concord, Ca. 94520.

Author's Profile

Cheryl Biggs lives in a rambling house at the foot of Mt. Diablo, California, with her very supportive husband Jack and their very weird but lovable five cats. She has always loved to read and now spends most of her day happily at the computer, writing her own stories, which include everything from historical and contemporary romance to time travel and paranormal romance.

Previous titles for Zebra include *Denim & Lace, Family Tradition, Mississippi Flame,* and *Across a Rebel Sea*.

In 1994, Cheryl will also begin to write for Pinnacle under the name Cheryln Jac, with the release of a time travel, *Shadows in Time,* and her first paranormal romance, *Night's Immortal Kiss*.

YOU WON'T WANT TO READ
JUST ONE — KATHERINE STONE

ROOMMATES   (3355-9, $4.95)
No one could have prepared Carrie for the monumental
changes she would face when she met her new circle of
friends at Stanford University. Once their lives intertwined
and became woven into the tapestry of the times, they would
never be the same.

TWINS   (3492-X, $4.95)
Brook and Melanie Chandler were so different, it was hard
to believe they were sisters. One was a dark, serious, ambi-
tious New York attorney; the other, a golden, glamourous,
sophisticated supermodel. But they were more than sisters — they were twins and more alike than even they knew
. . .

THE CARLTON CLUB   (3614-0, $4.95)
It was the place to see and be seen, the only place to be. And
for those who frequented the playground of the very rich, it
was a way of life. Mark, Kathleen, Leslie and Janet — they
worked together, played together, and loved together, all behind exclusive gates of the *Carlton Club*.